T0123722

To Dance at the Bridal

By
Roderick Bethune

O Come ye in Peace here, or Come ye in War,
Or to dance at our Bridal, young Lord Lochinvar?

authorHOUSE®

AuthorHouse™ UK
1663 Liberty Drive
Bloomington, IN 47403 USA
www.authorhouse.co.uk
Phone: UK TFN: 0800 0148641 (Toll Free inside the UK)
UK Local: (02) 0369 56322 (+44 20 3695 6322 from outside the UK)

© 2022 Roderick Bethune. All rights reserved.

No part of this book may be reproduced, stored in a retrieval system, or transmitted by any means without the written permission of the author.

Published by AuthorHouse 09/27/2022

ISBN: 978-1-7283-7509-0 (sc)
ISBN: 978-1-7283-7510-6 (hc)
ISBN: 978-1-7283-7508-3 (e)

Print information available on the last page.

Any people depicted in stock imagery provided by Getty Images are models, and such images are being used for illustrative purposes only.
Certain stock imagery © Getty Images.

This book is printed on acid-free paper.

Because of the dynamic nature of the Internet, any web addresses or links contained in this book may have changed since publication and may no longer be valid. The views expressed in this work are solely those of the author and do not necessarily reflect the views of the publisher, and the publisher hereby disclaims any responsibility for them.

To Dance at The Bridal

by

Roderick Bethune

A young Scot's involvement in Commodore Home Popham's decision to invade the Spanish empire of the River Plate in 1806

Dedication:

To the myriads of Mackynouns, McInnons, MacKinnings, McKinnons or Mackinnons, together with all other Scots and Irish forced to leave their homes in the 18th & 19th Centuries - emigrating to the Americas, North and South - this book is dedicated with respect and affection.

Author's Note:

This is a work of fiction – that is to say that the principal character, Lauchlin Mackinnon, is largely a product of my imagination. But, being set in a factual environment, much of the background is inevitably true and peopled by those who really existed. Britain did invade the River Plate on three occasions early in the 19th Century; Admiral Popham was Court-Martialled after the first invasion and General Whitelocke after the last; General Beresford went on to become Governor of Madeira and, eventually, Marshal of Portugal, serving under the Duke of Wellington; Juan Manuel Rosas was almost certainly the largest cattle baron at that time and became Governor of Buenos Aires. He almost certainly bore a large responsibility for the clearing of the indigenous people from cattle lands. He died in exile, at Southampton, in 1857.

The sketch in the cover design is from a contemporary source believed to have been present at the battle for Buenos Aires.

Postlude: (June, 1982)

Miguel Mackinnon is frightened. He has never been so frightened. As a twenty year-old conscript in the Argentine army he had expected to serve for eighteen months or two years in an office close to his home in Buenos Aires. After all, that was how his brother and many of his school-friends had spent their call-up. Not a pleasant experience and certainly an interruption to his education, but one that was more often boring than frightening.

Now, in total darkness, he finds himself in freezing, horizontal sleet hiding behind a rock with shells and gunfire making the very peat tremble around him. He is aware of some irony in being attacked by red devils from England! Although born on an Argentine farm, his grandfather had possessed a British passport; Miguel has no idea what took his ancestors to the country in the first place.

He puts down a comforting hand, but Carlos Caceres is dead. Carlos was the radio operator whom Miguel was ordered to help, heaving the weighty instruments to the top of Mount Longdon, which they were told was the highest point in all the Malvinas. Miguel's role was to protect Carlos and ensure that nobody interfered with his messages to base. The messages were initially scribbled out by Teniente Tandil but he made himself scarce as soon as the bombardment started. Not that Miguel was any good as a guardian – he had only visited the shooting range once in his training and fired a total of five rounds.

The bombardment is easing. Can he make a break for it? There are figures appearing in front; they are firing from the hip; he leaves the rock and starts running through the gorse. A jolt and agonizing pain in his head. He manages two more paces before blessed unconsciousness.

Chapter 1 *(April 1803)*

"Lauchlin! Where are ye? Still in yer pit you lazy shirker?"

Shocked into full wakefulness, he stumbles from his straw mattress in the corner to put on the outer clothing he removed last night. It is soon done. He sleeps in his thick shirt and under-things. The damp cold bites deeply. The only light – dark and grey even though it is nearly May - comes through the small window which rattles in the wind but fails to keep out all of the fierce rain cascading against it. Ewen, an older lad in the tenements bursts into the room.

"You sluggish idler! There's nae wood for the stove – get doon and fetch it up!"

From the other corner he hears his grandfather begin to moan and chunter his displeasure:

"Who let him in here? He has no right and no business speaking to a Mackynoun like that! Stand up for yourself, laddie – remember who y'are!"

"It's all right Grandf'er, he's only shouting because the stove needs wood."

Blundering down the communal steps of the two-storey Port Glasgow housing, he smiles bitterly to himself over the old man's words. In his dotage now, he has the memory of a house-mite for recent events; but for the past he can recall the finest detail. Lauchlin never tires of hearing how nearly sixty years ago the family had influenced support for Prince Charles Edward's march into England to regain the crown that properly belonged to him. Lauchlin knows that his Great grandfather, Ailpin, had helped the Prince in his escape after the ignominious defeat on Culloden Moor and been nearly hanged for his loyalty. Only his advanced age had saved him. After a year in an English prison he had been allowed back to his old country. But it had all been changed. 'Stinking Billy' – the butcher Cumberland, had destroyed the clans. The Mackynouns who had been 'Lords of the Isles' were banned from Mull and the islands around Skye and been forced, like so many others, to the mainland where they had made their way to the developing settlements along the Clyde river at Port Glasgow. They still keep the old man's kilt in the Mackynoun tartan. Treated almost like a religious Icon, it is hidden away. Wearing the kilt is now forbidden except, on occasions for the army that serves King George.

Outside he battles against the driving rain as he tries to collect enough dry wood to feed the communal stove upstairs. Normally a thick piece of sail-canvas covers the small stock of timber but the wind has disturbed it and most of the wood is now damp.

He pokes around the lower levels taking out the drier pieces. *'More smoke than heat for a while',* he thinks, knowing he will get the blame. He fixes the sailcloth in place; he needs to hurry as his job at the wool-yard demands a prompt arrival at six. In about a year, after his sixteenth birthday, he will be required to arrive an hour earlier, but his wages should increase to six shillings a week. He knows the rent on their bare room is seven shillings and sixpence. The earnings of his father and two brothers mean that his mother has an easier time than most in obtaining food at the market. The Macleans who have the large ground floor room had tried last winter to keep a pig but the rent-collector had found it and taken it away. It was a cruel act – the animal did no harm. Lauchlin wonders if there is some Irish blood in the collector's veins. There do seem to be more of them around these days.

It takes him three trips up and down the steps to fill the wood scuttles. He takes two spoonfuls of porage at each trip. His mother wipes his mouth after the last load. His other duties include checking the water in the high sump that feeds the basin in the communal kitchen. This is pumped up from a well serving a number of households. At this time of year the well is full and he knows he must do some thirty pulls at the lever to obtain the right volume. In August it will require twice that but the resistance will be lower. Until two or three years ago they used this water for all purposes, including drinking, but so many people were becoming ill that the Procurators' Office imposed a ban on drinking it. Now they have to rely on John Hankey and his cart carrying water from his farm. He sells it at a ha'penny a stoup. The trouble is that his "stoup" varies – sometimes it fills two of his mother's big pitchers, at other times it is an inch below the lip.

After completing the requisite number of pumps, Lauchlin knows that there is enough water for the essential washing and boiling. But his mother cannot let him escape without one final admonition:

"You should get yourself up with Fingal and Stuart," she shakes her head, referring to his brothers, "then you'd have time to let your breakfast settle and we could do more of your letters and reading. I want ye to memorize a page of the Shakespeare I've marked. Ye're no a wee boy any longer and ye could do well for yerself!" She runs a hand across his head and adds, "it's time I took a knife to your hair again, laddie, it's grown awfu' untidy!"

He agrees with a grunt as he picks up his cap. Being now full of porage he needs a quick visit to the privy and hurries out. When about to reach the rotting, wooden door, Mistress Mackenzie cuts across and slides in before him. He curses inwardly. *Wretched woman spends half the day in there!* Now he knows he will have to use the long channel at the mill which takes the waste to the river. He has done this before but needs to avoid being seen as the owner gets angry.

He will wash his hands on the way to work. He hurries down the side alley thinking about his mother's words. His letters are already better than those of his brothers. He needs more continuity at the numbers if he is to be able to obtain work in the office where the hours are easier and pay rumoured to be greater. Labouring for the juniors, as for almost everyone in the factory, is monotonous and, occasionally, dangerous. Apart from the cleaning and sweeping the floor, the youngsters have to do the initial washing of the fleeces when they arrive, generally full of dirt, stones and shit. Further cleaning and removal of the waxes is done by skilled men of whom Lauchlin's father is one. After drying they are sorted by the owner himself, before the carding and scouring can begin. The younger lads are used to sort out the "kemps" and woollen remnants which have to be carded, scarified and, hopefully, spooled. If a break occurs under the twin-treadles of the winders, a child will have to crawl under and retrieve the ends which generally results in frustrated kicking from the delayed operatives, losing pay by the minute.

As he leaves the building through the close he finds Ewen leaning against the wall talking to Annie Shearer a girl from the next tenement whom Lauchlin's mother dismisses as 'no better than she should be'. Ewen is showing off and immediately wades into Lauchlin.

"Ye're a lazy draggie, Islander – ye need a guid lesson to teach ye how to get up in the mornings!"

"Oh push off, Ewen. I've done the wood and now I'm off to my duties with the wool!"

Ewen puts his face into Lauchlin's and gives him a hard shove which knocks him into the wall. "Is that the push you mean? You're a frightened wee rabbit now, so you are, even with your smart highland tones!"

This is a surprise. It has never struck Lauchlin that he speaks with an accent learned from his family and different to the speech heard in these streets. "I've no the time for this! Leave me be or I'll make ye sorry!"

Annie gives a giggle. She loves imagining that the boys are fighting over her. Some in the alley have already begun to form gangs that fight with those in the next street. As Lauchlin tries to leave, Ewen grapples with him but he shakes him off. He is still small for his age – Mackynoun men tend to be 'braw' and strong – but he will grow and is already hard and wiry. Ewen now runs at him and delivers a hard kick at his groin which penetrates. Ignoring the pain, Lauchlin turns back and lands a punch on Ewen's nose. He goes down with a shriek of protest. Lauchlin rubs his aching parts which now make his need for a privy more urgent and runs to the yard. Mr.Arbuthnot, the owner is standing by the entrance in his long, black coat and high hat. Lauchlin removes his cap. "Good morning, Sir."

"Ah it's you, is it, Lauchlin. No need to run it's still three minutes to the hour!" He gives a friendly smile as he turns away. "I wish all were as keen to get to their work!"

Lauchlin goes through and reports to Mr. Johnson, the supervisor, who sets him to sweeping the floor. It is a task he quite enjoys as it enables him to move about the works, surreptitiously watching the several processes. The smell of urine, used in the curing, is almost overpowering but the workers barely notice it. The washing takes place outside where the various tanks can be emptied directly into the channel which carries the waste to the river. Taking his opportunity, Lauchlin squats behind a stack of fleeces standing in the rain. Ewen's kick still aches and impedes full success. Mr.Arbuthnot has been heard to say that he should put a roof over the washing tanks but there has been no sign of that yet and Lauchlin sees his father is getting a good wetting. It sets him to thinking about the work that awaits him once he is sixteen.

He arrives home just after six in the evening. It is still raining and he knows his father will want hot water for a warming wash in an hour's time when he returns with his other two sons. His mother's face is dark with disapproval.

"What's this I hear? Not content with getting up late, you've been picking fights with Ewen! Mr. McCorqudale has had a complaint and he may be coming this evening to talk to your father!"

In vain he tries explaining the true facts. He has to go and collect more wood for the landing and check that the large water chest is filled and warming. The stove is big, stretching across the whole landing. It has to serve four families and is a prodigious consumer of the wood they buy off the cart every week for three shillings. Some rent collectors supply the wood themselves, taking a further profit in the process, but Mr.McCorqudale is generally a fair man.

After lighting the oil lamp, Lauchlin's next duty is to empty his Grandfather's chamber pot. It is too much to expect the old man to traipse down the two flights of stairs to the communal privy. Unpleasant smells are no novelty in these apartments and the contents are soon on their way to the river.

Lauchlin washes himself and goes to help his mother as she stands over the big stewing pot. Ewen's mother, Mrs.Maitland, is on the other side cooking her own family's dinner. The other two wives entitled to use the stove are watching. It does not do to leave your food cooking unsupervised.

"Yon Lauchlin's a brute, Mistress Mackynoun! My Ewen's nose was spitting blood all morning. He had to wear a poultice over it when he went off to his work in the market."

"Boys will always be boys, Agnes, but his father will be speaking to him when he returns!" She smacks Lauchlin on the back of his head, but it is only for show and he feels no rancour. "Set up the room for dinner" she says quietly, "and see how your Grandfather's doing, then fetch out your slate and write out the first three verses of the 23rd Psalm. Then think about the meaning!"

He put+s up the small table they have in their room, laying out the spoons and knives. His mother had told him in the neighbour's hearing that there would be some bread and a piece of cheese to follow the mutton and potato stew.

"Shall we be able to find the meat this time?" Lauchlin teases his mother and smiles at Mrs.Maitland to show there is no ill will, but she merely purses her lips.

They have three small chairs for the table, one each for his parents and one for his grandfather if he feels like sitting up.

He finds his slate and chalk and writes the wording as instructed: *The Lord is my shepherd, I shall not want*. He completes the three verses. What would a shepherd make of his flock being cut up by Mr. Arbuthnot and his staff in the mill? That's what sheep are for…so would the Lord permit him – Lauchlin - to be cut up if it served a greater purpose? And why does He make him lie in still waters? What is the meaning of that? Have a bath? He muses on as he hears his father coming in. That reminds him of the fight with Ewen. His father may be angry. How could he not have fought? Run away? Lie in still waters, was that it?

His father returns with Fingal and Stuart. They seem in a cheerful mood but as they enter the room he sees they are soaked to the skin.

They strip off their wet clothing which will be hung on the landing ready to put on again in the morning. They use the warmed water in order of seniority. The eldest son, by tradition, is named Fingal, the second should be John, his father's name, but they broke the habitual rule when moving into the tenement. Lauchlin knows that the "auld" Mackynoun tradition had it that the eldest son inherited the land and titles, the second went into the church. Should there be a third he was to assist the eldest and, hopefully, make a marriage that would increase the family's holdings. They all know those days are long past.

Towelling himself vigorously his father stands over him. "What's this nonsense about you attacking young Ewen then?"

Lauchlin starts to explain but his father waves the comments away. "Mr.Arbuthnot told me you were in good time this morning. Seemingly ye were polite. That's good." He turns as his wife comes in with fresh, warmed clothing from the landing.

"Let me have the wet things, John, they'll need hours if they're to dry by morning." They move together behind the hanging sack-cloth that serves to divide up the living space. Lauchlin listens as their conversation continues. "Has Fingal said any more to you?"

"Aye, he has it all planned. We'll need to talk about things – all of us, together."

Fingal has had it in mind for nearly a year to marry Elizabeth Tempest, a sweet girl from further up the street. Lauchlin assumes they will simply move in with the rest of them. It will be a squash but he has never known anything different.

Stuart comes into the room also wiping himself down. "Och, the water's cold and dirty enough even for you now, Lauchlin!" He laughs and flings a pile of clothes he has brought in behind the hangings where the two elder boys sleep.

"A wee dram would just meet the spot." He proposes from behind the curtain, loudly enough for his father to hear.

"It's no' your birthday, lad and we've little enough to celebrate this day!" Their mother brings in the heavy stew-pan. Lauchlin fetches six plates while she sits. "Will ye no' sit up at table, Grandfaither?"

"Och I'm well enough where I am, thank-you." His son nods at his own eldest to take the vacant chair as he seats himself.

"As ye said, a dram would be good but," he sighs regretfully, "we need to discuss where you're to live with the wee lassie."

"I've spoken with McCorqudale, but he's nary another room free." Fingal's voice expresses his disappointment. "D'ye think the landlord himself has space?"

His father points at Lauchlin. It stays pointing while he chews and swallows. "Ye're near sixteen, laddie, we need to decide what you wish to do with your life."

Lauchlin looks up defensively. "I'm good with the letters, faither, and I hope Mr.Arbuthnot will give me a place in the office." His voice tails away as his father shakes his head.

"I've spoken with him today. I helped him with the sorting. Oh he likes you well enough, but he only has two clerks in the office and his daughter has been learning the business so that she can join him. There'll be no vacancies there for a long time."

The room falls silent for some moments. Lauchlin's father stares into space. Born in Skye but forced to spend nearly all his life seeking a safe haven he is defensive about their tenement. At the same time he is often tortured by doubts and a belief that he has failed his family. If just one of them can attain some kind of success it will restore his confidence in moving everyone to Port Glasgow. Then Fingal speaks up again. "If Betty and me can set ourselves up where Lauchlin sleeps, he can move in with Stuart…" He is interrupted by his mother. She looks at her youngest.

"That work with Mr.Arbuthnot was always a faint hope, Lauchy."

Lauchlin looks up. "But I can get a job in the factory! And when I'm sixteen I'll be paid more."

She shakes her head. "You're better than that, laddie. No disrespect but you're capable of more than six or seven shillings a week." She sighs, "but ye need a bit more polish to pass as a gentleman."

"Oh a gentleman is he - thank you very much!" Stuart struts around the room holding his plate away from an up-turned nose pretending offence but there is more humour than dismay in his face.

Their mother looks at Lauchlin. "I'm writing a despatch to my brother, your Uncle Andrew Drysdale in Edinburgh. I've told him you're a capable young man and asked if he can bend his mind to a suitable opening. By all accounts he is well set up and perhaps he will know persons who need a smart lad!" She scrapes out the last of the stew which she gives to her husband. "When I've finished the writing of it I'll need you to take it down to the Coach office at the inn. I'll have it wrapped up and carefully addressed to the castle. Perhaps the coachman will take it for a ha'penny."

From his bed the grandfather calls out: "Yon Drysdale's in the army – the English army!" The adjective almost sticks in his throat but he spits it out.

"Och there's only one army now Faither We're all in the King's service."

"The English king!" Grandfather nearly spills his stew, "or German!"

"No, no. Remember the lands were joined together when Mary, Queen o'Scots' son took the English throne!"

"Aye," Fingal agrees, "King James the sixth."

"The first!" His father corrects him absently.

"I'm no listening to you!" Grandfather mumbles away in disgust.

Lauchlin's mother looks at her youngest. "I cannot have any more people in this room. You do see that, don't you. There will be bairns…"

Fingal looks embarrassed. "Oh Mother…not for a wee while, at least. "Betty has said she doesn't want to be responsible for breaking up the family. Do you not think we could move in here just until McCorqudale or the landlord can find another room?"

His father shakes his head. "You've heard your mother. Now we'll speak no more about it!"

"It's not good too many people living in a confined space." Their mother sounds defensive. "And it's time we found Lauchy suitable work. We'll not rush things but if Andrew can think of something in the big city we'll all have to consider it. Now, who's for a wee piece of cheese?"

But matters were not settled as quickly as they had hoped. The letter to Edinburgh takes about four weeks to elicit a response which is not completely positive. It is clear that Andrew will do his duty by the family if he has to but he would prefer it if some other solution can be found.

Chapter 2

Some months pass before the final decision is taken to send Lauchlin to join his uncle. Now, on a grey, Autumn morning and in lordly isolation, he is perched on the top, rear-facing bench seat of the Edinburgh coach. Looking back along the road they have travelled, he watches the last sight of the high wooden "trees" of the ship-building dock gradually sinking beneath the horizon. It is the first time he has left and he blinks away signs of distress which he blames on the cold wind. He thinks of his mother bent over the stove and wiping the hair away from her face. He tries to pull himself together – *"Ye're no' a wee boy any longer…"* and studies the road where their wheels have cut into the muddy surface and disturbed small puddles. Two or three miles out of the town the road narrows to a single-way track and it takes the loud horn call to make oncoming traffic pull into the side. He sees a shepherd with his dog ease a small flock off the road. Is his life to be similarly disturbed? There are few travellers to be seen. He wonders about robbers, what are they called? Highwaymen – ah yes. He tucks his kerchief with the sovereigns more deeply into his mantle. The wave of homesickness continues to wash over him as he wonders about his future. *"The Lord is my Shepherd, therefore can I lack nothing…"* he thinks back. It will surely be a more exciting life than working the fleeces in Port Glasgow. With a lump in his throat he recalls his grandfather's embrace as he reminded him of the Mackynoun's motto: *Fortune Favours the Bold.* The family will be at supper tonight when he will be absent for the first time in his life. He misses them already. It has taken four or five months of patient discussion for his mother to agree that he should take the Edinburgh coach. She had always yearned for her youngest to move to a definite opening rather than a speculative hope, but she had given way in the end.

"I'm sure my brother Andrew will take good care and not let you work at anything unsuitable."

Last night Fingal had also embraced him and slipped him a half-sovereign which he knows the prospective bridegroom could ill afford.

This morning his mother handed him a bulky travel roll and explained that it held some new clothes as well as pieces of rabbit for his journey. She kissed him tenderly and gave him a knotted hand-kerchief which she said contained three Sovereigns. He thinks now about how she must have skimped to save that enormous sum. His mind ranges over his future, wondering about what lies ahead. It is brought back with a bump as the coach gives a violent lurch. It is a long time since the family had agreed that Fingal was entitled to bring his bride to share his life and that it was therefore clear that Lauchlin or Stuart had to leave. As the weeks passed, they had worried about the decision. Stuart had felt that, as the next oldest, he should go. But Lauchlin was the one who brought in little money and, secretly, his mother had felt he had the best prospects. *Fortune Favours the Bold.* Last night his father had not embraced him. He had formally shaken his hand but there had been a definite tear in his eye when he demanded regular news. Stuart had merely studied his feet as if feeling guilty and never looked directly at his younger brother.

Now, sitting high above the road, he nervously thinks about this uncle whom he has never met. On the other hand, he tells himself, the prospect before him is something to be excited about. This Andrew Drysdale, has been built up in his mind as a successful captain on the staff in the Castle garrison. His mother has told him that Andrew has always been a religious believer in the true faith, by which he decides she means the Catholic supporters of the Stuarts. Strange to think of such a man in the English army. Lauchlin fingers again the letter she has written, he does not know the detail but she will have praised her youngest whom she has coached so intensively and expressed the wish that fine employment with a good future will be found for him. He thinks over the whole matter again and nearly falls into a doze.

He feels the coach slow as the horn is blown and the driver shouts for the road to be cleared. Hanging on to the hand-rail, Lauchlin turns to see a herd of cows being driven towards the city. The castle is perched high on a hill overlooking a smoky congregation of house roofs shining in the damp air.

Having passed the two cow-herds, the vehicle has to slow again as they enter the outer streets of the city. With a caution born of experience, the driver brakes for the occasional bumps as they leave the basic, country highway, for city surfaces some of which are cobbled. The horses' hooves have a tendency to slide over these when wet and each corner gives him another sight of the castle, silhouetted here against a setting sun which has finally decided to put in a late appearance. It is perched high above them. He remembers his grandfather's tale of how the Scottish army had captured the city but left the castle untouched, merely looking in on itself. His grandfather had hummed *'Hey Johnny Cope'*, a reference to the English general who was left looking foolish while the clans rolled past him into England.

The coachman heaves on the reins as the four horses finally draw up at 'The Red Lion'. Under steaming flanks their hooves stamp the cobbles as if impatient for the passengers to alight so that they can pass through the arch to the stables where they know they will be rubbed down, watered and fed.

But out in the yard some of the passengers are slow to ease themselves from the positions they have been forced to occupy for so long. The coach advertises regular and leisurely stops for travellers to enjoy the views and for the 'relief of feelings' but, in truth, the driver and his attendant, "Roley", had been in a hurry to complete the journey. Only after breasting the hills at "Kirk o'Shotts" had the horses been properly rested, giving the passengers a chance to stretch their legs. Some of them ate a light meal to assuage their pangs, an egg, biscuits or even some kind of haggis.

Lauchlin had plucked up the courage to ask the driver about highwaymen. He and Roley had chuckled as they gave the horses a nose-bag.

"Bless my soul, young sir, they would not dare be in these parts!"

Roley had placed a foot on a wheel and stretched up to his seat and uncovered what Lauchlin recognized as some kind of elderly firing piece.

"If they did they might enjoy a wee conversation with my old Bessie here!" They both laughed again.

Although not in the least hungry, Lauchlin had forced himself to eat the rabbit prepared by his mother and he had imagined her in their room, her delicate fingers removing bones from the cold meat and popping them into the stock pot.

Pressing his cap back on his head, Lauchlin collects his bundle from between his legs and quickly descends from the high seat. It seems to be colder than in Port Glasgow. As the evening had begun to draw in, he had felt the wind cutting through his coat. The large backs of Roley and the driver had offered him some protection but he had felt the wisdom of removing his cap before it blew away. Conversation with them had been impossible and he had kept his arms braced across his chest while holding himself securely pressed into the edge of the bench. At this height, the rolling of the coach had often been alarming and he had wondered whether the journey could have been improved with a full complement of other travellers squeezed in as a solid block.

Four other passengers had travelled inside, on the relatively comfortable padded cushions. As they now emerge, chatting together, it is clear to him that inside travel for a gentleman is far more conducive to social exchange as well as being a sight warmer. In concert with the horses, he stamps his feet in the yard as he waits, allowing his body to warm, wondering about his next steps.

A tanned, almost dwarf-like man approaches him. His trousers had once been white and he is wearing a faded red jacket with brass buttons. "Begging your pardon, sir, might you be Mr.Mackinnon?"

"Er yes, Mackynoun, are you from Mr.Drysdale?"

"Begging your pardon, sir, the captain sent me down to escort you to your lodgings, my name is Bonnington."

Lauchlin sees his teeth are as brown as his face and there is a large gap in the centre. "How do you do, Mr.Bonnington, but how did you know when I was arriving?"

"Begging your pardon, sir, just Bonnington, but he sent Emily and me with the small wagon every day!"

"That's very kind of you, er Bonnington, I am obliged to you."

Leading the way through the arch, Bonnington takes care to avoid the small accumulations of wet hay and other detritus. There is a fresh, animal smell which Lauchlin welcomes. The small man merely nods,

"Begging your pardon, sir, but many may think this duty more agreeable than drilling in the square or washing a shirt."

A thin, brown mare is standing in the shafts of a small cart, her head buried in a nose bag. "'Ere we are, Emily – time to go 'ome!" As he takes off the nose bag which he throws in the back, he puts a cone-shaped cap on his head. It looks as dirty as the rest of his turn-out but Lauchlin can just make out the number "52" embroidered in red on a background that had once been yellow.

Lauchlin throws his bundle up on the seat. The cart leans over precariously as he hauls himself on. He looks down, "Oh, you're a soldier, Bonnington?"

He spits on the cobbles as he unwinds the leather reins which were wrapped around a post and climbs up beside Lauchlin. Making a clicking sound through his teeth, he murmurs 'walk on.'

"Begging your pardon, sir, I am the Captain's man, 52nd of Foot, sir, right of the Line! Would you happen to know, sir, the address of your lodgings?"

"No I don't Bonnington. I don't know what arrangements Mr.Dry… er the Captain, has made for me."

They proceed at walking pace through the old city. He pulls his coat tightly around him. Smoke drifts down from chimneys all the way, obscuring any sight of the moon. Bonnington clears his throat and spits again.

"Begging your pardon sir, I' that case we'd best go to the Captain's lodgings."

"Will he be there already? Not on duty at the castle?"

Bonnington makes no reply and seems to concentrate on the horse. Lauchlin looks around as the darkness deepens. Candles and oil lamps are being lit in several of the houses which are mainly two storey structures, many sharing a small arched entrance to the rear, presumably wealthy enough to have their own stables. The air is cold and he thinks again of his family who will shortly be coming home. Through the windows the houses look prosperous and comfortable. The mare makes heavy weather of the steep climb towards the castle.

"All right, Emily my dear, nearly there." Lauchlin sees no sign of control through the reins but, as if by habit, she turns down an alley to the right and draws up at a dwelling illuminated by an oil lamp reflected in a low, red-painted door. Two horses with blankets and nose-bags are tethered outside to iron rings in the wall. There are windows on either side and there would appear to be no shortage of candles.

"Begging your pardon, sir, but here are his lodgings. Will you enter first and I will take Emily to her stable, give her some oats and bring in your luggage."

Lauchlin turns the latch and pushes at the door. It makes a scraping sound and he has to lean his weight upon it. He blinks against the light and sees four men in the room seated around a square, gaming table. Rugs cover much of the plain, flagged floor. After the cold outside, the warmth seems excessive. He can barely breathe. The room is thick with smoke, partly from the open fire and, more heavily, from the long clay pipes which three of them are holding. One looks up.

"Well well, this must be the young scion of the Mackinnons! Something of a skinny-m'lynx I'm thinking!" He rises and comes forward. His tone of voice and welcoming, outstretched hand belying the severity of the spoken words.

"I am Lauchlin Mackynoun, sir," he says, taking the proferred hand and giving a small bow as his mother had taught him.

"Good to see you, good to see you!" Drysdale turns to look back at the others. "Allow me to introduce you to these gentlemen – if that's not stretching a point. First, here is Captain John, the Viscount Leadbetter, Highlanders, and 71st Regiment of the Line - just don't play cards with him!"

The Viscount makes a half-hearted rise to his feet. "Your servant, sir."

Lauchlin is taken aback. He sees a young man around his brother Stuart's age wearing plaid trews in dark green. He has fair, crinkled hair and a friendly expression. How should he reply? His mother had not prepared him for this. "H..how do you do, s.s.sir." Drysdale murmurs quietly in his ear: "just say my lord…" Lauchlin gives him a half bow and repeats "My lord."

Drysdale moves him towards a plump figure almost chewing on his pipe. He is darker with something like a sneering expression. He has a trimmed moustache and has removed a short wig which is on a chair by his side. But what impresses Lauchlin most is that the man is fat. Throughout his years in Port Glasgow he supposed the most influential individual was the rent collector. Although clearly comfortable, he could never have been thought of as over-fed. This man, however, overlaps the chair he is sitting in. Indeed, the chair is nowhere in sight. These people must be rich indeed. Drysdale intones: "Major Friedrich Beaudesert, King's Hessian Dragoons." The man nods at Lauchlin who half bows again and repeats "your servant, sir."

"Now we come to Captain Brian McNulty – 24th Foot!" Lauchlin sees a younger man with a tanned, freckled face. They bow to each other.

Raising his voice Drysdale calls out: "Mistress Judge, some ale if you please and is it time for our chops to be prepared?" With the question he turns to the Viscount with an enquiring look which receives a positive nod.

It has been a long day with novel adventures and Lauchlin is uncertain about how to react to these strangers who are clearly quite relaxed in their own company and not greatly interested in meeting him.

With a scraping sound, the front door is opened again and Boddington appears with Lauchlin's bundle. "Begging your pardon, sirs, I pass through."

He opens a door at the back and they hear the thump of his feet climbing stairs. The door to the kitchen is opened and a plump, red-haired woman of about Lauchlin's mother's age comes in with four tankards of ale, two in each hand.

"Ah, Mistress Judge, this is the gentleman we have been expecting – a flagon for him also, if you please, and I trust an extra chop which we shall eat as soon as it suits you."

Mistress Judge bobs in Lauchlin's direction while she lays down the tankards. "Right away, Captain Drysdale and will he be sharing your accommodation?"

"Ah yes indeed, for the present at any rate. My campaign bed will suffice," he takes a quick glance in his nephew's direction, "for him, of course!"

Lauchlin has another moment of homesickness. He wishes himself safely back at home. Then he pulls himself up. This is the adventurous life he sought. Mentally he stands straighter; he thinks of his mother's *Ye're no a wee boy any more*. Of a sudden he realizes he has not emptied his bladder since the stop at Kirk o'Shotts. He bends in Drysdale's direction: "Your pardon, uncle, but is there a garden here or a privy?"

"A garden! Great Heavens, sir." Clearly talking to the whole room, he speaks theatrically: "This is the capital city. We are enriched with the finest privies imaginable but, if it pleases you, there is a commode behind the screen there which saves us time when we are at the cards!"

Slightly shame-faced, Lauchlin goes behind a heavy curtain which acts as a screen. He finds a pot much like the one used by his grandfather. It is already nearly half full. There is some light-hearted ribaldry while they appear to deal out the cards. When he emerges, he takes up the tankard of ale which is very welcome and watches the game. It is totally unfamiliar to him but appears to involve them playing in pairs and recording their scores individually.

After the first deal, Drysdale turns to him. "This is called 'Whist' - a confounded old game, probably French – damn their eyes!" He consults the score and continues, "as a result of which we are down some four and a half guineas to my lord Leadbetter and Major Beaudesert!" Lauchlin feels somewhat intimidated by their attitudes. Drysdale seems surprisingly unfazed by the loss which, in Lauchlin's eyes is a life-changing sum, enough to have kept his whole family fed and warmed for some weeks.

"You have had a run of bad luck, Drysdale," Major Beaudesert speaks, without any sympathy, in a heavy German accent emanating from a mouth that is but a line beneath the moustache and above several chins. "Maybe it will change after our supper!"

Bonnington and Mistress Judge come in at that point bearing large trays. She is wearing a pale grey pinafore that covers her from neck to foot. There is more ale and she lays a cloth on a larger table at the back of the room. Bonnington puts out cutlery and uncovers a dish disclosing a mound of mouth-watering mutton chops.

"Come sirs, I am ready for this!" Drysdale stands and carries his chair to the table. The Lord Leadbetter does the same, saying, "so am I sir, as you see, ever following your lead!"

The others chuckle, Captain McNulty offers: "very good, my lord!"

Lauchlin sees the fat Hessian officer lean heavily on the card table as he hauls himself to his feet. McNulty moves his chair to the dinner table. "I'll wager our young friend here is ready for a cutlet or two, eh. Mackinnon?"

Lauchlin nods eagerly. "I had my breakfast porage some thirteen hours ago sir, and a wee snack atop Shotts Hill."

Mistress Judge pushes another chair to the table. "Sit yourself down, young sir, and enjoy the Captain's supper."

Lauchlin needs no second bidding but, before they start, Bonnington comes round offering each in turn a ceramic bowl of water into which he has squeezed a small sponge. They rinse their fingers, drying them on a linen napkin. Eating whilst seated is something of a new experience for Lauchlin but his mother has been briefing him on customs and codes of etiquette. The chops are served up with what he takes at first to be porage but it seems to have been cooked in a different way and tastes of onion. He watches carefully as they take up their knives and forks. The latter are new to him and he wonders why they had needed to rinse their fingers so carefully before eating since they do not appear to touch the food.

He forces himself to eat slowly, hoping that he will be offered a second helping. But the meal is taken leisurely. "The news from the Cape is not good, my lord," Drysdale opens quietly, "it seems that we have lost another transporter ship on its way to India with perhaps nearly four hundred men on board."

Lord Leadbetter is startled. "Oh God, another storm? Have you read anything of Colonel Ferguson himself? I always said we should never have handed the Cape back to the Hollanders. They're simply a French department again! That damned Bonaparte!"

McNulty agrees. "We had to lose some good troops to get it initially then went and gave it back!"

There is a general pause before Drysdale continues. "It was that dreadful treaty in Amiens. We know how the government wanted peace and, I imagine, agreed to whatever they asked. The Corsican is now seen in his true colours. We shall not make that mistake again."

Leadbetter smiles ruefully. "Still, we kept hold of Canada. And now we shall just have to go and take back the Cape."

The Hessian Major drums his fingers on the table and adds quietly: "It will take more than an explorative raid. It will need a stronger force and the Dutch Minheers will be expecting us!"

Leadbetter nods. "Disembarking on a beachland is often perilous. It's virtually on the Equator is it not. Just where the Atlantic meets the Indian Ocean. The devil for ships rounding it on the way to India. We must hold the Cape again!""

They concentrate on their food in silence once more. Then Leadbetter turns to Lauchlin. "And what do you plan to do with yourself, young man?"

"I have come to Edinburgh in pursuit of a career, my lord. I must seek an opening that will lead to a successful life."

Drysdale chuckles quietly in support. "We are yet an open book John. Clean pages awaiting the pen and ink of life to flow over them."

Leadbetter laughs. "That is beautifully put Andrew – damn me, downright poetic!"

The German major puts in. "Things are difficult in Hesse with this war. They say Napoleon is marching in all directions. The Austrians and the Russians should put a stop to his latest adventure. A youthful fellow with the means and with good health could do worse than join a fine regiment."

A young woman comes in to clear away the dishes. She looks at Lauchlin with open interest. Drysdale gives a quiet laugh: "It's all right, Margret, this is my nephew, he will be staying a while – no need to eat him up immediately!"

The maid colours up quite prettily as she carefully stacks plates on a tray. "Losh Sir – I meant no such thing!"

Drysdale merely smiles. "Well, come along Gentlemen, these cards will not deal themselves and I am feeling lucky!" John, Captain the Viscount Leadbetter, rises and moves his chair, back towards the gaming table.

Chapter 3

Lauchlin sleeps well on Drysdale's campaign bed placed some three feet away from his uncle. He is used to the sounds of others sleeping close by. Grandfather, in particular, was a constant noise in the night, caused either by discomfort in his limbs – settling his bones he used to complain - or simply the need to relieve his bladder. Here the building is generally quiet and the sounds of the city more remote than the noises in Port Glasgow where the clogs of workers trudging to their benches in mill, forge or yard were frequent. The Edinburgh air also, whilst smoky from the many chimneys, seems cleaner. Until getting clear he had not been particularly aware of the intense smells emanating from the wool mill.

Drysdale does not wake quietly. Apart from general body sounds that he emits in his sleep he generally passes a quiet night. But his consciousness returns with energy and a desire for activity which intrude on Lauchlin's gentle transition from dreams to reality. Drysdale sleeps in his shirt and he leaps from his bed shouting for Bonnington. By the time he has returned from the 'long-drop' privy behind the kitchen, Bonnington has brought hot water and prepared a chair for his master. He shaves Drysdale every other day with a vicious-looking razor about five inches long which he hones after almost every stroke. When the shaving is completed, he wraps Drysdale's face in a steaming-hot towel leaving only a small opening through which the remaining stem of a clay pipe containing only the residue of last night's final smoke is introduced. Drysdale chews and sucks on this under the towel while formalizing his plans for the day.

Lauchlin finds himself generally ignored during these operations and proceeds with his ablutions as he can.

Over breakfast on the second morning, he had looked up from his porage and biscuit asking for advice on how to find employment.

"Oh time enough for that young'un – I'm more interested in teaching you the rudiments of Whist – with the approach of Christmas and the New Year I shall be in need of a good and regular partner!"

Lauchlin is surprised at the seemingly erratic nature of his uncle's working day. Some mornings he goes up to the castle before six; at other times it can be nearly mid-day before he dons his uniform and strolls away from Mrs. Judge's. He explains that his duties are to act as a liaison officer between his regiment – The Northumbrian Fusiliers – and the several Scots regiments recruiting in the castle. Lauchlin uses his own spare time by walking into the city and identifying the commercial centre. He seeks work in rather an idle fashion. Several afternoons and most evenings are spent over cards and he finds the calculations and risk assessments of Whist stimulating. He begins to partner his uncle on visits to other lodgings. He is a careful player and only runs a 'finesse' when he feels the odds favour him. He writes to his mother twice a week explaining that he is learning about city habits and that it will not be long before he obtains full and worth-while employment. He sends the letters back by the Glasgow coach.

This idyllic life comes to a close during his fourth week. Lounging about after breakfast he is running over in his mind last night's success at cards when he overhears a worrying discussion between Drysdale and his landlady. Mrs. Judge is explaining that it is some two months since his rent and board were settled and she is finding it difficult to allow its continuance especially with an extra mouth to feed. A sheepish-sounding Drysdale responds by handing over some of the back-log and replying that recent Messing bills had been high and also that previous losses at cards are in course of being corrected. With a pang of conscience, Lauchlin reminds himself that the Sovereigns inserted among his clothing are not the results of his frugality. He is struck by disappointment at his own conduct and aware that he must begin to pay his way.

That evening he brings up the subject with Drysdale and asks him to accept a small payment for rent and board. His uncle is embarrassed and his face flushes but as Lauchlin presses the matter they agree on a charge of half-a-guinea per week.

By nine o'clock the next morning, Lauchlin is down in James Street where he knows the greatest number of lawyers and accountants keep their chambers. It is bitterly cold and has started to snow. As he walks along he takes such shelter as he can from overhanging roofs and balconies.

The quality of the buildings is high, many with wrought-iron railings. The paving beneath his feet is sound and the dampness reminds him that he will need new shoes soon if he is to wander the streets looking for work in such weather. He had passed some trading premises on his way down and is certain that at least one was a cobbler's workshop. With a decision made he steps out more confidently only to suffer a light deluge down his neck from a thawing balcony.

He stops to shake the water off his shoulders and his eyes alight on a small sign fixed to a door: *'Smart Lad wanted. Must be able to Read'.* He pushes the door and steps down into a stone-flagged room around thirty feet by twenty. There is a long counter behind which he sees three men standing at writing desks. The light is poor and lamps hang from the ceiling making the air quality poor. Their ages vary from about twenty to more than twice that. The eldest approaches him. He is wearing a dark, knee length jacket and black waistcoat over a pale shirt. From the light at the entrance Lauchlin can see the clothes are somewhat ragged and have been subject to careful darning.

Through the oily smoke, the old man's eyes are sharp and questioning and he stares up as Lauchlin stands before him. His neck is thin and heavily lined with an Adam's apple rising and falling from a soiled white collar. "Yes, s..si.." he lets the respectful address hang in the air when he sees the age of his visitor. "What can I do for you?"

"You have a sign outside, sir. You need a smart lad. I can read, write and do my numbers!"

"Mmm?" He peers keenly at the young applicant. "We want a lad who will deliver letters around the city. They are most important and we will not accept any dawdling!"

"May I enquire about the emoluments, sir?" It is a phrase he has heard used.

The man blinks. "Subject to a satisfactory trial period, the emoluments are nine shillings and sixpence per week – paid on Saturday evening at six pm. after satisfactory completion of six full days. The hours are eight a.m. to six p.m. Lateness will not be condoned. Do you have references from your last employer?"

"No sir. I have only recently arrived from Port Glasgow where I was employed in a woollen mill."

"No references eh! Well, we can give you a trial but the pay will be eight shillings and sixpence."

Grasping his courage, Lauchlin frowns: "Sir, I will accept the lower figure but for only the first week. If my performance is satisfactory I must ask for the full nine shillings and sixpence thereafter!"

There is a loud laugh from one of the others in the room – "Good lad!"

The older man turns from the counter: "Berenson! Any more of your wild behaviour and I shall report you to Mr. Kendrick." He addresses Lauchlin: "We shall see about that. Will you start at eight tomorrow morning?"

"I can start now sir!"

The man moves down the counter and lifts a flap. "Come through then and let me have a few particulars."

In this way Lauchlin is employed as a messenger for McCulloch and Kendrick, an established Accountancy office. Within thirty-five minutes he is back on the street with a leather satchel over one shoulder containing eleven letters all folded, sealed with the firm's official stamp in red wax and addressed to other companies in a variety of streets about which he knows little. By dint of enquiring he manages to deliver them all, even those concealed up small, hidden stairs in quiet and dark alleys.

He returns to the office just before one thirty to find only the young Mr.Berenson at his desk. He is told that Mr. Colquhoun, the older clerk and office manager is in with Mr. Kendrick. The other clerk, Mr.Treddle, is taking dictation from the senior partner, Mr. McCulloch.

Berenson slaps him on the back: "Well done, young sir! Don't you take any nonsense from Colquhoun – he's a bully and his heart died some five years ago, - his head perishes as we watch!"

After his rather meagre breakfast, Lauchlin wonders about some sustenance to keep him going until his return to Mrs. Judge's. Berenson advises him to carry a snack with him eating it while out of the office, perhaps on his morning round.

There are only six letters for delivery in the afternoon. All to local addresses. On his return, he is put to sweeping the floor area but advised to sprinkle a small amount of water to avoid any dust rising. The quantity of such water is a constant irritation to Mr.Colquhoun who fusses about with instruction.

Lauchlin follows this pattern for nearly a month. After his second week the pay is increased to the full nine shillings and sixpence, all of which is faithfully passed to his cousin leaving a shortfall of a shilling per week. Each morning he leaves Mrs. Judge's promptly at half-past seven with some small sustenance for his lunch. Sometimes Drysdale is still lying in bed. There are rarely many letters for the afternoon and he learns the storage system whereby the original, in-coming letters and copies of all outgoing correspondence are carefully filed.

Christmas Day in 1803 is on a Tuesday. It is the first of a two-day holiday. On the following Thursday morning Mr. Treddle, the more senior of the two juniors fails to put in an appearance. Kendrick, the younger partner is much troubled by the absence.

"Oh dear, Mr. McCulloch wishes to despatch a number of important letters today! You'd better attend him Colquhoun, Berenson's writing is not good enough for letters from the senior partner but he'll have to do mine!"

Lauchlin does not let the opportunity pass. "If you please sir, I have been complimented on the quality of my letters – and I am good with numbers too."

Kendrick turns and looks at him, perhaps for the first time. "Mmm… well, right then, come through and I'll see what you're like…"

As Lauchlin follows him through to the back office he cannot fail to see the blazing anger in Berenson's face. He realizes that his precipitative action has pushed his colleague out of possible promotion. He worries about the situation for some moments but soon concentrates on his new duties after all, he also needs promotion.

He is placed at the end of a large desk where Kendrick seats himself with his back to a window looking out on a bare yard. The light is not good but the air is less smoky. Then Kendrick lights a cigar and settles himself more comfortably in his large chair.

An inkwell, pens and paper are standing at the end of the desk. The system calls for Lauchlin to prepare the original, perfect letter after transcribing any copies that are needed.

"Right then, err…Mackinnon, this is a letter to MacBride and Thompson, address as before in Edinburgh…." He draws on the cigar whilst consulting papers on the table, then continues: "*..Pursuant to yours of 29th October 1803, it is our view that the tenancy agreement was for a de jure possession until...*" he pauses. "What's the matter? These phrases new to you? Well you'd better get used to them!"

Lauchlin is shaken but struggles on. He identifies the phrases as probably Latin but knows that he will have to seek help in their spelling.

Colquhoun, the senior clerk enters the room and whispers to Mr.Kendrick that he is wanted by Mr.McCulloch. Kendrick puts down his cigar and hurriedly follows Colquhoun to the senior partner's office. Lauchlin takes the chance to settle himself more comfortably and tidy up the headed notepaper. Suddenly the door is burst open and Berenson enters. He nudges Lauchlin aside and picks up the inkwell before spreading the contents over the desk where it begins to drip on the floor. He then hurries out again without a word.

Lauchlin does what he can to mop up the black ink which has spoiled many sheets of paper and is now staining the fine wood of the desk.

Kendrick and Colquhoun come back into the office muttering together. At first the senior clerk notices nothing but Mr.Kendrick starts forward with a bellow of fury.

"What the devil do you think you are doing, boy? You ..." He is lost for words as Colquhoun calls for Berenson to bring cloths and cleaning materials. Then he looks at Lauchlin. "Get out! Get out! Get him out of my sight, Colquhoun!"

After strenuous efforts for justification while helping to mop up the mess, Lauchlin is dismissed. He leaves without any references and knows that finding further employment will now be harder.

In something of a daze, he wanders around the area. He realizes that Berenson had seen his actions as a declaration of war. He tells himself it is a lesson he must remember but it does nothing to restore his confidence. He looks down at his ink-stained fingers and tries to clean them on damp railings.

Alexander Place is a turning off James Street and seems mainly populated by lawyers' offices. One of these, Rose and Mathewson, has a sign at the door saying '*Smart Boy wanted*' but it transpires that all the applicant needs is the ability to sweep the step and do such tasks as crop up. More to the point is the fact that the pay is a miserable four shillings and threepence a week. Lauchlin explains to the office manager that he has skills in writing and accounting and cannot accept less than twelve shillings a week. Without further ado he is shown the door.

He stands outside as the evening throws a chill dampness around his shoulders. The earlier snow has stopped but the air is freezing the wet pavement. There is a silence and a clarity of sound that encourages him to think he can hear the noises of Leith Docks coming up from below the city. It reminds him of Port Glasgow and homesickness again closes in on him. Should he have accepted the work in the office even though the pay was so low? What would his father advise? He longs for the security of his family. He feels useless at not being able to hold on to his work even as a messenger. That action of Berenson's was evil. His misery is compounded when he sees a young man of about his own age looking curiously at him. He has just come out of the offices. He is dressed in the smartest of city clothes which are quite unsuitable for this weather: a dark jacket with silver buttons over blue velvet britches with white stockings and dainty polished shoes. Their eyes meet and the youth addresses him:

"Ah Mr. Mackinnon, excuse me but I overheard what you were just saying to Mr. Rose. If you really can write and keep an account I think you might be the answer for my uncle Mr. Francis Reardon in his business at Malcolm Chambers. Perhaps you would care to come with me and let him look at your teeth and generally study your bloodstock!"

Lauchlin stares at the speaker. Is he some kind of clown? His build is slight and there is nothing to lose in accompanying him. He learns that the name of the young man is Struan Reardon. The uncle referred to is a tailor of some reputation in Edinburgh.

"He badly needs an accountant who will extricate him from current difficulties. I have spent some small time on his books but I must return to my studies in St.Andrews!"

Malcolm Chambers is a row of high class shops running between James Street and Upper George Street. Struan swings the mainly glass door open and calls out: "Hector! Kindly inform my uncle that I may have obtained the answer to his prayers!"

It is a room some thirty feet square with one small window set high in a corner. What light there is enters mainly through the glass door although a lamp swings over a low work table. The four walls are surmounted just above head height by a wooden pole bearing a line of clothes hangers on which a selection of half-finished suits with rows of white cotton stitching is displayed. The single chair is placed near a mirror standing on a small rug. Hector clearly works on the floor at the small table some two feet high. He rises immediately to greet them. Lauchlin is impressed by the effortless ascent of such elderly limbs. He is wearing an apron with a thin scarf around his neck to which is affixed what Lauchlin at first takes to be a brooch but which on closer examination is a black velvet pin cushion.

"Good evening, Master Struan, Mr. Francis is in his office." A small door at the side opens and the Master Tailor comes through. Francis Reardon is a thin, bent man of about sixty. He seems to be formally dressed in a fine white shirt and dark britches but much of it is obscured beneath a heavy cotton apron. His thin, pinched face peers through a pair of small, wire-framed spectacles. He blinks benignly at his visitors.

"Oh it's yourself is it Struan. It's good to see you, yes, yes indeed!" Just as Lauchlin thinks the greeting is at an end it continues: "Are ye not due back at St.Andrews? Those clothes are very fine for an evening at Court but a mite too elegant for dusty student lodgings – are they not?"

"They are, Uncle, and I shall be changing them soon. I dressed formally because I went to see some Counting Houses in James Street hoping that they would sort out the difficulties I have been outlining to you. Sadly their costs were higher than I felt justified. Instead I have been fortunate to encounter Mr. Mackinnon here who would like to carry out this work for twelve shillings and sixpence a week."

The discussions continue for another thirty minutes. Hector returns to his sewing early in the proceedings. Struan and his uncle, whom Lauchlin quickly learns to call Mr. Francis, take him through to the office and show him an untidy mass of trade bills and invoices. Some attempt has been made to enter them in Credit and Debit Registers and in a separate Record of Accounts but it all seems to have been abandoned.

Struan tries to explain: "My uncle is a fine master tailor and Hector has served him for many years but people have taken advantage of them. Mr. Francis is not good at administration – are you Uncle? – And you will see that it needs some sorting!"

Lauchlin has never been involved in accounting and, whilst dismayed at the prospect is attracted by the money. Also, it looks to be a more interesting job. With Struan he bends over the table and studies the documents. He notices that the Credit entries of money owed far outweigh the value of receipts. Interested he sits and starts sorting the mass of papers into separate piles. He finds that it is mainly straight addition and subtraction that is involved together with the need to separate outgoings and receipts in files.

In this way, Lauchlin becomes an employee of the respected business of Francis Reardon & Company, Master Tailor. The work is absorbing and he is soon writing letters to clients reminding them of unpaid accounts. Over the following weeks many of these result in an encouraging flow of monies. The three of them share in the delivery of the letters. Lauchlin is intrigued to see so many of them going to officers in the Castle Garrison. One of these is Captain Andrew Drysdale drawing his attention to a debt of forty-three shillings for bespoke woollen uniform britches.

There are also several unpaid accounts from wool and cloth suppliers. Mr. Francis explains that these must be paid as they cut off supplies after some weeks. "I tried doing the same thing to my own clients but they merely took their business elsewhere!"

In a loose discussion of the matter over Whist some time later, Lauchlin is shocked when Lord Leadbetter chuckles: "Well, nobody pays his tailor does he?"

He continues to find the work satisfying and feels that he is making a useful contribution to the business. Following a discussion with a client he decides to aim for an accounting qualification. One suggestion he follows is for an additional control. Mistakenly he calls it an Agenda but he opens an extra account book which includes every item – loss or gain - which, being strictly in date order gives him a daily summary of the figures.

But it is clear that Hector's health is not good. His breathing is laboured and on occasions Mr. Francis has to draw his attention to sewing errors. At an early stage, Lauchlin is keen to try his hand at sewing but soon finds it is not for him: his eyes ache from too much fine work; his fingers are clumsy and somehow prevent him from following close designs and, if these were not enough, a needle pierces his skin causing bloodstains on a fine piece of silk lining. He stays sorting the accounts, writing up to seven letters a day. But, as the weeks pass, Hector's performance deteriorates and, in a serious discussion, Mr. Francis admits that the problems of running the business are dragging him down. "I'm grateful to ye, young Lauchlin, but I am myself no longer what I used t'be." He confesses that he has received an offer for the business from a larger establishment that already has its staffing needs but requires more space.

"I tried explaining that you only joined us some four or five months ago and had already made a great impression on the business but they say they only want the premises and my customer lists. I'm so very sorry."

He goes on in a roundabout way to discuss Lauchlin's plans for the future and promises him an excellent reference.

Lauchlin is shaken by his words. These last months have been a useful experience and he is conscious of the value it has been to him. He had been planning to seek an increase in pay, confident of the value he was adding but that was clearly out of the question now. He determines once more to find a solid position where he can progress in a career that will make his mother proud.

Chapter 4

The loss of his interesting and well-paid work hits Lauchlin hard. Through the early Summer he continues seeking rewarding work. He fills some positions but through no fault of his own they lead nowhere. It is the loss of a full and useful day that he misses most.

As May turns into June, introducing a thin, warming sunshine, he remains lodging with Captain Drysdale at Mistress Judge's. Financially he does not appear to be suffering at all and is well able to pay the weekly sum to his uncle. Although he finds his life enjoyable, he remains determined to secure employment. He uses his eyes and ears constantly, hoping to hear of another opening suitable for his talents. He well knows that his winnings at Whist cannot be relied on.

Meanwhile he soaks up etiquette and customs and finds being waited on by Mrs. Judge and the girl, Margret who turns out to be Bonnington's daughter, a pleasant experience. Although his outgoings are minimal, he does find that he is spending too much of his savings on essential clothing, tips and small rewards.

He continues to sleep in his underwear recalling how after some initial weeks, Margret had pointed out that she could not find his nightgown to launder and she had, therefore, made him two new ones from her old petticoats. He had immediately recognized her account as a means of gaining his attention. Pretending a shocked severity, Lauchlin had hurried to her side in the bedroom knowing full well that she was merely playing a game. After all, Drysdale himself slept in his shirt. Giggling she had held up a new gown and asked him if it was the right size and style. Coyly she suggested he should try it on. He went to snatch it from her but she twisted away. Within seconds she was in his arms with his lips close to hers. He pressed hard against her. But his rapid passion had frightened her and she had made her escape. From that time there was a playfulness and a familiarity in their relationship which was not lost on the others. At one stage Drysdale overhears their exchanges. He strictly advises his nephew to avoid such an involvement – "the girl knows no letters or numbers" –*Lauchlin's sights must be set higher.* They nearly have a falling-out as Lauchlin reminds his uncle that his own roots are also somewhat shallow. Nevertheless he realizes the sense of his uncle's words.

Captain McNulty has been ordered to take his contingent of the 24th Fusiliers to Kent to join the major part of his regiment at Shorncliffe Camp. With his departure, followed by others, Lauchlin is increasingly needed as a fourth at Whist, often partnering his uncle. He has learned the game quickly and become adept. He continues to make a few shillings. More importantly he has established a good relationship with several of the officers. As the year progresses the longer evenings introduce another new experience.

They play their cards at different lodgings, enjoying their ales and suppers to a degree according to the status of the host, varying from Lord Leadbetter's rooms, actually attached to the castle State Rooms, to a somewhat small lodging in a seedier area used by a lieutenant of a lower Rifle Regiment. But the sense of family is strong and there is never a hint of criticism about social standing. He learns that the G.O.C., Major General Williamson, is related by marriage to Lord Leadbetter. Consequently his rooms are beautifully furnished and he is cared for by two Fusiliers who share the batting between them.

The quality of the cards they use there is also superior and they are cleaner. Lauchlin assumes that new cards are brought out before the old packs are soiled through use. The small chairs they sit on are something of a challenge for Major Beaudesert's figure but the table is a real pleasure – lightly gilded legs and a soft, green baize top. Lauchlin is convinced that he always plays better in these surroundings and this particular evening is no exception. He lays down the four last trump cards claiming the hand by four tricks over the 'book'. There is general congratulation about his play. Drysdale joins in the plaudits:

"Ah well, partner. You know what they say: Lucky at cards – unlucky in love!" This is a new saying to Lauchlin and it shows on his face. Drysdale continues: "actually very good, partner, nice play though I will concede we were fortunate in the position of those two queens before your kings!"

"I trust" Leadbetter intercedes, amidst laughter, "that you are not referring to the four of us when you say that!"

Later, during a lull over their supper, Leadbetter happens to mention his need to collect some property from a house he is selling in Eyemouth, a fishing village just North of the English border, perhaps seventy miles to the South-east of the city.

"It's an old family house used by two elderly aunts. They have both now died and the place is not of any interest to us. But there are some family pieces we don't want to lose. I could send a couple of the lads but there is some fine silver and glass and I feel the responsibility would be too great. I can't get away myself for at least three or four weeks. What is known about the larger city carters? – can they be trusted? - It's a bit of a problem."

"How much is there to bring back?" Drysdale asks. "Could Lauchlin do it with Bonnington and his old Emily?"

"Mmm…no, I don't think so. Need a bigger wagon and better with a couple of horses…it's a lonely area and I wouldn't want to be stranded out there. Also," and he rubs his chin, "some of the stuff is fairly valuable."

Having spent part of his morning in a lawyer's office whose main business seemed to be property security, Lauchlin asks whether the material could be insured.

"Oh certainly – I would do that. But the truth is that we'd like the silver here. Most of it was my grandfather's. Some of the glassware has precious memories too."

Lauchlin looks up. "I'd be happy to go, sir, but we'd need help with the wagon and I don't know if Bonnington can manage two horses."

"Oh I wasn't trying to palm the job off on you, Lauchlin, but thank-you – it is a thought. Two of my fusiliers – an older and more experienced pair – with their muskets perhaps…borrow one of the regimental carts, they're a good size actually…well, it would be doing us an enormous favour…"

Drysdale looks pensive. "I'm sure Bonnington would be useful there. I can spare him for a couple of days."

Leadbetter nods. "Well, thank you, we'll think about it. Now – back to the cards!"

Most of the other officers' rooms, like those of Major Beaudesert, are simpler and closer to Drysdale's so that they walk over as soon as his work for the day is done, often by about four pm. Occasionally he has duties that detain him, such as Orderly Officer or Stick Officer for the day. But Lauchlin now rarely misses his evenings at cards. About once a month he goes without his uncle. It is something he finds slightly distasteful though he knows it is a common enough event. He recalls the first time, about four weeks after he had come to Edinburgh, being due at Major Beaudesert's for a game, Drysdale had told him to go alone.

"I cannot play cards tonight, I …err have another engagement." To Lauchlin's look of enquiry Drysdale had continued "and please don't return before ten – I shall need the room to myself."

Lauchlin now always does as requested but he knows that on returning he will find the bedroom in some disarray and smelling of scented powder. No comment is ever made on the matter and Lauchlin maintains an appropriate silence, after all the rooms are not his. On one occasion he was privately amused when, clearing away the breakfast dishes the morning following one such evening, Bonington had bent quietly over and handed Drysdale a fine hair pin carved from something like jade and representing the Scottish lion:

"Begging your pardon, Captain. But I think this belongs to Miss Adeline." Drysdale had simply taken it from him and said nothing.

Lauchlin realizes that his presence is not always so welcome.

He likes to spend an occasional morning at a coffee shop in Princes Street where a daily newspaper is available to read while enjoying his drink. He studies the news and reads about job opportunities while carefully observing city life. He considers the minor expense worth-while.

About a fortnight after Leadbetter had raised the question of removing his household materials, Lauchlin learns that two fusiliers will be available in three days' time for the trip to Eyemouth. An elderly housekeeper will have the silver and glass ready for their collection and he is told that it will all be carefully packed in straw and boxed up so that there need be no delay at that end. He asks Bonnington whether he can manage the reins for two horses.

"Begging your pardon, sir, but I can't manage any 'orse. Old Emily she just axes me where we're going and I tell'er. That's it really."

Having discussed the route and consulted a map they decide to depart at six a.m., just before a fine September dawn which will give them some fourteen hours of daylight for the journey. Lauchlin would like to do it in the one day but realizes they may have to break their journey and sleep in a barn. The weather looks fine with no sign of rain.

The two fusiliers are somewhat unprepossessing and much of a pair. The term *Old soldier* fits them to perfection. Lord Leadbetter had warned him the evening before of this, explaining: "I've told them the stuff is precious and they are to guard it properly. For that reason I've authorized them to take their muskets. But you'll have no trouble – I've arranged for plenty of ale in the wagon so they will be quite content".

They bring the wagon round somewhat later than requested but Lauchlin says nothing. He sees the two muskets lying in some protective straw, side by side. There are several small barrels of ale at the back and he wonders if they have made an early start on the refreshment.

Bonington shakes his head when he first sees them. Both are big men with the square look of highlanders. Private Drewett – *'Drew'* - is sitting up on the box seat with the reins. He is around thirty-five, dark with a bad-tempered look. He seems nervous, perhaps not relishing this opportunity for a day away from military constraints.

Private Jameson –*'Jamie'* - on the other hand is a bundle of energy and apparently anxious to depart. Sitting next to Drew on the box his ginger locks bob about as he speaks. His hair is long and would normally be drawn into a tight bun. Bonington's disapproval is apparent. *Jamie* descends to talk excitedly about the need to depart. He has an angry scar running from his right nostril down to his chin. He would seem to have no teeth at all.

Equipped with a letter of authority from Leadbetter together with a sketch showing the location of the house, Lauchlin climbs in and positions himself on the left side facing inwards and opposite Bonnington. He indicates to Drew that they should make a start.

They set off at a gentle walk down the hill. The cobbles are as wet and slippery to hooves as usual although the day gives promise of warmth. Lauchlin notes that there is little concord between the horses and their driver. There is no friendly conversation as between Bonington and Emily. He says nothing, assuming that this attitude is probably more professional. There is some congestion in the lower streets near the market and they actually come to a stop in Princes Street but are soon on the road to Haddington and East Lothian.

But even on the open road, Drew makes no effort to get the horses cantering. To his enquiry the response is that they have a long day ahead of them. Lauchlin feels suitably chastened. Climbing the hill up to Cockburnspath, the horses proceed even more decorously and at noon Drew pulls off the road pronouncing that it is time for the horses to "'ave a chew". Lauchlin makes a face at Bonington but gets no reaction. The two privates take the opportunity to broach a cask. Lauchlin and Bonington eat some of the *iron rations* they have brought with them.

"Eh bonny lad!" Jamey enquires through a wet, toothless mask, "are ye related to His Lordship?"

Lauchlin admits that he is not but merely carrying out a favour.

"Ah ha! A favour eh. With perhaps a few shillings at the end o' it!"

"No, no. I can assure you of that." He looks for help from Bonington who continues to ignore the situation, though his eyes remain watchful.

They find the house quite easily from Leadbetter's sketch. Approached by a gravel drive it sits above the headlands looking out on a patchy, grey sea. But it is already after four in the afternoon and there are only five hours or so of daylight left. Lauchlin worries about wandering that unknown road in the dark. Bonington gives the animals a nose-bag with some hay while Lauchlin pulls the iron door knocker.

Dame Agnes, the housekeeper, checks quickly through the letter of Authorization and indicates the wooden boxes which are to go.

There are eight of them and they fit comfortably in the back of the wagon nestling in with the ale casks. Bonington ties them down securely with a piece of old rope leaving plenty of room for their legs as before. The housekeeper presses them to "a wee dram to keep out the cold" so that it is after half-past five with the beginning of a fine sunset before they leave the house and go carefully up the drive.

The horses seem to sense that they are travelling homewards and feel rested after their brief pause. Jamie now drives them on and they are soon cantering quite happily.

"Hey Bonny Lad!" Drew calls out from the box seat where he is openly drinking from one of the casks. "We'll have to camp out after all. D'ye ken a place to stay? A place wi' grass and water for the nags?"

Even on the open road the light is becoming poor. Bonington's head facing him is a dark shadow making no discernible movement. Jamie murmurs a quiet reply to Drew's comment. Lauchlin suspects they have both been heavily at the ale.

"Ah yes! Jamie's right. We'll make a call on Mr. Murray, just this side of Dunbar. For half a guinea or so he'll let us use a fine, big barn where the wee naggies can munch his oats!" Lauchlin thinks he hears a quiet hiss from the head opposite.

Without a moon, Jamie has slowed the wagon to a walk. For nearly an hour he and Drew converse in low tones. Lauchlin kneels at the side forcing his eyes to try piercing the total darkness. He moves to the other seat, nudging Bonington aside but it is no better. He cannot recall ever experiencing such blackness and a phrase about Stygian gloom enters his head.

Then, with apparent familiarity, Drew calls out "There!" Jamie turns the horses off the road and down a small track. Peering about him Lauchlin sees a light ahead and they enter a farmyard. Drew sends out a whoop. "Hey, Master Murray! Are ye at home to greet lonely travellers?"

Within a few moments a burly figure is silhouetted against the low lighting in the house. "Ah" It replies, with little evidence of surprise. "Is that you then, Drewie? How many of you are there?"

Bonington eases himself off the cart murmuring to Lauchlin as he passes: "This is not good - just stay there a while, young sir!"

Lauchlin watches the three of them approach Farmer Murray. All four murmur together. After about five minutes Jamie returns. He grasps the head of one of the horses and calls out to Lauchlin. "Ye'd best descend, bonny lad. I'm putting the animals in the meadow for the night."

"But what about the wagon?" He enquires, "it needs guarding and surely the horses should be rubbed down and watered!"

"Och it's only a few hours or so. They'll be right enough." His speech is becoming slurred and Lauchlin is certain that both have been drinking heavily.

He continues to protest. He senses something is not right. The animals will be cold. He knows he cannot leave the cart out in the field unguarded. "No, no! The wagon must be in the barn with us." He turns to ask Murray who has come out of the house: "can we not put the wagon in the barn where we're to sleep? The horses can then be watered and fed in comfort!"

Murray comes out to him. He puts his face an inch from Lauchlin. "Are ye an expert on the horse, then laddie? Ye'll do as ye're told or 'twill be the worse for you!" He grasps Lauchlin by the shoulder to turn him around.

"No, I'm not having this! There's something wrong here!" He breaks away pushing the big man with both arms while feeling behind him for one of the muskets. But Murray is an experienced street fighter and charges with his head down. Lauchlin has the breath knocked out of him and falls heavily banging his head on one of the wagon wheels. He rises quickly, just avoiding a kick to his stomach and lunges towards his adversary. With a scream of hate, Murray lands a blow on his jaw. It is from a man trained to fight and Lauchlin goes down again half in, half out of the wagon. He loses his senses as his head hits the gravel.

He is unconscious for an immeasurable time. When he recovers he finds his hands and feet are tied and he has been thrust into the well of the cart. His neck is twisted and his head aches severely. The "wee dram" pressed on him by Dame Agnes is now spread all over his coat. Apart from feeling ill he is overcome by a sense of his foolishness. But *Bonington,* he thinks, *how could he have been turned?* How long he lies there, passing in and out of consciousness, he cannot tell. His whole world is his mouth and nose buried in foul-smelling whisky and bile. Meanwhile he feels the cold beginning to bite. What an utter, total failure he has turned out to be! Cannot keep even the simplest of jobs and now he has been duped by a couple of simple scoundrels.

He is disturbed by a sudden jolt as the wagon is jerked into motion. There is nothing he can do. He is trapped, filling the space between two vertical wooden walls. Something presses uncomfortably into his back. By arching and switching his position he eventually calculates that he is lying on the two muskets. For a moment that gives him hope but he realizes that with his hands and feet bound he is powerless. The wagon jolts and sways as it is taken up the track. He forces himself to listen. He hears a man panting but it is all too disjointed for him to comprehend.

After perhaps thirty minutes he feels the wagon stop. Someone comes round to the back and it sways as he climbs aboard. He feels his feet being lifted and then released as the rope is cut. He is turned over and the bindings round his wrists are also cut. He drags himself into a sitting position. If he can just have the time and opportunity to reach for a knife or one of the weapons. He thinks he could use it as a cudgel. There is a tearing sensation in his back but he grips the seat and manages to look around him. It is still dark, the risen moon but a slight crescent.

"There we are, sir, reached the main road again." The voice is exhausted but is clearly Bonington's. "If only the moon were larger or could come out a bit more we could make real progress."

"Bonington! What the hell's going on?" His own voice is a rasping croak.

"Let me help you into a more comfortable position sir. There." He sits on the side bench with him. "I was always suspicious of them two larrikins, sir. I thought they was up to no good." He pauses awhile to catch his breath. "I doubt they was the two chosen by His Lordship. They will have slipped in somehow. Some money has spoken I suspect. We was always planned to go to that fellow Murray's place. They planned to be away with all the stuff – p'raps over the border."

"But how did you get us away – there were three of them?"

"And a wife in the kitchen sir. She was as rough as any! I took the precaution of purloining a flask of the Captain's brandy. They was all well sozzled up in the end so I walked out and ran the horses back here to the road. Now, we's best get on, but I don't know how the animals will react to me. Fortunately they're tired and we would all like to get 'ome."

They move to sit side by side on the box. Bonington shows him how to hold the reins for one horse while he tries to control the other but it is not a success. The animals need controlling by one driver. In this way, with Bonington calling out encouragingly to the animals as much as to Lauchlin, they manage to move together at a walk and, after passing through a sleeping Haddington, some kind of a slow canter. They reach the outskirts of the Capital about half-past ten in the morning and walk the animals gently up to the castle.

They are treated as heroes although Lauchlin goes out of his way to stress Bonington's role in the matter but the old soldier maintains that it was only when Lauchlin launched his attack on the farmer that the scale of their villainy became apparent. A runner is sent to the Procurator Fiscal, informing him about the Murrays' part in the affair but Lauchlin hears no more for some weeks. As for Drewett and Jameson, it transpires that, as previous fusiliers who had finished their time, they had continued to maintain a social contact with some of the current regiment and had thus learned of the goods being transported.

As a gesture of thanks, Lord Leadbetter gives Bonnington a sum of ten guineas which he has some difficulty in getting him to accept.

There is a tragic end to these happenings: three days after the arrest of Jameson and Drewett, Bonington's Emily is found dead in her stall at the castle stables. Both of her forelegs had been savagely broken and she has clearly been subjected to a manic attack. It is presumed to be the work of friends or relatives of the guilty men but nothing is ever to be proved.

Chapter 5

James Hogarth, Principal Secretary to the King's First Minister, William Pitt, clutches his heavy cloak to him and shivers. The sharp October winds have blown him along Downing Street to the familiar black door with the simple brass plate. He inserts the large iron key and enters the building. It is not yet seven a.m. but he can already see a light illuminating the corridor leading to the offices.

Hogarth is not completely surprised. Since his return to the greatest Office of State, Mr. Pitt has laboured tirelessly. On arriving from the House last night he set to work and was still drafting despatches when he allowed his Principal Secretary to leave. Hogarth sighs. There will be a large volume of correspondence for the clerks to copy and distribute when they arrive in about an hour.

He wonders how long the Minister can keep up this rate of work. The second son of the first Earl of Chatham has always been sickly. Hogarth knows he was educated at home, largely under the direction of his father and was quickly recognized as an exceptionally gifted child. His doctor prescribed a regular draft of sweet, Port wine as a cure for his ills and, to judge from the steady supply from Masons' Wine Merchants, this recipe for his health still continues.

On his way from his home in the Strand, Hogarth had diverted the coach to Buckingham House to obtain the latest news about the King's illness. It is not good. He seems no worse but the whole administration worries that matters will fall to a halt again as they did some three years ago when His Majesty was laid low for months.

In his small office he takes out the diary for the day. Although familiar with the programme it is as well to ensure nothing is overlooked. Pitt has a habit of slipping little items in where there is no opening. He tries to move silently as he hangs up his cloak. He listens to the sounds emanating from the room next to his. Having served as Principal Secretary ever since Mr. Pitt's resignation three years ago in 1801, he is familiar with every squeak and creak of the furniture. He pictures every detail of what is going on at the Minister's table. It is quiet but perhaps he can hear the scratch of nib on paper and the heavy breathing that accompanies it. A slight cough is in tandem with the clink of the Port decanter as Mr. Pitt pours out more of the libation. While sorting his papers, Hogarth worries about that perennial cough. His master is not a well man. He gives a slight tap on the communicating door and goes through.

"Good morning, my lord!" This is his normal mode of address. Whilst he knows Pitt is not ennobled, his main title is First Lord of the Treasury and Hogarth is firmly of the opinion that nobody in history has managed the nation's finances better. He also knows that Pitt has totally failed in the management of his own affairs. Hogarth is not privy to every detail of his minister's private life but he is fairly certain that he is deeply in debt.

Pitt barely looks up as he mumbles a greeting.

"Remind me, what's on the programme for this morning."

"The Marquess of Bute has requested an appointment when he would like to be accompanied by Baron Grenville and Mr. Addington. I have set it for eleven. I thought you would wish to leave for the Commons at about eleven forty-five."

"Yes, what's on their agenda?"

Hogarth gives a little cough of his own. This will not go down well. "Ireland and the emancipation of the Catholics, Sir, I understand that the Marquess is advising that His Majesty has not changed his mind."

Pitt bangs his fist on the table his anger rising immediately.

"It's worse than that - His Majesty will have none of it!" He gives an angry sigh. "Perhaps it will become a resignation matter again - Incidentally, is there any more news from Buckingham House? Is His Majesty recovered?"

He is told about Hogarth's call on his way. "There is another item, Sir. You asked me to set ninety minutes aside for it. "General Miranda, the Spanish officer is coming at nine together with General Wellesley."

"Ah yes...Mmm.... Get me the maps of the South Atlantic. This needs an element of thought."

It is the war that now occupies virtually all serious discussions. It is Pitt's belief that the Triple Alliance of Russia, Austria and the British is key to overcoming the threat of the French. It is barely a year since the so-called 'Peace of Amiens' was signed. Among the important points included, was the recognition of the ruling House of Orange Nassau. This was a condition insisted upon by King George. The restitution of full independence to the Hollanders had included the return to them of the Cape at the Southern tip of Africa. This had been taken by the British early in the war, wrenched from the French after a cruel blockade and invasion. The only stipulation Pitt had made was that the Cape should be open and available for use by all shipping, especially British ships on passage to and from India. But now, so soon after an agreement hard won by Cornwallis against the evil French minister Talleyrand, serving Joseph, brother of the Corsican fiend himself, the French had attacked the Low Countries again and Holland had ceased to exist.

Hogarth brings the required maps. He is relieved that Mr. Pitt has accepted the visitor without one of his alarming changes of mood.

The arranging of this appointment went back to 1799 during Mr.Pitt's first administration. Hogarth has carefully looked up the notes made after that meeting. General Miranda was an officer in the Spanish army. At the first meeting, five years ago, he had received a friendly reception. Pitt had welcomed his ideas on encouraging revolt throughout South America against the Spanish oppressors. But King George had been opposed to what he perceived as the Pitts' preoccupation with warfare – father and son. The short Peace of Paris, signed some twenty-two years ago with the young King's enthusiastic support, had not gone down well either with His Majesty's relatives in Hanover or, indeed, with many of the British people. Hogarth had been a small boy at the time. He remembers his mother cheering when she heard the news of the agreement but he still smiles when he recalls the shouts of 'Quad-loop!' by those against the signing. It had taken years for him to learn that the exhortations had been about the Island of Guadeloupe – that sugar-rich jewel which had been handed back to the French together with other successful conquests that had reverted to them and the Spanish, such as Florida and Havana. Many complained that these strategically important areas had been taken only after hard fights and handing them back for the sake of a so-called "peace which passeth all understanding" was an affront.

At least we had kept Canada – and Jamaica. Hogarth remains mystified about the Cabinet disputes regarding the loss of Guadeloupe. He had read all the files and studied the maps; Canada was clearly a far greater prize than a small island. He had heard the argument put forward by the Duke of Bedford that suggested it would be better to let the French control Canada as this would keep the Colonists in Massachusetts constantly fearful of a French invasion. Then their ambitions for independence might have been curtailed. Hogarth strokes his chin. Maybe Bedford was right. The New England settlements were surely lost for ever now. Anyway, the British flag still flew over Canada even if the dreadful Iroquois natives were a severe thorn in the side of the King's Peace.

Today, some four years after General Miranda's original interview, peace with France is something long forgotten. Great Britain is now engaged in a full-scale war against Napoleonic revolutionaries and is gently trying to negotiate an alliance with the Spanish. Bonaparte's dominance of their country has brought them little but poverty. Perhaps this is not the time to antagonize a potential ally. Besides, just examine this man's record:

Born a Creole in Venezuela, Miranda joined the Spanish army at the age of twenty-one and rose rapidly not only as a result of his burning ambition but through a genuine ability in the field, fighting against a range of invaders in Central America and the Caribbean. No doubt he was helped by a movement in the Spain of that time to encourage sons of the empire to succeed in the Military. For too long they had complained of being kept down in favour of home-grown pure-blooded Spaniards. But, as Hogarth had learned from the notes, at the age of thirty-two Miranda had been Court-martialled for selling arms to the American colonists. Strangely he was also charged with supplying the British Government with the complete drawings of the fortifications of Havana. His treachery had gained the racists in Spain even more support. Dismissed from the army without a pension he now devoted himself to putting forward arguments in favour of rebellion to all and sundry, especially members of the British Government. With passion and a satchel full of mad schemes he preaches the value of supporting revolution in South America against the Spanish and Portuguese rulers. The benefit to himself, personally, can only be guessed at.

Pitt had agreed to receive him again when the application was first made some four months ago. Now Miranda has returned for this second interview with Mr.Pitt and is hopeful that he will give him a good reception. As a help in this matter he has secured the presence of another Tory grandee whose reputation is currently on the rise. Major General Arthur Wellesley, lately returned from India and his successes in Mysore, has agreed to accompany him to today's interview.

They are shown into Mr. Pitt's office and seated around a corner table. Hogarth remains to take such notes or instructions as are agreed. They are offered a glass of brandy which Wellesley refuses. In truth he is more interested in the Minister's views on the war with France, particularly Britain's need to repossess the Cape than in discussing South America. He had studied the matter but it was now very secondary to his thoughts about the Spanish Peninsula itself.

Looking for an opening, Miranda spots the maps which Pitt had been studying. "I see you still look kindly upon my suggestions, Minister and I know that General Wellesley was asked to produce plans…" Pitt interrupts him, holding up a hand:

"Captain Home Popham also drew up some outline suggestions for me. I think you saw him recently. He was probably in a particularly receptive state bearing in mind his current situation. But time is moving on. General Fox is having some success in the Mediterranean. There is a limit to the number of troops we can put into the field."

Miranda looks up eagerly. "But, with respect Minister, his brother, Charles, also approved my suggestions! And General Wellesley here submitted a battle plan which…"

Pitt again holds up his hand. He looks at Wellesley:

"If we can but gain an alliance with the Spanish king, there are arguments for an army in the peninsula – to go for the very heart of the serpent – if they have hearts…in the meantime we expect to gain the Cape, I have been discussing the matter with Home Popham – he should be successful, after all it is only against a bunch of Dutch farmers…the French are hardly…"

His voice tails off as if realizing that he is speaking in the presence of a Spaniard and divulging more of his thinking than is proper. He remains uncertain how close Miranda is to the Colonists in the Plate or to anyone else for that matter.

"I'm still trying to sort all these campaigns into some kind of priority. I really cannot countenance any more haemorrhaging of our depleted forces by rushing off to South America and…", his face reddens, "I feel that His Majesty and the Duke of York would be unlikely to agree to such a thing."

He turns to other papers. Hogarth recognizes the instruction. He stands: "Thank you gentlemen, if you will come this way."

Miranda stands. His mouth opens and closes soundlessly. Then he storms out almost slamming the door in Wellesley's face.

"You are missing a golden opportunity!" He is fuming. "Attack in Spain by all means but have a parallel drive in South America! It will enrich your merchants and extend your empire. King George's rule will be greatly enhanced. Once you have the Cape, the route to India is secure." He calms himself. "Please help me – Could I, perhaps, see this Captain Popham again…or even the King?"

But Wellesley seems to have been attacked by a small coughing fit. "Harrumph" is all he can manage. But Miranda has not finished. Sitting in the carriage which has been graciously lent to him during his time in London, he continues:

"Do not pass up such a good opportunity, Wellesley. You know that when I saw Mr.Pitt last time, barely four years ago, he was convinced that this was the right thing to do! Apart from enriching your country-men with all the wealth currently passing to Spain," his voice takes on a sneering note, "it would secure a new empire for you – something you will need now that the North Americans have been showing you the door!"

But Wellesley's timely coughing fit still seems to prevent him replying. He knows that Miranda's words contain some substance. He is also aware that Pitt had been thwarted in the early development of such plans by that wretched colleague of his, Charles Fox, who seems to block everything unless his own family are involved. Wellesley himself is not above a touch of jealousy, family connections are so important. But overall he is not sorry at Pitt's decision. There are too many unknowns and this fellow Miranda is not exactly reliable with his record. Wellesley 'harumphs' again. He is no lover of an officer who can so easily betray his sworn Sovereign.

As Miranda drops Wellesley off at his club his voice takes on a bitter note:

"Just remember, Wellesley, there are a dozen generals unemployed like you sitting about seeking opportunities!" He settles back in his seat. He is not finished in London. He is certain the colonists would rise *en-masse* in support of a landing and Miranda knows the prospects for him, personally, should be superb.

Chapter 6

Edinburgh, 10th November, 1804

My dearest Mother,

Since my last letter the weather has turned colder but I am keeping well wrapped up and eating well.

I am sorry to say that my latest employment has not turned out well. I am truly sorry but the right occupation seems hard to come by. I have been trying to obtain a book on accountancy so that I can become qualified and that would open more doors.

Many of our evenings are spent playing a card game called whist. It is a great favourite of Uncle Drysdale and of many officers. We play in pairs and, I must confess, for a small amount of money. But I am careful! I think I am quite good at it but can promise you that I shall avoid the danger of addiction which would interfere with my career.

I spend time reading the Shakespeare you gave me and try to memorize selections. Many afternoons I go up to the castle and watch the soldiers marching. They are mainly recruits and I think I now know the drills better than they do themselves! It is interesting to see the Highland regiments are not yet wearing the kilt. The Officers' tartan trews make me feel very Scottish. Grandfather would be proud.

I hope he is well. Please give my respects to Father and my best wishes to Elizabeth and Fergus as well as to Stuart. For your dear self I reserve my love and respects.

Your son,

Lauchlin.

With the passage of weeks, Lauchlin has become a familiar figure, watching the recruits being drilled and instructed in the loading and firing of muskets. He thinks back to that night in the wagon when he had considered using one of the weapons. He knows now that it was as well that he had not had the chance. There are some particularly complex movements involving fire-power. He observes, impressed, as they perform *'Open Order', 'Forming Squares'* and firing volleys in column, or in line, although no powder or shot is ever discharged.

One afternoon he is casually standing under one of the arched entrances taking shelter from a light fall of snow. He watches as a trained Company drills with weapons and wonders if they are 'passing out' having completed their training. He recognizes the officer taking the parade. Lord Leadbetter, immaculate in his tartan, marches up and down the ranks with his sword held rigidly in his right hand. The drills are complex and involve much shouting by the NCO's. He realizes that much of it is now familiar to him and he can recognize the occasional error or delay by an NCO.

Cards that evening are at the Viscount's quarters. During a quiet lull Lauchlin mentions that he had been watching.

"I know – I saw you under the Postern Gate. Mind me now, those laddies have only been in the Regiment for some eight weeks. They are doing well!"

Over a late breakfast the next morning Uncle Drysdale tells him of private conversations he has been having with the Viscount.

"He is much beholden to you and has not forgotten your part in his property recovery. He is concerned that you have not been able to secure employment. He has made a suggestion that I feel you should consider very carefully."

Lauchlin keeps his eyes down as he chews purposefully on his porage. Drysdale takes a swallow of ale.

"He is prepared to sponsor you as an Ensign in the Royal Highland Regiment of Fusiliers. You know this is the seventy-second Regiment of the Line and one of the more senior of the Scottish regiments. This is a distinct honour. Apart from your uniform and accoutrements which he wishes to pay for, there is a fee of ten guineas to be paid to the Regimental Colonel who happens to be General Williamson. I think you know he is a relative of John's. Don't give me an answer now – I would just like you to think about it. Your pay, as an Ensign in the Royal Highlanders runs, I believe, to twelve guineas a year, and for a subaltern, twenty."

He coughs to clear his throat. "Actually, I think he is anxious to find a way of rewarding you, even financially, without you being insulted!" Lauchlin thinks to himself '*I might perhaps welcome such insults*' but he says nothing.

The news is by no means alien. He has become increasingly enthralled watching the military drills. He recognizes the spirit of comradeship which pervades and he is finding the lack of purpose in his own life depressing. He thinks about the Royal Highlanders. He knows they were supporters of Prince Charles Edward having been started about a hundred years earlier by the Earl of Mar, possibly related to his ancestral Mackynouns, to suppress the Covenanters. He wonders about his mother's reaction – she had always spoken well of Uncle Drysdale; Grandfather will not like his serving the King of England but a Scots Regiment might be a different thing; and a regiment started as supporters of the Gallant Prince? And twelve guineas a year…he does a rapid calculation, is nearly five shillings a week with much of his food and accommodation found…

He swallows and looks up. "I think I should like that very much!"

Drysdale is pleased. He seems to have been expecting a refusal. "It's not all drilling in the castle garrison, you know, there is travel and, of course, an element of danger that can be exciting. And away from here the food is all provided so you should be able to save a shilling or two!"

But matters are not as simple as Lauchlin had hoped. There is a procedure to be followed. All regiments select their officers with care and the more senior the regiment the greater the cost and the selection process; promotion and selection is rarely by merit; the Royal Highlanders may not have the seniority of the Scots Guards, but they have a history going back a hundred and fifty or so years and they have a number of important battle honours prominent on their Colours.

The first step is an official call on the Regimental Colonel accompanied by the sponsor. Bonnington arranges his hair, tying back an apology for a pigtail which is all he can manage; Uncle Drysdale lends him a fine coat in blue broadcloth and advises him to use the name Mackinnon. "The auld spelling smells too much of the rough clans and has gone out of fashion in today's Unionist environment."

Viscount Leadbetter sends a coach to fetch him so that they can travel to the General's apartments together. They arrive at a glittering reception room just as a fine clock on a mantelshelf is striking six. There are three other officers with the General. It is the first time Lauchlin has seen him and he notes with surprise that he is wearing tartan trews in a green pattern. He also notes that he has golden colonel's insignia on his high collar, having evidently dispensed with the Major General's crossed sword and baton. This must be a courtesy to the hosting regiment. A small, grey peruke sits smartly over deep set, but kindly, blue eyes and a hooked nose that Lauchlin has learned to call *Aquiline.* In his hand he holds a glass of sparkling wine and he waves at a uniformed servant with a tray to come over and serve the two new arrivals.

The Viscount speaks first: "Colonel, it is my pleasure to present to you Lauchlin Mackinnon, a gentleman whose family are known to me and for whom I am pleased to vouch."

"Good, good. Thank you John. How do you do, Mr. Mackinnon?"

Lauchlin gives a small bow and answers as counselled: "Your servant, Colonel."

The three other officers approach. Two are wearing similar tartan trews in what he thinks must be the full dress clothes of the Royal Highlanders; the third is in a formal Dress Uniform of the British Army. He is disappointed not to see the kilt being worn; he remembers how the wearing of highland dress was made illegal after the battle on Culloden Moor but was re-introduced some forty years later but only for the Highland regiments serving King George. It does not seem to be in vogue here.

He notes that one of the Highland officers is a Major; the other a Captain. The one in British Uniform is a Colonel. He has a challenging look about him but, in repose, it is a kindly face that studies him. The General turns to them, "Colonel Beresford, allow me to present Lauchlin Mackinnon, an aspirant for the Regiment of Royal Highlanders. Now I'll leave him to your tender mercies while I talk to my nephew." He takes John's arm and they walk out of his hearing.

Lauchlin thinks at speed. He knows he is now on his own and is grateful for the briefings he has been receiving. He bows in their direction: "Your servant, Colonel."

The Highland Major smiles, "yes, good to meet you. Let me top up your wine!" He signals to the servant. Lauchlin has the sense to take care. This wine is not simple ale. He is unfamiliar with it and it behoves caution. "I believe you play a fair game of Whist, err… Lauchlin?"

Is this a trick question? It is not something he has prepared for. Is there a suggestion that he is a gambler – even a wastrel?

"I have a simple knowledge of the game, sir, and I certainly enjoy such an evening but I could not claim to be expert."

The British Colonel speaks quietly. "I believe your uncle is Captain Drysdale of the Northumbrian Fusiliers." Lauchlin confirms the fact. "Yes, a gallant officer I have heard. We shall be needing many such judging by the news!"

Lauchlin is enjoying the wine and thinks the evening is going well. He accepts another glass. He twirls it gently in his hand, responding confidently to their questions. Then he notices the eyes of the two Scots looking down at his feet. With horror he realizes he has spilt wine down the front of Uncle Drysdale's broadcloth and some has dripped on to the General's carpet. At that moment a Sergeant of Fusiliers enters the room. Over a shoulder he carries a leather despatch case. He marches up to the General and they talk in low tones. The General nods as the sergeant hands letters to him. He keeps the thicker part of the despatches and turns to the other officers.

"Urgent despatches, gentlemen! I fear this little *soiree* must be cut short!" He hands a despatch to the Colonel:

"Colonel Beresford, this is addressed to yourself. It has come from General Baird. I have despatches to read from the Secretary of War. May I suggest we break off and re-convene in my office in an hour." The General stamps off, calling for his *aide de camp.*

The other three officers go into a huddle. Lauchlin looks helplessly towards the Viscount who takes his arm and says: "I feel we are somewhat *de trop* here m'dear fellow. Let's go back and see if we can arrange a game of cards!" As he escorts him out of the room, Leadbetter murmurs, "we've been expecting those orders…wonder what this means…." Leadbetter hosts him for the evening and Lauchlin does not reach his bed until the late hours.

Rising the following morning, he is surprised to find his uncle already up, eager to find out what transpired at the castle. He is trying to explain his somewhat mixed feelings when there is an urgent rattling at the front door. Bonington opens it to reveal a messenger from the castle. He has a letter addressed to Lauchlin. Bonington accepts it at the door and hands it to him. It is from the 72nd Battalion of the Royal Highlanders:

"If Mr. Lauchlin Mackinnon would care to call upon Colonel W.C. Beresford at Garrison Headquarters at eight in the forenoon, he will be pleased to receive him."

Bonington looks expectantly at him. "Begging your pardon sir, but Is there a reply? The messenger is waiting."

Lauchlin is somewhat flustered. He shows the letter to Drysdale and quickly nods his head. "Yes, tell him I will be pleased to attend upon him!"

As Bonington looks from one to the other, Drysdale whispers to him: "Well done, but you should give the messenger a penny for his trouble!" Lauchlin has left his small cash upstairs and goes to fetch it but Drysdale forestalls him. "Never mind, just give him this, Bonington – thank you."

At seven-thirty they walk up to the castle together. "You must decide now if you wish to join them. It would appear that Colonel Beresford has received marching orders - some major activity is imminent." There are already a number of wagons drawn up outside the Stores area and men are carrying a variety of materials which are being loaded. On the small upper parade ground a group of recruits is being drilled; Lauchlin wonders if it is his imagination that suggests a new urgency about their training. From the elementary stage of their drill, he supposes they are new arrivals.

Drysdale continues: "He will likely give you four minutes of formal acceptance and hand you over to a subaltern for the substance of the matter. I may or may not see you tonight but perhaps you will find a way to let me know what is happening!"

As they round a corner from the gatehouse, a lone piper is just assembling and testing his pipes. He gives a short burst on the chanter.

Drysdale holds a hand on Lauchlin's shoulder. "A piper! My goodness. It's what your grandfather would have called 'the Piob Mhor'. Its playing has only recently been made legal again – with the kilt. Let me stand and listen – you'd better go on!" He gives his nephew's shoulder a final squeeze. "Incidentally, you should be formally dined in to the Regiment and I would be invited but with all this rushing around there may not be time!" And he pats him on his way.

Lauchlin stands before him. "Words cannot express my thanks to you for all your tolerance and understanding…"

Drysdale pushes him away. "Get on with you! You've saved me a fortune at whist – how am I to cope in future? Hope to see you this evening."

The office is a hive of activity. He presents himself and is asked for his card. He has to confess that he has none. The clerk gives a toss of his head, murmuring "Confounded nobodies!" And goes through a door at the back. He does not return for ten minutes and then directs Lauchlin to wait. An officer with a sword at his waist but with what appears to be the English Royal Coat of Arms on his sleeve sticks his head out of a side door and barks: "Keep a civil tongue in your head Mackay or I'll know the reason why!" The clerk looks down at his paperagain, "Sorry Mr.Browning, sir." Lauchlin wonders what rank the officer was.

He is pleased to have some moments to watch and compose himself. Most of the men he sees are wearing the badge of the Royal Scots or the Highlanders, and he concentrates on their rank badges and how they are addressed. In most cases he is quite familiar with the meaning but he is left wondering about the mysterious one with the Coat of Arms. But he was no outsider since the Saltire appeared proudly on his cap. Before he can ask, he is called to come through into the office.

Colonel Beresford is seated at a desk surrounded by clerks. A captain stands at the end taking notes. Despatches are being dictated to the officers commanding a range of battalions and detachments. Several are to be copied to Captains of bodies as diverse as the Artillery and the Stores and Medical services. He looks up as Lauchlin is brought in.

"Good Morning, Mr.Mackinnon, I am sorry that our discussion last evening was interrupted but, as you will have gathered, we are under orders to move. If you will be kind enough to confirm to me now that your interest in joining the Royal Highlanders Regiment remains firm I shall be pleased to accept your oath in affirmation and welcome you to our numbers in the rank of Ensign with seniority as of this day's date."

He stops expectantly and the others around look at Lauchlin waiting for a reply.

Once more he is grateful for the warning talks over recent days with the Viscount and Drysdale. "Thank you, Colonel, it will be an honour and a pleasure for me to serve in the Royal Highlanders Regiment of Fusiliers. I swear on my honour to serve His Majesty King George, his heirs and legally appointed officers and ministers as a junior officer in the Royal Highlanders, on my honour, sir!"

"Good. That's done then. Welcome to the family. I am a Gunner but have been adopted by this fine body! Perhaps you will just make your mark here…Now I'm going to hand you over to Subaltern McKechnie…" he stares around him… "where is the wretched fellow? Ah there you are Duncan. Good. Off you go then – no doubt we shall meet again soon!"

The young officer referred to comes forward and extends a hand. "Duncan McKechnie, how do you do?"

"Lauchlin Mackinnon, your servant."

Lauchlin sees a friendly young man in his early twenties with fair, slightly unruly, hair and the beginnings of a moustache. His ears stick out suggestive of a young bird about to try flight. His uniform jacket is in green instead of the scarlet of the Royal Scots. He leads him away from the Colonel's office. "They tell me I'm to be your mentor. Do you have a uniform? No, a sword?...No…History of the Regiment?...Drills?... Loading of weapons?..Naming of parts?...We have some way to go, young sir!" He gives a giggle. "Don't worry about it, when I arrived two and a half years ago I barely knew one end of a pikestaff from the other. We'd better start with the Regimental Tailor – you can kit yourself out with a smarter suit and equipment in your own time but this will have to suffice for the present!"

The tailor's shop is behind the main stores and connected to them by a double doorway. Facing away from the parade ground is a sign indicating its private nature. Lauchlin knows that tailoring needs for officers are conducted on a commercial basis but all other regimental needs are supplied under public funds with deductions from future pay. He wonders what debts he is about to accrue, thinking back to Francis Reardon and the new words Lauchlin had learned. But the Viscount had said he would pay so there was no going back now.

They enter through the private door by a large sign announcing:

'J.J. Arthur – Quality Military Tailoring – By Appointment'.

A selection of uniform jackets hangs on racks, mainly in red but some in the dark green of the Royal Highlanders Fusiliers. All are without badges of rank and, after studying Lauchlin's figure, Mr.Arthur selects one for him to try on. Next must be the black, bearskin *Shako.* Mr.Arthur points out the differences between the officers' cap and that for other ranks. It already carries the white cockade and Saltire. The Regimental badge would be borne on the broad head straps. Finding the white uniform trousers takes only a moment but fitting of his trews in the regimental tartan takes up most of the time. He has to stand and sit so that the precise length can be measured. "Some are worn over the boot, young sir but at other times over a neat and presentable shoe!" Lauchlin is disappointed not to be ordered to wear the kilt. He imagines the feel of the thick wool in a garment designed to protect the wearer from winter blasts high on the hills. They also take care in the selection of his black leather boots to be worn with white puttees.

Details as to white leather cross strappings, gold frogging and stockings are quickly resolved and Lauchlin again wonders about the total costs of such magnificent clothing. There must be a limit to Leadbetter's generosity. A heavy cotton white shirt completes the fitting and Duncan recommends that he should get two of these.

Mr.Arthur promises to complete the work within four hours and they undertake to return for fittings at the end of the morning. The tailor will prepare a summary of the account which they can collect at that time.

Lauchlin is excited at the prospect of wearing such heavy quality materials which surpass much of what he has used during his short life. He is brought back to earth by Duncan's next comment.

"I don't suppose he does a morning's business like that too often! Set you back something like forty-five guineas I suppose…still, that's nothing against the cost of a half-decent sword…"

"I believe I can have time before settling his account?"

"Of course, of course. And perhaps a grant of some kind from the Regiment. Still, you know what they say, nobody pays his tailor!" The comment takes him back again to Mr. Francis and his failed business in Edinburgh. He wonders how Mr. Arthur's accounts are handled.

The matter of the sword is put behind them as they continue the training discussion. Lauchlin feels more confident when they come to drill movements but realizes he has to learn the necessary commands and the positioning on parade of 'supernumerary' officers which is what he will be.

The Regiment is proud of its history and this subject keeps cropping up throughout the morning. But their visit to the Armoury is very complex since he needs to know about basic artillery movements as well as full details of musket loading, commands and firing in ranks.

Duncan is keenly interested in every aspect of the musket and confesses that he has been shooting on his Grandmother's English estate since childhood. It is obvious from the way he holds the gun as he talks that it is something of a passion.

"The fusiliers have to be totally familiar with their weapons. How to take them apart, keep them lubricated and re-assemble them. All that has a huge effect on their ability to load in the time, aim and fire to order!" In his enthusiasm he discusses the benefits and drawbacks of modern developments. "I was able to try a rifle once, that is where the muzzle has been rifled, with machine-cut grooves on the inside. It makes the ball exit in a spin so that it has less of a tendency to wander away from the target. It's good for shooting competitions when you have time to load with care and are keen to hit a particular target perhaps a hundred yards in front. But loading a rifle is too slow for fusiliers in line ahead, and they don't need to be especially accurate either, since we generally fire in volleys!" As he enthuses about the effect of such mass volleys, he gives a light laugh, "Does nothing for your hearing, of course. That's why fusiliers are nearly always deaf!"

He names the critical parts to Lauchlin. "These are the jaws that hold the flint and fusiliers need to be inspected so that they have a decent piece of flint in the first place!" He demonstrates what he means and shows how the jaw screw adjusts for the flint and how the fusiliers have to be shown to watch that aspect. He demonstrates insertion of the powder, loading a ball and how the explosion takes place in the pan; the use of the frizzen and the frizzen spring.

"Mind you, as an officer you will have to rely on your sword, so that is another aspect of our training! But for now I think it's high time we went back to Mr. Arthur's emporium and then we may get something to drink. Incidentally, every new member of the Mess has to be *dined in* but, since we're under orders to move that may be difficult."

The fitting goes well enough. The feel of the trews and jacket is different to that of any clothes previously worn and the boots although heavy and almost clumsy, give him the confidence that he can surmount any obstacle.

Mr. Arthur has not prepared his account and promises to send it on to Lauchlin's lodgings within a day or two.

Feeling altogether more secure in his Ensign's uniform, he follows Duncan to the Officers' Messing Hall for a glass or two of refreshing ale. There is an atmosphere of urgency and most of the officers to whom he is introduced are clearly occupied in preparing for a new activity. To every request for clarification Duncan is fobbed off with the promise that he will receive his movement orders from his superior.

Duncan's appointment is under Captain Arthur Grant but there is no sign of that officer and he feels he should leave Lauchlin and go to report to his Company Headquarters.

As he is leaving, Colonel Beresford enters the room. He stands in the doorway scanning those inside as if seeking someone. As Duncan is almost in the doorway he turns to him. "Ah Duncan, how has the mentoring gone – is our newest member now fit for foreign service?"

Duncan stands smartly to attention. "I believe he is well on the way, sir, to being a most useful addition to our gallant band, but I could not say that he is totally equipped yet for the field."

"No. no, quite so, but welcome again er… Lauchlin. I think you had better stick close by me until we find something more important – I need a good runner at my shoulder just now so that must be your first appointment and it will help you to recognize your fellow officers and the general disposition of our troops!"

Duncan bravely asks him the question he has already put to various officers. "Do I understand you to say, sir, that we are being posted?"

"You'll hear officially from Captain Grant, Duncan, but I can tell you we are off to join the main dispositions of these Regiments at Shorncliffe Camp in Kent. After that…" he smiles as he turns back to Lauchlin, "I hope you're a good sailor! Now then, er Mackinnon, go back to your lodgings and make your final dispositions, we are off to war!"

Bonnington shakes his head at the sight of him. "Begging your pardon, sir, but you must let Margret press that jacket. It doesn't look good. The buttons require attention too. I'll just need a half-hour!"

It takes Lauchlin only moments to pack up his possessions although they are now greater than when he arrived. He sits and composes a letter to his mother. He tries to justify his actions in joining the army and stresses the regimental history for his grandfather's sake. He is unable to give her an address but promises to write with further details when he knows them. He gives the letter, addressed to his father, to Bonnington who will get it to the coaching inn. The cost has now been fairly well established as one half-penny. Then he gives Mrs. Judge a half-crown together with his grateful thanks.

Bonnington returns with his jacket. It has been sponged and carefully pressed. The buttons are shining brightly and give him a pleasant feeling of military smartness. "Begging your pardon, sir, but if you will let me have those boots I think I shall be able to transform them!"

Margret watches from the back door as Lauchlin replaces them with his old pattens which now feel insubstantial. He is still padding around when uncle Drysdale returns home. He grasps Lauchlin's hands in his…

"My word, you do look fine. Now, I have something for you." He calls to Bonnington and nods his head. The servant goes back through the door. "This is by way of being a farewell present. I have enjoyed your company and…" there is a danger of some emotion creeping in. He collects himself before continuing, "and I know my friends have begun to admire your skill at whist." Bonnington returns with an armful of polished straps and a sword in its glittering scabbard. They both hang it around his waist and adjust the straps so that it needs but a light touch to control it as he moves around.

"Good – there are many better swords around but I think this will serve you well until such time as you feel the need for another!" He sits down and studies Lauchlin's full regalia. "The sash is perhaps a shade long, Bonington, but it'll serve. I'm glad to see you and be able to say goodbye. Don't forget the Shakespeare plays, they will offer company during lonely nights and may help you to remember us. For now it's as that fellow Burns wrote: "Auld Lang Syne". I must return to the castle. I am engaged in writing despatches on the General's behalf. You must get back too. You will be leaving tonight... I know where you are going."

Lauchlin leaves one of his last shillings with Margret and then all of his remaining small change from Fingal's half-sovereign with Bonnington.

He shakes his hand and thanks him with all his heart. He now possesses just the single sovereign that remains of his mother's gift.

There is a suspicion of moisture in Bonnington's eyes as he promises to bring Lauchlin's kit up to the castle together with the campaign bed which Drysdale advises him to take. He holds the street door for the two officers to walk up to the castle together. Drysdale puts an affectionate arm across his nephew's shoulder.

"You're off to the Cape with Colonel Beresford but Home Popham is in naval command and that can lead to anything – Good luck!"

Chapter 7 *(May 1805)*

In one of the smaller offices in the Admiralty, Commodore Home Riggs Popham is studying, once again, the orders he has received from the First Minister - William Pitt, from the elderly Duke of York - Head of the War Department and the special advice from Lieutenant General David Baird, the Senior Army Commander. Baird writes from India but is already hurrying back to take overall command.

Home Popham's preparatory work is now completed to his satisfaction. He has studied the history of this Cape of Good Hope, its constant internal wars between Dutch settlers, local tribes and some people called *Bushmen.* He remembers its capture by the British some ten years ago at the request of the Prince of Orange but its modern involvement with the Napoleonic Batavians has placed at risk its importance as a refuge for ships rounding the continent to and from India.

The papers on the table are mounting: numerous replies from Admiralty and War Office officials to his questions on regiments and ships being provided, and the larger pile of copies of his own despatches, scribbled out feverishly by the junior clerk allocated to him.

Hitting his elbow on a corner of the table he swears as he knocks some of the papers to the floor. Leaning down he notices again the low quality of the scrawled ink. Why only one, fourth grade clerical officer? He feels his resentment rising again; why has he been alloted such a poky little office? He is in command of a major task force. This should have been recognized.

A light tap on the communicating door precedes the entrance of his clerk:

"The Army List, sir. You wished to check on Colonel Beresford..."

"Ah yes, let me see the detail!" He almost snatches the paper. He is greatly relieved to see that the entry for William Carr Beresford, Royal

Artillery, shows he was gazetted Colonel in the 71st Royal Highlanders only three months ago. So, his own appointment as a Naval Captain pre-dates Beresford by four years.

Now he is Commodore over a relatively junior army commander. His irritation rises again. He should have had a say in the appointment!

He has already sent despatches ordering him to begin the movement of his troops from Edinburgh and to join the rest of the fleet at Cork. He places the copy neatly in the appropriate manila file and glances at his own instructions: He is 'requested and required' – how well he knows that phrase - to carry troops firstly to Shorncliffe Camp near Dover, he cannot remember which old, dead-leg admiral is now in charge there. Popham is quietly delighted with his own appointment - another joint army-navy co-operation and he knows that he has been successful in such undertakings before. He has great faith in his own abilities in the use of land troops and believes the Duke of York looks favourably on him. Perhaps it is the opportunity for a new beginning – *prize money* is *t*he thing, so far he has been unfortunate in that aspect.

Commodore Popham is a man of mixed reputation. He likes to boast of his simple roots and of how he joined the navy at sixteen as an ordinary seaman. He neglects to add that he had been a student at Trinity College, Cambridge and abandoned his studies at the behest of Captain Edward Thompson, a family friend, so that his service on HMS *Hyena* was less onerous than might otherwise have been expected.

Under the overall command of Admiral George Rodney his initial duties had been largely in the West Indies against the French, the Spanish and the American Colonists. Later he was taken prisoner when HMS *Shelanagig* was captured by the French off a lee shore near the island of St.Lucia. He smiles to himself at the recollections. He certainly put his time on the island to good use. His study of naval charting and surveying started there over fifteen years ago as did his initial experiments in ship to ship signalling. Thinking back he frowns to himself. There is still scope for further development and he vows to continue working at the problems after the present operation is satisfactorily concluded.

He could have made progress before but, not having been in a permanent appointment, had been dismissed from the Navy after the American war. He remains resentful; not even half-pay. He had continued with his work in surveying, charting and map development until the rise of Napoleon resulted in his reinstatement at twenty-eight as a lieutenant. He leans back in his chair now, thinking of those years. It was probably his experience in surveying that first drew him to the attention of the Duke of York when campaigning in the Low Countries. Popham believes he had been key to the success of several joint naval and army operations. But some of his fellows, presumably out of spite and jealousy, had privately spoken against him, especially to the First Lord, St.Vincent. But the Duke had stepped in and personally promoted him to the rank of Commander over the heads of others higher in the Navy List. He recalls his delight when that appointment was made but, inevitably, it had resulted in more opposition.

Now, following his appointment as Commodore, he remains suspicious and convinced that his enemies are continuing their efforts to bring him down. Though skilled in his own fields, Popham is not an easy man to befriend and he is bad at leading more junior officers.

The latest despatch from Mr. Pitt puts him in mind of his meeting with him in 1799. William Pitt had asked him for his views on making a landing in the area of the River Plate. Did he think it would be heavily defended by the Spanish who had now joined forces with Revolutionary France. Obviously, Popham could not produce detailed plans for such an operation out of his head. He knew the huge River Plate was beset with shoals and sandbanks that made traversing it difficult. He spent some time analysing the river. Pitt stressed he was only after his initial views but Popham needed time.

Subsequently he had sent full plans to Downing Street which he thought had been favourably received. Then he heard that other suggestions had been put forward by some wretched Major General Wellesley, countering with landings in the North of Brazil. In the end, Pitt had prevaricated and nothing was done.

Ever conscious of the need for care, Popham again forces his orders into his head: *Requested and Required* - yes, he knows full well the glee with which his opponents would grasp any failure. He is to enable the troops under Colonel William Beresford to take and secure the Cape of Good Hope rendering such assistance as may be necessary. Current intelligence suggests that it is only lightly defended by a handful of ill-trained French dragoons and Dutch Irregulars known as *Boers* but this information may be out of date. Following success at the Cape, he is to patrol the sea area – and the orders stress the need to cover it properly – from the West African coast North to the Equator and Westwards to the coast of South America ensuring that no enemy counter-attack can take place. Really! Do these people have any idea of the size of that ocean?

He now awaits two senior staff officials from the Admiralty who will "sign off" his final orders for the operation. Why are these nobodies keeping him waiting? Popham has secured a large force – others say too large – and he remains bitter about Admiral Lord St.Vincent who has stated that half the quantity of men and materiel allocated – i.e. those already on their way to Cork, should have sufficed. So be it! We had taken the Cape before and given it away in peace negotiations. This time it will be for keeps!

Satisfied that he has met all the criteria, he drums his fingers on the table; where are these officials? It is time to depart for the Kent coast and take up his command - yes, he likes the sound of that! His carriage will take him to Dover but he will spend one more night at his home, Titness Park near Windsor. His wife, Lucy, is ten years younger than himself and they already have two children. He rubs his eyes. He is tired. It will be good to see them before he goes away.

Chapter 8

Holding his sword carefully to avoid it becoming entangled in his legs, Lauchlin hurries to report to Colonel Beresford's office. His stiff white stock and leather cross straps make him stand squarely. The clip of his boots leads him to feel military. Under the surprisingly comfortable shako, he thinks about his new situation. He knows that without the intervention of Lord Leadbetter he could never have aspired to it. He grits his teeth determined to make a success of the opportunity.

He is received by Captain John Dirleton, the Colonel's *aide-de-camp,* who is occupying the colonel's chair behind a small, folding campaign desk.

"Ah come in - Lauchlin isn't it…yes, Mr. Mackinnon, good to meet you…welcome to the King's Scottish army!"

Dirleton is a Royal Artillery gunner as is his superior. He sees a young. bright yet cautious face, under a *'bonnet'* that has slightly slipped over one ear. There is a liveliness that he approves and a set about encouragingly broad shoulders.

In reply to a question, Lauchlin advises that his kit is arriving shortly but that it consists only of a small bundle and a folding bed.

"Folding bed eh. Oh that may be handy in a small cabin" he looks slightly doubtful – "It'll probably be all right then. You can share with our two subalterns, Crowley and McKechnie – they'll look after you. Do as they tell you. I think you know Duncan McKechnie? Ah yes."

"Are we to sail in a ship then, Captain Dirleton?"

"Call me John when we're not official - Indeed yes, tide at eleven tonight. Out of bonny Leith to join the rest of the flotilla at Dover where we will arrive, God willing after a pleasant Summer cruise, on Friday morning. Meanwhile we have a lot of despatches to write. Do you have a good hand, Lauchlin?"

Without the chance of a reply, he is given the edge of a table where a civilian clerk is busy writing; a chair and a selection of quills and nibs is presented. The clerk moves sideways:

"Some prefer to use these new nib things in a holder, this paper is smooth so both work well." He sniffs as Captain Dirleton leaves the room. Picking up another despatch he murmurs quietly: "Colonel Beresford's writing is appalling – just 'cos he's a full colonel! God I don't know!"

Lauchlin sets to copy a letter written by Beresford to the Artillery Commander. He is told not to use any form of greeting. "The Colonel will choose how to address it; here it will probably be 'dear Stuart' but you write everything else until the final salutation. Remember this may be just a copy of a letter already sent or may turn out to be the original. There are always many copies to be made for others' information or for recording purposes in London."

Leaving a space for the Colonel's opening, Lauchlin faithfully copies:

You are requested and required to bring your three troops of horse artillery to the number six Dock at Leith by four this afternoon for loading on Transports as directed by the attached Movements Order. As already discussed, limbers will need to be detached for loading; ball and powder to be conveyed separately as directed by Ordnance, but horse provender for seven days to be provided by yourselves.

The letter he is copying continues over three pages and Lauchlin finds the task demanding. There is little hint about the original letter's addressee. He realizes that Staff work involves a considerable amount of writing. He wonders if this is what Colonel Beresfod meant about using him as a runner but he remains resolved to succeed. While leaning across after dipping his nib in the ink-well he drips a blot on what he has just written. The clerk notices and instantly lays a soft cotton blotter over the mess by which it is largely absorbed. He mutters in irritation, "just stay well away from that area until it's properly dry, and take care to wipe the nib on the side of the well!"

Lauchlin's thoughts return to his first dismissal when Berenson deliberately spilt the ink. That's not going to happen again. Captain Dirleton hurries back into the office. He leans over. "Oh you've a fair hand Lauchlin – good, carry on. Incidentally, your carter has been up with your kit it's been left with the subalterns' chests."

For the next hour he is occupied with copying despatches from which he learns that at Dover they will join the remainder of the forces already being prepared at Shorncliffe Camp. They will then sail in a huge convoy of over sixty transports, including store-ships, escorted by nine men-o-war to Cork for further stores of powder plus meat, flour and water. The route thereafter is not included in any of Lauchlin's copying but it seems likely that the bulk of the force is being prepared to supplement the East India Company's forces.

At five o'clock Captain Dirleton announces that they are now to move to their Messing Hall for a light supper. He will have the opportunity to meet the bulk of the other officers, following which they will march to Leith Docks for their Transport vessels. All their letters and despatches are collected and protected in a leather envelope before being placed in a large shoulder bag. Lauchlin is to carry this to the ship and guard it with his life.

There is great activity as the troops assemble on the parade ground. He continues to hold himself upright but the sword and the despatch case are both on his left side. The carts have mainly left the Stores and are presumably already at the Docks. He estimates over five hundred men on the parade ground. He slides anonymously past Colonel Beresford who is standing in the Entrance Hall of the Mess engaged in conversation with other senior officers. Inside he sees that many of them have laid down loaded packs which they will carry on their shoulders. There are some sea chests marked with owners' identities which are being collected and put on the carts. He sees his camp bed with the rest of his rolled up kit waiting with Duncan McKechnie and hurries to join him.

"Is this your wee bed, Lauchlin?"

"It is, yes. I was advised to bring it."

"I fetched you a greatcoat from the stores before they closed. I'd hate to see ye chilled at sea." He chuckles and points to a heavy uniform overcoat lying by the other kit, then goes on, "I doubt you'll have the space for a bed, my bonny wee boy – reckon we'll all be on the floor, or the deck as they say, among the rats and cockroaches – unless we rate a hammock!

The navy looks down its nose at army officers and we are pretty low in that scheme. Looks like it's beginning to blow too!"

There is a smell of soup coming from the kitchen area. Lauchlin realizes he has not eaten for some hours. He asks about going in for supper.

"Aw, I think that might be unwise – if we're off to sea the less there is to come out the better."

Lauchlin wonders about the remark but thinks it best to follow. He thanks him for the coat and wonders at the cost but he is too nervous and wound up at the prospects before them to raise the subject. He has never seen a big ship close to, let alone boarded one. On the order to fall in outside he notes how even the captains are picking up their own gear. He decides to leave the folding bed where it is - Drysdale will be able to recover it in the morning.

The march to Leith Docks takes them over two hours although mostly down hill. Many of the officers have fallen in with their own detachments. He assumes their horses will have gone separately. He and Duncan march at the back. There are a number of large transport ships awaiting them. They are tied up four or five deep as far as Lauchlin can see in the evening twilight. The air is full of the smell of caulking tar, fish and rotting sea-weed with overtones of the horses already loaded. It appears that to reach the outer ships they have to go aboard one of about eight actually moored to the jetty and cross over the intervening vessels. There are some lights, presumably oil lanterns, but it is difficult to see much detail.

"Captain Dirleton said we were to go aboard the *'Scottish Flame'...*" Duncan intones "he says we'll have duties on board though how in Heaven's name are we supposed to know where that is!"

The columns of men are halted and marched in turn to points where three planks have been placed against each of the ships moored at the dock. Lauchlin learns they are called *'Gangplanks'*. Duncan snorts "I'll no be gaing awa' in a hurry to cross over a wee plank! I just hope the wood's no' rotten!"

They agree that the horses will all be on the first ships so they choose to mount the middle entrance on the second ship. There are sailors pushing men on board and others waiting to catch them. They have to climb up and Lauchlin hears one seaman saying that he could see the tide already rising. Duncan shouts to him: "Is this all right for the *'Scottish Flame'*?"

"No mate. Three or four then inboard! Look lively there!"

They move on as directed, the area is a hive of activity and they clamber up to the next ship but one. There is a slight breeze rising so that the ships rub gently against one another like cows in a field sniffing a newcomer. The planks between them move as if in opposition; occasionally both ships rise together but more often there is an awesome irregularity.

Lauchlin shouts out the enquiry to a seaman and receives the confirmation he wanted. He has wrapped his new greatcoat around his neck and clutches his sword and bundle to his chest while holding on to the leather satchel. He has no arms to help him balance but is relieved as he jumps down safely enough into the waist of the ship.

He is grateful to have Duncan with him. Although knowing no more about the ship and their accommodation than he does himself, he has a confidence that leads them on to a fourth ship tied up almost out at sea. The ship is busy and they are relieved to see Captain Dirleton leaning down and shouting a welcome. He points to a lit corner near some stairs ascending to a higher deck and tells them to deposit their kit inside the passage reached by the small door in front of them. They pass through into a narrow access passage where the ceiling is no more than four and a half feet high. They bend to pass along towards a small oil lamp where some kit is already stacked which Duncan recognizes: a sturdy box belonging to Tarquin Crowley. There is a small recess either side of the passage way and Lauchlin worries that they will be required to sleep there. The lamp makes the thick air stick in his throat. At the same time he is increasingly conscious of having missed his supper. He hears a succession of high-pitched whistles followed by myriads of feet thumping around overhead.

"It sounds as though we're on our way." Duncan makes a move back. "Let's go and watch!"

As they emerge through the small door they are almost knocked over by a rush of men clambering into the rigging. A loud voice from further away shouts at them: "Belay there! Don't get under the crew's feet! Foresail Team two, haul away! You two skulking there begone! Mizzen crew! All of you, here now on the capstan – wait for the order!" There is another piercing whistle.

There are three naval officers above him on what he learns is called the quarter deck. One shouts down at them to clear the area. Lauchlin backs into the passage again. "Let's see where it leads." They make their way past the stacks of their kit as the passage narrows, ending in a blunt point with a small trap-door perhaps eighteen inches square. On top a heavy iron clamp screws it shut. The light is poor but Lauchlin sees that undoing it would enable the oak flap to drop on a hinge. He tries unscrewing it and although managing the odd half turn, it is too rusted up with salt to open further. He grunts this information to Duncan who is kneeling behind.

"Here, let me try!" They have to reverse some way before the passage widens sufficiently for them to change places. Duncan heaves at it. "This would sweeten the atmosphere if we could get it free!" There is a burst of air as the door behind them opens and another subaltern worms his way towards them.

"Ahoy there, landlubbers! Ah, what a sight! Keep those rears pointed away from me, if you please. You must be Lauchlin, the Ensign, detailed to look after us two officers! Good to meet you even if it is only your arse I can see. Two glasses of chilled Rhenish if you please!"

From his position at the end, Duncan calls out "Ah there y'are,Tarquin, I was beginning to think you'd missed the boat! Lauchlin Mackinnon meet Tarquin Crowley!

"Loch Lynne eh? That's a new one to me, I know Lomond, Ness and Katrine! I shall call you Lomond, I think, or Lochinvar! That's it – Young Lochinvar!"

Duncan calls out to him. "Ho Ho, Tarquin – have you been at the rum already? Help us here - I've been trying to open this confounded window thing and get some air but it's too rusted over – needs a spanner of some sort."

"You are a land-lubber Duncan! That's for a sharp-shooter to draw a bead on the French captain if the ship comes into action! This is the rearmost section. I reckon it'll be cold enough down here once we get going. So, no farting! Just have to put up with it for the present!"

"Oh is there a present for us then? I thought there must be a reward for lying in this creepy dungeon with you!"

"Very good, Duncan. Who's been at the rum now? It'll be a while before we reach the Forth. We are apparently being warped along. They row a line out to a stone bollard thing then wind us towards it on the capstan. One ship at a time – take a month or so for all these I imagine!

We'll feel the wind when we get out. I'm going for a pee. There's a thing they call a head just along from the quarter deck." He reverses out of the door and Lauchlin decides to follow him.

"How do you know so much about this ship, Tarquin, are you a secret sailor?"

"No, Sir Lomond," Tarquin undoes his buttons while looking up at the sky, "is this the right place? Can't pee into the wind you know! I like to know what's going on so I came aboard earlier." He relieves himself and comments: "that's better – we're to sleep in what they call the 'after'sail locker. At first they offered the fore-sail locker. I thought they said 'Foreskin' locker – that's clearly too limiting isn't it. So I chose the other! Much relief don't you know! Actually, junior officers like ourselves should be accommodated with the Midshipmen but the Captain has decreed that we must stay in the locker. It's only a short journey."

Lauchlin has not yet had a proper look at his new companion but he seems a jocular soul. "No commodes below so watch your drinking before bed!"

Back in the locker there is a lot of noise overhead from running feet and clanking of iron as the capstan is turned. There is a sharp ring on a bell and a voice calling. Tarquin mimics it: "Ship's Bell. Every half-hour, ding-ding!"

They decide to get some sleep, Lauchlin feels physically exhausted and looks back on what has proved to be an extraordinary day. By lying sideways across the passage they can all stretch their legs fully, and they use the softer parts of their kit to make themselves reasonably comfortable. They decide to sleep in their clothes.

The air remains stuffy; not particularly hot but the oil lamp starts to flicker before finally extinguishing itself with an acridity that blends with the sickly sweet smell of the timbers surrounding them. He is conscious of the odours of people crowded together. He sleeps lightly and wakes several times affected by the rolling of the ship. His head aches from lying badly and the lack of supper seems to make little difference to the feelings of nausea which keep rising in him. He is keen to avoid waking his sleeping companions and forces himself to lie still. He wakes fully some hours later with the sound of six bells ringing through the ship. He has a momentary lack of recollection. The ship's movement is alarming on what he imagines is the ocean. Without the oil lamp the blackness is almost complete.

Further sleep eludes him and he decides to put on the greatcoat which he has been using as a pillow and seek fresh air. He hangs on to the wooden supports at either side of the narrow passage, finding difficulty in working out its geography. At last he negotiates his way to the door.

It is a cold, clear night but with perhaps the faintest hint of sunrise. Each roll of the ship provides him with the sight of a classic crescent moon the other side of the mainmast. The air is fresh and he is glad of his coat. The wind beats continuously through the sails and rigging giving an occasional sharp slap. Above him he hears a slightly irritated voice grunting "watch your helm!" And an unconcerned reply: "ay-ay sir - sorry!"

Lauchlin risks going up two of the steps to see what is happening. A door opens and military feet stamp to attention. There are lights burning around the quarter deck and a figure he knows moves down some steps towards it.

"Good morning Sir, it is Colonel Beresford, I think?"

"Indeed yes, just came to see what is happening. A fresh morning. You are the Officer of the Watch?"

"Lieutenant Carmody, sir, at your service. We are making good progress. The wind suits our sailing point, roughly from the North-East." He is silhouetted against a light as he takes his telescope and peers back. We are the leading vessel, there are three in sight, two and three points to larboard. Just make out their lights".

"Good, good. Hm…Hmm… A calm sea."

"It is, sir. Your men seem to be in fine fettle. They have their wives with them?" It is more a question than a statement.

"Hm…Yes, some…campaign wives really though some have been around for a long time. It's good for morale and they do the laundering and a lot of the cooking."

Beresford stamps around on the deck as though warming his feet before looking over and seeing Lauchlin who immediately pretends he was climbing the stairs. "Hello, who's this?"

"Ensign Mackinnon, sir. Just taking some air."

Lieutenant Carmody snaps at him. "You're not allowed up here and you're not supposed to be wandering about the ship – get below!"

Much chastened, Lauchlin turns away. Beresford calls down: "Come and see me at about nine, Mackinnon, that's err…two bells in the forenoon watch, have I got that right Carmody? I've a lot of despatches to get off and my secretary's sick." He chuckles, "Heaven knows how he would cope with a real sea. Golly, I remember once in the Indian Ocean…!"

Lauchlin does not hear the end of the sentence. He is already crawling in the dark towards his snoring companions.

They rise together when four bells ring out, he thinks about six o'clock. There are more running feet overhead and the shrill sound of the Bosun's whistle. Duncan professes a need to empty his bladder and, since he is furthest from the door, the others perforce do the same. They emerge carefully through the door next to the steps up to the Quarter deck. There is a pump being worked by two seamen feeding a hose while a dozen others are on their knees scrubbing the deck. The seamen are in bare feet and in a playful mood. The hose is casually waved at the three soldiers before an authorative voice shouts at them.

"Sorry Mister Spragg – just an accident – thought there was a lump of dried sick just there!"

The sky is a lot greyer than it had seemed earlier and the wind has increased. It blows almost from one side so that the ship is keeling over. Lauchlin finds it a touch alarming but none of the seamen appears concerned. An older sergeant approaches them, he has a heavy limp and drags one leg on the deck. He is not wearing a cap so merely holds a finger to the side of his head. "Begging your pardons, gents, but I'm told your breakfast is being served in the Port-side Dolly room, just along there." Lauchlin is secretly amused, that phrase…clearly Bonington went to the same school as this sergeant who seems to be allowed the deck.

"Thank you Sergeant Robinson," Duncan speaks for all of them, "we'll attend directly but there is a more pressing need first!" He leads the way. "That's Sergeant 'Hoppy' Robinson; an ex-dragoon - had his horse killed under him but it fell on top and trapped him. Good fellow!"

After using the heads, they find a small bowl and catch some water from the hose to have a brief wash. The water is salty and Lauchlin is conscious of his appointment later with Colonel Beresford. He will need a shave after breakfast. The rolling continues to cause slight ringing in his ears but he manages to keep the nausea under control.

Beresford is already at work when Lauchlin goes up to the Quarter-deck to report. He occupies a comfortable saloon, reached by six steps up from the Quarter Deck. This wraps itself around the stern of the ship immediately below the Poop but above the Ship's Captain's quarters. Lauchlin estimates the head height at about five feet; Clearly, he thinks, a naval career would be ideal for a dwarf.

Seated at a portable desk, Beresford welcomes him with a handful of some five despatches which he has already written and which require copying. Most need two copies but there is one which he says must be copied three times. Sadly, Lauchlin notices it is the longest at four pages. The area is small and there is only a collapsible table for him to use He sits on a cushioned seat that curves around the rear wall and puts him in mind of the bench at the top of the Edinburgh coach. He sets to work. There is plenty of paper and a selection of nibs but the ink is only in a moulded pot which forms part of the Colonel's desk. He is forced to position himself close to the folding desk and is very careful to wipe the nib on the side to avoid any blots which would result in starting again. The first letter is one of the shortest. It requires two copies and is addressed to Commodore Home Popham,R.N. commanding fleet operations. It is copied to the Secretary for War at Whitehall, London:

Sir, *3rd June 1805*

I have the honour to confirm that in accord. with yourDespatch of 14th ult. seven hundred and twenty men are being conveyed to Shorncliffe Camp, Kent, to arrive by the 15th inst. This total comprises:

Two hundred of the1st Regiment of Foot, The Royal Scots, One hundred and eighty of the 55th, Regt.Cheshire Yeo'y.,Two hundred and fifty men of the 71st/72nd Royal Highland Regt. And forty men Roy. Art'y. All complete with equipage and materiel. Balance of fifty officers and NCO's.

As directed, I shall communicate with yourself on arrival and place this detachment at your service.

I have the honour to be
Sir
Your Obedient Servant, William Carr Beresford, Colonel.

Copying the letter the first time takes him over fifteen minutes; he reads it through and is pleased with the result. Copying it again takes slightly less time and, comparing all three of the despatches leads him to think his hand is the neatest. He lays the three letters aside and takes up the next. Colonel Beresford is engaged in writing a further despatch which will, no doubt, also require copying.

By the end of the morning Lauchlin has copied out some thirteen despatches. He finds difficulty in maintaining the same standard of neatness. His arm is getting exhausted. The Colonel sits back:

"Good! A fair morning's work, Mackinnon. Let me see what you've done and we can seal them up and address them." He quickly scans through what has been copied and nods his acceptance. "There are two more I need to write before we reach Dover tomorrow. Come and see me again this evening at six!" Lauchlin stands and knuckles his forehead in salute. Beresford studies him. "Is that your best uniform, Lauchlin? It's not really up to the standard of a Staff Officer.

He confesses it is his only uniform.

"Mmm…get another complete outfit in Shorncliffe. The tailor there has tartan – Mr.Briggs – … and that shako I saw you wearing the other day…needs refreshing!" As an apparent afterthought, just as Lauchlin reaches the door, "charge it to the regiment's account on my say-so".

He rejoins his companions and they have an acceptable lunch in the same 'Port-side Dolly Room'. He is beginning to find his sea legs. Time is hanging heavy. They are not supposed to wander around the ship but the area of their 'After Port-side Locker' is not conducive to social exchange. The troops on board are brought up in batches of forty at a time roughly every three hours for food, exercise and use of the ship's heads. He studies the highlanders of the 72nd; which of them will be his men? There are about thirty women with them and two have small children. On board they are all supervised by a squad of about a dozen marines.

At six he reports back to the Quarter Deck for Colonel Beresford and is directed to mount up to his quarters. He returns to the same corner of a table. An oil lamp has been lit and hangs, swinging slowly in the centre. Beresford smiles at him. "They tell me that the lamp is hanging still, it's the ship that is moving – I don't know!" He looks down, "There's only one Despatch to be copied – two copies please – then we can perhaps call it a day!"

This despatch is an order to the Majors commanding the other two Regiments in the detachment. "They've already received these orally so we'll just hand them over when we get to Dover."

He finishes the copying about forty minutes later. Beresford holds them under the lamp and checks them. Lauchlin wonders how he never appears tired. "That's fine, thank you. Will you take a wee dram?" He pours out two small measures from a wide-based decanter wedged in the corner of a shelf, *"Slai-nge"* he salutes. "D'ye play whist laddie?" To Lauchlin's reply he suggests an evening with Captain John Dirleton, Major Malachi Mackenzie and himself. "These voyages can become very tiresome. Being down in hammocks the men can't engage much with their ladies…all right on a short trip like this." He settles back in a comfortable chair. "On a longer voyage they have to take part in highland dancing – it stops them getting stiff!"

Five minutes later there is a tap on the door and the other two card players arrive. Neither seems surprised to see him. Lauchlin rises to his feet finding it simple to balance lightly against the ship's movements. He realizes that Major Mackenzie is the officer he met in the General's quarters at the castle. Privately he wonders at the name Malachi. They receive a dram and, with practised ease, set up the small table Lauchlin has used for his writing. The top is reversible and it has a fine baize surface underneath. They cut for partners and Lauchlin finds he is paired with the Colonel. His reaction is to be nervous and to realize that it could all go so wrong now. Happily, the cards are kind and at eight there is another gentle tap on the door and Colonel Beresford's batman serves up a light supper of some smoked fish which they consume with another dram. It is a convivial evening which is broken up by Mackenzie at ten-thirty saying he would like to do his rounds.

Back in the locker he finds his companions stretched out filling the space. The oil lamp has been re-filled and provides ample light but the air quality is very poor. Tarquin looks up as he crawls in.

"Ah ha, here is Mr. Lomond, our absentee! We thought you must have fallen overboard. Tell us, have you been writing letters for the old man all this time? You've missed your supper!" Lauchlin explains. He tries to speak carefully but is conscious that a wall might be being built up between them. He tries to minimize the quality of the evening and makes no mention of the supper or of the small drams.

"If I survive this night," he jokes, "I shall have a crick in my spine leaving me about three feet tall. Also, the air in here with the fumes of that wretched lamp, not to mention certain body odours, is giving me a head that will challenge those that stick out over the sides of the ship!"

"Ah…so do we conclude that Sir Lomond is now so high and mighty that the subtle bouquets which Duncan and I produce are no longer his 'parfum de jour'?

Lauchlin knows he must go carefully. His friends – and he needs to keep them so – must be wondering what he has been doing all evening. "Alas…when a man with a crown and pips on his arms fixes an eye on you and says sit there, I am not bold enough to argue! It is good to be home again even if the smell reminds me of certain farmyards."

Duncan lashes out at him with his substitute pillow and good humour is restored. It is agreed that the lamp will be extinguished when they have completed all their arrangements. Lauchlin selects the furthest corner. He feels he will sleep well and does not want to be disturbed by weaker bladders.

Chapter 9

As the white chalk cliffs come into view, the *Scottish Flame* is the leading ship in the convoy. Descending the stairs to the Quarter-deck Lauchlin sees the officer on watch carefully observing men on shore through his telescope. He recognizes Lieutenant Browning a fairly elderly man who has always been friendly. The men appear to be constructing a huge circular base. Browning lowers his telescope and nods to him.

"D'ye know what they're doing there, M'lad?"

Lauchlin is mystified as much by the question being directed at him as by the demand itself. He pauses on the last step. "N...No sir. Is it to be a lighthouse?"

Browning gives a small chuckle. "Aye, it looks like that doesn't it. No, it's what they are calling a Martello Tower. I was in Cornwallis's attack on Corsica some ten years ago now. They had one or two of those. The very devil to get past! Stuffed with men and weapons all firing at you through small slits you can't reach! They say we're building them now all round the coast. That'll put a stop to any Frenchie ideas!"

They shorten sail as they arrive in the ancient port of Dover. Its geographical position as the nearest harbour to Continental Europe has resulted in a certain wealth coming to the town from the movement of taxed goods. At the same time, that benefit has been offset by the threat of invasion. The town itself lies under the protection of the huge Norman castle, together with its Roman lighthouse still looking out to sea from its high position on the cliffs. The wooden harbour screen is being replaced by stone blocks which provide shelter and a good anchorage. The wind is changeable, bouncing off the great white walls as they try to reach their anchor point about four hundred yards off shore. The Bosun's whistle and shouting are very evident as For'sails and Royals are lowered and reefed.

Although supposedly in their "safe" accommodation, the three young officers have found a small space where they are unobserved while they watch the constant rise and fall of the Mainsails. The anchor is released after about nine o'clock as the sun sets in a blaze of golden light reflected off the cliffs to change the colour of the sea from pale blue to a yellow green.

They pack up their kit with the last light from the open door, expecting to be called to disembark, but learn that they are to remain on board until the rest of the fleet arrives.

Lauchlin sleeps well during what he hopes will be his last night on the *Flame.* He wakes at about six, disturbed by the sounding of the ship's bell. It is almost light and the ship is unusually quiet. There is a steady breeze as he ventures out to the Heads. Up on the quarter deck there are the familiar figures of the Watch officer and his men. No lights can yet be seen in Colonel Beresford's quarters.

As often, there is a line waiting to use the facility. Clambering back through the small door he disturbs his friends. The confined space only allows one at a time to try and dress.

A watery sun breaks through as they finish their porage. The castle walls change from grey to a pale gold, occasionally sparking a glint on the bronze barrels of cannon. Tarquin has duties with his "lads" and disappears but Duncan's time seems to be free. During the next three hours the two are able to watch as other ships in the convoy arrive and anchor in close lines behind them. Duncan snorts, "they'll all have to scatter quick enough if the wind comes up!" Lauchlin watches as a ship's boat is rowed across to the other ships; he assumes his copied despatches are being delivered. The soldiers and the families are allowed up. Lauchlin sees men of the highland divisions. The red-coated Royal Marines line up to prevent anyone escaping. The discipline is more relaxed now that they have made land but there is no evidence of anyone going ashore. The highlanders are big men and laugh among themselves as they squeeze through openings designed for slighter men and take deep breaths. Two children, about six years old, are running freely among the soldiers crowded on the deck in the ship's waist. Similar crowds can be seen on the other five transports that have arrived. He assumes the rest are to follow. "No horses yet." Duncan suggests "all on other ships I s'pose. Or have they been sent somewhere else?"

A naval officer he recognizes as Lieutenant Carmody leans over and calls out: "You, Mackinnon, Colonel wants you – come up here!"

Duncan scoffs. "More letter writing, Loch. Tell him you want to be an army officer, not a clerk!"

He goes up the steps to the lieutenant who, without a word, jerks a thumb up the stairs to the Colonel's quarters. He taps on the door.

"Ah Lauchlin, good. I've got to go and see the Port Admiral. I shall need you to come with me. There will be despatches to deliver and collect. The Captain is lending me his barge – I'd like to get away at once."

"Very good sir, will we be coming back or should I take my kit?"

"Mm…" he is uncertain. "Better leave it with Captain Dirleton. He can stow it with mine." His eyes crinkle as he smiles, "in the army you must be ready for anything!" As Lauchlin leaves he adds "full and smartest rig, please."

Duncan checks the position of his sword straps which have not been worn since leaving Leith. His bulkiest item is the greatcoat and he leaves it all with the Colonel's a.d.c. while taking up a position by the taffrail where he sees men sitting in the boat. He is told to climb down. It is not difficult. The Colonel descends after him. He has changed into a smarter uniform and carries a leather despatch case on a strap over a shoulder. He eyes Lauchlin and hands him the bag. "Here – you take this, it's getting entangled with my sword!" Lauchlin is pleased to take it -he appears more involved. He hangs it over his right shoulder so that it is free of his own sword belt and sits lightly on his uniform trews which are badly creased. They cast off and are rowed smartly towards a small stone jetty just below an official looking building with a large naval ensign blowing proudly in the wind.

Beresford takes the bag from him as they mount the steps. "You'll have to wait outside while I am with the Port Admiral. Shouldn't be more than half-an-hour."

In fact, he waits in an adjoining office where a naval lieutenant, somehow uncertain of Lauchlin's rank, seems keen to talk. "You've been leading that convoy just down from Leith? Where are you bound?"

"I couldn't say I've been leading! As for where we're bound – again I couldn't say. I've heard mention of India."

"India. My word…I joined the Navy in the expectation of sea service but I have been Flag-Lieutenant to the Port Admiral for nearly two years.

Lauchlin simply nods. Are the words a cautionary reminder of Duncan's mockery about merely writing letters?

"D'you understand naval signalling? The Admiral is being harassed by your Commodore about the flags we used to signal him in. I gather your chap's a bit of a stickler for the new methods!"

"Err no. I'm in the army and I'm not up with signalling yet."

"Mmm…" The lieutenant nods in agreement. "D'ye ride? Army officers always seem to ride here. I like horses…" he pauses in thought, "perhaps I should try to transfer to the army…what do you think?"

"I…er…can only say I find it an engrossing career." He begins to suspect that the young man is of a simple disposition. Perhaps the admiral is a relative.

Fortunately there is activity in the corridor and the lieutenant jumps to his feet. "Hey-ho, meeting's finished." They go to stand outside.

Beresford emerges. He looks perturbed and hands the despatch bag over without a word. They move slowly down to the jetty and climb back into the boat. Beresford looks at the coxswain as if thinking. Then makes up his mind. "Back to the ship, please, Mr.O'Neill!"

As they approach the ship the coxswain makes various signals with his mooring pole and calls out: "Flame of Scotland, Colonel Beresford!"

The Colonel has been silent all the way across. As they climb up through the taffrail he says: "A number of despatches to go, Mackinnon – two or three before five o'clock, others by about eight tonight." He stomps away without another word.

Lauchlin calls out after him, "I'll come along in about half-an-hour then Sir?" Beresford stops on the steps and looks back. "Make it an hour and you can write to your mother and family; one of the ships is going back to Leith."

Lauchlin is left wondering what to do. The opportunity to send news home is not to be lost but he has no paper, no quill, no ink and certainly no suitable space to sit and write.

Duncan and Tarquin are watching for his return and eager to learn if there is any news. He tells them of the ship returning to Leith and of the opportunity it presents to send letters. Duncan is pleased, "I brought a sheet of paper with me but I'll have to write in pencil!"

There is a cold meal in the Dolly, of old mutton, cabbage and carrots. When it is over he thinks it is a reasonable time to go back up to the Colonel's quarters.

He has now changed back into his work-day clothes and seems more cheerful. "There's one, fairly long, despatch on my desk there. Five copies please!" He goes outside and calls down to the Officer of the Watch.

Lauchlin sees the letter lying open on the desk and takes it to the corner table ensuring that he has a good nib and can reach the ink and paper. Making himself as comfortable as possible he draws everything towards him and starts to copy.

My Darling Cynthia, 11th June 1805

He has written three words before realizing that it is not the Despatch referred to. Quickly he stands to move everything out of his way and hurries back to find the right letter. He replaces the personal letter where he found it but cannot resist the opportunity of reading how a senior officer writes to his family.

I write in haste from the "Scottish Flame" in Dover
Harbour. The news is not encouraging, from here we
go to Cork for re-victualling and to join up with the
rest of our forces. But the command is not to be mine.
The naval responsibility remains with that wretch
Home Popham who is confirmed Commodore and S. David Baird
is to follow and assume command at the Cape.After that, who
is to say? Perhaps India or home…

He hears the colonel coming back up the stairs from the Quarter Deck and ensures that everything is back in place. Then starts copying a Despatch to all Regimental Commanders in his Division listing their next destination and what supplies are to be taken on each ship. It is a mighty list and must have taken him, or more likely Captain Dirleton and his staff a considerable time and calculation. Lauchlin wonders how the food and provisions can be obtained. It consists of many tons of fresh beef, in barrel; twelve tons of fresh mutton, six of fresh pork, ten of salt pork, potatoes in barrel, carrots, flour, sugar, butter, fruit and fresh water. There is a reminder that old water barrels are to be scrubbed out and bleached before re-filling.

He hears the shrilling of the *Bosun's* pipe while he is barely half-way through the third copy. In a panic he puts the work aside and, drawing a fresh sheet towards him, writes to his mother.

Saturday 11th June 1805
My Dearest Mother,
I write from Dover Harbour in the County of Kent.
They tell me that there is a ship going back to Leith
and this gives me the opportunity to write and tell you
what has been happening since my last despatch.

He has to think back to his last letter, it was written at speed from Drysdale's lodgings and so much has happened since. He tells them that he is about to cross to Ireland for supplies before setting out perhaps for the Cape or India. He cannot resist a small measure of exaggeration in describing his duties and ends with his deepest respects to his father and grandfather and hopes that Fingal and his bride are settling in well. Lastly he sends his affectionate respects to Stuart.

I must end this letter and continue my duties and hope
that this will be in time to catch the next sailing for Leith.
I shall address this care of Andrew Drysdale
In the hope that he can get it to your dear self.
Ever your loving son
Lauchlin.

He reads it through and wraps it in a covering before addressing it as described. Writing the letter has brought memories flooding back and he feels homesick. He thinks of his mother's cooking and of her constant presence and comfort whenever he was in doubt or in difficulty. With a deep breath he finds himself longing to feel her strong arms around him.

Shaking his head he continues copying out the long list of stores to be taken on each ship. It helps him recover from his melancholia. He sighs to himself – *still a wee boy then, Lauchie?* At length he finishes the copying and goes out to find the Colonel. He is holding a meeting in the Captain's cabin with what appears to be a number of his own commanders and captains of other ships. The Officer of the Watch prevents him from going in.

"You can wait there, nothing is going to happen now the *Glorious* has gone back."

"Gone back where, sir?"

"Back to Leith – her base, you idiot!"

With a sick shock he realizes that his letter home has missed the ship. It will now have to wait until the release of another ship – hopefully at Cork.

They sail that night. Their accommodation unchanged. Day follows day as the eight ships in their convoy proceed Westwards along the Channel mainly hugging the South Coast. During the third night Lauchlin wakes to sounds of the *Bosun's* whistle and of feet pounding on the deck. He finds the ship rolling quite violently. His companions are already awake and complaining. Duncan has retained a flint box and, after struggling with the pitching, manages to light the oil lamp. He stares at the locked gun port they had struggled with on their first day. They can all hear the waves reaching up outside trying to break in. "Good God, I'm glad we didn't leave that open we would all have been drooned!"

Tarquin Crowley is on his knees backing towards the door. "I'm not waitin' here to be drowned – I'm going outside!"

As he leans his weight against the door it is swept out of his hand and opens with a violent crash that pulls him out as he tries to minimize its severity. Rain and wind rush in. Tarquin tries to find shelter, hurrying back into the lee of the doorway only to receive a shout from above: "You there, get below, keep that door secure!"

"Is the ship going down? We don't want to drown!"

There is a burst of laughter which carries through the noise of the wind. "You stay there, mate, we've decided you're the first to greet Davy Jones!"

Another voice calls out. "Belay that, Smith! Explain it's only a squall!"

"Aye aye, sir, just a bit of fun. Sorry mate, it's just a squall and we're taking in a couple of Top-gallants!"

Tarquin crawls back pulling the door closed behind him. "Bleeding clowns, it feels much rougher down here. D'ye know they've got sailors climbing up the masts – bloody monkeys!"

During lunch the next day they reach the shelter of the huge natural harbours of Southern Ireland. Under reduced sail they leave the basin of Cobh and enter the protection of Cork. Lauchlin, who is standing with Colonel Beresford on his small exercise deck is astonished at the sight of the ships anchored there. Even Beresford is impressed. "There must be over fifty ships here already, and when the others arrive behind us… quite a force to be reckoned with!"

Lauchlin thinks back to the Colonel's letter to his wife. The tone of regret - even fury – that the command was not to be his. A seaman is up on a cross tree above them, signalling with flags. The officer of the watch is staring with his telescope at another ship. He looks up and yells "Right Yeoman – Acknowledge!" He turns with an oath under his breath, "I shall never get the hang of this new signalling of the Commodore's. I now have to consult the Code book! – ship flags with just numbers have been good enough since……" He goes to the door of the Captain's cabin behind him, "Captain Sir, message from the Commodore, must just decipher it."

After a pause, the captain emerges. Lauchlin cannot remember seeing him before. An overweight, red-faced man he looks as though he has been disturbed from a post-drunken sleep. He looks back at the officer, wiping a hand across his face. "What's the signal, Farthing? Get a move on!"

Lieutenant Farthing emerges holding a paper in his hand. He brings a hand up to his cap. "All captains to repair to the flagship at four bells, afternoon watch, sir."

"Oh sh…! Lay the barge on please." He turns to re-enter his cabin then stops. "And please advise Colonel Beresford of the signal... he might care to accompany me."

After an early lunch they watch as Captain Shoebridge and Colonel Beresford, both in their best uniforms, are rowed away to a ship on the far side of the harbour.

Crowley takes a pack of cards from his pocket. "Let me show you a trick." He looks around trying to find a suitable surface that would serve as a table.

Duncan looks perturbed. "Better not out here, they might think we're gambling for money."

He pushes the cards back into his jacket. "You're really a bit of a scary-arse Duncan. Tell you what, when we can go ashore we'll find a good inn, away from the port area. We'll have a few Mothers' Milks, meet some of the local Delilahs and I can show you a trick or two!" He chuckles, "some even with cards!"

Duncan looks back at him. "What a thrill that'll be! How long do you think we shall be here Loch?"

"Well, I do know there's a pile of stores to be taken aboard as well as some live animals."

"Live animals? You mean the horses?"

"No, cattle for eating. Apparently some of these ships have stalls – some for horses yes – but others in the charge of butchers."

He goes on to explain that Colonel Beresford had told him to get a new uniform at Shorncliffe. Should he try to get one in Cork?

"I'm told this is a great place for riding too. I'd like to learn to ride a horse!"

"Oh that will be especially useful when you are a senior clerk!" The other two laugh at him.

Two hours later they see a boat rowing towards them. It has a small burgee flying in front. Tarquin calls out, "I think that will be the Despatches boat – if our families had known we were here they could have written." It reminds Lauchlin of the letter he has to send home. He goes to the foot of the Quarter Deck steps and calls out to the Watch Officer. "Pardon me sir, I have a letter to send back to Edinburgh, can I hand it to the Despatches Boat?"

Lieutenant Munro leans down. "That would be about as useful as throwing it into the sea. Don't worry, laddie. There'll be other chances – we'll be here for some weeks."

On the Flagship, Commodore Home Popham is chairing a meeting of some twenty-five of the more senior captains in the group. Colonel Beresford is placed at his side, uncertain whether this is a recognition of his seniority or to keep him under control.

"Gentlemen, my purpose this afternoon, is to acquaint you with the current situation as outlined to me just recently by the King's First Minister, Mr. Pitt. We are a formidable force – in total we shall be something over six thousand men. As you have seen we have around two hundred Dragoons with their chargers. These are to be installed in ten of the transports of the Derby Class. I look to you Captain Ponsford for assurance that you have the stalls, men and provender for these animals." Captain Ponsford is seated at a point half-way along. He nods his agreement. He is young for such a senior role – a slim thirty-five year-old who spent two years under Nelson blockading Toulon. Personally he feels demeaned to have been appointed to command a fat, slow, almost unarmed transport ship when most of his service has been in Frigates and 'Seventy-fours'. He knows Nelson is still out in the South somewhere, blockading the French ports. "You will also have the officers and men of the Dragoons to accommodate, I suggest they are equally divided among your ten transports." Ponsford is irritated. How else should the men and horses be accommodated? But he looks at the Commodore and nods his understanding.

"Captain Ponsford!" The Commodore is showing his displeasure, "with so many of us crammed in this cabin, it would be helpful if proper courtesies were addressed to this number of senior captains! Many of whom do not know you!"

Captain Ponsford stands. His bowed head and bent knees a tribute to his height and the low ceiling rather than respect for the Commodore. As he speaks, one hand idly fingers each of his two golden shoulder epaulettes demonstrating his own seniority.

"I apologize if my conduct was deemed disrespectful, Sir. Perhaps I have been too long at sea where we have grown accustomed to remaining seated even for the Loyal Toast. Your orders are understood, Sir, although the Dragoons will not be coming aboard until the day before we sail."

"Right then." Home Popham realizes he has made something of a blunder. This puts him in a bad mood. "So, some six thousand men, the cavalry I mentioned, three hundred gunners with their wherewithal which includes another thirty horses. You have the pleasure of their company, Captain Beauchamp." The man named staggers carefully to his feet. Close to fifty his eyes somehow show a tolerance lacking in so many of those present. One sleeve of his jacket is folded over and pinned to his breast. "It will be my pleasure and my privilege, Commodore. I have arranged to meet with Major Carruthers of the Gunners to ensure that they can be received aboard the sixteen ships stipulated in good time." He sits down heavily.

The meeting continues with staff plans for the loading of men and *materiel.* "I wish to reach the Cape at the time of their harvest – they will be under some pressure to remain on their farms – that will require us to sail before the end of August, gentlemen!" His Senior Staff Officer, Commander Staveley, brings out a large map which he hangs on an easel. "Now, the general situation as outlined to me by Mr.Pitt." He proceeds to give an outline which even Colonel Beresford has to admit is accurate and all-embracing. "The Austrians and the Russians are to hold Bonaparte but we must be prepared in case he breaks through at Austerlitz. Perhaps he will now be emboldened to try and take Russia itself – we hope he does, I believe it will be a dish too large for his digestion." There is polite laughter at his humour. He continues. "We have our orders, gentlemen. The first is to take and hold the Cape thus protecting our route to India. After taking the Cape I anticipate receiving further instructions which will likely mean sending at least a proportion on to the sub-continent, or it may be to Jamaica – Villeneuve shows signs of trying to break out through Lord Nelson's blockade. We are then required to patrol the seas between West Africa and South America. " He gives a sigh and looks around. "We have a large number of men with us. It will be scandalous if they are not put to good use. Also, if not kept fully occupied they will get up to mischief. Recreational ideas will be welcome – perhaps some kind of sporting competition, I have heard football is popular – perhaps polo for the officers. Exercising the horses is most important." After some more minor points the meeting ends as the ship's bell sounds eight times to announce the changing of the watch.

Beresford expresses his thanks to the Commodore and turns to Captain Shoebridge. Privately he had thought it likely that he would be invited to stay on the flagship for dinner but clearly that is not Home Popham's style. They wait for their boat to be summoned before returning to *Scottish Flame.* They are received at the taffrail with all ceremony, *Bosun's* whistle, Marine Guard of Honour and the First Lieutenant lifting his hat. As is customary, Beresford joins the captain in acknowledging the courtesies by raising his own hat but he is not satisfied. He feels it essential for his own staff officers to check that all the stores and materials are loaded correctly. Once they are ashore at the Cape it will be his responsibility if some essential item is missing or faulty. The stage is therefore set for some gruelling weeks as first the stores and then the animals are brought aboard.

For Lauchlin and the two subalterns it is also a busy time. Tarquin and Duncan are needed at their Divisions where a daily check is carried out on each man to ensure that he is fit for duty. Both are then heavily involved in supervising the tally of stores coming aboard. Bringing the barrels of salt pork, beef and mutton is dangerous and demanding work. From the warehouses ashore the stock is taken by the soldiers to the boats and rowed out. When they are in position, the seamen use slings powered by the capstan manned by twenty-eight of the watch to hoist one barrel at a time to the deck where the soldiers manhandle it towards the deep holds where the seamen stow it under the supervision of one of the ship's officers. Each item is carefully checked against a list at the warehouse, at arrival ship-side and again as it is stowed. Inevitably, items fall overboard and are largely lost. On occasions one of the soldiers or a seaman gets injured and has to receive treatment. One of the barrels of rum is dropped heavily on the deck and springs a leak. Lauchlin is surprised how quickly small bowls and bottles appear to collect the spillage almost, he thinks, as though they were expecting it. The lists of stores are audited and compared. The errors are adjusted, usually by accepting an average. But each list has to be countersigned by an officer. The result is that the administration for something over seventy ships is considerable.

At four bells in the forenoon watch the mainbrace is spliced. Under the guard of armed marines a barrel of rum is brought up and each seaman receives a small cup-full. This is not extended to the soldiers. It is a traditional difference and, although leading to some grumbling, it is accepted. Work is usually brought to a close at eight bells of the afternoon watch, - four o'clock. As routines become established, and the days continue to lengthen, occasional outings ashore for troops and seamen become advisable. Desertions among the seamen are still a fairly regular occurrence when many have been recruited by the Press-gang. When caught they are usually punished by a flogging. Desertion among the troops is rarer and viewed more seriously, flogging for a minor absence without leave; desertion in the face of the enemy by hanging in front of a parade.

Following the Commodore's suggestion, an inter-service football competition is arranged. This takes place under the supervision of armed marines. There are four large fields within the Cork Military establishment. Lauchlin is rarely free from duty by eight bells so only becomes involved in one match. But it is an entirely new experience for him and the fierceness of the tackling and the competitiveness among the ships astonishes him. He is also conscious of the Colonel's instruction to obtain a new uniform and has to allocate some of his afternoons off duty to this. Colonel Beresford has confirmed again that the cost of this should be charged to the regiment on his authority.

Tarquin still wishes to explore the inns away from the port area and they agree on a date for this. Lauchlin's inability to ride limits their range and the landing is not a success. Every inn and public house is crammed with troopers or seamen who have quickly establish rights of use over selected establishments.

The subalterns discuss how to correct Lauchlin's inability to ride. Sergeant Robinson overhears one such conversation. He approaches Lauchlin privately and offers to teach him the rudiments. "Begging your pardon, sir, I was a Sergeant of Dragoons for seven years!" He knows where suitable mounts can be obtained from within the barracks and a session is arranged for two days' time.

Lauchlin explains to his companions that he will be occupied in Beresford's service. Accommodation in the boat ashore being limited they all take the first one available so that Lauchlin has to pretend he is visiting the Camp Registry while they go off on their own expedition. There is rarely a shortage of mounts. The animals need daily exercise and in advance of a major expedition such as this there tend to be more horses than riders.

He meets Sergeant Robinson behind the Sergeants' Mess. Keeping a sharp look-out for the subalterns, he follows as his instructor limps to the Riding 'Hexercise 'All. "Begging your pardon, sir, but Hi squared it with the Corporal of 'orse – provided we leave no mess, the 'all is hours for has long has we likes!"

Robinson selects a mount he thinks will be suitable. "This is *Jessup,* sir, he has a kind eye". He talks to the animal continuously, inevitably reminding Lauchlin of Bonington with his Emily. He fits the bit and reins speaking as to an old friend: "'ow's my boy this morning then? You're a good boy ain't you, Jessup – goin' to be nice to the young Ensign?"

As the reins fall into place, Jessup politely nods his head up and down.

They start with the correct saddling procedure. "Begging your pardon, sir, but when doin' hup the girth you 'ave to hensure that hall the gases that hare always present, hon account of what 'e heats, are, so to speak, hexpelled! Hotherwise hit'll be loose and you'll fall hoff!" Matching his actions to his words he delivers a sharp dig in the ribs and yanks the girth another notch.

Mounting and riding are not as easy as Lauchlin had expected. Strong and healthy as he is, even mounting up with one foot in a stirrup is demanding. Just sitting on Jessup's saddle stretches his legs apart and when Robinson encourages a light canter the motion unnerves him and his feet come away so that he too often finds himself hitting the ground.

They have an hour of it until Robinson decrees that they have had enough. "Next time, begging your pardon, we might try a little jumping!" Lauchlin's thighs and rear appeal for a long rest but he makes no mention of it.

On his way back to the harbour he passes one of the inns which the highlanders seem to have made their own. He becomes aware of being closely examined and, looking up, recognizes a face he had hoped never to see again. It takes him back to that evening nearly a year ago when he had gone to collect Lord Leadbetter's property. It is a shock and he steps back to challenge the man at once.

"In very truth you're Jameson aren't you! What are you doing here?"

Jameson smiles at him totally without guilt. "Well, bonny lad – it's Sharpshooter Jameson now and I've joined the 72nd Highlanders! And I see you've moved on too!"

"But you…" for some moments Lauchlin is tongue-tied. Jameson continues. "Aw me and Drewett did our time then I went back to Glasgie and joined up again. They'se glad to have me with my experience."

He feels helpless and looks about him but there is no authority nearby. He sees signs of the boat for *Scottish Flame* and hurries to the jetty. All the way back as the men row in perfect unison he finds himself trembling half with remembered fear but also with fury. Can that tale be true? Should he report the matter to someone?

Back on board, the others fail to notice his stiff movements and surreptitious rubbing of a sore back but are interested in his description of meeting Jameson.

Duncan chuckles. "Well it's a coincidence right enough, but ye canna take action aboot it. It's not as if he was on the run or anything!"

"But his sentence must have been very short!"

"Mmm…not necessarily…I imagine there's a few of the lads here have a background of some kind. Best to put it behind you."

Day follows day as he becomes increasingly familiar with the duties of the Colonel's Secretary while his riding skills improve to the extent that Jessup is exchanged for a livelier mount. Jumps little more than a step are practised and, eventually jumps up to some three feet high are tackled with greater confidence.

As preparations for the departure of the convoy are completed, Beresford applies pressure on the Captain so that accommodation for Tarquin and Duncan is moved to hammocks adjacent to their platoons and closer to the Midshipmen's Mess. As a result, Lauchlin has sole charge of the rear-sail locker.

Chapter 10

Commodore Hugh Popham's aim of sailing before the end of August is achieved – but only just. The convoy, consisting of sixty transport ships escorted by seven frigates and three larger men-o-war, moves ponderously away from the coast of Ireland as bands on shore and on two of the larger '74's' play martial airs.

Lauchlin stands with Beresford on his *poop* deck area. The Colonel listens to the music and shakes his head: "If I hear *Heart of Oak* just one more time it will be too often! I expect you'd rather hear the pipes, wouldn't you."

Lauchlin dutifully agrees as he watches the officers on the quarter deck below doff their hats in salute to the Port Admiral's Pennant while surreptitiously staring up at the sails, gauging the wind and controlling the *coxswain* at the wheel.

After working so closely with the Colonel, Lauchlin has noted that he has a weakness in one eye. He has become accustomed to the Colonel's habit of turning his head to use his good eye when reading a despatch but it is still unnerving to see his head at an angle when looking further afield.

Beresford has chosen to retain his accommodation on the *Flame of Scotland* so Lauchlin's world has remained very much as before. His sleeping space is greatly improved and on most days he is still able to have breakfast with Tarquin and Duncan but thereafter they are increasingly involved with exercising their platoons while he is kept busy recording Beresford's instructions.

For several days they move in a Southerly direction. The gentle winds blow generally from the West and he becomes accustomed to the deck sloping permanently down to his left. For a couple of days he suffers from mild seasickness but, he tells himself, it is principally a headache from reading poorly written correspondence in a bad light. He is excited at the prospect of being close to Africa as for some days gentle zephyrs control their way. Then the wind shifts so that they are forced to tack. The crew seem to be eternally aloft adjusting the sails as directed by the Bosun's shouts as they are hit, sometimes fiercely, by hot and, somehow, dusty gales.

The Commodore is determined to keep the ships together and the flagship is constantly observed signalling to stragglers to close up. The officer on watch is often heard complaining that the Commodore is still developing his new system of signalling. On occasions, strangely at the same time in the forenoon, just as the sun is approaching its apogee, the winds die altogether and the Commodore sends boats around the fleet with orders that sometimes countermand those given earlier. But generally the weather is sublime and with plenty of supplies on board and no enemy encountered life for the seamen is acceptable.

Some three weeks after leaving Cork, the fleet anchors outside a harbour in Madeira. The men-o-war fire signal guns in a salute to the Portuguese ally which is returned. Home Popham and his senior team go ashore at Funchal to learn the latest situation from the authorities. Beresford and Dirleton stand together and watch the proceedings while admiring the greenery of the hills. The *a.d.c.* closes his eyes and stares up at a warming sun. "What an idyllic spot, Colonel! You've been here before, of course."

"Oh yes, John, but a long time ago....you know...if it weren't for the fact that Portugal is so fiercely against Spain and therefore our ally, we should have taken these islands. Only lightly defended – not a bad harbour...we could hoist guns up on those mountains and...altogether a pleasant posting for a retired senior officer!"

"Not making plans for your retirement, surely sir?"

"Well, the years roll by, John. It's a different age. I begin to think I've gone as far as I'm likely to now. Heaven knows what troubles people like the Commodore and his brothers will lead us into! Mind you I never said that."

"Understood sir. What stores can we obtain here, water of course."

"They have animals, I'd be going after more fresh meat - and flour of course. No rum for the sailors but they have a sweet wine which has a good reputation. I expect the odd bum-boat will put out to us - see what they offer. But it's down to H.P. what the fleet buys."

The next morning there is a general signal for the senior captains to attend a meeting with the Commodore. Once again Beresford joins Captain Shoebridge in his boat and they are rowed across. The only stores they have been ordered to replenish are the water-butts.

Home Popham informs the meeting of despatches he has just received. "The government of Portugal is still supportive of our efforts and generally on side. There need be no delay to our onward progress. I have undertaken to carry despatches for them to Bahia. The only reports they have here are unreliable suggestions that the French and Spanish navies are collaborating and threatening to come out and face Nelson down in the roads of Trafalgar, but I doubt the veracity of such tales. All things being equal, gentlemen, we should make a rapid crossing and make our final preparations for the assault on the Cape." In reply to a question he comments that as an island group prices for most commodities are high and they will only replenish their water stocks.

After five days the convoy puts to sea again. It crosses the Equator on 15th October, entering the Southern Spring just as Autumn is trying to establish itself in the North. But there is no discernible change on board. Lauchlin finds the heat oppressive even as the officers are permitted to leave off their jackets. The winds also begin to play games with the convoy. Lauchlin marvels as a ship only some two hundred yards distant, or twenty cables as he is learning to call it, can be observed making good progress under full sail whilst their own situation is becalmed with sails flapping uselessly. Once again the crews are forced to spend much time aloft as the *Bosun's* whistle and his rope end urge them to rapid alterations of sail. The evenings are pleasant idylls. The soldiers are allowed up in rotation and occasionally a highlander will dance on the covers of the holds. When he returns to his accommodation under the quarter deck, the heat is unbearable and he finds small areas where the pitch has melted and dripped on the deck below. He wedges his door ajar to gain a modicum of fresh air.

After a week of such weather the wind veers to blow violently from the South-west. The sea changes from its reassuring blue to one where lashing waves crash over the ship causing some flooding where the soldiers below decks have broken rules and opened up the gun ports.

In spite of the Commodore's insistence, the weather prevents the ships staying together and it takes a full week for the last straggler to work its way into the huge bay after the leading ship has anchored in Bahia. One of the transporters carrying over two hundred men of the Leicester Yeomanry and one hundred and ten seamen never arrives and is registered as lost at sea. Other members of the convoy have been severely damaged and much valuable equipment broken beyond repair. The fleet spends some five weeks in the Brazilian bay effecting repairs, with the Commodore becoming increasingly bad tempered – two ships need actual careening on a beach. Stores are replenished and several conferences held on the flagship before they are able to put to sea again on 5th January.

Beresford pounds the rail in fury as he looks at the array of shipping trying to achieve an orderly departure. "Four and a half bleeding months of this to achieve precisely what, John?"

"Well, we've been a bit unlucky with the weather, sir but I s'pose the Commodore is now expecting us to take the Cape from the Netherlanders once and for all! Assuming, of course, that another treaty is not negotiated…"

The Colonel looks thoughtful. "He was at the Cape before, of course, about ten years ago when we first captured the place. But," he snorts with contempt, "now we've got to fight for it all over again. It's a bit of a mish-mash. Hottentot tribes farm the northern parts and trade with the Dutch Burghers who are quite a mix…Calvinists speaking their own kind of language…the place was run by a sort of Dutch East India company but never really got it together. Now the Hollanders are on Napoleon's side again it's essential for us to keep the French away or lose control of the Indian Ocean!" He bangs his fists together. "We shall have to replenish a lot of stores before we try to make it to Calcutta." He swings round to lean his back on the rails. "I would have thought a monitor might have been coming here with despatches from London. Not heard a word for over three months. War might be over for all we know!"

"I wouldn't have thought so, sir. God, I hope not anyway! A load of us for the half-pay lines and even more for the rubbish pile!"

Beresford chuckles ironically. "Not much chance, anyway. Now, where's that young scoundrel, Lauchlin – nose in a book? He's as bad as my wife!"

"I lent him a copy of my "Rules of Engagement" Sir, makes a change from Shakespeare - you know he still maintains he wants to be a soldier, not your clerk. Not that he's complaining – just a bit ambitious."

"Ambition's all very well, John, but he's got no family connections to help him along."

John Dirleton smiles and nods. "I'm not aware that your connection with the Peerage gave you much of a leg-up!"

"Mm….well you know very well that my mother could not be married to my father but he has been good to her…and to me. Right, we'll try and have him out in the field then…mind you, I still need my secretary!"

Five days later, when still three hundred miles short of their destination, *H.M.S. Whippet* achieves its purpose in finding them. The Lieutenant in command signals the flagship that he is carrying official despatches and some private mail. Happily the weather remains kind so that several ships' boats are able to cross and collect their relevant canvas sacks. Beresford retires to his cabin with a heavy stack following which he summons his staff and sends out slight revisions of his earlier battle plan.

"Sir David Baird's arrival has been delayed. His instructions are that we are to proceed with the operation. Accordingly, I have decided to launch the main attack on Saldanha Bay. The water can be rough there. Let us pray that the wind is not from the West and that our boats can make a safe land-fall. Gentlemen!" He pauses for a moment, "most of us will go ashore at that point. We expect to draw the enemy's principal response there. An alternative landing will be made on the sands at Bredasdorp, to the East. I am told there are sand dunes all the way round and Captain Dirleton will command that operation. My hope is that we shall be able to advance North from both beaches, joining up twenty miles inland having drawn the Netherlanders out of Cabosvoort."

After two days of copying out despatches, Lauchlin is surprised to find Beresford watching him with a benevolent expression. "They tell me you want to be more of a soldier, Lauchlin."

"Indeed, Colonel. I feel I could be more use out in the field than doing mere clerical duties that any child just out of the schoolroom could do." Realizing he has been outspoken and somewhat rude, he collects himself to add. "I'm very grateful for the opportunity to act for you, Colonel, but simply feel it is time I moved on."

"Mmm…yes, well. We shall make a landfall against an enemy

tomorrow. As you will have read in the orders, the 28th Foot and half of the 72nd Highlanders will be landing at Saldanha Bay, here, at first light." Using a large map he points at Bredasdorp to the East. "This is almost the Indian Ocean and should be smoother. Captain Dirleton will go ashore here with the balance of the 72nd and the 75th, to be followed by the Artillery and as many of the horses as can be safely conveyed. There are ten of the American Sharpshooters as well." He folds the map. "Subaltern Crowley's Division will go with him and I would like you to serve as Captain Dirleton's Runner – carrying out such duties as he gives you. I know you will use your head in what could be a tricky fight." He smiles again. "Take your sword and stay out of the line of fire!"

He is too excited to sleep much and his dreams are composed of mad dashes against the enemy with himself in the van. He rises at eight bells, four o'clock in the morning, roused by the sounds of the two regiments preparing to leave the ships. There is much shouting and signalling. Running feet show that the sails are being adjusted. He forces some porage down his throat and reports to Captain Dirleton.

"Right, Lauchlin. Just stay where I can see you and jump when I say so! Colonel Beresford has already left the ship, joining the two Infantry Regiments who will make the first landing." He suddenly grips Lauchlin's shoulder: "There – can you hear that?"

Faintly, fighting against the wind he can just make out the sound of a bagpipe being played near the shore.

"One of the other ships had a piper… Lucky devils!"

But there is no time for dawdling. Everyone has his weapon checked and is issued with a small amount of food. It is a dark morning and the breeze, although still relatively gentle, is from the dreaded West. There is no attempt to minimize the lights being shown. He cannot see any detail of the shore and the ship dips its nose in the sea as it continues sailing East towards the Indian Ocean. Spray washes over them and he feels his heart pounding. He blames the roughness of the sea for the bile and nausea which insist on rising in his throat. He hides his trembling hands. Troops will be lowered away only about twelve miles from where the earlier landing was launched but, owing to the shape of the Southern Cape, the point of Bredasdorp is more than twenty-five miles by land from Saldanha.

The sun makes its slow appearance over a grey sea. Captain Dirleton gestures for Lauchlin to precede him down the ship's side and into a boat already brimming with nervous Highland Fusiliers fingering their muskets and powder horns. The packs on their shoulders take up valuable space and there is some irritated shoving. The craft rises and falls violently with the sea. As he times himself to drop in, he scrapes his wrist on the ship's side. The roughness tears his jacket and removes a layer of skin eight inches long from his right arm. He is angered by his clumsiness and conceals the hurt. There are eight boats in all. His eyes meet Tarquin's sitting with his platoon but there is no reaction in the slightly nervous stare. As the rowers clear the ship he sees the other transport coming up. The sounds of whinnying show that the horses are beginning to be hoisted over the waves.

His sword rests between his feet and he hugs his sore arm but then has to grip the boat with both hands. The shoreline looks sandy.They reach the edges quickly. The big boat is grasped by huge waves surging towards the shore before being released as quickly to be gripped by another irresistible, almost unnatural power that throws the craft into the shallow surf with a jolt, before withdrawing to regain its strength and return with a terrible vengeance which heaves them on the beach. The oars are raised and Dirleton shouts out "That's it! Out of the boat – with me!"

But the sea has not finished with them. Even as Dirleton and a few eager fusiliers leap into the water, the boat is sucked back into the waves before being thrust forward with even greater violence catching two fusiliers who go under. The oars furiously try to control their position. Most of the troops leap out. Lauchlin lands almost waist deep in the surging sea as the undertow sucks at his boots. He staggers ashore trying to keep up with Captain Dirleton who is well ahead trotting up the soft, dry sand towards a path leading inland. He feels a strong hand grab him clear of the water. "This is the way, young sir!" It is an accent he does not recognize. His uniform is the same red jacket and white trews of the Foot Regiments but one shoulder bears a badge "*Loyal American Rifles*". Lauchlin sees he is a Sergeant.

"Not a good idea all going down a path like that!" He gestures to other men around. "Spread out! Over to the right or left there – not on the path!"

Lauchlin realizes the sense of what he is being told. This is the kind of warfare to which the American Colonists would have been accustomed. Although there is no sound of firing it would be a natural spot for an ambush. He expresses his thanks. The man nods to him. He seems mature, even old for this kind of running. Lauchlin breasts the top of a dune and sees a grove of pine trees stretching ahead. Dirleton and the first of his men are consolidating a few hundred yards away, recovering while he peers through a telescope at the land ahead. Lauchlin hurries to his side and squats down. His trews feel moderately dry but his boots are full of water and sand and his sore arm stings. The heat is becoming oppressive.

"Good man, Lauchlin!" He turns round to talk to those near him. "Well done lads. We've made it ashore. I can't see any sign of opposition yet. Spread out among the trees – check your equipment, clean your weapons. We'll wait here and see how the cavalry and guns have coped." He bends towards Lauchlin "Now, nip back and see if the horses are making it. Tell them where we are. Then let me know the situation!"

He jumps to his feet and trots back the way they came. Leaving the shade of the trees brings him into the full glare of the sun. At the top of the dunes he lies down to survey the beach, ignoring the burning sand on his knees. His heart thumps and he feels strangely sea-sick as if the dunes were rising and falling.

It is something of a chaotic scene. Over on his right, about three hundred yards distant, he can see four or five horses swimming ashore with riders hanging on. There are three big boats attempting to reach the beach, each with two masked horses who are being forced to keep their heads down by attendants grasping reins as they try to rear up. One is kicking out and appears to have knocked a rider into the water. One boat is about ten yards off shore and the animals are being urged to leap into the water. He runs down to the first horse and rider to make it ashore and tells him where Captain Dirleton and the leading party have gone. There is no sign of the artillery. He grasps his sword and trots back. He can feel the sand grinding blisters inside his boots and hopes the party will give him time to clean himself up. He reports to the captain who nods.

"Right, we'll give it another thirty minutes before moving off. Sergeant Matthews – set sentries please!" Lauchlin sees the man named is the *Loyal American* who correctly steered him off the beach.

They can be heard well before they appear; rearing horses with foam dripping from their mouths making a somewhat unmilitary sight as a collection of about twelve of the Dragoons arrives. As they dismount they use rough cloths to rub their mounts down and this helps calm them.

At Saldanha Bay, the situation for Beresford is not as straight-forward. Under a fierce gale blowing from the West the surf rises and falls by some four metres tossing boats up before crashing them down with splintering force. Men try to leap ashore but are violently thrown about. One of the ship's boats loaded with twenty-five of the Royal Scots is swamped whilst still some distance offshore; the men, including an officer, are thrown into the sea to be dashed away.

In desperation, Beresford calls for one of the transports to use its protective bulk to shield them from the westerly gale. The ship is deliberately sailed inshore rising and falling with the power of the waves until finally settling in the shallows to provide a breakwater. In the lee of this shelter, boats can eventually be landed where they immediately come under fire from members of the local militia. These are mainly *Boer* civilians, shop-keepers and local families, who have been called forward at the first sighting of the convoy. But their aim is poor and although some casualties occur, as the landings continue they are forced to withdraw.

The principal centre of the colony is Capetown which is defended by a motley group: The Governor, General Janssens, has little experience of warfare and his attempts to develop the skills of the local farmers and *Burghers* have met with only limited success. Ever since his appointment, he has tried to cope with the several warring factions in the colony They have no more love for their French masters than for any other power trying to interfere with their way of life. Exactly as the British had planned, it is time to harvest the grapes and thresh the wheat.

The Governor had been expecting an invasion and during the first rumours of an imminent attack, had circulated plans showing how his troops were to be summoned and assembled. At the first sighting of the ships he had signal guns fired in an agreed pattern. But rumbling thunder and the force of the wind distorted the sound giving his troops an excuse to ignore the calls.

Janssens' main, trained body, is a battalion of *Waldeck* mercenaries about four hundred strong. He also has around two hundred French infantry, largely elderly and seeking retirement; nevertheless, they are professional soldiers. Around one hundred and fifty mercenaries captured in various skirmishes almost complete the defensive wall put up to resist Beresford's landing. Few are committed to the Batavian cause and have been generally enjoying a pleasant and undemanding interlude. In addition, the new year, 1806, has just been celebrated and many are sleeping off the effects.

Only Janssens's artillery can be identified as having any real loyalty to the Governor. It is composed of light howitzers which, although commanded by mercenary officers, are in the care of locally trained Hottentots. Most of these speak the *Nama* language which is almost unintelligible to their officers.

The Summer heat is at its height and most recent training has been done during the cool of the evening. Most of his force are unwilling to risk their lives in such conditions.

After forty-eight hours of somewhat haphazard re-arranging, this small force sets out from Capetown early in the morning hoping to meet the advancing British troops before they can be properly consolidated. However, the detachment under Captain Dirleton has been so much more fortunate in its landing that they are encamped on the very route chosen by Janssens. His scouts bring him reports that the number against them is not large; he assumes this is the main British force and plans an immediate attack before the heat of the day hits them.

Sergeant Franklin Matthews of the *Loyal Americans* has been charged with the responsibility of posting appropriate sentries. His briefing has included the information that the main threat will be from the fort at Capetown. He is provided with a sketch map which indicates its location and he knows that the direction of the advance will lead to its Western corner. He places three of his 'chosen' men two hundred yards apart watching the northern approach, with himself at the centre. They are about half a mile ahead of the rest of Dirleton's detachment and settle themselves out of sight and camouflaged as best they can.

Although physically exhausted, Lauchlin had felt too excited to sleep. In spite of his thoughts, eventually he falls asleep under his greatcoat with his head resting on his small pack. His neck stock is removed as are the white leather cross straps; his trews are loosened. Everyone carries supplies for three days on the assumption that they will be able to sustain themselves either from the land as they advance or from stores on board the ships. He dreams he is still on board and feels the gentle rocking of the waves.

After a full moon, the sun rises brightly from behind the British camp. Sergeant Matthews is making his rounds when one of the sentries whispers to him. "I think I can hear our lads coming Sarge, but it's queer – they're in front, and coming back towards us!"

Matthews joins him in creeping forward. They are adjacent to a sandy road which is little more than a track, some thirty feet wide with bushes either side merging into pine trees planted years ago to reduce erosion. Progress along such a surface is easy and fairly silent which is one reason for Captain Dirleton's decision to use it.

The Hollanders' three light howitzers being towed by six horses make most of the noise. The jingle of bridles and reins together with the deep beat of twenty-four hooves is what first drew the attention of the British watchers. Additionally, the men advancing are not keeping silent but talking animatedly among themselves as though on a peaceful ramble. Sergeant Matthews has the experience to recognize their mixed Afrikaans speech as alien and not part of their own force. He orders the sentry to run back immediately and warn the Captain. Then he takes the other two men and places them in a commanding position round a bend on either side of the track, ensuring that the sun is directly behind them. Calmly he supervises the loading of their muskets. As the first of the lines of men come into view they are well within range some thirty yards ahead. Matthews fires first, being closely followed by the others.

The effect is immediate. One of the *Waldeckers* goes down, the remainder dive into the bushes either side calling to each other as they try to load their weapons. With the sun in their eyes they fail to see the small ambush disperse and scurry back to the main force.

Captain Dirleton makes a mental note to recommend the Sergeant for a decoration and congratulates him for giving them the time to form up. He orders the dragoons to walk their mounts quietly through the trees towards the North-east so that they will be able to attack the Dutchmen from the rear. Then he forms his men up in three lines, ensuring that the edges into the scrub on either side cover a sniper's advance. Dirleton positions himself centrally at the front and Lauchlin, with sword drawn, stands closely behind him.

The Dutch are not lacking in courage. After staying down for five minutes their leader realizes that only two or three men were holding them up. They form up again on the track but he sends an advance group of fifteen to scout ahead. When this detachment comes into sight of the lined up British troops they are almost annihilated by a single fusillade from kneeling and standing lines. The front line then moves to the rear to re-load. The next line are kneeling and ready to fire in an operation they have carried out a hundred times on the parade ground. Those Dutch who are able turn to run back to their main force. In a continuation of the drill, the British form a line abreast and, with muskets re-loaded, advance at walking pace to meet the enemy's main body.

The Dutch force awaits them, in position on the track, hidden in the scrub at the side and concealed among the trees. They fire as the Redcoats come into view but, fortunately, the range is too long, they are poorly trained and few of the shots find a mark. But one or two do go down in the front rank. Holding his place at the front, Lauchlin has raised and lowered his sword in time with each command to fire. He feels it is pointless but it is the correct drill for a supernumerary officer who has to hold the front as lines change. Re-loading is a slow and cumbersome process. The British have practised it so that it is second nature. And, relatively, they are fast. The fastest in Europe. When Captain Dirleton orders the cease fire as the Dragoons come up from the Dutch rear, the battle is over.

It is just in time forLauchlin. He feels sick with reaction. His head is ringing through the incredible noise of the muskets behind him. He replaces his sword in the scabbard and turns to see the full horror behind. One of the men he knew, Grahame was it? Is lying holding his stomach while his insides run out through his fingers. Other wounded are stretched out crying with pain. As the lines break up he sees only dirty uniforms. No proud band plays its way through this awful scene.

At the same time he feels some elation at having come through his first engagement under enemy fire. Although conscious of not having done anything useful, he is pleased that he has been able to behave properly and not disgraced himself. He stayed in front just behind Captain Dirleton and tells himself that had Dirleton fallen he would have needed to step up himself. It is a sobering thought as he finds his sore arm has re-opened. There seems to be a wetness and the arm is steadily dripping.

One of the Highland Fusiliers looks at him. "Good God, Sir, you've been hit!" Lauchlin sees his lips move but can understand little of what is said. He tries to speak himself and realizes that he has partly lost his hearing from the noise of the firing. As he watches he sees a fusilier take something out of each ear. It proves to be a lead shot wrapped in a piece of soft leather.

"Always use this, sir, stops you going deaf. But you've been hit in the arm!"

He is about to deny the fact when he sees his sleeve is soaked with blood. "Here sir, let's have a look. Sit ye doon!" He does as directed and the man eases off his coat. The arm is aching and stinging. "You were lucky, sir, and no mistake!" Along the side of his original wound when leaving the ship, there is a perceptible line of burnt flesh marking the route of a ball. Several of the Highlanders are impressed. "You're a lucky one sir. I'd like to stand by you in the line!" It is a superstition he has heard others speak about – some are born lucky and there is competition to be close to them in the line of fire. His arm is beginning to burn but the wound seems to have self-cauterized.

As the ringing in his head begins to subside, he asks how they can hear their commands when they have plugged their ears.

Some look shame-facedly at each other. One, bolder than the rest speaks up.

"Well, you see sir, that's why you're there – waving your sword about – when you bring it down we fire!"

Two days later with further cavalry landed at a spot between Robben Island and the Blueberg, Beresford takes the bulk of the mounted men to besiege Capetown itself. The plan was to reach the Capital before the bulk of Janssens' force is able to return.

The defence left inside the fort is seriously depleted and soon surrenders. In the hope of an early end to the campaign, Beresford sends a courteous letter to the Governor, General Janssens. It compliments him on the quality of the defence but points out the uselessness of further resistance. It ends by offering honourable terms of surrender.

Commodore Home Popham and Colonel Beresford duly receive the surrender documents. After some days, Janssens and several of his officials, together with their families and staff are escorted to one of the British frigates which will carry them to a neutral port on the West coast of Africa.

Many of the French Infantry and most of the mercenary sharp-shooters elect to serve the British Flag under the same terms as before. Their daily pay is thus somewhat higher than that of the rank and file British soldiers but the adjustments for food and housing allowances quickly keep them in line.

Four days later in clean uniforms and polished boots much of the army parades in Capetown to march through the centre of the town with colours flying. The bands play and make a brave sight including three pipers and the drums of the Highland Regiments.

Beresford despatches two battalions of the infantry and the Light Brigade up country to secure the province as far as Glassings. Much of the land is almost desert there and the heat of the long Summer has dried the rivers into trickles. The Eastern side of the colony is subject to attacks from several tribes, especially the ferocious Xosas, and the troops have orders to push them back. The burghers and farmers resent the stealing of their cattle by the *Bushmen* but seem content to transfer their loyalties to the British Crown. Orders are issued that until a British Governor is appointed, the country will be placed under a system of Martial Law but this fully respects their established Roman-Dutch laws which continue to be administered by Afrikaner *landdrosten.*

Beresford's despatches to London report the successful completion of the task. He is cautious about aspects of the Afrikaners who seem quite amenable to his instructions which are mainly guided by the need to hold the Cape against any French or Batavian attempt to recover the territory. Defences are improved and the old wood and earth fort in Capetown is strengthened with stone slabs brought down from Beldorf. Troops are placed to cover strategic points. The principal bone of contention concerns the Afrikaners' treatment of the Hottentots which Beresford compares to the slavery issues currently being debated in London. But he decides to leave that problem for another day.

Chapter 11

Commodore Home Popham surreptitiously begins his search for personal prize money. He remains convinced that true financial benefit has been denied him throughout his naval career and he is determined to correct this.

For ten days Lauchlin is ashore with Beresford. There are many despatches to write and copy. He finds writing with his injured arm is not a problem and when they inform him that he will carry the scars to the grave he is quietly pleased at the prospect of showing his injuries to his family.

Then shall he show forth his arm and say, these wounds I gained on Crispin's Day.

The despatches to London take three months even on a fast Monitor, and probably four months for the replies which are eagerly awaited since they will surely include the appointment of the new Governor. Home Popham wonders if he will be in the running and considers the actions he would take if it were so.

Many of the sultry Summer evenings are spent enjoying a game of whist in the newly prepared Officers' Mess and, in spite of his low rank, Lauchlin becomes quite widely known as a serious player. The hospitality of many of the officers leads him to learn caution in his consumption of strong drink.

Early in the occupation, the Commodore invites a number of the senior officers to a lunch party on board the flagship. Sir David Baird has taken a detachment to the East coast to investigate Durban as a major refuge for shipping. In the Supreme Commander's absence, Home Popham feels quietly self-satisfied. The conquest has been achieved at a much lower cost and at greater speed than had been expected.

He sits back and surveys the group. "Well, Gentlemen. We have now some four thousand men more than we need for controlling the Colony. We await despatches as to how they are to be disposed – sent to India? Back to England? Or perhaps dispersed around Europe in the war against the Corsican. Until we are told where they are to go, we have the problem that they are eating their heads off at the Crown's expense and beginning to get into trouble in the inns and *bordellos* of Capetown!" He pauses to sip his wine.

"Pass the Port round, gentlemen!" He is coming to the tricky part. "I have been reminded of the reports prepared by General Miranda for Mr. Pitt some time ago. He convinced Mr. Pitt that a landing by a force as small as two thousand in the area of the River Plate would be welcomed by the inhabitants who have been trying for twenty years to throw off the yoke of their Spanish oppressors!"

He reminds them all that his orders now require a careful coverage of the Atlantic Ocean to ensure that no counter attack can be mounted by sea. "I have heard…." He gives a slight but, somehow self-important, cough, "that the French fleet has suffered a severe defeat off the coast of Spain…we could, of course, merely comply with our orders and set off on patrol, but…" he pauses.

A naval officer down the table looks up. "But are the Spanish not our allies now, Commodore?"

Home Popham plays with the stem of his glass. He had been expecting this question. "Well, we're not absolutely sure of this, are we? The situation in the Iberian Peninsula is fluid, to say the least."

Someone else pipes up. "The wealth pouring into Spain from the River Plate is immense. Gold and silver from lands to the North-west are sent down the big rivers to where they can be loaded and shipped straight over the Atlantic into ports like Palos and Corunna."

Home Popham frowns at him. The truth is that this closely follows his own line of thinking since it is that wealth from the mines of Potosi that he would like to get his hands on. But that is not an ambition that would be acceptable to London. He must avoid any suggestion of self-interest in this expedition.

"Yes, yes we know that but this is not a matter of mere piracy. I am speaking about an expansion of His Majesty's interests. The American

Colonists dealt us all a severe blow…" he pauses to allow another comment from the table.

"What resources could Spain bring against us if we did take over the River Plate area? The odd Treasure ship, perhaps." The room gently laughs at his humour. "Possession is nine points of the law, after all."

Home Popham frowns again. "I am speaking of assisting this area to independent nationhood, gentlemen. We are not Sir Francis Drake singeing the king of Spain's beard!" He chuckles in the hope that he has convinced them that his own aims are altruistic.

"I understand that the town of Montevideo has a fort that is effectively a ruin. I believe we should land there, re-build the fort and begin to expand our forays from there, where we would be well able to obtain supplies by sea and, indeed, from inland." He looks down at the table as if thinking aloud, "after a successful landing, a proportion of our ships will be able to continue patrolling the ocean."

Another voice chips in: "We could possibly be back in Capetown after completing this mission before despatches arrive from London."

It is agreed that the Staff should prepare preliminary plans.

In mid-March, before the Autumn rains have properly broken, the fleet puts to sea. Some three thousand men and five ships are left to police the Cape. The fleet's supplies have been greatly enhanced – more fresh meat, salt cod, butter, cheese, some grapes, raisins, potatoes, carrots and many butts of fresh water. But the colony has a shortage of corn and wheat. The weather has been disappointing and there was little rain when it was needed. The supply officers bemoan the lack of flour; fresh biscuit is a staple of a long voyage.

Lauchlin joins some four hundred and fifty of the 75th Royal Highlanders under Colonel Beresford together with some light artillery and cavalry in what he only gradually learns is a speculative crossing of the Southern Atlantic. He has, at last, won a break from his duties as Colonel Beresford's Secretary. A volunteer from the new Capetown Naval office has been recruited. Lauchlin has gained a place with a platoon of his 75th Regiment and sleeps in a hammock among them. News of his new accommodation is accompanied by secret ribaldry among the troops.

"You'll have to behave now Nancy, you and Franny must stop your little games!" Whatever Lauchlin hears is not understood and goes over his head. Increasingly he is being torn in half by those sentiments that want to be an officer and the elements within him that would prefer to join in and simply be a member of the group whose company he is beginning to enjoy.

Two days after leaving Capetown the weather changes alarmingly. The wind strengthens to constant gale force head winds. All ships are forced to shorten sail and to change direction. The adverse weather continues for forty-eight hours and when the storms have finally blown themselves out many of the ships are dispersed. One of the big transports is thought to have gone down with the loss of a full crew and over two hundred fusiliers. Other ships have suffered damage and the Commodore orders all ships within sight to put in at St.Helena for repairs.

They arrive on the twenty-fifth of April and Home Popham knows he should no longer delay sending despatches to London advising of his actions and intentions. He stresses the need to occupy the number of men under his command and that only a moderate cost will probably be expended, which will likely result in a massive advantage to the Crown.

Colonel Beresford writes to the War Office principally seeking advice on how he should treat the civilian authorities in the River Plate area.

After waiting in vain for the lost transport, Home Popham appeals to the Governor of St.Helena for help with building up the strength of his force. After promising that he will pass a most favourable report when he is next in London, the Commodore persuades the Governor to allow him to take some two hundred men from his garrison to replace those lost at sea. The repairs take longer than expected and the fleet cannot put to sea again until the twenty-first of May. A monitor ship with news, mail and despatches arrives at St.Helena at the end of their stay. It advises of the victory at Cape Trafalgar and, of greater personal interest, informs that Commodore Home Riggs Popham is promoted Vice Admiral of the Blue – a dramatic improvement since the logical step up would normally be Rear Admiral.

The reason for his new rank becomes more apparent when at the same time, Colonel Beresford is promoted Brigadier-General with a separate note from Sir David Baird informing him of the War Office's approval of his actions.

Lauchlin finds himself sleeping as well as at any time in his life. Apart from being battened down during the storms, he is able to take his men up for air and exercise several times a day when some demonstrate their skill at Highland dancing. They sleep in tiers of hammocks in a deck height of four and a half feet, but there is a comradeship which he finds most agreeable. A proportion of the men are Lowlanders of the Royal Scots whose speech is so different from his own. There is only limited light down below from two oil lamps so that "non-exercise" time is spent in the hammocks. In the cramped conditions, access to a "head" is difficult and restricted to what is little more than a hole down the side of the ship. The racks of muskets are at the end of the deck secured by a chain through the trigger-guards and he has made himself more familiar with the cleaning, caring and loading of the firearm.

In fact, he has become something of a mascot with the older and more experienced Highlanders. The near-miss of the musket ball has led to him being called "Lucky Lochy" and there is a genuine competitiveness to stand behind him in a fight. The attitude of Scottish soldiers to their officers has always been more relaxed than that south of the border. Lauchlin is not yet even a subaltern, his rank still being little more than a cadet.

He is also intrigued by the stories of two of the Loyal Americans. Sergeant Franklin Matthews whom he first encountered in the landing at Bredasdorp and his confederate 'Chip' Parker.

"We prefer to call ourselves Virginians," he opens, "My pa was a small farmer near a little town called Whaddon, just outside Norfolk. I had two brothers older than me so I knew I had to find myself some kind of work." He stops as if thinking back is painful. "I joined the army – obviously the only army there was then – the King's army. This was twenty-five years ago and although there had been that so-called declaration of independence, a lot of us in the South didn't go along with it. You might remember that Virginia and other Southern states chose to follow the advice of Benjamin Franklin and stay loyal to the Crown. He's some kind of distant relative and I was named after him." The sound of the Bosun's whistle announces that they are to go up for exercise and there is a rush for the narrow steps.

He sees another platoon on the other side of the deck. They are in lines and doing physical exercises which take up most of the available space. Lauchlin tries to get his men doing jerks and jogging. Franklin Matthews joins in with some enthusiasm: "Come on, look lively lads. You'll never stand up to the march unless you stretch those muscles!"

Later, when they are back below decks, Lauchlin seeks him out to thank him for his help. He is curious as to how a colonist whom he thought would have been against the British should choose to be a soldier of the King's.

"Well, it's not a pretty story and certainly doesn't reflect well on anybody." He shakes his head slowly. The recollection is clearly painful and Lauchlin wonders what is coming next.

"We were down in the Floridas fighting the Spanish. The Bastards had come across from Havana… I hate the Floridas – bogs and crawling with snakes and crocs. Anyhow, we beat them Spanish back into their boats and then we were sent North to Virginia where there was real fighting going on…while we had been busy keeping out them Spaniards, a detachment of the Colonist army had come down and laid about…made an end of Whaddon and Norfolk. Their artillery destroyed any buildings they could find. They weren't Colonists – they were God-damned revolutionaries on the French model! You think the Duke of Cumberland was hard on your family? Nothing to what those mad dogs did to us!"

In a slight pause Lauchlin asks him about his family. Matthews stops and his face screws up.

"They blew up our home and killed my whole family. I made it back just in time to see my mother as she died…It's no wonder I stayed supporting the Brits…we were sent up to Canada and then…" He gestures, clearly making an end to his recollections, – "we were promised reparation for our lost property but we never got it. Some of my cousins followed the army to Canada – settled in good farming country near Niagara." There is silence for some moments. "Ah well, here we are now!"

After two weeks, the voyage from St.Helena is becoming tedious. Their supplies of flour are exhausted and the biscuit which is now being issued is stale and over-run with weevils. Some mutterings take place below decks. The Admiral and Beresford are aware of the dis-satisfaction but there is little they can do.

Lauchlin's sources of information are greatly reduced since he is no longer in a position to read and write the despatches. Around the fourteenth of June they come up to a frigate whose foremast is bursting with signals. Gradually the news seeps down but it is simply a repetition of that received at St.Helena. Lying in his hammock Lauchlin often finds himself wishing for an invitation to join a whist four in Brigadier Beresford's cabin.

At last they arrive at what Home Popham refers to as the target area. He has temporarily transferred his flag to one of the smaller frigates and now uses his experience of charting and surveying to go forward and investigate the state of the river and ascertain the most appropriate course through the shoals and mud flats of the shallow River Plate.

At *Cabo Santa Maria,* on the northern side of the broad estuary, there is shelter and the Admiral, who has gone back to his previous flagship, summons some of the senior captains to a conference. Beresford sits in on it. While Montevideo is the nearest large town, and was his original objective, his observation now tells him that its defences are in better condition than his original information had suggested. He is also informed that the cereal crop has been greatly reduced through a fungal attack. This means that the flour needed throughout the fleet is not available. Additionally, his surveyors support his opinion that the approaches would be difficult for many of the larger ships. Home Popham's reputation as an experienced surveyor is well founded. While advancing further up- river is probably just as difficult for larger ships without charts, the possibility of getting the supplies they need incline him to changing the objective.

Beresford is perturbed by the alteration of plan but mainly because of the reason being given. "How reliable is this news of the cereal crop being decimated?"

Commander Alderton, the Admiral's Chief Staff Officer looks down at reports in his hand. "They say it's been destroyed by a pest called *Hessian Fly,* sir. They say it comes from Prussia and, I suppose, Hesse. It's a fly that lays eggs which hatch and destroy the crop. The news suggests a better crop further up-country." General Beresford sniffs at the statement.

"You sound more like a farmer than a senior naval officer!" He picks up the map lying on his table.

"Yes, I'm sorry General. I was giving you the fullest information as stated on the despatch sent by one of our Intelligence people landed some days ago."

After detailed discussions with Beresford, Home Popham decides to take the fleet up river and make a landing nearer Buenos Aires. He drums his fingers on the table.

"The weather can be gusty and when the winds ease, it often gets foggy. We should have arrived earlier and not at the end of Autumn!" He turns to scowl at the window. "It makes traversing this river even more difficult!"

He decides to move his flag back to the frigate and, with the most skilled of the lead swingers constantly checking the depth, personally leads the fleet in line astern.

"A damnable shame!" He mutters to Commander Alderton, "this will warn the Spanish of the size of the invasion force but the conditions make any hopes of a covert arrival impossible!"

The sighting of the fleet advancing towards them comes during a difficult week for the Viceroy, Juan de Alzada. He has been the subject of unpleasant cartoons in the local journal, mocking his habit of keeping his nose in the air as if the people around him carried a noxious odour. The truth is that a condition in his eyes makes vision from the top half of the pupils more difficult. His corrective lenses are little help but certainly make the cartoonist's work easier.

He has also been receiving unhelpful and what he considers exceptional demands from the local Council. They are increasingly seeking rights of self-determination and lower taxation just as Madrid is demanding an increase to cover the costs of maintaining troops in the Plate area. In fact, as he has delicately tried to point out to them, there are now few Spanish soldiers to be seen as they have increasingly been sent up to Callao to guard against the possibility of invasion from the Pacific Ocean.

Madrid's response is to send a consignment of muskets and supporting materiel with the suggestion that he train a local militia but this is alien to his manner of government. An armed militia could easily mount a revolution against Spanish rule.

His first notification of a foreign invasion comes in an urgent message from Captain Martin de Liniers, the local naval commander based at Montevideo, that a force of what seems to be a hundred ships, is advancing up the river. Liniers is attempting to follow their progress with those armed men he can immediately call upon. He states that he will attack any landing but needs all the resources which can be raised.

In some strange way, the news is not unwelcome to the Viceroy as it justifies the warnings he has been sending for some four years. Liniers is the senior commander; he must make the best of those resources at his disposal. The Viceroy quickly collects his family around him, packs up such wealth and treasure as he can lay hands on and departs the area in four carriages. They travel for three days until they reach the city of Santa Fe. They camp overnight in large, military tents with all the men positioned outside acting as sentinels in case of Indian attack. The children think it is exciting and greatly preferable to life in the dull city. The Viceroy's intention is to make for those North-western parts of the empire which are better guarded by the mother country. Access to Spain from the Pacific is clearly more difficult but the intensely Hispanic lands up that coast as far as the Canadian border are deemed by His Excellency to be much safer. He plans to stay in Santa Fe until the situation becomes clearer. They will then either return to Buenos Aires or continue to Callao. He left his intentions clear with his junior office staff. He would come to regret this when a British patrol was sent up to bring him back.

Chapter 12

The nationality of the invaders is not immediately apparent to the citizens of Buenos Aires. Many of them are dismayed at first in the belief that it is a French fleet. As time passes and flags begin to be recognized there is a feeling of relief. Many of the colonists have a sense of deliverance. For over three hundred years they have argued with increasing fury for freedom from the constant demands of Madrid. The endless stress on treasure started with the original *Conquistadores.* Spain itself being well endowed with a wealth of farming land and sunshine, rarely sought the import of grain or cattle products from these huge basins of rich soil the size of Western Europe. Much of this is now covered in rigorous grass, feeding the herds of wild cattle and horses descended from escaped or abandoned animals first brought from Europe upwards of two hundred and fifty years before.

The lack of ploughing and soil aeration over millennia, together with long dry seasons, has encouraged the grass roots to descend to depths unknown to European farmers. Consequently, while the soil is undeniably rich, the establishment of more delicate plants takes years of heavy digging to get rid of the hardy grass roots. This demanding work has engendered a hardness in the country settlers and a determination to hold on to what they have earned. The indigenous people being almost entirely mobile farmed very little of the land living off the animals, lightly-rooted vegetables, herbs and the plentiful fish.

The damp and foggy weather makes the fleet's progress difficult, even perilous. As the afternoon advances, Beresford is anxious to effect a landing before the bulk of the Spanish troops can be organized to meet his advance. A small tongue of land at *Punta de Quilmes* offers a sheltered spot for the boats to reach the shore. Beresford's Intelligence has advised that there are some two thousand Spanish infantry trained and ready to engage him. He has been told that they are of poor quality but they are professional troops and armed with some artillery which, as yet, is undefined.

Lauchlin and the twenty or so men that are now his constant associates are on the central well-deck. With Sergeant Matthews he is carefully checking their muskets and equipment when he finds himself facing two highlanders he does not recognize. They are strangely out of place and their hair, though properly tucked under their 'bonnets', is clearly very long. With a shock he realizes these are two women. For a second or two he is paralyzed. He has been told about army "wives" following their husbands but he has never had to face the question of their actual fighting. He swallows and accepts the situation.

Although conscious that his sword must be his principal weapon as it is needed to give his troops the signal to fire, he has also equipped himself with a musket on a sling hanging on his back, together with powder and shot in two pouches on his belt. He plans to stand in front, giving the appropriate signals until the battle is almost over when he can experience the full effects of firing in the line.

He can see activity from the other ships and hears a horse whinny but still they are held Then Brigadier Beresford gives the order to go and they swarm into the boats. Although the water is relatively calm, the boats do rise and fall to an alarming extent. He avoids the rough scraping from his fiirst descent and makes an exemplary plunge into a press of men which forces him to the stern. They are quickly rowed ashore by the seamen. He leaps into a light surf and finds himself on a rough pebble beach which he can clearly feel through the soles of his boots. The surface slopes upwards towards what appears to be an open field on a hillside. They hurry to reach cover. Beyond this, for at least five hundred yards distant, the land continues its upward slope.

Major Dirleton is standing on a small rock and sees Lauchlin as he comes towards him.

"Well done lads! We have a report from scouting parties that there are signs of Spanish cavalry arriving and taking up position on the top of the hill. Keep your wits about you!"

Lauchlin and his men continue up the slope. The climb is harder than it had appeared and he appreciates that their exercising has not been sufficiently demanding. Forced to stop and catch their breath he looks around studying the ground. The climb seems to end in about a quarter of a mile and, hopefully, their progress will be easier on the level. There is no sign of Spanish cavalry but he sends two men ahead to act as scouts. The darkness falls quickly and orders are received to bivouac for the night.

A light mist starts to fall. Through it Lauchlin can see that General Beresford has placed light cannons on the flanks in case the cavalry decide on a last minute charge. A young trooper hurries up to him: "Despatch from Major Dirleton, sir, please take four men and post sentries up the hill, covering on the northern side – three hours on, he will see they're relieved!"

Lauchlin looks around slightly helpless. *Four men? Which four men? Oh God!* He can see no sign of the two women.

Sergeant Matthews is nearby. He has removed his cap and for the first time Lauchlin sees his hair is already grey. Probably in his forties. He is tall, something not apparent in the cramped conditions aboard ship, over six foot and fairly broad in the shoulder. He calls out for the sergeant to join him in setting four sentries. "I'm with you, sir..." he murmurs, "Fredericks, McCorquran, Woodburn! With me, three hours - on watch!"

With a grateful Lauchlin in attendance, they quickly move towards the top of the hill. The men are positioned some three hundred yards ahead of the main force and placed where they can observe without being seen. Sergeant Matthews takes Lauchlin some fifty yards back and eases off his pack. "This is a good spot for us to keep an eye on them, sir, and still be in touch with the C.O!" Looking back, Lauchlin can see the camp beginning to close down for the night. He does not feel that he has covered himself with glory. He attempts to correct this impression with humour. "Nearly the end of June, Franklin and it's cold, misty and wet!"

"Ah well, heck! In these heathen parts the seasons are stood on their haids. Come January I 'xpect it'll be hot as Hades." Lauchlin is about to mention the problem of the two women but thinks better of it.

Like everyone else he only has a light cape in his shoulder pack. The grass is so wet that he tries to wrap himself up in it but it fails to protect him fully. Beresford sends round orders forbidding the lighting of fires. Their supplies consist of some pieces of cold meat which are difficult to identify. Sergeant Matthews, at Lauchlin's elbow, mentions the men's concerns about the lack of biscuit.

"You can't eat this muck withat some bread to take it down!"

It is a cold and hungry force that is roused before first light to continue the advance. Lauchlin's small team of observers had been relieved half-way through the night and they had made their way back to the main group. Matthews now shakes him awake.

"They're all rising, Young sir. There ain't any breakfast but we must load up". Lauchlin feels exhausted. He is both mentally tired and feeling as if he has not slept for a week. The plaid cape has moved off him during the night so that he is now cold and wet. He murmurs his thanks and tries to look active as the advance begins. It is a damp, misty morning with a light rain making the ground difficult. Near the summit of the hill the land develops a fold and becomes boggy. To avoid the swamp means a slow, scratchy move through thick gorse and bramble which cuts uniforms. It is the heavy mud that protected them in the night since the small force of Spanish cavalry could not cope with it at speed. But it now has the effect of preventing Beresford from progressing his artillery.

Lauchlin feels wretched. His boots sink in the mud trying to suck them off his feet and he is becoming fearful of the battle which he knows must lie ahead. His first experience, at the Cape, was of only short duration but it had left him feeling sick with reaction. Now he knows what is to come. He sees himself standing in front of the line with his sword raised. Surely they will not miss him this time. 'Lucky Lauchy'! He acknowledges to himself that he is frightened. What would a ball fired deep into his stomach feel like?

The main force of fusiliers proceeds to pick its way through the swamp but the horses pulling the guns are forced to take a circuitous route lower down the hill which puts them out of touch with the General. Eventually the infantry reach a small stream which gurgles its way down-hill in a vain attempt to drain the bog into the larger river, the *Chuelo,* some forty yards across their path. Enemy troops can be seen massing on the single bridge but the light is still poor making it difficult for either side to fire with any accuracy. The British artillery has not yet made its lengthy way around the hill. Whilst grape shot from the cannons might clear the enemy off the crossing, it could also destroy the bridge which Beresford studying it through his telescope sees is constructed entirely from wood which looks well rotted.

Meanwhile, as the light strengthens, the Spanish howitzers open fire on the British infantry which is advancing towards them through the gorse and rough bushes which have taken over to provide the only cover. The sun rising over the hill behind them makes range finding difficult for the Spanish guns and their shooting is poor, indicative of a lack of practice. As the Scots continue their descent towards the river, the surface of the ground improves allowing better progress. Beresford orders the muskets to be loaded and primed. He forms his men into line abreast and their pace quickens. Lauchlin again takes up his position in the front of his platoon. He fights to control his apprehension and there is some comfort in the warmth of the sun drying the clothes on his back. When only fifty yards separate them, Beresford gives the order to halt and open fire. The front line kneels. The first two salvoes are only partly successful as many of the weapons have been affected by their watery progress.

Lauchlin strongly dislikes his position and would prefer to be one of a line. His duties require him to restrict his activity to empty sword thrusts at each order to fire. He cannot protect his ears knowing that he must listen for these commands. Turning his head he sees that Beresford and Dirleton have had their horses brought up. Once again the order to fire is given. Lauchlin is surrounded in acrid smoke which causes him to cough. He hears Dirleton ordering them to re-load but await the order to fire. Lauchlin stands with his sword raised. Why is there an interval? Let's get it over and done with! He is central to his men and the delay lasts forever. The order comes within perhaps thirty seconds. The noise continues to be deafening as salvo follows salvo.

The British muskets are now warm and dry. By around the seventh detonation the Spanish have retreated, abandoning two artillery pieces but taking their mules with them. Beresford orders a *hold fire!* And trots back up the hill on his grey. The greater height enables him to search the ground with his telescope. He concentrates on the left seeking his artillery. An outrider returns with the news that he is less than ten miles from the centre of the city. He is reluctant to cross the river without his guns. He gives orders for the bridge to be secured. As the troops move forward, flames can be seen licking up the sides. The Spanish have withdrawn to take up positions in the reeds and bushes on the other side of the river but Beresford's men are too late to save the only crossing for miles. Another messenger rides up to the general, informing him that his guns are some two miles distant on his left and are also seeking a crossing as they work towards him. As the General orders the firing to be resumed, the Infantry lines form again to fire on the Spanish across the river. They are met by strong musket fire which causes several casualties.

Lauchlin sees a wounded man being tended by a comrade. There is a gap in the line. His musket lies nearby and Lauchlin takes it up hoping to stand in line with his men. Following orders from a lieutenant he fires across the river in tune with his fellows. He believes his prowess with the musket is improving but as individual targeting is not possible he simply joins in the batteries of salvoes. The Spanish defence continues for another forty-five minutes but seemingly half-hearted is securing hits. At last Beresford's artillery arrives having given up the attempts to cross the river to the West. In less than fifteen minutes the howitzers have begun a steady and accurate rate of fire. As musket shot and grape start clearing the area, the Spanish complete their withdrawal.

Lauchlin is dismayed to see how his own lines have been diminished. Going round with Sergeant Matthews he finds several of his soldiers nursing injuries. Some are seriously hurt. Matthews's face is set in a grim frown and he feels himself totally overcome by the sight of so many wounded. His ears begin to clear and the sounds of screaming from the other side of the river show that much of their own shooting has been effective. From the corner of one eye he sees a soldier lying spread-eagled in the grass. Looking closer he is horrified to see that it is one of his own men who has been nearly cut in half by musket shots. His muddied tartan trews are casually crossed suggesting someone sleeping. The upper half is ugly: mouth open and eyes staring. A strange lack of blood. Lauchlin cannot prevent vomiting. But the injured need help and he calls others to assist in trying to make them more comfortable. One of the women "soldiers" has strips of bandage in a leather satchel and she moves around the casualties doing what she can. Lauchlin is trembling with reaction but knows he must help. *Is this what real soldiering is about? What is he doing here?* From somewhere deep within he hears his mother's voice declaiming lines from her favourite Psalm:

He maketh me to lie down in still waters – He restoreth my soul

As he tries to help the injured he learns to restrain his shaking and to get himself under control. He is supposed to be *an officer for God's sake!* Gradually the shock begins to ease.

Crossing the river is a slow business. A small dinghy with a broken bottom is found which is roughly repaired and they produce a number of rafts on which some are able to cross. The horses swim over but they require guiding and those pulling the guns need to be released from their burdens. There is a delay of some four hours before boats arrive from the fleet enabling the crossing to be completed. Beresford orders the boats to carry the British wounded out to the ships and for everything possible to be done for the injured Spanish.

The fortifications at Buenos Aires have not been needed for a long time. Principally facing the river, a defensive wall, largely of stone with sections of timber, mainly provided by wrecked ships, was erected in the seventeenth Century against attacking tribesmen, Portuguese seamen or marauding Nordic whalers. Areas of it are seen to be rotting away. The few indigenous people now are generally peace-loving and spend their lives hunting for meat and hides which they exchange with the European settlers, principally to the latter's benefit. These include herbs such as *mate,* which regrettably is sometimes traded for liquor.

Beresford personally takes his troops into the centre of the city where considerable fighting continues, especially in the main square, *La Plaza Mayor**, around the Cathedral and the ancient building known as *El Cabildo.* This fort is the seat of local government and Lauchlin sees men up on the roof firing down at them. One of his men, Hargreaves, goes down with a scream of pain. Lauchlin's anger replaces his sense of fear. He is so enfuriated at the injury that he calls his platoon to follow him and break down the old wooden doors. Inside he finds stone steps leading up and a man in Spanish uniform standing at the top with a musket trained on them. He is only about three metres away when he fires. Lauchlin cannot see where the shot goes but the Spaniard is cut down by three of his men firing almost simultaneously. Brandishing his sword, Lauchlin takes the steps three at a time.

There are only seven men with muskets on the roof. They drop their weapons at once and Lauchlin screams at his men not to fire. Only as his

* Subsequent to the Declaration of Independence on 25th May 1810 this was renamed Plaza de Mayo.

personal control returns does he see that they are not in uniform. One looks about twelve years old.

Beresford forms his forces into three lines as they advance but it is soon apparent that they are being fired upon from a number of rooftops around the square. The attackers take cover behind walls and corners but it is only when the 72nd Regiment consolidates its position in a side street that they are able to break down the doors and enter the houses. The defenders are few in number and the Highlanders find several families huddling together in kitchens and bedrooms.

A number of white flags are waved from around the square. Beresford strides through the main doors of the fort and congratulates Lauchlin and his men. The terms of the surrender are agreed with the Council within three hours. Beresford explains that the aims of his expedition were to remove the Spanish from its wealth-producing colony. He believes that the British Government will not wish to occupy the area permanently but to encourage good relations with an independent state. The Council explains that the military commander, Captain Liniers, is "unavoidably" absent. Some of the Council mutter among themselves that Liniers has deserted and left them to their own devices. The total number of professional Spanish soldiers is fewer than Beresford's Intelligence had warned and he soon learns that Liniers has taken the bulk of his forces to Montevideo, no doubt to try to mount a counter-attack.

Beresford takes over the Viceroy's large and sumptuous office in the fort and his secretary is comfortable in an adjoining chamber.

The first despatch is written to the Vice Admiral on the flagship, informing him of the city's capture, that the populace is generally friendly but warning of the dangers still mounting in Montevideo. With accompanying covering letter the Despatch is soon on its way to London and to General Baird at the Cape. Beresford explains that he needs to cover the dangers from Montevideo and will send detachments up country for perhaps seventy-five miles or so to guard against any other attacks from the Spanish. He also seeks advice on how he should treat the locals.

He then informs his troops that their capture of the city is a small element of the war against Napoleon and the Spanish. There is no long-term plan for occupation and they must remain vigilant against an attack expected from the other side of the river or from inland. In the meantime property will be respected, good relations should be observed and no bad behaviour will be tolerated.

For two days there is something of a silence. There are delegations from the Spanish and from the colonists themselves. As if by a signal, on the third morning the city sets out to celebrate its independence from Spain. Banners and bunting fly from many houses, including some British flags. There are spontaneous marches in the streets and British soldiers are welcomed with free drinks in some homes and inns.

Full disembarkation of the ships continues and some of the troops are housed in buildings in the area of the river frontage where a small, wooden harbour is being constructed. Some inhabitants protest; these are noted but they are rapidly moved on.

A week later a delegation from the reformed Provincial Council seeks a meeting with General Beresford who is viewed as Supreme Commander. He invites them in for the following day and lays on bottles of Whisky and nine fine glasses that are found in a sideboard.

It is a crisp morning with perhaps the faintest indications of a frost. The sky is clear blue without a cloud to be seen. Beresford and Dirleton chat together reminding themselves that it is virtually mid-Winter. A sentry announces the arrival of the Council.

Ten men enter his office. They are affable and introduce themselves. The leader is Ernesto Puerridon, a man Beresford likes at once. An athletic-looking forty year-old he maintains a scholarly look with a thin face and a dark beard. He is dressed in formal clothes which would be the height of fashion in Europe. Jorge Parranto, is the Clerk. A priest comes with them, introduced as Father Paulo: "I speak the English and will be happy to translate." He bobs up and down a permanent smile in his almost spherical head. Puerridon speaks two sentences or so at a time which the priest translates.

"General Beresford! We are here to thank you and your men for helping us to Independence!" Beresford makes no effort to correct their interpretation of the British presence. He is still uncertain about Home Popham's intentions. Puerridon fumbles with a thin parcel he is carrying. The Clerk helps him by holding the packaging from which Puerridon brings out a small silver tray. It has been polished so that it reflects the low angled winter sunshine coming in at the window. Puerridon bows as he presents the salver and the rest of the party applauds. Beresford sees that it bears an inscription, in English:

Presented to General William Carr Beresford
And the People of Great Britain
By
The Citizens of Buenos Aires with grateful thanks
July,1806

Beresford is quietly delighted with the gift but is nervous of the effect it is likely to have on Home Popham. He invites the Council to be seated while Dirleton tries to organize additional glasses.

After some general and complimentary conversation, Beresford is able to assure them that property will be respected and citizens should proceed on their normal way of life.

"The defence raised against us was a noble fight and we are pleased that many of the soldiers have chosen to join our ranks."

This leads to a rather uncomfortable silence. Puerridon looks around at the other members and coughs while he thinks of a suitable response.

"Err…Captain Liniers is now at Colonia and conferring with the citizens of Montevideo…we cannot be certain that our Agreement extends to him…he is a very warlike officer."

Beresford smiles accommodatingly. "It was a gallant defence against a well-trained and equipped army. My superior in this matter is Admiral Home Popham who, I feel sure, will wish to meet with you shortly. It would be sad to risk the lives of more young men in what can only be a very one-sided conflict. If you can get a message to Captain Liniers please assure him that I will be pleased to discuss the situation with him and can send him a Pass to ensure his safety."

There is some discussion amongst themselves which is not translated. Beresford raises the subject which he knows is uppermost in Home Popham's mind - that of the Treasure ship's sailing to Spain. A satisfactory resolution of this would probably assuage his personal needs and certainly make him lose interest in a solitary silver salver. There is another embarrassed silence until Puerridon coughs again to clear his throat and his thinking.

"That, my General, is something of a fable…yes, I believe in past centuries it was the practice to load up one ship a year and send it to the mother country. But the risks of storms, pirates and…err…even your Francis Draco, were such that the system had to change. Several, smaller consignments took its place…much now leaves from Callao…in the North, you know…the journey by mule from Potosi was always perilous of course."

"Ah yes, I see the logic of that. My Admiral, Home Popham, is most interested to know the situation regarding these sailings. He has… err, expended much of his wealth on this operation and may well view such treasure as a lawful prize of war."

There is more quiet muttering around the room. Father Paulo, looks up.

"But this is now the property of the State, my General. Whether it belongs entirely to the State of the River Plate, or to the areas further to the North-west is…something to be discussed but surely not a prize of war…!"

Beresford stares at him. "My own interest is purely professional, of course, but if you speak of property belonging to an area further north… we have not yet conquered that and it is still subject to Spanish rule – and therefore at war with my country." He looks down at his papers for a moment before continuing, "I am in process of sending men in pursuit of the Viceroy who, I believe, is residing some three hundred miles to the North-west."

A meeting that seemed to have started so well ends in disagreement. Beresford sees them off the premises. As they leave, a small Guard of Honour of his own Regiment, the 71st Royal Highlanders has formed up for them. The Sergeant of the Guard calls them to attention, then to the 'Present Arms!' The Council walks out somewhat stiffly without a backward glance although Puerridon lifts his hat.

Beresford returns the Guard's salute. He is conscious of having failed in his initial meeting with the Council. As he does, he sees Lauchlin standing to attention at the very back of the parade, his sword pointed outwards in salute. He realizes he has not spoken with him for some time. "Ah Mackinnon! Have you a moment, if you please."

Lauchlin's heart sinks at the summons. He had thought he was well clear of the boring clerical duties yet now, here he is again… He follows the General to his office. Beresford flings himself into a chair, removes his hat and shamelessly massages his eyes.

"Sit ye down! Now, I saw your attack on this fort and have heard of your conduct. You should know that I shall mention you in my despatch. How d'ye feel things are going? You have your own platoon, I understand. I think it time for you to be promulgated a subaltern. Seniority 12th July – that suit you?"

"Indeed yes, sir. Thank you very much!"

"I'll send a despatch to the War Office at once, copied to the Vice Admiral. Get your uniform altered. Joe Lapston the tailor will be following us ashore. He can make the necessary alterations." He looks through some papers on his table, then continues. "I'd like you to serve under Captain Murdo Cameron. I think you can make a real contribution as part of that team. He's just lost one of his officers – you'll have to fill the vacancy."

He offers Lauchlin a small glass of whisky in celebration as he pulls out a map of the river area.

---"This is somewhat sketchy, I'm afraid. We don't have any maps of the interior. We need to correct that situation. After we have had time to consolidate fully our occupation of the city, I would like you to lead a small group of twenty fusiliers and go up country. Take five cavalrymen in case of trouble and to get urgent messages back to us. I suggest, and I can only make suggestions to you at this distance – you will have to make your own decisions based on what you find – so, I suggest you follow the river up to where we believe it splits. Secure the position at the junction, here." He shows him a spot on the ill-drawn map. "At the same time, and this is important, sketch every detail of the country and send your reports in daily. Take paper, pencils and ink and writing materials." He smiles, "now you see why I am entrusting this important work to you. Get it back to me *pronto!*" He smiles again, adding, "that means soon – you see, even I can learn their lingo! I shall send the appropriate orders to Captain Cameron within a day or two."

The conversation takes on a friendly, casual note. After fifteen minutes Lauchlin takes his leave and goes in search of Mr. Lapston, following which he plans a meeting with Captain Cameron.

Beresford turns as Major Dirleton enters with a despatch case over his arm. "This has just arrived on the monitor *Whippet.*"

Together they open it and spread the letters over the table. Beresford takes up his private letters to be read later.

"Despatch here from Lord Wyndham, sir."

The War Minister writes that he is responding to Beresford's reports from St.Helena dated 3rd May 1806. He notes that they are planning to land in the Plate area as a result of Commodore Home Popham's decision. He states that there are many demands for troops in several theatres of the war and the aim must be to return as many as possible to the Cape by the earliest possible date. The occupation of the Plate area should NOT be considered a permanent placement but until he hears how the local inhabitants react he cannot give Beresford any instruction as to how long he should stay. It is a generally friendly despatch and states simply that if they are repulsed by the Spanish he should return his troops to the Cape and go to England himself on leave when he will look forward to hearing his further reports.

The despatch ends by saying that on the assumption that the event has been a success, he is despatching a further two thousand men to the Plate under Colonel Auchmuty and that he hopes it will include some cavalry.

Beresford shows the despatch to Dirleton. "This leaves the decisions here. Return troops but I am sending you some more!" He runs his hand through his hair.

Chapter 13

The next morning Home Popham sends a despatch to Beresford informing him that the location of the Treasure Ship must be disclosed and that its ownership is to be transferred to his care.

The Admiral has received despatches from London that have not put him in the best of moods. They are sent in response to his own from St.Helena and are not couched in the friendly tone used for the response to General Beresford. As Home Popham carried out this operation entirely at his own volition he is virtually informed that it is down to him if it is a success or a failure. Either way he is told that the ships are required at the Cape and he should hold himself ready for an early return.

The Admiral had also taken the opportunity to write to several London merchants and bankers advising them of a whole new continent awaiting their development. Some of these have now replied. They send their warmest congratulations and assure him that they will be taking early advantage of his advice and they will be pleased to reward him handsomely for his gallantry and assistance.

Three days later Home Popham decides to take a ceremonial drive through the city. An open barouche has been found in the Viceroy's stables. They quickly paint out the Spanish coat of arms and find two reasonably matching horses that can be managed by the veteran Light Brigade Corporal. The Admiral wears his finest and most ornate ceremonial dress with his cocked hat topped with egrets' feathers. He places Beresford in the seat opposite him and chooses to face the back of the driver, the better to wave to anyone in the street.

If he had expected a massed crowd of cheering populace, he is disappointed. Now that the Spanish have left, the citizenry feels quite capable of managing its own affairs. A secretly trained body of irregulars has maintained a stock of weapons and for some years tried to threaten the Spanish. This was the background to the Viceroy's disinclination to maintain a local defence force. There is a growing belief that they are quite capable of overcoming the relatively small force occupying their country. It wants all foreign troops out. There are now too many British installed with little to do and there have been complaints about drunken behaviour.

The tour takes little more than forty minutes and leaves Home Popham in an even blacker mood. An ugly scene is avoided when a woman prevents her small son from throwing a stone at the carriage.

He sits in Beresford's office and compares it with his own crowded accommodation in the flagship.

"I think I ought to come ashore – this will suit me splendidly. You can have the office next door. I think we should be seen to act together." He moves around restlessly, opening and closing drawers as if assessing the value of each item.

"Tell me," he finally faces the army commander, "how do you manage all these confounded Scots? How can you trust them when it's only a few years since they were in revolt against the Crown?"

Beresford tries to explain that there have always been soldiers with particular difficulties but it is his duty to train them and use them as directed.

The Admiral continues roving around the room like a caged lion. Suddenly his eyes alight on the silver salver which Beresford has inadvertently left on top of a cabinet. "What the Hell's this?" He reads the citation and his face is a mask of fury.

"Where did this come from? Who's promoted you to supreme commander? I'll take this and have it melted down – it's a start!"

Before Beresford can think of a reply, there is a tap on the door. His Secretary comes through, quickly followed by an agitated Major Dirleton.

"Bad news, sir. Bit of a fight in an inn near the river. Two of our men from 29th Rifles. One dead, the other in a bad way. I've sent a column under Sergeant Bell to keep things under control. He'll report to me when he returns. I thought you'd like to know at once."

"Damme!" Beresford rubs his eyes. "I'd hoped this wouldn't happen. Try to keep everything calm and let me know immediately!"

"Yes, of course, sir!" Dirleton withdraws dragging the Secretary-clerk with him.

"Your bloody infantry, Beresford! Comes of having too many men with nothing to do. Time you moved some of them up-country. Blasted Spanish will be coming back if you're not careful!"

In fact, for some days Beresford's Staff have been drawing up plans for just such expeditions. Lauchlin's orders are but a small element. There is a threat from the South of the city where a force of Spanish sharp-shooters is believed to be re-forming. More serious, however, is the lack of intelligence from the North-west. That is the direction from which the main rivers flow. A flat-bottomed boat could sail down with five hundred men on board and re-capture the city in half-an-hour. Beresford's main problem lies in the fact that he has no knowledge of whether such troops exist or even if there is such a thing as a flat-bottomed craft or even if the rivers have cataracts which would make such expeditions impossible. He has already sent a senior Intelligence Officer to investigate the situation and his despatches to the War Office in London cannot expect an answer until October at the earliest.

Home Popham takes his leave. "I'll return tomorrow morning, Beresford. A full meeting of the Senior Staff, I think. Maps of the whole area – decision time!" Beresford stands to watch him go and notes that he has not forgotten the silver salver.

Damn the man! Beresford says to himself, *and where's the local Spanish navy? They'll be around somewhere!*

With his promotion, has come Lauchlin's responsibility for organizing, under Captain Cameron, his small platoon of twenty or so men. At the first opportunity, he goes to report to him. He finds a man of large personality hidden behind a dour, ginger-haired near-caricature of a highlander. The ends of his moustache are twirled to long points which project well beyond his rosy cheeks.

He shakes Lauchlin's hand warmly and claps him on the shoulder. "Right then, Lauchlin!" His eyes sparkle, "ye know yer replacing Lieutenant Grant? A guid man, sorely missed – but not by a sniper - bugger 'im! - I'm told ye'll fill his shoes! Now - ye're as welcome as the February rain in Inverness! That's to say better than the ice but all depends on your disposition! Your men are lined up there – get to know them, ye'll have six of the cavalry as well and ye've got yer Sergeant Matthews y'asked fer, and I'll see you when I get back."

He struts away to a full briefing with the General. As his name implies, he is a full-scale Highlander. He says little and, although he is from the North, his speech betrays a considerable time spent in Glasgow. A physically big man his nose shows that he has not always been averse to a spot of hand to hand fighting. In fact as Lauchlin finds later, he had initially made his living that way, but a combination of dishonest fight arrangers and pugilists even bigger than himself had led to his being enticed to join the army. The date is burned into his mind. On 26th August 1784, he had been successful in a bruising contest with a hard street fighter known as 'Knuckles Gravestone'. While recovering from his injuries, his rightful winnings were stolen by the fight arranger. He had spent a fruitless night trying to trace the thief and morning had found him unable even to buy his breakfast porage. In the square he listened to a smartly-dressed officer accompanied by someone from the Procurator-Fiscal's office. They were announcing the formation by a Colonel Montgomerie of a new regiment to be known as *Glasgow's Own*. They were handing out sixpences to all who joined. Without hesitation, the seventeen year-old Murdo Cameron held out his hand and put his mark. Since then he had served in the Netherlands under the Duke of York and in the East Indies under Cornwallis. As a private soldier he had seen his pay rise from sixpence a day to a full shilling which was reduced by one penny three farthings for bread and meat; in time this was further reduced by four shillings a week for what was described as "messing". Theoretically he remembered his net pay was supposed to be one and a half shillings a week. Such a sum was quickly lost in the taverns and brothels of Europe. The latter had gained him a glancing taste of a disease which had kept him clear of the worst ravages of the Indies. His recollection of pay changes was sharp as he had been deeply involved in negotiating and calculating details with the Regimental Treasury officials working under strict Government limits. He had always been careful and courteous so had avoided *'Arrest for impertinence'* or *'Dumb Insolence'* which had beset so many of his fellows. To avoid charges of being a Barrack-room lawyer he had been encouraged to succeed as a soldier and this had gained him a steady progression in which his experience of the common life made him a better leader. The move from Senior Sergeant to Lieutenant had been especially hard and was mainly a reward for saving the life of his colonel after the disaster of Yorktown; three Americans had captured him and Murdo had shot one and slammed the others into unconsciousness. That had been the moment when he had been advised to move regiment and he had been a 71st Royal Highlander ever since 1st January 1790. He well knew that as a Captain in a senior regiment of the Line, his pay was just over twelve and a half shillings a day. He was without a family and had made sure that the bulk of this was entrusted to a London Banker named Cox whom people said was trustworthy.

Lauchlin salutes as Captain Cameron leaves. He sees his men lined up waiting for him. Franklin Matthews steps forward and salutes him. It is the first time he has received the respectful greeting and he has to hide his shocked surprise.

"Thank you Sergeant Matthews. If you will stand them in Open Order and at ease, please!"

The platoon is too junior to merit a corporal as well as a sergeant and Matthews accompanies him down the lines introducing each man. Lauchlin recognizes some from his days of sleeping in the hammock. There are two others from the Loyal American Regiment with *Sharpshooter* badges on their green jackets. Lauchlin hopes the colour will not clash with the green of the Spanish.

"These will be very useful in a rural and unknown environment, sir", Matthews murmurs to him out of their hearing, "and Johnson speaks a bit of Spanish too." The rest appear to be mainly Lowlanders from the area of Port Glasgow but he suspects that they have origins going back to the islands. Certain it is that one or two will have roots very like his own. He wonders what his family would think if they knew about his present situation. Life has many forks in the road. Some choices are forced upon you and some are simply opportune but many can be critical.

Suddenly he comes face to face with a man he had not expected to see: "Jameson!"

"That's me sir, and happy I am to see you again!" The scar on his face twists in what he imagines is a friendly expression.

"Face the front, Jameson!" Sergeant Matthews barks sternly at him. Lauchlin feels it safer to say nothing but he vows privately to keep an eye on the man he last saw as he was being tied up at Eyemouth with Lord Leadbetter's property.

In spite of his shock he does his best to remember each man's name. Some have a particular characteristic to help him. One called Bentley has his hair neatly oiled down to the regulation pig-tail. Trying to recover his position and be pleasant Lauchlin asks him what he uses.

"Ear-wax, sir!" Comes the instant reply from a straight mouth. But was there a hint of a twitch in the face of the next man? Were they trying to intimidate the new, young officer? He moves away without giving any sign.

"Eyes front, Bentley!" Sergeant Matthews is having none of it.

Lauchlin's kit has been moved to a house near the city waterfront. He shares it with three other junior officers and they are served by two batmen.

On the day following he is called to Captain Cameron's billet and his orders are spelt out.

"Here's a copy of the map ye saw in the General's office, such as it is. Your task is mainly to survey the land to the west and south of the River Plate up to where we believe it is fed by another biggish river – the *Currents* we think it's called – prevent any Spanish from infiltratin' and check what people inhabit the country, whether European or indigenous – dinna antagonize any of them! That means ye canna lose yer temper with anyone! Find out what the land is good for. Right? You are to report daily by means of one of the cavalrymen and to sketch and correct the map of all the land as you travel. And your reports must tell us where y'are – if we have to recall ye we can't go wand'rin' aboot the countryside looking for ye. Right? And do it *PRONTO!*"

"Understood. And I'm to have five or six of the cavalry as well sir?"

"Five – Aye, and the name's Murdo except on parade. And ye'd best take a wagon and two mules to carry yer victuals and powder and shot. Take food for twenty-eight days although I expect you to be relieved within fourteen. I suggest you use two of the cavalrymen to scout ahead. Frank Matthews's a good man – he'll sort out the feed ye need for the mules and horses. Best take one of the Regimental ponies for yourself. I canna say how high is the risk of meeting any Spanish but ye must be ready at all times!"

"Right, Murdo, thank-you. Can I ask you something else that I find a mite troubling? It's the presence of women among the troops. Is it all right? And who feeds them?"

"If you've got a woman or two you're fortunate. They make the men behave, they wash their clothes for them and – often as not – do the cooking for everyone. And some of 'em can shoot as well as anyone! Time'll come when you'll be glad enough of their company!" He turns as if to leave then comes back to Lauchlin. "Ye'll see that you've two more of the American or Canadian Loyals in their green jackets. They may be strange in their manner o'talking but – like Matthews - they're good where it matters – value them!"

"Thank you Murdo. I'll go now and brief Sergeant Matthews and we'll leave sharp after breakfast tomorrow!"

Captain Cameron grows pensive for a moment. "One other thing, laddie. Ye'll know where the Spanish sympathies will rest – but the Creoles… they're people born here, maybe of Spanish descent or other European - maybe even half Indian. Watch them! Pay particular attention. Ye won't know where their loyalties are. Trust them only as far as ye can throw 'em."

"I understand, Murdo. And thank you."

"Aye, Good lad, Lauchlin. Just one thing: don't merely brief Frank Matthews, brief the whole party – it's small enough... They'll work for you all the better if they know what it's aboot! And one other thing, laddie: get one of the locals to teach ye a few words of the lingo, like 'what's this called' and 'what's your name' and even 'have ye seen any Spanish soldiers'? You'll probably find that Matthews, Johnson and Thurlo speak it a bit – those Southerners often do -- And don't worry your pretty head aboot the women! Just think where could they go if they lost their man – like as not they'll have to find another!" He winks as he turns away, "You could be the lucky one!"

Lucky or not the next morning dawns cold but, more seriously, with a thick blanket of fog. Lauchlin is eager to be off but in a discussion with Captain Cameron, he is urged to delay his start until noon.

"Whatever's the use of crawling aboot in the fog? Ye canna do any surveying and, like as not, the enemy will be feeling his way doon a river or road with which he <u>is</u> familiar. He might fall on your laddies and ye'd be wiped out without knowing a thing aboot it!"

They are sentiments with which Lauchlin can only agree and in a briefing with Sergeant Matthews, they decide to push their plans back by five hours. Lauchlin goes to find a local who will teach him some phrases and he writes them down.

Chapter 14

Later in the morning, a watery sun breaks through the fog. After a somewhat hurried dinner of boiled beef and vegetables, Lauchlin signs for a pony of about sixteen hands called *Heroic.* It is described as calm and obedient. The name comes from that of his sire – *Courageous* and that of his dam – *Diana.* The veterinary officer in charge of the regiment's horses prides himself on a sense of humour. The pony is naturally rather reluctant to leave his fellows in their lush paddock. It is too early for him to be put back in the stable block. Lauchlin draws a saddle from the Stores and proceeds to dress the animal using the method taught him by Sergeant Robinson. Tightening the girth does not go as well as predicted; when Lauchlin gives him a gentle punch in the belly, the animal merely turns to gaze at him with an enquiring look. One of the grooms comes across and speaks sharply to him: "See here, *Heroic*, if you're going to be awkward the nice officer won't want to tak' ye oot!" So saying he delivers a very sharp blow which enables Lauchlin to move the girth two holes tighter.

The shock seems to freeze the animal to the spot, making mounting easier. The groom adjusts the stirrups for him and he urges *Heroic* out of the stable and towards Matthews who is standing by the wagon with two mules between the shafts and a driver on the box seat. The other eighteen men of the party are drawn up behind as Matthews calls them to attention. He salutes as Lauchlin rides up. He tries to return the salute but jumbles the reins in his hands and it is only due to the horse's firm stance that he does not fall out of the saddle.

"Our five huntsmen with their steeplechasers await us at the port exit area sir," The Sergeant pronounces with a straight face.

"Very good, Sergeant, we'd best go and join them!"

Lauchlin dismounts. His sword almost catches in a stirrup but, once again, he is saved from looking foolish by *Heroic's* attentiveness. He holds the reins and murmurs "I think I'll march on foot for a while, Sergeant Matthews!" He stares around ignoring Jameson who is standing like a rod. He tries to see if there are any women. He sees none and, remembering Murdo's words, dismisses the thoughts from his mind.

"Very good sir." He turns and calls out: "Browning!" A fusilier in the rear rank grips his musket in his right hand and runs round. "Here Sergeant!"

"Right, Fusilier Browning. You've often been heard to say that you wish you were in the cavalry, you are hereby appointed Officer's Groomsman. You will lead and care for this animal. You will feed him and rub him down as he needs it – understood?"

"Aye Sergeant, thank 'ee very much Sergeant!" Matthews takes his musket and places it in the wagon. Lauchlin with a sense of relief hands the reins to him, "thank-you, Browning."

"My pleasure, sir!"

With muskets at the *trail* and in three ranks they march down to the port where they move to the Cavalry barracks. A number of horses and riders move round a make-shift arena. But he sees a group of five who seem to be waiting for him. As he approaches they grasp their horses' reins and climb lightly into the saddle. One of them salutes him, calling out: "23rd Dragoons, sir, Trooper Littlejohn!"

Acknowledging the salute, Lauchlin nods at him. "Good afternoon, Littlejohn. We shall have an inspection please, introduce everyone to me." Trying to get to know his men he rides slowly through their line memorizing each name and face. "Very good, Littlejohn. Will you please fall-in behind the wagon. We shall proceed on foot for a short distance. I wish to be fifteen miles clear of the town before we bivouac for the night."

Leaving the port area behind, they move off in a North-westerly direction keeping the river on their right and following a reasonable road which suggests the regular passage of traffic. The mist is beginning to form once more and the pale sun takes on a weak, yellow tinge. The temperature is ideal for a brisk march and the surface although firm is slightly sandy and yields gently to the horses' hooves and is kind to their boots.

After some ninety minutes, when he calculates they have covered about six and a half miles, he allows a fifteen-minute rest, telling Matthews to set up a sentry north and south. He takes down from the wagon a piece of board and a sheet of paper. He has little idea of how to survey the land but can note the gradual slope up from the river to low hills on their left. There are few trees and he is quite pleased with the way he shows the small curve of the river with the angle of the road and the numerous little rivulets that seem to feed into it from their left. He is about to include a crescent moon hiding behind a misty cloud when he remembers that this needs to be of military use and is not just a piece of art.

Fortunately the mist does not get any thicker so they are able to proceed for perhaps a further seven miles. Lauchlin discusses their need for a good camping spot which can be guarded on four sides.

Matthews agrees then carefully passes a comment which Lauchlin knows he should have thought of himself - the need for a rider to be ahead of them by perhaps five hundred yards. This would avoid the danger of marching into an ambush.

Lauchlin nods in agreement, silently chastising himself when a small flickering light ahead indicates some activity. As they advance it reveals a small town. Thinking of his chart drawing, he estimates it at roughly seventeen dwellings in length with perhaps six or seven stretching behind. He mentally calculates a population of, perhaps, two hundred and fifty to three hundred. A town of some substance then. Of particular note is a crude slip-way down to the river which he estimates would certainly be an excellent landing place for a boatload of troopers. A smell of wood smoke draws their attention to a smoking chimney with a wooden barn behind. They stop just short of the slipway and he gives Matthews the order to fall out again with appropriate defensive posts. Lauchlin goes up and bangs on a front door which, even in the failing light, he recognizes as of superior quality. It has small glass panels either side of a brass knocker made in the shape of a bull. Flickering lights through the glass suggest candles or an oil lamp.

It is a glowering face that opens the door and looks out at him. Dark skinned with a full beard, the man is wearing a light-coloured shirt, tucked into loose, baggy trousers that disappear into a fine pair of leather boots. Remembering his orders not to upset the populace, he doffs his hat.

"Good afternoon, sir. We are men of the British army and are passing through your town."

Following the gesture of Lauchlin's arm, the man leans out to look, "*Que quieren aqui? Soldados de bosta!*"**

Lauchlin smiles again, trying to be charming. "Ingles" He points at his men. "Do you speak English?"

The man turns and calls out: *Maria, veni aqui, Hay carajos! Y no se de dondes vienen!****

The woman summoned comes to the door. Whether she is his wife, servant or daughter is hard to tell. Lauchlin bobs his head again and smiles. Pointing back at his men in the road, he repeats: "Ingleses!" He takes out the piece of paper on which he had written some Spanish phrases. He asks the name of the village: *"Como se llama aqui?"*

At his crude efforts to communicate, the faces clear. The man excitedly says: *"Ah no son españoles...La Villa se llama 'Las Conchas'" (They're not Spanish; the town is called 'The Sea-shells)*

It is now virtually dark. The woman looks out at the men in the road and speaks quickly. He seems to ask a few questions then nods his head. He points at the barn making motions of a head resting on his hand. *"Se quieren dormir alli?" (Would you care to sleep there?)*

Lauchlin can hardly believe his luck. What had seemed an alien, even agressive, image is now transformed into a friendly, hospitable face.

He makes gestures of thanks and acceptance indicating that they have their own food. The man nods again but signs that no fires can be lit in the barn. *"Sin fuego en el granero!"*

Lauchlin nods his head again and calls Matthews over. He introduces him: "Sergeant Matthews". The Sergeant holds out his hand which is grasped as he says: *"Sargento Franco Matthews – a sus ordenes!"* The woman claps her hands *"Ah si,habla Castellano – Sargento Franco Matador!"*

The man leads them to the barn. He is chatting away to Matthews but it is mostly unintelligible. He is consumed with interest about their destination. The interior is dry and there is plenty of hay for them to sleep comfortably. Somehow Matthews has found a means of gaining permission for a fire to be lit beyond the line of houses on the edge of the river. Their animals can be put at the back in a field which is currently unoccupied. Matthews appoints sentries and the wagon driver takes his mules with the

** *What do you want here, shitty soldiers?*

*** *Maria, come here, I've got some bastards-and don't know where they're from!*

horse into the field which contains a water trough. Wood for their fire is in the wagon but it is slightly damp and there are problems

Lighting it. Their host, whom they find is called *Señor Carnero* shakes his head and takes an armful of hay from the barn. Their fire is soon crackling merrily and their food is giving off a very tempting aroma. The man takes more of his hay which he puts in the wagon – *"para mañana!"*

Lauchlin is planning an early night with a good sleep in the warmth of the barn, but the noise and smell of cooking attracts a crowd of other inhabitants. A man brings out a guitar and there is soon singing from the locals in which the soldiers join. One of his American or Canadian Loyals sings a soft ballad which takes Lauchlin back to his Scottish roots.

He is astonished when one of his highlanders rises and, alone and unaccompanied by any music, dances a solemn *Fling.* The locals clap and cheer but Lauchlin notices none of his men join in the applause. In the deep recesses of his memory he recalls the 'Tullochgorm', an island dance supposedly done by a lonely shepherd imitating the fighting of stags. Although none of the men can possibly remember its banning after Culloden, it is a nostalgic reminder for all highland people and they are deeply affected.

As soon as he can, he writes a short letter to Captain Cameron reporting on the day, naming the village they have reached as Las Conchas and that the locals are overwhelmingly friendly. One of the Dragoons will be sent back with it in the morning.

He is awake before dawn and creeps out to look at the weather. It is misty but not like yesterday's fog and there is a pleasant smell of old wood smoke both from the house and the remnants of their fire which had been carefully extinguished last night. The men prepare their breakfasts while Lauchlin completes his despatch and adds another sheet to his map. The village has three or four 'long-drop' holes and Matthews has ensured that all signs of their fire the night before are cleaned away. A Dragoon called Ickerson is entrusted with the despatch for Captain Cameron. He is told that they plan to continue with the present route but, if forced to divert, a sign or a rear marker will await him. Lauchlin watches as he canters back towards the city. The rest of them form into order on the road. He sends two of the Dragoons forward to act as his eyes and ears. They are carefully briefed to stay no more than one mile ahead and one must return at once if there is anything to report.

The whole family comes out to wave them off and other villagers shout their good wishes as they leave the area. Lauchlin feels very satisfied with the detachment's progress, they have behaved well and not disgraced themselves; the weather is cold with a touch of frost but it is dry and excellent for marching. The road they travelled yesterday evidently ended at *'Las Conchas'* but they are now on a perfectly serviceable track that causes no difficulties for the mules with the wagon. In the mud at the sides there are many signs of cattle so he searches for a farm or some kind of habitation. The track diverts slightly from the river leaving a gentle slope down to a stony, circular meander; if the cattle are brought here to water, their access is easy. He also sees horses' tracks but there is no sign of any wheeled vehicle. *This is Winter,* he thinks to himself, *would the river be much lower in Summer?* Matthews has told him that the men are in good heart, having noted that 'Lucky' Lochy is able to charm good accommodation out of the locals. *"He may not be so good on a horse but he's al'reet on his feet!"*

As they proceed, he uses the opportunity to get to know Matthews better. A loyal American he was astonished at the decision not to follow the advice of Benjamin Franklin when they revolted against the government of King George III. "It was bringing in the Stamp Act that did it – not the tax on tea which was only being raised to pay for the army actually in the Colony!"

The invasion of Virginia when his family were killed cost him everything. "The army's my family, sir. I wish for no other!"

It is a sentiment he hears from others. Matthews's two American colleagues who also describe themselves as Virginians explain how they were sent up to the Canadian East coast when the War of Independence ended.

They march briskly for two hours covering an estimated eight miles. They rest for fifteen minutes while Lauchlin starts another sheet for his mapping. He is careful to put a prominent *"Sheet number2"* and the date at its head. While drawing a line for the track they are following, he notes how it follows the river almost exactly. Where there is a diversion it soon returns. He is aware that there has been a slight but steady turn towards the north and estimates that their direction now is North-north-west. He grumbles to himself at the lack of a compass. Use of the sun is only approximate. Occasionally, no more than once every mile or so, there is another track descending the hill and the animal tracks generally follow these. They make another stop after a further two hours and such a track descends near them. He calls for one of the Dragoons, "Dyrham, I'd like you to ride up this track and see if there is a farm or anything I should include in my survey."

"Yes sir, how far up should I ride?"

"No more than a mile at most. Be cautious – have a look then hurry back and tell me what you've seen. Likely we shall have moved on but if the track forks we'll wait for you or leave a sign."

Dyrham mounts his horse and trots up the hill. He is soon out of sight. Strangely there are no trees but the grasses are long. Duly rested they resume their march along the river. He assumes Dyrham will canter the mile or so up the side track, have a good look round and return – fifteen to twenty minutes.

His reckoning is accurate. Dyrham is back in less than a half-hour.

"We canter a mile in six minutes, sir. Slightly slower if it's hilly. I allowed ten minutes for the slope but it's a gentle hill. Nothing to report, sir, just clear grass lands." He had seen no animals.

"What about fences, Dyrham – anything likely to contain animals?"

"No sir, but there are a number of ditches that could be used in that way. They probably drain the higher land down to the river. They don't look natural to me but dug out years ago – could they be by Indians, sir?"

"Indians! Great Heavens man…I don't know. But you saw no sign of anyone?"

"No sir, no habitation of any kind."

Two hours later they stop for a meal break. He calculates that they have covered sixteen miles since leaving the village and uses that as the scale for his map.

Matthews sends Dyrham to relieve the two dragoons checking their advance. Within five minutes they hear them shouting as all three gallop back: "Enemy approaching! Armed cavalry Sir!"

Lauchlin leaps to his feet. "Collect muskets from the wagon! Form two lines in defensive positions! Load but await my command!" He then calls out: "How many Dyrham and how far away?"

"Difficult to say, sir. At least ten, mounted, perhaps..." His report is cut off by the arrival of about a dozen fierce horsemen, with knives tucked into black sash-belts. His first reaction is that they must be Indians but he soon dismisses the thought. A nondescript group, dressed very like Señor Carnero in the village last night. Their tops are again the colourless, loose shirts, something like blouses but over these they wear a leather waistcoat with a fleecy lining. They wear similar baggy trousers tied under their feet tucked into a lightweight slipper, perhaps with a rope sole. Some have black berets on their heads, others have wide-brimmed, leather hats tied under their chins to prevent them blowing away. That this is a real likelihood is demonstrated by the number of front brims turned up rather like trees bent against a prevailing wind.

They rear their horses up somewhat theatrically as they see the two lines of armed troops facing them. Lauchlin immediately steps out in front holding up his hand.

"No shooting! Order Arms - Sergeant Matthews!"

"Aye sir! Front rank, steady. Rear rank: Order Arms!"

The apparent leader of the group is a youth of perhaps sixteen. Riding a large, black stallion much higher than those of his fellows, he sits easily in a sheepskin covered saddle. He is fair skinned in contrast with most of the party who are swarthy. Also, he seems to have blue eyes that bore deep into Lauchlin's face. There is no fear or respect in his face.

"Que hacen aqui – de adonde vienen?" (What are you doing here – where are you from?

Lauchlin feels somewhat helpless. The youth is angry yet has an air of authority over these men who look like rough farm labourers with a touch of the indigenous people. But they seem to be trained and disciplined. He removes his hat and bows. "Soldados Ingleses!" and tries to indicate his goodwill with a frozen smile as his right arm waves for Matthews to join him.

"Ingleses? Y que hacen aqui?" (English? And what are you doing here?)

Matthews stands at his elbow, cleverly showing his deference. He speaks passable Spanish asking where they are.

The young face remains unimpressed but with a thumb he gestures over his right shoulder.

"Ibicoy – mi padre es Caudillo de todas estas tierras!" (My father is Caudillo over all these lands)

Lauchlin feels at a loss. Is the first word the name of the village or the name of the youth? Or is it merely part of an unintelligible phrase? If they are to spend much time in this country he is determined to learn more of the language. The youth smacks his chest and sits proudly in his saddle: *"Rosas! Juan Manuel Jose Domingo Ortiz de Rosas!"*

Lauchlin bows his respect: "Ah Señor Rosas — yo" and he indicates himself, "Mackinnon; este, gesturing to Matthews, Sargento Matthews."

"Macagua! Que tonto." (A Macaw – what an idiot)

The horsemen behind him dutifully laugh. Lauchlin has no idea what has been said but understands the contemptuous way it was delivered.

In his crude Spanish he asks if they can proceed up the track. Matthews repeats the request.

"No, pasaje prohibido!" And he pulls his horse's head around. His men make room for him. With a commanding gesture he leads them away.

Lauchlin is left feeling rather foolish. He is conscious of his orders not to antagonize the locals but here he is being prevented from carrying out a survey of the country. The sun is high and he calls for another break and a meal, posting a sentry to the north, following the party but to stay out of sight.

Now these were presumably Creoles, those people born here that Murdo warned him about. He could write a despatch for Captain Cameron, basically asking for instructions, but what reaction would that cause? Also, can he really spare another dragoon to carry a fresh despatch? Ickerson, who went off earlier, will barely have arrived. Lauchlin feels disinclined to set up a situation which may escalate. He must be cautious. Also, as he comes to realize, who is the best person to make a decision on this question? Surely the man on the spot – and that is himself. Silently he debates the situation.

He decides to spend another fifteen minutes thinking it through while the party ahead disappears totally from the scene. He fears appearing an idiot before his men. Perhaps it is time to show some authority, improve his riding and exercise *Heroic.* He talks to the horse trying to emulate the gentle tones of Bonnington back in Edinburgh. As the animal strolls quietly for some two hundred yards in each direction, he falls to thinking about Drysdale and the evening card games. This causes his thoughts to wander back to his family in Port Glasgow. It gives him a spasm of homesickness although he knows full well that he made the right decision at that time and must do so again. The progress of a British military operation – no matter how small – cannot be held up by a band of twelve herdsmen under a youth. The youth will be one of the dreaded Creoles – the others indigenous…is that right? Yes, they must go forward – armed if necessary.

His reverie is interrupted by a call from the sentry placed up ahead. "Horsemen coming sir! About fifteen I think." They both trot back briskly and Lauchlin hands the horse over to his groomsman. Matthews is calling the troop to line up with their muskets at the ready. Once again Lauchlin stands in front of them.

The party soon rides in. It is almost the same group as before but this time it is much more sedate. The leader is a serious, middle-aged man formally dressed in a dark dress coat and tight fawn trousers tucked into beautifully polished black boots. As he draws his men up he removes a fine dark leather cap with a gold ribbon and bows his head with a gesture of respect. He calls out for someone at the back to come forward. As Lauchlin draws his sword and salutes in return, he sees an elderly monk ride a small pony to the leader's side. He is simply dressed in a brown robe with a cowl thrown back and a plain length of rope around his waist. His face is nearly as brown as his habit but lined with life.

"Good days, I am Father Ignacio Loyolla. I am here for translate. You English soldiers?"

For a moment a saintly halo lights the back of his head as his shiny scalp reflects the sun yet, when he looks more closely, Lauchlin can see small, grey hairs in clumps. "Yes, Father, although we prefer to be called British!"

His eyes, deep in the lined, leather skin, seem to sparkle with amusement. "Many apologies, I feel it." He turns and explains to the man at his side. "Allow me introduce you to Don Leon Ortiz de Rosas, the Caudillo and owner of all these lands!"

Lauchlin bows in respect. Inwardly he puzzles is this a Spaniard or one of the dreaded Creoles? "I am Lieutenant Lauchlin Mackinnon of the 71st Royal Highland Regiment, serving under General William Beresford."

The monk translates before turning back. "The Caudillo enquires what you do here and what you planning. Also, where Spanish soldiers?"

"We are a small scouting party sent ahead to map and survey the land and to enquire about its people. It is an honour for me to meet the Caudillo and I would like to assure him that we mean no harm to his lands or properties." He rests for a moment, planning his next phrase while the translation is made. Don Leon nods his head in understanding. Lauchlin continues. "His Excellency will be aware that my country is at war with France and Spain. It was therefore decided to attack the Spanish army here in the hope of bringing freedom to all the people of the old Viceroyalty of the Rio de la Plata."

After a few moments of discussion:

"Don Leon says no need to map the area – he has many at his *Estancia, - La Chacra Fortaleza.* He says if you come call on him he will be pleased to show them to you."

"That is most generous and helpful, Father. Tell me when would it be convenient for me to come."

This time there is considerable chatting between them. The monk looks at the sky. Eventually he turns to Lauchlin with a smile. "Don Leon says it going rain very hard tonight. If you wish your men can be sleeped in one of his outbuildings. He will send food out them and he says that you join him and his lady for dinner and discussion."

Lauchlin hears the small murmur of pleasure from behind him. "That is a most generous offer which we shall be pleased and honoured to accept with gratitude. How shall we find this estate?"

After more translating and nodding between them, Father Ignacio explains that he will stay with the soldiers and guide them to the Farmhouse. The Caudillo nods his satisfaction, lifts his cap before turning his horse and leading the group away. Father Ignacio dismounts heavily from his pony. He holds on to the reins while he approaches. As Lauchlin sheathes his sword he asks if the monk would like them to care for the pony.

"No, no. When others out sight she loose to water in the river and pull up some this poor wintery grass."

"Won't she run away?"

*"Esta verguenza?** No. Where go she, this her land."

Lauchlin wonders whether the monk's use of that phrase, copying that of the Caudillo, was completely coincidental. Father Ignacio looks up at the leaden sky and gives a shiver.

"I not a man of Winter. God sends me this beautiful country from my

**This disgrace?*

monastery near Valencia. I love doing His work here but on cold days I reminded of my old home, sit on the banks of the river *Magro*."

"Your English is very good, where did you learn it?"

"Ah, I always interested in language – and literature! Before I twelve years, the Prior at *Villar del Arzobispo,* Father Pedro, send me to the big university at Valladolid. We read books in the English and in the French." He shakes his head in recollection, "I a boy at thirteen, that age, you know, I enjoyed the writings of people like Francois de Malherbe and Pierre Bayle – especially Bayle, he ...oh...rude for a young boy!" He chuckles quietly.

"And English? You read some of our writers too?"

"Oh yes, Chaucer to start, very strange" He stands to declaim: *"If t'were a kibe t'would put me to my slipper!"* He laughs out loud – "Good eh? – and the modern Scottish poet...Burns...yes, very good but strange languages, old English and new Scottish! Ah but your Shakespeare, like the Frenchman Mathurian Regnier, much hidden meanings. Is really wonderful for me speak English again, Shakespeare yes: *Oh for a muse of fire!"*

"I like Shakespeare, I have a book with most of his plays, and poems too."

"Oh I like see it, a wonderful memoria!"

"I left it in Buenos Aires with my kit. I would like to learn to speak Spanish. Is it very difficult?"

"Oh no, here all young children speak it!"

"Ah you jest with me, Father. How can I best learn to speak it?"

"Jest? – ah joke, yes, a jester. You must live here for twenty years and speak nothing else. I could give you lessons in conversation Spanish if you stay here but it need take three months at least." He turns his eyes on Lauchlin; they seem to bore into his very soul. "That if you good student."

"Alas, we shall only be here for a short while."

He hears a shout and turns. Dragoon Ickerson who carried his report this morning has returned. The sweat on his horse suggests that he has been riding hard. He salutes and hands his leather despatch case over. It has just the one message. "You will excuse me, Father."

"Si, si – como no!"

Buenos Aires, July 15th, 1806.

Your Despatch from Las Conchas, which we have numbered 1, has been safely received and read by General Beresford and the Staff. You are congratulated on establishing a relationship with Mr.Carnero. We may send an emissary to develop the contact. Suggest you carry on in a similar way. Please continue to report particularly on the map handed to you and how it compares.

Sgd. Murdo Cameron, Captain,
71st The Royal Highland Regt.

He turns back to the Priest as he puts the despatch away "Forgive me, but I have to check my orders!"

"*Claro,* that is perfectly understoodable."

"How far do the Caudillo's lands stretch? We had a visit earlier from a young man who forbade us from proceeding further."

"*Ah si,* that be Juan Manuel. He is the Caudillo's son. A remarkable young man – he not yet eighteen… but he something like Shakespeare 'Posthumus Leonatus'!"

"Posthumus what? I don't know him, Father!"

"Yes, Leonatus – *'All the learnings that his time could make him the receiver of – which he took as we do air.'* Juan Manuel is that kind of student. Most quick to learn! Not only that, he ride better than a *Gaucho!*"

"A what?"

"That is what we call the men who work the land for the Caudillo. Not the *Esclavos.* They are the indigenous people and have a finity with the horse. They originally caught *animales ferroles,* I think you say wild, err, feral horses, escaped from the early Spanish. Juan Manuel was nearly born in the saddle and he much respected by all the men. How did you converse with him?"

Lauchlin introduces Matthews and explains about his small check list of phrases.

"Ah Matthews…*si, el Discipulo mas Bueno!* that very good! Allow me to give you some more. If you learn ten phrases a day you will speak the language passably in two weeks!"

The three of them discuss this matter in greater depth for some time, exchanging phrases and verbs as they walk along leading the men and horses. Father Ignacio, after looking up at the sky, collects his robe around his legs.

"It perhaps time we move to the Estancia, dinner will be at the nine hours" – He draws himself up imperiously and repeats the phrase like a butler: "Dinner will be at the nine hours! That is what you say?" He chuckles. "They eat later in the summer but they only spend some two months a year out here. The family normally resides Buenos Aires and another estancia to the Sud. We returning there *prontisimo*, perhaps tomorrow."

"May I ask who will be at the dinner tonight?"

"Oh just small family affair. Don Leon and Doña Agustina his wife and her mother, Doña Valenciana Lopez de Osornio. Juan Manuel whom you have met and perhaps…" his brow seems to darken, "perhaps if he is still here, Don Bernardo de Amuñecar he Spanish *Grande,* Don Leon think he make husband for Alicia, she sister of Juan Manuel, Alicia Daniela. She just seventeen years and a lovely person. Perhaps she will attend to see you. Honour if family allow. She and I often speak English each other."

"Really, and how is that possible?"

"Oh she always a bright child. And I privileged to be tutor for some years. Juan Manuel is so very gifted but, for the present, he more interested in learning management of horse and estates. He full de ideas. He believe he will sell his beef all over world. At present he export only the leathers. All say it the best beef, reared on these great grasslands and with climate very… *clemente."* He pulls his robe around him again, "except in winter!"

"But the only way he can send the beef without it going bad is by salting it and that may be fine for soldiers and seamen but people at home like their food fresh."

"That true." Father Ignacio moves his head up and down, "but he have science ideas about processing the beef in a *fabrica*, and…oh it is beyond my thoughts, but I think we should make move to settle your soldiers before storm arrivings. Now, what is the phrase again for 'I am so *agradecido*'?"

Matthews calls the troop to order. The monk tells him to follow the track along the river for a mile or so until they find a path up to the left. "I teach *Oficial* here more verbs. You no need! Take that and I will guide you again!"

Father Ignacio leads his mount by hand and they walk along behind the soldiers as they discuss some regular verbs their usage and exceptions.

On the stump of a dead tree there is a small mound of mud and Lauchlin sees a bird fly out. The monk looks up. "Ah you see him? He is *Hornero.* Bird that make nest like that and sing very good."

"Hornero, that's a strange name. I don't think we have anything like that."

"Hornero, Yes his nest make like what you cook bread…*Horno,* yes…. an oven, that right. Your Mr.Matthews should know! Juan Manuel very interested in birds…but he most interested in an independent country,"… he talks seriously: "he say Buenos Aires should be the capital of the region – a country the size of many European nations, of course. Now, here we are at Ibicoy."

They have reached the turning in fifteen minutes and Father Ignacio goes forward to speak to Franklin Matthews. They move up towards the estate, leaving one of the cavalrymen with his horse to guide any returning Despatch Rider.

Chapter 15

Baron Grenville, the King's First Minister, has called a meeting in the Cabinet Room in Downing Street primarily to discuss the latest situation in the war against the French. But first, in deference to His Majesty's expressed interest, he has invited William Wilberforce, the Member for Yorkshire to address them on his constant preoccupation with slavery. King George has reportedly expressed outrage at the number of slaves still conveyed by British shipping. At the same time, His Majesty is anxious to avoid any changes that could lead to an increase in political disagreement.

Grenville barely listens as Wilberforce drones on about the cruelty he has personally witnessed. He is familiar with all the arguments and could support either side. It is a problem for another day. In the meantime he quietly enjoys the soft Hull burr of Wilberforce's accent. He is respectful towards this forty-seven year-old member because he is close to the Foreign Secretary, Charles James Fox whose enormous bulk is filling a chair just three along the table. For the present Grenville must avoid antagonizing Fox. His friends in Parliament can make things difficult for him. At length, following a general nodding of heads from the Whig supporters present, Wilberforce is able to take his leave.

The main business being the war against France and Spain. Lord Wyndham, the War Minister, brings them up to date with the latest situation and commends certain actions which are generally agreed.

Then, as is so often his practice, Charles Fox turns his disagreeable face and vast number of chins towards Lord Wyndham. He wishes to raise a relatively unimportant detail of the War. With his deep and perfectly enunciated vowels he demands to know on whose authority the main body of ships has been withdrawn from the Cape.

"I have it on good authority that a counter attack is even now being planned by the French together with Hollanders and Flemish hangers-on and our troops are liable to be under-supplied!"

Grenville allows Wyndham to respond. He quotes from the despatches just received from Vice Admiral Home Popham and General Beresford, sent by fast frigate from St.Helena. They are dated 19th May. Popham had explained as carefully as possible that he deemed the opportunity to attack Spanish possessions in the River Plate too good to ignore, that the relatively few troops involved had been agreed with General Sir David Baird and that the ships had been needed to cover the vast Atlantic to ensure that no counter-attack could come from that direction. The inclement weather they experienced was exceptional, the total loss of a Transport ship with all lives was not something that could have been foreseen. Beresford, writing to Wyndham, had explained his reasons for begging the replacement men taken from St.Helena with the full agreement of the Governor.

Grenville is angry at Fox's intervention and tries to take the question over. "Why is there nothing from St.Helena's Governor? Surely handing over seven hundred of his men for an operation right away from their designated posts is something he should be telling you about! Suppose there were an attack now on the island?"

The Duke of Grafton, a previous First Minister and supporter of the late Lord Rockingham considers himself one of the few "King's Friends" still in power. He expresses the views which he believes His Majesty would support:

"I agree, My Lord. Additionally, I have heard that Sir David Baird has arranged for some two thousand men of the 38th and 47th Regiments to be sent from the Cape together with artillery and two Squadrons of the Light Division."

Lord Grenville is appalled to hear this. He knows it is true having just received the information himself. But where do these fellows gain their Intelligence? It does not help him in the Commons when opponents are so well informed.

"Dammit Wyndham!" He turns back to his War Minister, "this is a situation that is growing out of hand. These despatches were written two months ago. All sorts of things could have happened. This is precisely what I warned everyone about! Popham was sent with generous weaponry to capture and hold the Cape. What the devil does he think he's doing dancing off to the Americas on some damned foolish capers of his own!"

The Foreign Secretary repeats his shock. "There is also the problem of Popham's friends. With respect I would comment that Mr. Pitt was able to control them but now that we have lost him…" He leaves the se ntence unfinished. Grenville knows that what he says is true. Pitt was close to the King and in many ways they worked together, hand in glove. He knows that His Majesty detests Mr. Fox but he has had to be invited to join Grenville's Cabinet so that it can survive.

Grenville worries about Mr. Fox's aggression. He remembers the difficulties over the Stamp Act when the King supported the American Colonists on the assumption that it would end their moves towards Independence.

"You will have to take him in hand, Wyndham. His siblings in Parliament will be protecting his corner but, My God! Doesn't he realize we are fighting a war for our very existence against Bonaparte? We are spreading ourselves too thinly!"

Wyndham is cowed. He has never seen the First Minister in such a fury. "I shall ascertain from Sir David Baird what resources he needs to hold the Cape. The excess can be sent to the River Plate until the area is calm and fully under control. Then they can be brought back and sent to serve under Sir John Moore."

Fox shakes his head in exasperation, the chins continue wobbling even when he stops. "And St.Helena? Get the troops back! But I believe Sir John is in need of those men now. They are not to be squandered away in the River Plate like this! And – if we should happen to be successful there, against the Spanish, what then? – The Colonists will have to be encouraged to set themselves up! We really do not have the resources to defend them."

The meeting is in agreement that it is not in the Crown's interests to retain these lands although their independence from Spain should be encouraged.

Lord Wyndham hides his dissatisfaction. Lord Grenville has not really supported him and too many other opinions have been allowed expression.

Chapter 16

Lauchlin cannot avoid being impressed with the estate at Ibicoy, He is just settling his men in a large barn about three hundred metres from the main house which is a splendid building. Someone he assumes is a kind of senior House servant, wearing the clothing that appears to be symptomatic of the country, right down to the smooth leather boots, has directed them here and by signs indicates that their food will be brought out to them shortly after nine o'clock. He leaves a lighted oil lamp hanging from a central rafter. Lauchlin knows that his men prefer to eat earlier and had been trying to enlist Father Ignacio's help.

The monk had screwed up his eyes as he thought the problem through. "That might be...little... *dificil!*. I mentioned they normally live in Buenos Aires. Here there is only limited staff and they have meals all planned. Could your men not make an exception today?"

He had turned to Matthews. "Look Sergeant, I don't want to make difficulties with this important family. It's extraordinarily kind of them to feed us and I think we're all going to have to wait."

"That's all right sir. We're not children. What's it likely to be?" His warm, North American tones appealed to the priest, who quickly answered.

"I can tell you *seguramente* what it will be: *Puchero!* That is kind of thick soup boiled up with masses of beef and vegetables. It is a staple with the gauchos and very popular!"

There had been murmurs of approval from all round the barn. Matthews asked if they should offer to go up to the house to collect it.

"No, no. It will be cold and raining. They are used to delivering meals out to the workers and their families. They have big iron boxes filled with hay and the bread baskets will be covered."

"Goodness Gracious," had come a Highland voice from a corner, "it sounds like Heaven has arrived to whisk me awa'!"

As the monk departed he turned quietly to Lauchlin. "I shall see you up at the house at perhaps ten minutes before the hour?"

"How formal will the dinner be? I only have my present uniform!"

"Oh there will not be *inspeccion* – it will be good to be clean, *quizas!*"

"And I have no little gift for the ladies, no flowers, no special trinket."

"I don't think that will matter – it is a normal family dinner…unless, quizas, some small military memento – a button perhaps!"

There is a gust of wind as he leaves. A couple of them heave on the big doors to close out the weather. There is a rumble of thunder and they hear the first rain drops spattering on the ground outside. Sergeant Matthews calls out: "Who'd rather be outside in this then?" Someone else starts to sing *"For he's a jolly good fellow…"* Matthews takes him quietly aside. "Let me have your jacket and your boots, sir. I'll see they're brushed and polished. Can't have an officer turning up all dishevelled!"

Just before the appointed hour, there is a discreet knocking on the door. Lauchlin is being inspected by Sergeant Matthews as he examines a spare uniform button. The doors are dragged open. A lad of perhaps eleven is waiting for him with a large cape and an oil lamp on a rod. He is dressed in somewhat grubby white clothes but what catches Lauchlin's eye is a large necklace around his neck. Subsequently he learns with shock that it is the mark of a slave. As he steps out he finds that the rain has eased but the youth insists on spreading the cape over him. The boy wears rope-soled canvas slip-ons several sizes too large which are clearly soaked through. The house is illuminated with a number of lamps although some windows are flickering with light suggesting a copious use of candles.

The young lad knocks on the front door which is opened immediately by another man in gaucho clothes but they are much smarter – the shirt seems to be of silk and the boots are in the softest black leather. He bows to Lauchlin but ignores the waif who escorted him. He waves a hand in dismissal.

*"Andate, Ticho. Sali de aqui!"** He takes Lauchlin's cap and shows him into a warm salon with a blazing log fire. The room is lit only by candles. Father Ignacio is there before him and explains that the family will

congregate here and go into the dining room together. Then he explains quietly that the Spanish *Grande* he had mentioned before will be present.

Large double doors at the end swing open and the youth who gave them such a rough reception earlier stands there. He holds both doors open and makes no move to come in. Finally his lips part in a welcoming smile but his sharp, penetrating blue eyes are wary. Lauchlin gives a small bow *"Juan Manuel, un placer!"*

He remembers this word from his lesson earlier as it is so close to the English 'pleasure'. Juan Manuel makes a remark that Lauchlin finds unintelligible but from the manner in which it is delivered it is presumably pleasant. His long, blonde hair is oiled and the beginnings of a moustache are just discernible. He is wearing a rather ornate tapestry jacket under which a pale silk shirt can be seen. His loose silken trousers hang over ankle-length boots in black leather which shine like a mirror. He squats to warm his hands at the fire and speaks to the monk who replies before turning to Lauchlin and translating: "He says the rain is very welcome for the grass."

"Don Leon was very accurate in his prediction, my men are most grateful for your hospitality."

The Father translates but before he has finished, Juan Manuel nods his head dismissively and stands up with a torrent of Spanish.

The monk translates. "He says it is a very basic need for anyone caring for the land and its animals to be able to read the weather."

Lauchlin is left to wonder if there is a touch of jealous condescension in the comment. But the doors are opened again and a man around Lauchlin's age enters. He is immaculately dressed in evening clothes that are probably up to the minute in Madrid or Paris. Long, thin legs are beautifully encased in lilac britches frogged down the sides and ending in pale cream stockings tucked into light evening shoes. He fixes Lauchlin with a gaze that makes no pretence of cordiality. The monk moves forward and speaks in Spanish.

"Don Bernardo de Amuñecar y Valencia, may I introduce Lieutenant Lauchlin Mackinnon?" The Spaniard looks down his nose and turns to the monk.

"Mackinnon *de adonde?"* Lauchlin knows enough of the language to guess that it is a question regarding his ancestry. He bows and replies "de Glasgow y Edinburgh, Excelencia!"

The situation is saved by the entry of Don Leon with a lady on each arm. Remembering the monk's words, Lauchlin assumes that one is his wife, the other his mother-in-law. Don Leon gives a short bow to his guests and escorts the older lady to a small arm-chair. She is dressed entirely in black, her grey hair piled high under a prominent comb. She takes out a black fan but does not open it. She taps one of the arms and leans back to gaze proudly at Lauchlin. He recognizes the source of the piercing eyes and bows to her and repeats his phrase again:

"Doña Valenciana, un placer". Don Bernardo struts over to her and gives a formal bow as he kisses her hand.

She emits something between a groan and a grunt. Don Leon introduces his wife: "Doña Agustina."

She smiles and nods her head towards Lauchlin, "Un honor, Señor!" Lauchlin stores that word away as another one that should be easy to remember. She is wearing a dark, silk formal dress with a lace mantilla over her shoulders. She smiles up at her husband and murmurs a short phrase.

The door from the hall is suddenly opened and a young woman hurries in evidently later than planned. She holds her head down until near her father when she pauses, seeming to express an apology. Lauchlin has the impression that he tries to express a disapproval for her tardiness that he does not entirely feel. He senses rather than sees a mischievous understanding between father and daughter. What can that be about? He glances quickly at the Spaniard. His mouth is set in a straight line – his lips pursed reminding Lauchlin of Agnes their neighbour back in Glasgow. Then he gives her a formal smile and kisses her hand with the slightest shake of his head. Lauchlin thinks this is a daughter who can do no wrong in her father's eyes but he finds the Spaniard a mystery. He does not seem to be a soldier.

This will be the sister, Alicia. As she turns towards him he sees a young woman with fair skin but an appearance that loves the outdoors and fresh air. Her hair is long but dressed up as if to fit under a cap or riding hat. Her dress is formal, ankle-length in dark blue silk over a white blouse whose collar can just be seen. He feels a physical kick in his chest. She is not beautiful in the formal sense but has a striking yet humourous expression that appeals to him He reminds himself she is the daughter of a proud family, a creole, possibly destined to marry a Spanish grandee; but he likes the twinkle in her eye and cannot avoid the thought that she is truly beautiful. He bows to her repeating "Señorita Alicia Daniela."

She stands behind her grandmother's chair and looks him straight in the eye. She has the same direct and somewhat disconcerting stare. "Sub-altern Mackiñon!" Her accent is poor and she pronounces his rank as if it were a German phrase, then stresses the final syllable of his surname but it is a brave effort and Lauchlin's face breaks into a smile as he bows again in admiration. The major-domo in the silk shirt opens another set of double doors at the side and announces: *"Don Leon, se sirve la cena."*

Lauchlin hangs back while Don Leon leads in the two ladies; Alicia takes the Spaniard's arm. Father Ignacio stands beside him and says "I will sit near to you."

It is a very pleasant, family-sized room with furniture that reminds him of the castle state rooms in Edinburgh. One window at the side is heavily curtained and the table and chairs are in a substantial, dark timber with seats in fine tapestry. There are two polished brass, oil lamps illuminating the room, one at each end and a candelabra of six candles is set in the centre of the table, again in polished brass. Don Leon's chair at the head is held by the major-domo while Juan Manuel stands behind his Grandmother's ready to help her in on Don Leon's right hand. Alicia is opposite her on her father's left with Don Bernardo beside her. Lauchlin finds himself sitting on Doña Agustina's left with the monk opposite him and next to the Spaniard. Juan Manuel takes his chair alongside Lauchlin. The table is set with lace mats and generous, linen serviettes. A small vase of flowers is positioned at each end. Father Ignacio moves to the head of the room to pronounce the Grace in Latin then returns to his seat.

Two dark-skinned serving maids sweep in with the first course: a selection of thinly sliced, cold meats. They are dressed in clean, white dresses but have the same, small chains around their necks. All the cutlery is in gleaming silver and Lauchlin reminds himself: *From the outside inwards.* Two wine glasses sit at each place setting and a white wine is poured while one of the maids comes round with a basket of small loaves. He takes the opportunity to study the necklace more closely. It is very strange. Can it really be a mark of slavery?

Lauchlin is surprised to find the wine sweet but thinks it goes fairly well with the meats which he considers delicious as he realizes how hungry he is. They are salty but not excessively so and the red colour which dominates leads him to think that there is a lot of blood in the recipe. He is careful not to praise the food at that stage remembering his Uncle Drysdale's training that the wealthy always assume the food will be of the best and make no comment. Don Bernardo hardly touches the first course.

Doña Agustina who had been served with a very small helping notices Lauchlin's enjoyment. "These meats are all from our own cattle and processed within our butchery at Rosario." After this has been translated, Lauchlin feels able to comment how delicious he had found them.

She beams with pleasure. "The recipes are our own and Juan Manuel is trying to perfect the production so that we can have them more widely known."

Lauchlin nods his understanding and turns to compliment the young man, but Doña Agustina smiles again and asks a question which is translated by the monk: "How long are you staying in this country?"

He replies that he is uncertain. His country is at war with Spain and they have come to the River Plate merely to cut off that source of wealth.

Don Bernardo leans across and asks what their intentions are regarding the people of the country.

"Oh to the best of my knowledge it is our aim to free the people of the River Plate from the Spanish yoke so that they may pursue their own aims and, hopefully, that they will retain goodwill for the British nation that enabled them to achieve this situation!"

The Spaniard almost chokes. "In that case why are you some fifty miles from Buenos Aires, fully armed and mapping the country? There are no Spanish soldiers here! You are spying."

Doña Agustina gently chides Don Bernardo. He shakes his head and looks down at his plate. Juan Manuel takes a similar line causing Don Leon to speak more abruptly and his son has to accept that. Later the priest mentions that Don Leon had told his son that one could never have too many friends and that the British might well help them achieve their ambitions both in the business and as a nation.

The serving maids come back into the room almost staggering under the weight of a large tureen which they place on the sideboard. The major-domo returns with a decanter of red wine from which he pours a small amount into everyone's glass. He hands the decanter to one of the maids who takes it away, presumably for replenishment, while he occupies himself with the tureen.

Using the monk to translate her words, Doña Agustina comments that the wine is also made in their own *Bodega.* Once more Lauchlin nods his enthusiasm. The old lady, Doña Valenciana, looks up and announces: "It was my husband's *Bodega,* he was rightly proud of our vines – until he was killed by the savages!" As she speaks she glares at the serving maids.

"Now Mother, you know all that is in the past; we work very well with them now."

His mother-in-law glowers down at her plate: "You are foolish to trust them."

With just a hint of bad temper, Juan Manuel turns to Lauchlin, "You are eating and drinking the finest food in the world. Make sure you remember it but not so much that you decide to stay! I will not pretend that we are not glad to have the Spanish banished but..."

Don Bernardo raises his glass to the light studying its colour. "Not all Spanish I hope..."

Don Leon smiles benignly as he interrupts: "Now then, gentlemen, this officer is our guest it behoves us all to be welcoming."

Don Bernardo looks across and says in passable English: "You are a *Teniente,* I think. I was a *Mayor*!"

Lauchlin looks directly across at him. "In that case, Sir, I salute you!"

The next course, the *Puchero* mentioned earlier by Father Ignacio, is served. Lauchlin sees a thick soup with potatoes and vegetables which gives off a wonderful aroma. Most prominent, however, is a knuckle of bone with beef still adhering to it. He tells the monk that this is the first time he has seen this dish and, to general amusement, he replies "Just wait until you taste it!"

Lauchlin watches to see how the dish is being eaten. They use a soup spoon for the liquid but a knife and fork for the more substantial items. But he is astonished to see them use a long, thin spoon for the bone marrow. The monk murmurs "you must get right inside and enjoy it with a dash of salt!" At the end, any greasy fingers are wiped clean by the majordomo leading all the serving staff in attending with a silver dish of rosewater and a linen doily. That concludes the meal and, as the ladies prepare to leave the room, Alicia holds up her glass of red wine in Lauchlin's direction and with a heavy accent pronounces in English "God save the King!" There is no irony in the phrase and everyone, except Don Bernardo who ignores the comment, gives a light chuckle. As she leaves she has to pass Lauchlin's chair. He looks at her and raises his glass: "Thank you Señorita." The others are largely involved in assisting the old lady to leave the room. Lauchlin bows and hands over the polished button – "A small memento." As he steals another look he murmurs quietly in English, "I wish it were more". She stands so near that he is conscious of her delicate perfume.

She responds with a whisper in the same language, "It will be treasured." But Don Bernardo has been watching. He rises and snatches the button which he flings across the room.

The men move up to Don Leon's end of the table and their glasses are refilled as the majordomo goes round with a cigar box and cutter. The Priest murmurs "these are not from the estate, we do not grow tobacco." It is another new experience for Lauchlin and once again he carefully observes the manner and conduct of his hosts. Coffee follows served in small porcelain cups. Don Leon looks at the smouldering end of his cigar and says "I like to do these things in the European style." Then gives a light chuckle, "Juan Manuel prefers to end his meal with a *mate.*"

Don Bernardo looks quietly at his coffee cup before murmuring rudely. "You have no idea! Only in Spain are matters arranged properly!"

The son soon pushes back his chair and stands. He holds the gourd of the *mate* in his left hand and holds out his right to Lauchlin. "Goodbye" he says in passable English, "I think we shall likely meet again." Then puts his mouth close to Lauchlin's ear and adds "Confounded Spaniards!" He says a casual goodnight to Don Bernardo and embraces his father, kissing him on both cheeks. As he leaves the room, he turns and adds: "It is perhaps as *Sietemesina* foretells!" He laughs as if at the Spaniard's expense but Don Bernardo merely glowers, saying nothing.

Lauchlin stays standing, looking enquiringly at the Priest. Father Ignacio shakes his head. "*Sietemesina La Vieja* is an elderly woman who makes ungodly predictions. The people should not listen."

Don Leon looks up. "You know she was old when I was a boy. How old can she be?" Then looking directly at Lauchlin he adds, she is an old witch, part Moorish, part indigenous, part gaucho and, yes maybe, part Spanish." The priest translates though clearly unhappy.

Don Leon continues, she lives alone and the people consult her. They give her food." As the priest intervenes Don Leon cuts him off, "No no, Father, she has said many strange things that have come to pass." He pours himself a drop more wine, "she is the reason I cannot clear those wretched Indians off my land!"

Lauchlin bows and s ays, "I must not overstay my welcome. Please convey my grateful thanks to Don Leon and say that I hope I may be of service to him some day." The Spaniard makes a rude noise but does not rise. The Father frowns but nods before translating and adding "yes, I understand you will want to get back to your men, Francisco will give you the drawings and maps you wanted. You will find Ticho waiting to escort you" With renewed thanks and another bow to his host, Lauchlin leaves the room. He finds the land-agent waiting for him with his cap and cape and carrying a leather case. Stealing a glance at the old clock in the hall, he is astonished to see it is nearly midnight. Francisco opens the door to him and bows. The youth with the wet feet awaits him outside.

As they walk smartly to the barn, Lauchlin says : *"Tu, Ticho?"*

Ticho looks at him startled. He says nothing but half nods his head. Lauchlin repeats the phrase to make sure he has it right. This time the reaction is marked.

"Si, Ticho. Esclavo de jardin."

As they reach the barn he smiles and looks at Ticho and says: *"Muchas gracias!"* Back inside he finds the men asleep but Matthews slides up to him with a silent questioning look. Using the oil lamp, he cannot resist showing him the full display of maps presented to him. He will try to discuss the issue of slavery with someone in the morning and, particularly, the difference between house slaves and field slaves. Presumably a garden slave like Ticho lies somewhere in between. He knows that in Britain the issue is being debated. Meanwhile, his priority must be to get the maps to General Beresford as soon as possible.

Chapter 17

In Buenos Aires the Vice Admiral sits in a large chair at the dining table where he has just eaten an indifferent lunch. He stares at General Beresford while his hands idly twirl the stem of a wine glass. He turns his head to look out of one of the small *Cabildo* windows and thinks over what they have been discussing.

"Don't these wretched people see what we've done for them? We've sent their oppressors away and are allowing them virtual self-government!"

"I fear they don't altogether see it like that, Admiral. They are beginning to wonder if they have exchanged one set of oppressive rulers for another."

"Oppressive rulers! That's hardly the thing is it. How many men did we come with? Barely a handful and we have the prospect of conquering a land mass the size of Western Europe!" His hands clench open and closed. "Does that not prove how welcome we are?"

"Mmm. - the limited number of troops at my disposal is one of my principal concerns. If they decide the price of our presence here is too great they may rise and throw us out!" He stands and stares out of the same window. "I am conscious of the main Spanish army which this Captain Liniers is training at Montevideo. I have a report from a scouting party saying that they number at least fifteen hundred men. Please excuse me for a moment." He hurries out of the room to his office where he picks up a manila file and returns.

"I've had another complaint from Puerridon. As you will recall he's one of the leading Councillors. He states that our constant demands for gold and silver plate are stripping some of the poorer people down to unprecedented levels."

"Oh for God's Sake!... People are forever moaning about taxes. Can't they see it's only right that we should receive some compensation for everything we've laid out for this operation? I would expect them at least to pay the costs of our soldiers! Why should they not pay for their own defence? What's more, I'm hoping for great things when the London merchants see the opportunities for setting up here. I've written to a number of them, you know. Make your fortune!"

Beresford nods and says quietly: "Yes, I've heard." He also recalls that it was precisely the tax to cover the costs of the British troops that started the whole business of the American War.

Popham steals a quick look at him but says nothing. There is a quiet knock on the door and Major Dirleton comes in.

"Excuse me, Gentlemen, but Major Urquhart has come in with his latest report. I feel you would wish to hear it at once."

Beresford immediately stands. "Good - James Urquhart is a specialist in interpreting political intelligence. I sent him to Montevideo to get some views of their thinking on the other side of the river."

Home Popham chuckles sarcastically. His humour has not been restored. "I always say, Beresford, you worry too much. I don't give a tinker's cuss about what people the other side of the river think!"

Beresford looks again at the despatch. "It is my practice to try and see ahead. There is talk of troops – and ships – massing at Colonia, here, West of Montevideo." He tries to show him the map but the Vice Admiral is not interested.

"Major Urquhart is a special envoy of the Minister's. His opinions are respected. He was a delegate at the Amiens Conference."

"And my word didn't we do well there! God we gave away everything we'd won!"

The door opens again and Major Urquhart is shown in. He stamps his feet to attention. Beresford offers him a chair. "Come in James, good to see you again. Now what have you to report?"

Urquhart is a studious looking man. More professorial than military in appearance. He has a heavy Glaswegian accent that immediately arouses Popham's antagonism.

"I went across in civilian clothes, General. As you know my Spanish is reasonable but my accent would have given me away. I therefore said little or nothing but simply looked and listened."

Home Popham chuckles again with contempt. "I bet you stood out like the proverbial sore thumb. They will have said exactly what they wanted you to hear!"

Urquhart is unmoved. Wisps of grey hair betrays an age beyond that of most serving officers. "That is, of course, very possible, Sir. But I was also able to observe great movement in the port area and there were numerous indications of armed militia, including their weapons, assembling just off the city centre. Their commander appears to be a Captain Santiago de Liniers, I'm uncertain whether he is Spanish or a Creolle. One report holds that he is, actually, French. But they seem to be quite enthusiastic about him. He's a Naval Captain, of course. I believe he was in Buenos Aires originally but is now in Colonia. I believe they are planning to sail across the river, Admiral, or hug the coast, they have fishermen who are cunning seamen, familiar with the river's shoals and banks."

Beresford pulls another letter from his file. "I have a despatch here from one of the small forces I sent out. Lieutenant Carnegie has written that there seems to be a similar massing in the area of Pedriel, about twenty miles to the south of us."

"Well, you'll have to deal with them Beresford. I issued an order two weeks ago that massed demonstrations are illegal."

"The troops will not be keen on firing upon civilians. You can be confident that we will do our duty but Spanish soldiers are one thing – civilians may be another!"

"Civilians! Where do you think they are getting their weapons from? Probably got nothing but a few scythes and the odd catapult!" He stands up. "I'm returning to the flagship. I must say that I am disappointed in the lack of optimism shown to me this day. The army seems determined to see an enemy around every corner. I would have wished for better. I will bid you good day!" With that rebuke Home Popham takes his hat and leaves the room.

Later that day General Beresford calls an urgent meeting of his senior staff and, while they are convening, sits to write a despatch to the Admiral in the flag-ship. It is copied to London.

Buenos Aires, 31st July 1806

Sir,

I have the honour to acquaint you with details of further information sent to this office this afternoon.

I am advised that something of the order of 2,500 men are drawn up at Pedriel Point with artillery, and are waiting to march to the relief of this city. I am therefore taking as many of the troops as I deem safe, to engage them before they have the opportunity to form up.

May I further advise that indications are that a fleet upwards of twenty vessels with militia and light artillery is being prepared at Colonia to cross the river and join up with the Pedriel force. At this time there is no indication whether they are Spanish or Platine in origin. May I respectfully ask for this fleet to be attacked and prevented from crossing.

God Save the King.
I have the honour to be
Sir
Your obedient Servant
(Sgd.} William Carr Beresford, Major General.

Having sent the Despatch, Beresford loses no time in attending the Staff meeting, following which orders go out to all officers with details of the situation.

Beresford is disappointed at this turn of events. He had hoped that his relationships with the Council were good enough to secure the colonists' co-operation in building up their own defences against the Spanish leaving the British to consider either a withdrawal or further advances elsewhere.

Although Puerridon had tended to go along with this overall plan, there were elements in the Council who were strongly opposed to them. In particular Martin de Alzaga led a group of the wealthier merchants to whom the loss of the Spanish market was ruinous. For some time they had been meeting in secret trying to fathom ways of restoring the old Viceroy. Supreme among these plans was the arming and training of the local militia. Madrid had been recommending such a course of action for at least three years but the Viceroy had been nervous about too many weapons in circulation. Distribution of them and training in their use was now set strongly in motion.

Martin de Alzaga has been plotting an additional scheme to terrorize the occupying army. From a house on the corner of the *Plaza Mayor* he had begun the construction of a tunnel which would enable a large *cache* of explosives to be placed under the area of Beresford's office. His haste in having this carried out causes its discovery. At seven each morning, after the *seven o'clock and all's well* tradition, the 26th Rifles carry out a guard-changing drill which often draws a small crowd of observers. An altercation breaking out between a nurse/governess with two children and a supervisor of slaves removing soil to a wagon around the corner exposes the scheme. The woman is angry at the dirty pavement and calls a soldier who reports the matter to a sergeant. Alzaga denies any knowledge of the diggings but the plans for moving the troops from Montevideo are advanced. These have started with the landing at Pedriel Point which is demanding Beresford's immediate attention.

After making disposition for the continued defence of the city, the number of troops Beresford is able to muster total five hundred and fifty. With two paid guides the army sets out in frosty air at two o'clock in the morning. It is now 1st August. They are accompanied by six guns drawn by twelve horses. At best marching speed of the Light Infantry battalions, they cover the twenty or so miles in under six hours. Beresford's vanguard informs him that the enemy is composed of a mix of Spanish army clerks and locally trained militia who have ten guns set up on a small hill overlooking a pebble beach, clearly assuming an attack from the river.

Without giving the men a pause for breakfast, Beresford orders an immediate engagement. With the lately-risen sun shining directly into his eyes, he studies the dispositions through a telescope. He is satisfied that the guns are trained in the wrong direction and decides on a full frontal open order of march. The enemy troops are busy clearing up after their breakfast with many of their weapons stacked in fours out of reach. With maximum fire and reload the British advance up the hill to a scene of confusion. The battle is soon over. Within twenty minutes the enemy forces have broken and abandoned their position leaving their cannon at Beresford's disposal. He walks the ground with Major Dirleton, shaking his head.

"This is a bad business, John. They have over a hundred dead and we have – none. See that all the wounded are properly attended to, ours and theirs, and send our men to breakfast. I fear this morning's tragedy will reverberate on us!"

"The Spanish are not the best of fighting men, sir. The locals seem to be much more aggressive."

Beresford is angered by the comment. "For God's sake, John! Look at the age of the Spanish – they're not soldiers – probably civil servants and customs men, switched here at short notice. Remember, it's about thirty years since any shipping was allowed in here. It was all the Vice-Royalty of Peru! The only shipping coming in here would have been smugglers!" He kicks a stone out of the way. "I was trying to establish a relationship with Puerridon – this will have scotched it!"

As he re-mounts he turns back to say: "And where's this Liniers? He'll be coming along from Colonia – we need intelligence. Where's Urquhart? We must get up to speed and tackle the next lot!" So, accompanied by little more than his staff officers he returns to the city. All are in a depressed frame of mind.

Two days later, Beresford learns that Captain Santiago de Liniers has crossed from Colonia, near Montevideo, with thirty small ships and two transports loaded with men and weapons. Their fleet chose a dark night without a light being seen and quite unobserved by Popham and his ships in the bay. Liniers's force lands at eight o'clock in the morning principally on the pebble beach below Señor Carnero's village at Las Conchas.

Once again Beresford prepares his men to move out and attack before the enemy can establish their position. This time the weather plays a defining role. Torrential rain and gale-force winds make travel almost impossible.

As well as spreading their tents around the area, Liniers and his troops occupy the buildings used by Lauchlin's men barely two weeks earlier. But Lauchlin is now some fifty miles north of the landings and knows nothing about them. He is battened down in tents using the steep bank of the river to gain some protection from the howling wind. Sergeant Matthews makes an attempt to post sentries at guard points but is forced by the weather to keep everyone together.

Floods and mud prevent the movement of heavy equipment and guns, but individual militia men from Buenos Aires are joined by others who escaped from the fighting at Pedriel and manage to join Liniers on his difficult march towards the city. Somehow he contrives to send a message to Beresford, informing him that the whole city has now risen and that the British forces should surrender immediately to prevent further bloodshed and avoid unnecessary damage to the buildings. It contains an assurance that the troops, and British traders who followed them, will be allowed to make an orderly withdrawal to their ships. Beresford is out inspecting his Western guard but hurries back to receive the emissary in his office. While composing a defiant response, he learns that his northern city outpost has already been over-run and fallen to Liniers.

The British form a strong defensive line using the fort as a base and watch-tower. On the night of 11th August, Beresford orders that the wounded together with the women and children and civilian British should be embarked. He sends a despatch to Home Popham advising that they plan to fight for two more days until the night of 13th August when he anticipates a strong march to the shelving beach at Ensenada, to the south, and he asks for ships' boats to assemble there under the protection of the ships' guns so that he may embark the army.

Urgent messages of recall need to be sent to all his outlying detachments. Dragoon James Buchanan is one of those summoned. He is young and fresh-faced but a determined soldier. All are given a detailed briefing, explaining the full situation. Buchanan is shown the maps together with an explanation of where Lauchlin's troop is likely to be found. But he is given nothing in writing – no despatches which, if captured by the Spanish, would betray the British plans.

Without exception, the cavalrymen are given one final order: "Just remember, you must get yourselves back here in time or you'll be left behind!"

Buchanan leaves at once. The darkness, the wind and the rain are his friends as he must somehow pass by the massed enemy troops making their way from the landing at Las Conchas. With perhaps over sixty miles to travel before he can hope to meet up with Lauchlin's troop, he knows he has no time to waste. In the darkness he is able to lose himself in the first of Liniers's troops making their way towards the city but, as he approaches Las Conchas itself, the dawning day makes an anonymous passage of his red uniform, even under a large cape, much harder. He walks his horse through the massed array busy with breakfast or landing stores and equipment from boats drawn up on the small beach. Though largely dressed in green, it is apparent even in the poor light of early morning that not all are in the Spanish uniform. Many are militia – civilians trained up to be of support in loading guns and even firing upon the foreign invaders.

With his cap removed and by keeping his head down he progresses well. He had asked Beresford about the possibility of leaving the main track and travelling cross-country but this would have been so much slower that the point of the mission could have been lost. For a brief moment he considers returning and reporting that he had been unable to find them. But he calls himself back to his duty and presses forward. In the melee of troops he is able to pass through Las Conchas itself with barely a shouted greeting and the track then becomes quieter although small groups of outlying Spanish and locals are still moving down to join the main force. The growing daylight enables him to move faster but he has been trained over several years to conserve the energies of his horse. After perhaps thirty minutes' cantering, and the occasional gallop, he walks for an equivalent amount of time. He would like to make a thirty minute halt to rest the animal properly – even to water and rub him down - but the risk of being observed is too great as is the exchanging of the animal for a fresh, local mount.

After one such stop he is climbing back into the saddle when a group of three *gauchos t*ravelling down from the Rosas *estancia* challenges him. Buchanan feels his only hope is to push his heels into his horse's side and hope to out-run them. But it is a short race. Their animals are fresh and one soon rides level with him and, with a cheery laugh, leans across and grasps his reins.

They soon realize he is British. Although they were not involved with Lauchlin's visit it had been a source of much speculation. They decide to take him up to the foreman. This is the individual Lauchlin thought of as the land agent. Buchanan is frantic at the loss of time and tries to explain his situation but it is all dismissed with a laugh and much nodding in agreement.

They soon meet up with Francisco, the foreman. The family returned to Buenos Aires two days ago and he is now in charge. He has just been informed about the landings at Las Conchas and was arranging to go and investigate. The sight of three of his *peones* bringing up a prisoner at first alarms him. He insists on Buchanan sitting and telling him exactly what he is doing there.

Language is an insoluble problem at first. Buchanan is so taken up with the urgency of his mission that he fails to think about the best way of communicating. Eventually he mentions the name Mackinnon and the foreman becomes intrigued. He gradually absorbs Buchanan's orders and the need for urgency. He knows exactly where the detachment has been bivouacked. In fact he has followed their progress ever since they slept in his barn. He makes a gesture with his hand trying to indicate six hours to reach them but is uncertain whether that message is understood. He orders one of the men to fetch a fresh horse and to saddle it up with Buchanan's equipment. He is instructed to guide the cavalryman to where his colleagues can probably be found.

In the event they meet up with Lauchlin by noon. The southern sentry notes their approach when they are still a mile distant and rides in to sound the alarm. The troop has fallen out for a meal while Lauchlin sketches in what he thinks could be the final point of his advance. When about four hundred yards away, Buchanan starts to shout, waving his cap. He clatters into their midst nearly hysterical with his exhaustion tinged with relief.

"We are commanded to withdraw immediately sir!" He calls out even before dismounting and jogs up to Lauchlin. "Orders from the General, sir, the army is withdrawing to the ships. All are ordered to make the best possible speed back to the city by tomorrow evening at the latest – if you arrive after that the ships will have gone without you!"

"Buchanan!" Matthews is incensed. "How dare you speak to an officer like that! Pull yourself together. You know better than to shriek out to the world! Who is this you've brought with you?"

Buchanan's training soon calms him down and he explains the situation. Lauchlin intervenes and with Sergeant Matthews at his side, questions the young dragoon. He explains how he was detained by workers from the Rosas ranch who lent him the fresh horse and guide.

Lauchlin welcomes the gaucho and invites him to share their meal. After examining their dried meat and biscuit he politely refuses. Buchanan explains about the strong Spanish forces at Las Conchas. Lauchlin speaks quietly with Matthews and decides to brief the detachment.

"We shall make all haste to return the way we came but it may be our duty to engage the enemy when we meet up with them."

He calculates from his own survey and from recollection of the Rosas maps that they have about sixty-five miles to cover to Buenos Aires.

"From what we have been told we must get back in thirty hours. It will be a long, hard slog lads but we can do it!"

They will start by jogging the first two or three miles. Their loads are eased by placing all weapons and heavy items in the wagon. One cavalryman will scout ahead. Should he encounter any obstacle, he will ride back to inform them in time to re-possess their weapons. Lauchlin has nineteen men under his command plus five cavalrymen, including the lately arrived Buchanan. The gaucho, whom he finds is called Juancito, seems content to ride along with them. The wagon is to follow the cavalry making the best speed it can for as long as possible. Lauchlin will go behind that. Matthews will bring up the rear, ready to place any faller in the wagon. The order of march is settled and they are on their way within fifteen minutes.

In Buenos Aires, Liniers's men have over-run Beresford's outlying forces. The British are trying to form a solid defensive line from the old *Cabildo* fort right across the *Plaza Mayor* in front. The tower of the fort is filled with British sharp-shooters, much as the Colonists had used that high point. They are charged with preventing the attackers from entering. Beresford is still hoping to create a neutral zone which will ensure the safety of the townspeople and all non-combatants. Unfortunately, there are houses outside the *Plaza* overlooking the fort and even commanding its high points. Soon there are several attacking snipers positioned to pick off the men on top of the *Cabildo* building who have little to hide behind.

Liniers brings up his artillery and places them at the corners of the square where they begin firing *grape* at the lines of fusiliers drawn up in parade-ground style with the files alternating as they fire. Many of the civilian householders have joined in the battle, lying on their flat roofs, picking off isolated targets. Beresford's men suffer heavy casualties.

Eighteen fusiliers from the 2nd Battalion, Royal Scots march in single file towards their designated post on a corner overlooking the square. Reaching the edge of an alley, allowing a good view of the houses they need to cover, they suddenly suffer a hail of fire from a line of irregulars who appear before them. Eight of the fusiliers go down. Sergeant Meek immediately takes up his position at the head and raises a sword to signal the order to fire. At that critical moment, a group of women and children emerges from the houses on either side preventing the fusiliers from seeing their assailants.

With sword raised, Sergeant Meek just has time to shout "Hold your Fire!" He wonders how to rid the street of the townsfolk who have clearly come to block his view of the target. He is about to command men to charge the fifty metres to clear the way when, evidently by a pre-arranged signal, with hardly a pause, they move as one, back into the houses. The interval has allowed the militia time to re-load so that almost before the street is clear, another salvo brings down a further five of Sergeant Meek's troop. He tries to organize a responding fire when the women and children intervene again. It is a rehearsed scene which is being practised at several strategic points around the centre of the city. The British are unable to fire upon these civilians.

After half-an-hour Beresford gives the order for the white flag to be raised. Liniers orders his men to cease firing but for some of the townsfolk the order is unwelcome and is ignored. Their blood is up and, having been shamed by the quick departure of the Viceroy and his staff, they are now set on proving their own ability to gain independent control of the city. After all, some say, Liniers is a Frenchman in the pay of the Spanish. With the ending of accurate fire from Beresford's troops, the civilian militia are encouraged to greater risks and forays so that the British casualties continue to mount. There are isolated instances of troops under a white flag being fired upon resulting in their taking up their weapons again. It is a further forty minutes before Liniers gains full control and the firing ceases.

An hour later, Beresford and Liniers meet to draw up the terms of the surrender. It is somewhat galling for the British Commander to meet as a petitioner in the very office which he has been using for some weeks. The agreement is soon signed and a copy carried to the flagship. The British will relinquish all local property that has been seized and, carrying their unloaded weapons, will be escorted to the ships which will carry them away.

The Vice Admiral receives this news with mounting fury. He cannot see that it was his failure to intercept Liniers's ships that caused the terrible outcome. During the night the ships are moved to lie off Buenos Aires while the wounded are tended and carried to the beach.

At about ten o'clock that night, three members of the Ruling Council, under Ernesto Puerridon, arrive for a meeting with Liniers. He is thanked for his efforts to procure the victory but, as merely a Naval Captain, and foreign at that, his work is now complete. The Council are agreed: there is no question of any of the senior British Officers being allowed to escape; their crimes are too severe and, with something approaching three hundred of the local colonists lying dead or wounded, they must be formally indicted and tried for their crimes.

Early the next morning, Beresford, Major Dirleton and about ten of his senior staff are allowed to collect personal items before being herded into three coaches and, escorted by eight horsemen from the militia, are taken to the town of Lujan some sixty miles from Buenos Aires. They are confined under guard in five rooms with communal facilities and attended by a guard commander assisted by a chef and four cleaners.

The troops so recently fighting under their command in the streets of Buenos Aires are forced to lay down their weapons and are marched under guard for thirty-five miles where camps are being prepared to hold them. Their regimental colours are seized and put on display. In due time some will give their parole and accept freedom and an allocation of land on condition that they never again fight for the Crown. Others are eventually allowed to return to their European homes.

Vice Admiral Home Popham is able to embark a number of British wounded together with women and children and some of the traders but, other than that, he can do little but watch proceedings from afar. His ships are moved to another anchorage where the guns can do no harm and, with a heavy heart, he settles to write his despatches to London.

Chapter 18

On a blustery September morning, James Hogarth, the First Minister's Secretary opens the shutters of the Cabinet Room but leaves the windows closed. There is to be a full meeting of the War Cabinet and, as this will include the new Foreign Secretary, the Duke of Portland, Hogarth must anticipate his demands for a warmer room. They say the Duke maintains fires in all his principal rooms throughout the year.

Baron Grenville's War Cabinet meets at regular intervals in Downing Street to negotiate plans for executing the war with France which will be acceptable to the King and to the two principal parties in Parliament. Whilst all are agreed on the necessity for a full and final defeat of the new Republic, there is a gulf between them as to the methods to be employed. Always present is the War Minister Lord Wyndham.

The news is rarely good; the triple alliance of Britain, Russia and Austria has virtually collapsed with the battle of Austerlitz. Almost desperate for good news, the despatches from General Beresford dated several weeks earlier present a welcome distraction. His reports centre on the capture of Buenos Aires, the apparent overwhelming goodwill of the populace and the likely danger from Spanish troops still in Montevideo. With this background he seeks fresh instructions as to the disposition of his forces and what his attitude should be towards the colonists.

The news has been widely welcomed in the City of London. It confirms the circulars put about by Vice-Admiral Home Popham and bears out the hopes of opening the door to a major new market well away from the difficulties of the European war. Some indeed speak of the expansion of the British Empire. The agreeable news raises the Government's approval ratings so that, although always against the project, Lord Grenville now tries to make political capital from it. Commercial speculators are quick to send off samples of their wares to the traders travelling with the army, proposing partnerships in the River Plate market. Some younger sons are packed aboard ships with instructions not to return without contracts.

The Cabinet's principal business continues to be the war with Bonaparte and the battles in Corsica and other parts of the Mediterranean but Grenville hopes that they can obtain some benefit from a situation that he originally opposed on the grounds of a shortage of ships and troops.. They have now also received a copy of Beresford's appeal to Sir David Baird in the Cape where he asks for a further two thousand men and cavalry. The Cabinet learns that Sir David is to send him what he asks under Colonel Sir Samuel Auchmuty . This information is not well received and the Prime Minister's mood alters and he becomes angry and ill tempered.

"Here we go again! Having to spread ourselves too thinly. Vice Admiral Home Popham had no business circulating that news about the capture of the River Plate area! This is secret war intelligence. How dare he make pronouncements without our authority!"

Lord Wyndham privately agrees but It is his belief that Grenville would have liked to announce the news to Parliament himself.

"I have little doubt that he took such action precisely so that the merchants and even the Bank would apply pressure on us to approve this latest request for reinforcements!"

Lord Grenville taps the letters with the end of a penknife. "This is a small, far-off country of which we know little. Why-ever should we become so involved?"

"It is a fairly large country actually, my Lord and a keystone in the Spanish economy. Our troops should, perhaps, be complimented on their success."

Grenville studies his papers. "I suppose these troops from the Cape have already been sent?"

The Cabinet Secretary, James Hogarth, consults another file.

"I have no firm information on that, My Lord, but I understand that Sir Samuel Auchmuty was commanded to leave as soon as possible. Perhaps we could send him a despatch at Cape Verde, copied to St.Helena, instructing him to await further orders."

Lord Wyndham intervenes gently. "I have instructed Colonel Auchmuty to place himself under the command of General Beresford and to aid him in securing the area. But I have stressed that as soon as possible the troops should return to the Cape. Should, by chance, the situation have changed and Beresford be in difficulties he is to do what he can to correct the position. I have made clear that we have no wish either to antagonize the Colonists or the Spanish since we cannot open another theatre of war in South America. But, if possible, he should leave the Colonists with a good feeling about the British; encourage the traders and, finally, the defensive force for St.Helena should return as soon as practicable."

"That's another thing!" Grenville explodes again, "What did the Governor - Mayhew is it - think he was doing letting seven hundred of his trained men go off on such a wild goose chase!" He continues muttering to himself then bursts out: "I am minded to recall the three of them, Baird, Popham and, yes, even Mayhew! If they're not fit for office they should be replaced. Popham, in particular, should face a Court Martial for thinking up the whole scheme in the first place! Admiral Murray should replace him."

There is some discussion on this role; after all, it seems probable that the operation has been a roaring success. It is decided to try and hold all the reinforcements until such time as Admiral Murray can review the situation and make proper and long-term disposition.

The Duke of Portland, ever the calming influence, speaks gently reminding the First Minister that an attack on Spain's American empire was once favoured by William Pitt.

"Sir, your predecessor was himself half-minded to allow such an undertaking ...and Mr.Secretary Dundas.... And other friends of Popham's in Parliament will not easily give way, particularly since the affair seems to have been so well managed and crowned with success.." Is it Grenville's imagination or did the wretched fellow lay a special stress on the word 'crowned'? *Yes,* he thinks, *the King may well like it and in his present sick condition force us to throw everything in to secure an enlargement of his empire.*

"Ah, Parliamentary friends...yes. I wonder whether it is not time for General Fox to be recalled from the Med., things are not going so well there, are they!"

Another Minister murmurs quietly, "General Fox indeed." He looks across at Lord Wyndham, "Would you not consider General Moore a more suitable commander?"

Lord Grenville bends studiously to his papers. There is almost a sly look on his face as he intervenes:

"As you may know, Mr. Charles Fox is strangely opposed to re-joining this administration. It might be good if his relatives have cause to complain about his behaviour!"

There is an unpleasant chuckle from across the table.

"Sir John Moore is achieving great things under Fox," Wyndham muses in reply, "if we are serious about recalling Fox we need a good man there to replace him. The Duke of York has many thoughts on the matter but I am not privy to his final decision. There's Abercrombie and Dalrymple – and Wellesley, of course...and..."

Grenville interrupts. "Wellesley's a good Staff and planning man. I'm not sure he'd be good enough in the field! Just remind me of the position of Sam Auchmuty's troops. They were originally to go to the Plate but we recalled them for the Portuguese invasion. Now that we've cancelled that... they could be held at St.Helena as suggested or...yes, sent to the Plate. But it must be understood, it's only a holding situation! We're not taking over in the Plate. We'll help them to independence – it's in our interests, of course, to weaken Spain's economy since that may encourage them to join us, but we cannot commit sufficient troops to defend them if Spain attacks again – let alone France! In the meantime, how do the discussions go between Cornwallis and the Spanish, will she join the Coalition against Napoleon?"

The meeting returns to its original agenda.

Chapter 19

By alternately marching in quick time and double time, resting that first night at Ibicoy for a total of just three hours, Lauchlin believes they have a good chance of achieving their objective. It has not been easy and has called for discipline and resolve. After three hours one of his Fusiliers had been clearly about to drop. Lauchlin refused his pleas to be left behind but allowed him to sit in the wagon. "You may rest there for an hour but then it will be someone else's turn!" In fact, after less than an hour's rest he had recovered and rejoined the march. Other drop-outs were few but were allowed a similar period of rest. The mules had started off well enough but were now clearly very tired. It would not be long before they refused to move and all weapons would have to be borne by the men themselves.

The detachment had finally reached Ibicoy, the Rosas lands, just before ten the firstevening. Juancito broke away. With many cheerful but exhausted shouts he returned home. Matthews had murmured that more than one of the men would have been happy to stay with Juancito and he kept a watchful eye as they laiy down for little more than an hour. The gaucho's company had been quite enjoyable. His dislike of their food and eating habits had brought some relief until hunger eventually forced him to participate. His toughness when undergoing the same rigours as themselves had been notable.

The Rosas horse lent to Buchanan is left with the British. Although it was initially intended to be exchanged for the animal he rode yesterday, Lauchlin thinks that the big Rosas brand on its flank might prove useful as a number of alternative plans begin to form in his head.

During the short halt, many simply fell asleep but, since they were eating on the march, any rest was helpful. Waking them gave rise to complaints and arguments but Matthews is bigger than they are and well able to cope. Lauchlin constantly calculates the distance they have to travel against the time available. If they can continue at their present rate, and assuming no opposition, it is just possible they will be able to reach Beresford in time. He believes they have twenty-five miles to travel in an absolute maximum of twelve hours. But the men are tired and some are close to collapse. The cavalrymen in particular are unused to hard marches and with the sole exception of his vanguard, he has kept them behind the main body for their mutual defence. But the time is approaching when he will have to release them. He has a quiet conference with Matthews, whose opinion he has come to value.

"If we let the cavalry go, sir, they should be well able to meet the deadline. But if we run into any trouble here or at Las Conchas…" he leaves the question in the air. "I'm not sure how long the mules can go on at this speed either."

Lauchlin thinks the problem out aloud. "If we can just keep going at a normal marching pace, we may be able to slip through the main landings at Las Conchas. They will be settled for the night now and will not be expecting an approach from this side. Once we're through the main body I'll let the horses go. Then it'll be every man for himself to try and reach the General."

Privately he is much impressed with the way he has, himself, been able to stand up to the demands of the march. He believes much of his strength has come from the sheer responsibilities of the command. He considers going into the Carneros' house and begging for horses and even some sustenance but knows that the delay would be unacceptable and he has no way of knowing how their sympathies lie after the landings in their front yard. He quietly goes round his resting men and tells them of his decision.

"If it comes to a fight our concentration must be on breaking through to the city!"

One or two are asleep but when woken express their ability to continue. After half an hour he calls them to order and, on Matthews's suggestion, agrees that the cavalrymen can mount up to walk their horses; his own pony continues to be led by his groomsman, Browning.

They approach Las Conchas around three in the morning. The moon is bright and their eyes are well adjusted. They see no guard as they try to hug the river's edge. There are small pockets of tents where men are presumably snoring their heads off. He wonders about stealing a boat and floating past any dangers but there is none drawn up on the pebbles and, in any case, he doubts if any of his men can row. Lauchlin is surprised to see muskets stacked in the open. The occasional lamp shows where the guards are located but they appear uninterested in the approach of shadowy figures.

For a moment he thinks about removing all or some of the muskets but soon dismisses the thought. There will surely be a chain securing them and any extra noise must be avoided. The mules' eight hooves beat the sandy path quietly. There is a gentle wind rustling the reeds by the river where it comes close to their path. It is a happy sound. He finds his head nodding and pulls himself up. He needs to check constantly if he is to prevent a kind of narcotic sleep taking over. He feels so tired.

Almost inevitably as they continue, his mind starts wandering again. The wagon wheels still being drawn by the gentle mules have him thinking of Bonington and his Emily; he dreams of Port Glasgow and images of his mother dominate. Suddenly he is jerked to wakefulness. Clouds are obscuring the moon and there are patches of deeper darkness.

Something must have disturbed him. Then he hears raised voices ahead. The cavalryman who had been their vanguard has been challenged by aggressive voices shouting in Spanish. Lauchlin's mind quickly recovers. He hurries back and wakes the men who seem to have been sleeping as they marched. He whispers instructions for the issuing of the weapons from the wagon. Matthews gets the men drawn up and as silently as possible the muskets are primed. He hurries forward. Before he can see what is happening, he hears a musket shot and simultaneously the urgent sound of hoof-beats galloping away. Uncertain whether to bless or curse the darkness he crouches down to move quietly forward round a slight bend in the road. The way is illuminated by a large brazier with two men bending over a third who is lying prone. Wondering how his lead rider could have fired a shot, Lauchlin takes in more of the scene and appreciates that it must have been a sabre slash that injured the man on the ground. The shot was, therefore, fired by the Spanish. He hears more shouting from ahead and realizes that his hopes of moving through Las Conchas unobserved are at an end.

He returns for a whispered discussion with Matthews. They can no longer stick to the path by the river hoping to pass through secretly.

"Form a column ahead!" He whispers. With most of the Spanish asleep they should have a good chance of shooting their way through. Matthews quietly reminds him that one salvo is all they have. They must hope the enemy assume that the cavalryman was on his own. Their main chance must be the darkness – and silence.

Even in the dark it is not an option. If they are to reach Buenos Aires in time, they must abandon the wagon with the mules and proceed through the fields on their right cutting through Señor Carnero's lands. Three or four hundred yards back he had remembered one of the rough tracks leading up, away from the river. They must retrace theirsteps to find that track. The remaining cavalrymen will walk ahead; should they be attacked they are ordered to charge the enemy and ride for their lives to the city. They go back about half a mile before finding the first path going up the hill. Lauchlin resents the backwards search but the danger of their situation has given everyone a new burst of energy.

The wagon is emptied of everything they need, particularly weapons, powder and shot. They are forced to abandon some food. Lauchlin gives the order for the mules to be taken out of the shafts. The straps and reins are discarded into the wagon. The mules make their own way immediately into the river and noisily start to slake their thirst.

A voice whispers: "You're not going to shoot them, sir?"

Lauchlin hesitates. By all the rules of warfare he should leave nothing that could be of use to an enemy. But he knows it would upset the men and the noise would certainly attract attention. In silent darkness he shakes his head and hurriedly collects them.

They start climbing the hill. The Winter rains have made the ground soft and the going is difficult. They continue for about a mile until he hopes they are far enough away from the Spanish to leave the path and turn south again. At first there is a bank about two metres high on their left but as they progress its height reduces. He hopes for a flat field. The horses in front are making progress harder for the men. In places small springs actually wash out on the path. He is forced to reverse his order of march. The jingle of bridles and harness puts all of them on edge. He orders complete silence knowing that it is a pointless instruction. There is occasional moonlight as the clouds pass and he wishes he had a telescope to survey the situation. The only sound apart from their own is the soft soughing of a light winter breeze. The Carneros' animals must all be in barns. The group proceeds again. He sees Matthews has the arm of one of the exhausted fusiliers around his shoulder with two muskets over the other. While looking at him he senses rather than sees a figure move to his side. A voice he does not recognize whispers in his ear:

"Mind if I join your group, sir? Major James Urquhart, Inverness Rifles, ninety-third."

It is a physical, electric shock. Lauchlin's head jerks as he spins around. He can just make out a shape, slightly darker than its surroundings. "Where in…" his voice is too loud, he starts again "Where in God's name have you come from?"

"I've been visiting this ranch, Señor Carnero. You must be Mackinnon, My hat - good to see you – you've done well! We've got to press on if we're to get back to Quilmes Point in time!"

"Where the hell's that – please God it's nearer?"

"Nnno… About seven and a half miles south of the city".

They continue to walk on. Lauchlin's mind is in a whirl. How did this man see them when they have moved invisibly through a small Spanish army?

"Oh I'm used to creeping around. It's my *habilidad* as they say here. *Mon metier* as that villain Talleyrand taught me. My hat! I was actually in his service for three years! Anyway, Quilmes is on the river. It's where the fleet's anchored. Popham's making General Beresford fight his way to him! Bastard! As far as I can make out from what Carnero has told me, the city is literally up in arms. Yes, by Jove! We'll have to try and get round it to the south. There's a river, the Chuelo, which will take a bit of crossing but we should be able to send to the ships for boats by then. Should be all right if we can conserve our energies!"

Lauchlin is silenced. They press on as best they can. He learns that Urquhart had been sent to sound out the people around Las Conchas and had been surprised by the Spanish landings. "Carnero himself is not reliable. Oh he's a nice enough man but naturally wants the best for himself and his people – won't push in any direction until he sees the way the wind blows. Who can blame him. Anyhow, after the landings right by his front door he provided me with clothing so that I could pass among them. Thought I could spend a day gathering information before making my way back. Lost me uniform as a result but it was good to see you – My hat yes! Don't want to get shot as a spy!" He gives a light chuckle.

Casting a careful eye over all his men, Lauchlin sees that Matthews is no longer supporting the weight of his comrade. He is moving among them exhorting them to greater effort. Lauchlin recognizes that he should be doing the same. He moves to the rear of the group, whispering encouragement.

The ground becomes increasingly boggy. The men mutter among themselves but there is no alternative to continuing this route until they can reach the summit. The mud comes over their ankles. He senses they are in a ditch flowing towards them down the hill. They are a sorry sight as they eventually reach the higher ground where progress is much easier.

Two hours later, when he is beginning to think they have made it past the Spanish lines, the fusiliers leading the way stumble into an outpost. Both sides are more than half asleep and the British weapons are hanging on slings around tired shoulders. The Spanish get off two volleys before the cavalry behind Lauchlin charge through with sabres flying; but it is still too dark for them to see much and, in accordance with their orders, they ride off into the darkness.

The Highlanders are soon over-run and for some it is a relief to surrender. People are running around thinking they are under attack. The situation is soon resolved. A Spanish sergeant previously skulking in a hut now takes a particular delight in shouting and pushing them about. A figure heaves Lauchlin aside, whispering: "You save yourself, Bonny lad, we'll be all reet!" Jameson stumbles out of the darkness trying to use his weapon as a club. He puts up a good fight but more Spaniards arrive with oil lamps and he is disarmed.

As a final gesture he grabs the sergeant butting his head hard, crying out "Have a wee Glasgie kiss then!" One of the Spanish hits him with a stone, there is the sound of a musket and the fight is over. Matthews mouths quietly, "that's Jameson for you – crazy hero. He'll be lucky to survive!"

Urquhart moves like a cat and disappears, whispering: "this way!". Lauchlin can sense that Matthews is shaking with shock. He tries to follow but Urquhart is nowhere to be seen. Lauchlin drags his sergeant into the shelter of an overhanging earth bank and lies on top of him, whispering into his ear:

"Stay down!" The noise level rises until an officer arrives and calls for order. He is addressed as *Capitan* and has clearly been called from his bed since he is dressed only in a cream-coloured nightgown surmounted by a military cap with a sword belt and scabbard secured tightly around an ample waist.

Lauchlin lies still, trying to think of what his next move should be. Even more oil lamps are brought up and lit in a babble of excited voices, his men are mainly just lying around exhausted and covered in mud. He cannot identify Jameson and watches as they are ushered forward, jostled into ranks and marched into captivity.

With Matthews, Lauchlin gently slides backwards as they ease themselves cautiously away from the intimidating noise. As the lights drift into the distance, the two of them crawl quietly back. By good fortune they find some farm buildings and feel their way inside to stand and shake themselves. But the wet mud is deep within their clothes. After forcing themselves to wait some thirty minutes they move cautiously back to the muddy path down the hill. Once again a figure slides in to their side.

"Well well, there's two of you anyway. Well done! My hat!...May I join you?" Major Urquhart has returned to the fold.

Chapter 20

Following the last Cabinet Meeting, and the Government being still completely ignorant of the true state of affairs in Buenos Aires, despatches have been sent by fast Monitor ship to Colonel Samuel Auchmuty to await his arrival at St.Helena or the Cape Verde Islands. They are copied to General Beresford at the River Plate. Auchmuty is ordered to proceed to the Plate and to place himself under Beresord's command. Should the situation have changed in any way from that reported in July, he should make "every endeavour" to secure the safety of Beresford and his men. He should obtain control of a port which would enable further forces to come to his assistance. Should he deem the operation hopeless he should return without delay to the Cape where the three thousand troops he is commanding are urgently required.

To Beresford they write that whilst they do not hold him personally accountable for the expedition and that his conduct is approved, they try to explain that they are not anxious to initiate action in South America since it would need an overwhelming army to hold it and these troops are urgently needed elsewhere. The colonists should be told that they must defend themselves against any counter-attack and that British troops are not to be involved more than deemed absolutely necessary. Should he deem it useful, he may use his troops in a training capacity for local militia for a limited time. He must be aware, however, of the possibility of Spain now being an ally in the war against the Corsican, so he should avoid disputes with the Spanish authorities, if they still exist.

As if to underline the list of problems, two thousand men sent by General Baird from the Cape arrive in the River Plate where their ships move quickly to join Rear Admiral Home Popham's fleet still waiting at anchor. The new arrivals are sent expressly in answer to General Beresford's appeal at a time when he was master of the city and still welcome among the colonists. The new arrivals are commanded by Lieutenant Colonel Backhouse who, on reporting to Popham, is amazed to learn that Beresford and his men are held as prisoners and that he is now the senior army commander in a land about which he knows little and with no orders from London telling him what to do.

Popham is pleased to have the additional ships together with the stores they are carrying but does not want the worry of all the extra men sitting about on his ships. He therefore encourages Backhouse to effect a landing.

On a bright Spring morning at the end of October he leads four hundred of his men on a beach landing to the south of Buenos Aires. He is immediately opposed by six hundred colonists and Spanish under Captain Liniers, together with two light cannons. . The encounter is brief. The British are on an open shore with the defenders lying amid grasses and sandy dunes. The opportunity to advance in close order is thus denied since only a single volley could have been discharged in the time available. The order is therefore given to advance with the bayonet. The defenders are not prepared for this reaction nor are they accustomed to this form of attack. They fall back yielding their two cannon.

Backhouse and his men take control of the small town of Maldonado and endeavour to fortify it against a Spanish-Colonial counter-attack. But Maldonado is a town without outer protective walls and Liniers eyes it and prepares to add these latest British soldiers to his list of captives.

* * * * *

Within a few days, Lord Wyndham receives despatches from General Sir David Baird in Capetown, confirming that he has ordered Lieutenant Colonel Backhouse to take two thousand men, surplus to his immediate needs at the Cape, to the Plate area and to place himself under Beresford's command. Wyndham is becoming increasingly nervous about the situation and has recently been made aware that Spain has refused the request that it should join the allies against Napoleon. He decides to consult the Head of the Army – the elderly Duke of York. He now proposes a breath-taking scheme to expand the attacks in South America. The Duke is impressed with the notion and without studying it further gives it his blessing.

On 30th October Wyndham writes secretly to Colonel Robert Craufurd ordering him to take four thousand fusiliers, one hundred cavalry and fifty cannon and effect a landing in Chile, on the west coast of the continent. After securing his position he is to advance north into the very heart of the Spanish American empire. Craufurd, a relatively junior colonel in the Army list finds certain of the orders difficult and makes an early call on the Minister.

"This is a large continent, My Lord and four thousand fusiliers will struggle to hold it!"

"You've seen what Beresford's accomplished in the Plate! The news of the superiority of British arms will certainly have been heard across the Andes! However, if you feel it is beyond your capabilities I am sure I can find someone else."

"It's not that, Minister…but I must study the topography and see what is achievable."

"Be assured, Colonel, the Ministry has studied the 'topography' as you put it. Your task is to land near the port of Valparaiso and to assure the population that your mission is a peaceful one. You are not there for booty but to show the colonists that beating the Spanish is easy and they can govern themselves - having no need for rulers in Madrid who take their gold and pass it to Bonaparte, funding his attacks on ourselves! At the earliest opportunity you are to send messages to Beresford on the Plate, informing him of your arrival. It is the Ministry's wish for a line of armed forts to connect Valparaiso with Buenos Aires. This will effectively give us control over the continent. The manning of those forts will be the limit of British expenditure, apart possibly from a detachment left there in a training role!"

"It sounds a trifle Roman to me, Minister. If I…"

"If it's beyond your abilities, Craufurd…"

As surprising and ludicrous as this scheme sounds, and one can understand that Wyndham wrote secretly on its proposal, Lord Grenville, the King's first Minister, must have had some inclinations in the same direction as he calls in Major General Sir Arthur Wellesley to consider and draw up plans for an attack firstly on Havana in Cuba, to be followed by simultaneous landings on the Pacific coast and the Eastern coast of Mexico.

The difficulty, as Wellesley writes, is to arrange for the two Mexican attacks to occur simultaneously since they would be from separate oceans at locations hundreds of miles apart. Nevertheless he proceeds to draw up plans as ordered, and also includes, again, his earlier suggestions for an attack on Venezuela. The troops being suggested for all these operations include some five thousand British, supplemented by two thousand captured French and Corsican soldiers who have agreed to serve the Crown, some three thousand locally enlisted and trained troops from the West Indies and some four thousand Indian Sepoys.

* * *

Such international plots and plans have no effect on the perilous situation that Lauchlin, Matthews and Urquhart are facing. They are alone in a foreign land, without supplies and virtually without contacts. Urquhart speaks the local language better than he will admit and he has twenty years' experience of Intelligence work involving secret negotiations, often at a high level. But he is nearly fifty years old and the other two wonder privately if his gentle, educated tones, will be able to stand up to a hard journey. Matthews is, perhaps, the greatest asset since he speaks a moderate amount of Spanish and is the most able in terms of coping with the physical hardships likely to face them. Whilst Lauchlin's background could never be described as privileged or protected, he is only nineteen years old and Franklin Matthews wonders if he will be forced to carry both of them.

A growing cloud cover keeps them in the darkness which has been their sole protection so far. The noise and light from Spanish camp fires shows where they are bivouacked. Urquhart murmurs that they must have had their sleep disturbed by the British presence.

"My hat – they won't like that – after their steaks and red *vino!* Probably a bit bad tempered – hope they don't take it out on our lads!"

They stumble as silently as possible back to the mules and the wagon. The animals stand face to face sleeping peacefully having left the river to crop the grass. However, they are calm enough as Matthews encourages them back between the shafts, replacing the reins and harness while Lauchlin, with some relief examines the stores which seem untouched.

Surreptitiously the darkness is yielding to a sullen, grey dawn. They start immediately, eating a breakfast of chewy, old meat and stale biscuit as they proceed at the start of what they still hope will be their last day in South America. Formalities between them are soon reduced. Lauchlin and James have no difficulty in addressing themselves in that way but it takes longer for Franklin.

James's dress, which they can now see for the first time, is completely in line with that of local labourers. Size was not a problem since the whole is loose and baggy. On his head he sports a black beret with the peak pulled forward. Lauchlin and Frank know they will have to change their torn and muddy uniforms. As a start they turn their jackets inside out but, as the day begins to warm up, they are discarded and hidden in the detritus at the bottom of the wagon. Although they are tempted to travel northwards, away from the Spanish, they agree that their duty lies in continuing the fight and, as James admits grimly, it is the only hope of attaining a beach where they can contact the ships which they hope are still anchored in the river. He goes on to admit in dry tones that his news is several days old and only obtained from Señor Carnero. He feels that if they can darken their skins and change their clothing they might be able to pass as labourers.

"Not that I've ever done a day's labouring in my life! My hat no! I'll just adopt a husky voice and spit a lot, that should help me to converse! Don't want to get shot as spies though!"

With stones, grass and mud they obscure the military arrow markings on the wagon. The mules carry small brands on their flanks. Lauchlin tears his shirt into strips but there is no hiding the fact that they need two changes of clothes. Frank sits on the box seat and chivvies the animals into continuing, albeit at walking pace, making their way again towards Las Conchas and the Spanish and colonial troops guarding the city.

While still about two miles short of the first Spanish outpost, the light drizzle turns to steady rain. James counsels them to turn up towards the Carnero *pueblo.* "If we sneak in between the houses we should be able to wander in the back way and I think I know a place where many of them hang their washing in the rain. A biggish barn and the weather will keep those who aren't at work tucked away preparing lunch."

Mention of the meal makes Lauchlin realize how hungry he has become but he keeps it to himself. The only sign of life is a solitary horse with water dripping from him but with his head deep into a nose-bag. While still some distance from him, James directs Frank to turn once more, parallel to the river, The rain increases in volume before James murmurs, "go a bit slower now, Frank, I think it's about here." But they have two more turns to make before he leaps off the back and tells them to go on slowly and wait around the corner on a wider track down to the river. Lauchlin watches him enter a barn which is somehow familiar to him from the happy night they spent here singing songs as the sun went down at the side of the river. The village is silent now. The heavy rain continues and the two in the wagon are soaked. They are also cold and wish they could use one of the capes lying on the floor. James's absence seems to last for ever and they feel exposed huddled in the wagon. The mules start tearing at the grass around their hooves and shake their heads free of the rain. The noise they make is slight but alarming.

Eventually James appears clutching bundles of clothes. He looks up at the sky as if seeing the rain for the first time. He throws the collection of rags into the back and climbs up. "Home then, please Francis." The mules are reluctant and slow to respond to the commands. "In your own time, Frank!" And Lauchlin thinks that for the first time there is almost a note of urgency in James's quiet drawl. He leaps out to grasp one of their heads as, with a jerk, the animals go forward again.

They make their way back to the river and turn towards the city. The mules have settled to a steady pace which exactly matches the speed of a marching column. James moves to sit on the box seat with Frank.

"We must be coming close to the Spanish. I think you should change into your working clothes!"

Lauchlin had been having the same thought. Although the track curves in places where it follows the winding river, it is open and there would be no chance of hiding if an enemy troop appeared. He wonders about the absence of trees or even a hedge – they simply do not exist in this part of the world. They look through the disguises James managed to find. Without showing it, Franklin allows Lauchlin to have first choice. The blouses are in a coarse cotton canvas and Lauchlin thinks they will begin to itch after an hour or two. The colours are neutral, pale shades of grey and he chooses the slightly smaller version. He removes his wet uniform shirt and slips into the blouse, wondering about its owner. It is loose, especially around the arms – *these gauchos are very muscular,* he thinks. Franklin's fuller frame fits the larger size and Lauchlin hopes James's choice of the baggy trousers will have been as accurate. He need not have worried – once again the baggy nature of the costume minimises the need for fine tailoring. They hide the muddy uniforms at the bottom of the cart. They have not shaved for two days but their skins remain pale.

In less than a mile they come across the first of the controls. This is James's moment of truth. He understands the question, where are they from? In a coarse imitation of a rough farmworker he coughs and spits before replying *"De Las Conchas".* The soldier nods and waves them forward. In this way they pass through two more controls but nearer the city there is more evidence of local colonists rather than those shipped over from Montevideo. Their plan was to avoid the city itself and move further south towards the Quilmes Point James had indicated. But they are constantly thwarted by small streams which force them northwards towards the river.

Conversing under his breath, James says "If we were on foot we could probably get across but we'd soon be spotted and caught!" They agree to carry on through the centre. Getting there is surprisingly easy. There are so many people simply keeping their heads down against the weather, while trying to cope with the sheer difficulty of surviving in a war situation that they are unmolested. It is when they are attempting to cut through the new port area and down towards the south that military and armed irregulars interfere. Fortunately James's Spanish suffices but they soon realize that a wagon apparently so empty is liable to be commandeered. Moving through a particularly busy passage-way, Lauchlin is alarmed to see James halt the mules and start shouting down to some troops and locals. He jumps down and says something in Spanish to Frank while handing him the reins. He gestures to Lauchlin clearly signalling him to descend. Pushing after him Lauchlin soon sees what has caught his attention. There are two British soldiers badly wounded that the locals are trying to move on improvised stretchers down to the river. The men carrying the litters are clearly exhausted so that James's offer to take them in the wagon is rapidly agreed. One of them explains that he is a doctor and needs to get back to the hospital. The city has decreed that those seriously hurt and incapable of further fighting are to be repatriated. James nods his understanding and confirms that he will take them down to the ships.

"Si, si, entiendo. Los lluevo a los barcos!"

Lauchlin helps to load the two men who are barely conscious but is able to remain silent. They now give an impression of being involved in some official activity and are hardly halted at the check-points.

Some three hours later they reach the small town of Quilmes. There is a shingle beach and Lauchlin is surprised to see that two of the ships are anchored less than half a mile out. The shallows prevent a closer approach. James climbs down and starts wandering down to the river but he quickly returns. He puts his mouth close to Lauchlin and murmurs "I'd better stay by the wagon. You go down and see if you can find a boat that will take us all out."

Lauchlin tries to avoid the eyes of any of the locals. He looks at the ground with an angry expression. There is a ship's boat drawn up about fifty metres away with six oarsmen enjoying a rest. They are all looking in a certain direction which he follows. He sees a figure in a blue naval uniform walking up the beach with a Spanish army officer. They are not far away and he assumes the Spaniard is approving the casualties who can be carried out on the boat. He wonders how he can converse with the British petty officer without drawing Spanish attention to their own situation. James strides towards the Spanish officer, calling out that he has two wounded men with him:

"Eh Capitano! Aqui tengo dos heridos!"

Lauchlin grasps the plan. While James occupies the Spaniard in discussing ferrying the wounded out to the ship, Lauchlin and Frank must try to identify themselves to the British seamen. He moves quickly down to the boat. Six pairs of unfriendly eyes watch his approach.

He stands with his back to the boat and speaks to one of the oarsmen but loudly enough for others to hear.

"We've got two wounded troopers but there are three more of us Brits who also need carrying out." Half a dozen heads jerk in shock and the Petty Officer walks round to study his face.

"Well, keep your heads down then - we'll try and fit two of you in the bottom of the boat but you'll have to get out of those clothes!"

"We've got uniforms in the wagon but if they see us in them we'll be grabbed!"

"Yeh – I don't like it. The town is cock-a-hoop about defeating us and they say they're ready for the Spanish now. It's too dangerous – likely we'll all get shot!"

Another one comes across and seems to be in charge. He heard what Lauchlin said.

"Right - Two of us will come up with you and collect the wounded. How bad are they, can they walk?"

"No, barely conscious. They're on stretchers."

. "Right, Jack and me'll come up to fetch them. Then we'll make a great song and dance putting them in the boat while two of your blokes climb in and hide at the bottom – plenty of room we'll lay the stretchers sideways. Right?"

"What about the uniforms – and the third one of us?"

"Hope to get him next trip. We're back and forth regular-like. Not worth trying to change clothes, it'll cause a scene."

Getting Frank off the box seat is the hardest part. To lauchlin it is clear that James is the obvious one to leave behind. He is the only one to have any chance of merging into a crowd. They can only hope that he can be collected on the next run ashore.

Leaving the mules at the waterside is also a risk, suggesting that something unusual has happened. James decides to take them back and leave them unobtrusively in the city centre. He promises to try and dispose of their uniforms. With no show of emotion they wish him good fortune and climb into the boat.

Chapter 21

In London the Cabinet is seriously divided about the assault on the River Plate. Both of the schemes for expanding the scale of operations have been abandoned. Lord Grenville takes some pleasure in reading the Summary, produced by the Duke of York's Senior Army Group, about Lord Wyndham's proposal.

"Your hopes of a landing in Chile from the Pacific have been exposed as being beyond the capabilities of a limited army, my lord. The number of men needed would far outstrip the capacity to keep it supplied with the necessary *materiel"*.

Lord Wyndham is not surprised. In the cold light of day his thoughts do appear over-ambitious. But he is determined not to look ridiculous in front of his fellow members of the 'Government of all the Talents'.

"I have to acknowledge that it did over-state our current abilities, my lord. However, we shall place the outline plans on file and – who knows – they may be called up again in the future together, I understand, with your own suggestions, my lord, of a landing in Havana and then Mexico. Our hopes of a punishing blow into the very heart of Spanish America need to be put on hold."

Grenville shuffles his papers. He regrets the decision. Such plans might have been rolled into the discussions now occupying much of Parliament's time about the cruelties of slavery. The King's health continues to cause concern and Grenville is secretly toying with the idea of raising the issue of Catholic emancipation while he is indisposed. This would bring Charles Fox and his supporters back into his government.

Reports of the failings in Buenos Aires and, particularly, of the capture of General Beresford, have filtered slowly into London but they lack definite despatches. The Cabinet's patience with Vice Admiral Home Popham is now exhausted. They agree to recall him but there are differences as to his replacement. They revert to discussing the manning of the army. Wyndham is mindful of Major General Wellesley's comments about the danger of having too few troops in Europe. The Cabinet is reminded that Colonel Robert Craufurd who was initially ordered to take troops to the Plate, is currently awaiting their decision in a safe harbour in the Cape Verde Islands.

"Their condition will not be improved by sitting on board a transport for weeks on end, Gentlemen!" Lord Grenville fulminates.

After a fuller discussion it is decided to send Craufurd orders to place himself and his troops under Colonel Auchmuty, currently believed to be hastening towards the Plate area. He has been told to review the position and, if necessary, recapture the city. The cabinet also worries about the position of General Beresford; should Auchmuty find him at liberty he is to place himself under Beresford's command. Should the situation be confused he must decide matters for himself.

It is decided to recall General Beresford. After a successful recapture of the Cape and now a year's campaigning in the Plate, he must be allowed home .This leads to a discussion about a new Commander-in-Chief in the Plate. The Cabinet is uncertain: Sir Samuel Auchmuty is as yet unproven in a senior role; Robert Craufurd is far too junior; Baron Grenville suggests Sir George Prevost who has been successful in the West Indies. Privately, others wonder if they should send one of the senior, successful commanders to what is only a minor campaign. Finally, the choice falls upon the current Inspector General of the Army, Lieutenant General John Whitelocke.

General Whitelocke is not a popular choice among the senior officers: a genial-looking man with a florid complexion he believes himself much loved by the rank and file. To this end he tends to swear publically and likes to regale the company with bawdy stories. In fact his success in the field has not been great.

Finding the necessary troops to go with him is not easy. In the event he is despatched with a single battalion of Fusiliers, about one thousand men, five hundred raw recruits to be trained 'on the job' and a battery of horse artillery. His orders are to find and release General Beresford and his men and, together with the forces already despatched under Auchmuty and Craufurd to hold as much of the Platine Region as can be held in future by a force no larger than eight thousand men. He sails from Cork at the very end of March, 1807.

The major forces with Colonel Auchmuty arrived in the River Plate some two months earlier in the midst of a heat-wave. He receives the first definite news about the situation with understandable dismay. Learning how the small force under Lieutenant Colonel Backhouse is continuing to retain its foot-hold at Maldonado is initially cheering but other reports are not encouraging. Their supplies are dwindling and they are constantly facing a force of over four hundred cavalrymen whose style of fighting is new to Backhouse's men.

"They come charging at you; you prepare the appropriate response, but they halt and dismount to use their horse as a protection and a firing rest. Then, as quickly, they mount up and are away! My fellows don't like firing at horses and it's catching us out, sir, I can tell you!"

Auchmuty studies the situation in detail, sending out small parties who are to return within ten days. Two detachments studying the area near Buenos Aires are attacked and suffer casualties. On the basis of the reports and in consultation with his Staff officers, he decides on Montevideo as the first objective. The town's position is ideal being the nearest to the ocean so that large ships can bring in supplies and reinforcements. It is not affected by the sandbanks and shoals of the river and, while believed to be heavily defended by a professional Spanish army, it is not thought to be composed of experienced fighting troops. Based on Beresford's initial dispatches he hopes that the colonists will be pleased to have their Spanish oppressors off their backs.

As part of the initial siege of Montevideo, he sends a battalion to attack the town of Colonia, about one hundred and fifty miles North-west and nearer Buenos Aires which remains the prime target. He is advised that Colonia has been largely depleted of troops sent on to Buenos Aires to make that city impregnable. Colonia surrenders quickly and the town is held by Colonel Pack with several hundred troops.

Vice Admiral Murray who has been ordered to take over the command of the naval ships still anchored uselessly off Buenos Aires has not yet arrived at the Plate. Notwithstanding this, Vice Admiral Home Popham is ordered to England. There is some quiet sniggering that his involvement has led to such ignominy that no recommendations have been made regarding his return to England. As a result he is forced to arrange passage home on his own account in a small monitor ship.

Some of the new arrivals are sent across the river to withdraw the men at Maldonado under Lieutenant Colonel Backhouse. Their recovery is made without incident and they join the massed troops attacking Montevideo, where they mount a major assault. But the fort is well defended and the attack is slowly transformed into a kind of medieval siege taking many weeks.

In these circumstances, the return to active service of Lieutenant Mackinnon and Sergeant Matthews is a matter of little note and their arrival at *HMS Monarch* is not propitious. Lauchlin is disappointed to find nobody of his acquaintance on the ship but, worse, no one who knows where the rest of his regiment is to be found. He is anxious to make his report and, in particular, to commend the conduct of Sergeant Franklin Matthews but there is nobody who cares to hear it.

The elderly transport has been virtually taken over as a hospital ship. The two strangely-dressed arrivals are not welcome but none of the officers seems at all interested in suggesting any alternative or sending them to another ship. They are put to work assisting the wounded, many of whom are in a pitiable state having lost limbs or eyes. The death toll continues to rise as infection takes its toll and the ship is unable to move to a proper spot for burial at sea. Requests to the Colonial authorities to allow them back on shore to be buried are not welcomed and are dealt with "in rotation".

Lauchlin cannot understand the number of ships seemingly doing nothing and is surprised to learn of the movement of much of the fleet to Montevideo conveying many additional troops and stores. Gradually he learns that a sizeable part of that force is centred on Colonia and that it will shortly be involved in an attack on Buenos Aires following success at Montevideo.

His near imprisonment on the *Monarch* continues for some weeks. He is unable to ascertain whether Major Urquhart has been safely carried aboard. After a while he learns that the wounded are now being carried from shore to another of the transports but his efforts to gather further information are unsuccessful. The whole atmosphere is one of a defeated force short of food and water but having little thought of what to do.

His uniform from the bottom of the wagon has been handed back to him but it is so torn and disreputable even after cleaning that he feels he has become a *Punch*-like comic figure. He is unable to replace it – the regimental tailors were evacuated with the wounded – he is retained as a supernumerary officer but with little regard for his rank. Frank's position is better since he has been able to obtain a proper uniform on which he has sewn his sergeant's chevrons. But, lacking any regimental or corps identification, he feels almost naked. They are shocked to hear about the capture of General Beresford.

After some weeks, the Mail catches up with him and he is delighted to receive six letters from his mother. He lays them out in date order and starts with the earliest. It is filled with news of local goings on including details about Fingal's impending wedding. The whole family was interested in his last letter home and they hope he will find his military work rewarding. Most of her letters are along similar lines except that as the date of the wedding advances she starts to worry that their style of living will be too simple for a modern young lady like Elizabeth Tempest. She hopes he is looking after his health and washing properly. Above all, she counsels, *you must always look your best.* He smiles at this, if she only knew.

As the Provincial Government slowly grants permission for the burial of individual casualties he is increasingly charged with commanding the cortege that moves slowly landwards for the interment. They are strictly supervised by the Colonial Irregulars – sometimes an officer or a sergeant but no displays of honour are permitted and certainly no firing of salute volleys.

Chapter 22

At the detention house in the town of Lujan, General Beresford wakes with a splitting headache. It is not unusual. He knows they drank too much of the red wine last night over their endless games of whist. The wine is reasonably palatable but, being the only drink available, it has become somewhat uninteresting after these months of imprisonment. So has the company he is forced to keep. There are twelve of them in five bedrooms and one common room where they congregate for breakfast at seven, then take their turn in the washing room and 'privy' before returning to the common room to play cards until a light dinner at two. Where possible they take a chair outside for a 'siesta' but it is now mid-winter and there is no heating. A light supper at eight after which they generally play – cards.

He picks at the worn tapestry of the sole chair in his room. *Everything is old,* he thinks, *like the rest of us.* Many have developed a cough which they cannot shake off. Proper exercise is what they need; he often sees horses being ridden on the road. A good gallop would set him up. Some of the cards at whist can barely be identified. *Much more of this and we won't be able to identify ourselves.* He smiles to himself as he thinks of the pleasure of shuffling a new pack of cards...... the smell as they come out of the box...

He remembers that today, 6th June, they are due another visit of inspection from the Provincial Council. Once again he will hope to ask Señor Francisco Puerridon, quite casually, if it is not time for them to be released and repatriated to England under parole. It surely cannot be in their interests to keep these senior officers under lock and key, feeding them three indifferent meals a day. Additionally, all of the other expensive resources must be an inconvenience. It is possible Puerridon will not come this time. Beresford has no way of keeping track of the political changes sweeping over the territory. He knows the British have enabled them to shake off the Spanish control at least in the short term – it remains to be seen if they come back. It is acknowledged that many local lives have been lost but there were also many British casualties. When will they call an end to this Shakespearian tragi-comedy?

In the Common room later he eases his head against the back of the big armchair, there are two of them with well-worn tapestry matching the chair in his room. His uniform is the same - worn through. The laundry facilities are as kind as they can make them but fine materials wear out. He hears hoof-beats in the road outside and levers himself upright to wipe the dust off the window with his hand. He can just identify the coat-of-arms on the side of the coach. He draws back to watch without being seen. Four of them. There is the portly figure of the clerk - Parrado is it? - Two others he does not recognize but he is pleased to see Puerridon walking round from the other side.

There is the usual reception committee greeting them outside: Captain Bilbao, the senior officer in the camp, is there welcoming them, *Good journey? Would they care for refreshment? Perhaps mate or some chocolate? Certainly all the British officers are well and no, no complaints.*

He hears them trundle into Bilbao's office. He knows they will be about fifteen minutes with him after which they split, half going to the kitchen and half round the rooms. His eyes meet those of John Dirleton, his adjutant of so many years. His hair is going grey.

"What Ho John? Another month passed – here they are again!"

"I hope they enjoy the privy, William, Charles has been at it again. Probably the red wine!"

Beresford is about to make a suitable rejoinder when he sees Puerridon coming into the room. He has to bend slightly coming through the door. Beresford thinks: *Never noticed that before – he must be over six feet.* He rises.

"Good morning, Gentlemen. I know you are well."

They converse together in their broken Spanish and his English. *Strange benefits from war between the nations* he thinks.

"Please a *pequeño paseo* in ze *jardin!*"

He wants to speak privily with Beresford in the garden, such as it is. Whilst the halting conversation takes three times as long as it would normally, they always manage to make themselves understood. He shakes himself into his old greatcoat and follows the senior councillor into the garden.

"*No me encanta...*" he starts to say he is not pleased to see a senior officer like Beresford trapped as a puma in a cage. He has a proposal to put to him in the strictest confidence. He is trying to get the Council to agree to send all the prisoners back to Britain provided they promise never to fight against the Rio de la Plata again. But his hopes have been dashed by the never ending siege and bombardment of Montevideo. This was all news to Beresford and he is very surprised to learn about new troop movements to the River Plate. Puerridon continues. If Beresford will give his *parole* promising to take no further part in the conflict, he will secretly arrange for him to escape. Puerridon adds that he would like, in this way, to send a secret despatch to Baron Grenville. Pretending to give the matter deep consideration, Beresford eventually agrees if he will permit Major Dirleton to escape with him. Puerridon screws his face up as though the suggestion is new or gives him difficulty. Beresford knows it is neither. They reach agreement and shake hands.

Five weeks later, on board *HMS Monarch,* Lauchlin is sitting disconsolately in the Midshipmen's Mess sewing a fresh patch on his torn trousers. They are permanently stained from being immersed in the mud. He receives a summons to the Quarter Deck and sighs internally assuming another funeral party. As he approaches the steps he notes the cold, grey river and thinks of how in late July the flowers will be bursting out in England. What on earth is he doing wasting his life like this? Not that he ever saw any flowers in Port Glasgow. It makes him think of his mother and how she might be sitting on her threshold in the sun. What would she think of this country? He stands to attention at the top of the stairway. A bad-tempered lieutenant informs him that he is to report to the Flagship at noon.

"We're sending the 'jolly-boat' across as usual at four bells in the forenoon watch. You'll travel in that – you'll be nearly two hours early but that can't be helped!" With that he turns away disdainfully having expended too much of his superior time on this unprepossessing figure who will, no doubt, catch it good and hard on the flagship.

Lauchlin calculates that this means leaving at ten in the morning.

With his experience that the boats never delay their departure he will have to hurry in trying to smarten himself up. He stands ready in the well-deck fifteen minutes before the hour. He wonders about the summons but his existence on the *Monarch* is so pointless that surely, any change will be beneficial. The boat is lowered but stops when level with him. The Petty Officer in charge gives him a smile and a waving gesture into the boat. He recognizes the man he had first seen on the beach at Quilmes and doffs his hat as he gets in. The ropes scream in the pulleys as they are lowered into the dull, muddy water. As they approach the flagship he is able to see it is called *HMS Thisbe.* The Petty Officer stands in the prow and does strange gymnastics with his barge-pole calling out "Monarch, sir!" A figure on the flagship waves to him to tie on.

Lauchlin climbs up the crusty side, hand over hand. A voice calls out: "Who is this ragamuffin coming aboard? My hat it's young Lochy himself!"

He is delighted to see James Urquhart. They pump each other's hands in pleasure. Another voice from the Quarter Deck calls down, "What ho there, well - Lauchlin Mackinnon, I am delighted to see you!"

Major John Dirleton trips down the steps and shakes his hand. "Well well, Lauchlin. I've seen better dressed scarecrows in a field! What have you been doing for the last few months? General Beresford will be delighted to see you, around noon. He is busy writing his reports and has a secretary with him. He will certainly want to hear your report and will have to include that with his own despatches. He and I will be off to England shortly."

Urquhart smiles mischievously. "General Beresford and John Dirleton have but lately re-joined us. They have made a gallant escape from their captivity!"

Over the next two hours, Lauchlin is brought up to date on the situation. The escape from Lujan was uneventful in the extreme. With an escort of three irregulars they had ridden fine horses through the night straight into the port area.

He learns that the new army Commander, Colonel Auchmuty, is heavily occupied with the attack on Montevideo. The bulk of his troops are currently held at Colonia, a nearby town on the north side of the river.

"When he has completed his business there," Urquhart opines, "he will quickly assume his duties as Provincial Governor whose principal aim will be to gain and hold the goodwill of all the people in the region. Prelude to Spanish rule again, I imagine, since word is that they are now our allies" He sighs theatrically, "it will therefore be a good thing if the troops all behave honourably…"

While they talk, the three of them move slowly up the steps to a quiet corner of the Quarter-deck not without some scathing glances from the officer of the watch.

The door at the back opens and Beresford comes out. He breathes deeply as he looks around. Lauchlin sees he has aged considerably and is much thinner. He sees Lauchlin standing between Dirleton and Urquhart.

"My dear Mackinnon! I hardly recognized you in your new uniform. It's good to see you made it in time. Please come through, I must have your report." He leads the way through to the admiral's quarters. "Admiral Murray has not yet arrived. He is to replace Vice Admiral Popham. I am being allowed to use his cabin until he arrives. As you see it is sumptuous. I shall likely return to the United Kingdom on the ship that brings him." They seat themselves on small folding armchairs. A clerk in civilian clothes is writing at a table in the corner. There is ample light from the sweep of window that covers the rear of the cabin. "This is Mr.Kennedy, Admiral's Clerk. You will recall the press of duties that keep him busy all day." He gives a short chuckle.

"I am sorry to learn that you are returning to Scotland, sir."

He grunts. "I don't know about Scotland…My time here is done." He looks out of the window and rubs his eyes. "We had control of the city and, I think, a good relationship with Ernesto Puerridon and the Provincial Council." He shakes his head sadly, "some of the merchants held to a different opinion but…I think we would have convinced them in time. I do believe the good Vice Admiral made many mistakes…" He looks over at Mr.Kennedy who gives every impression of being solely occupied with the despatch he is writing, then brings his gaze back to Lauchlin and shrugs.

"I'm not certain when exactly Admiral Murray will arrive, or indeed when General Whitelocke will complete the business in Montevideo, but I could not in all honesty suggest that you appear before him in those clothes. I realize a lieutenant's uniform is not available here, but while the city remains quiet I would suggest you find a tailor ashore and fit yourself up with a suit of clothes and light boots. Clean shirts there are a'plenty on board. Go to the Commissariat and tell them I sent you. They'll hand over the necessary. There is a British tailor who has hung on not two hundred paces from the shore. Treasure, I think. Strange name. Now, fill me in. As I recall you were able to receive some maps of the area from Mr.Rosas…?"

For thirty minutes Lauchlin gives him a full account. When he mentions the encounter with Major Urquhart Beresford interrupts:

"Yes, after your report on Las Conchas, I sent James to assess the depth of their loyalty. It could have been a useful contact but…things move on. You did well, I shall mention your work in my despatch. Tell me more of this Rosas family."

"Before I do so, General, may I draw your attention to the outstanding conduct of Sergeant Franklin Matthews, Loyal American Rifles!" He goes on to illustrate the nature of that conduct. It is all noted down and Lauchlin continues with his report.

Four days later, he is supervising a funeral interment. He has learned that another boat will be coming ashore in three hours and decides to seek out this British tailor mentioned by the General.

Armed with his 'chitty' from the Commisariat he finds the small premises down the side of a street leading off the river. He enquires in English if he is addressing Mr.Treasure.

"Yes, yes that's me! 'Golden' Treasure at your service, Sir. I was certain that business would flow if I could just hang on!"

They discuss the details of Lauchlin's requirements. Samples of cloth are examined. A number of measurements are taken. He decides on a swallow-tail style for the jacket – but nothing too extreme. Treasure will have the suit ready for fitting in forty-eight hours.

"I'm sorry that my stocks of cloth are still a trifle limited. If I become fully established here I will send for more. A sophisticated gentleman-about-town such as yourself will find my cloths most appealing."

"What brought you out to Buenos Aires, Mr.Treasure?"

"Oh, do call me Golden! I read all the pamphlets put about that this represents a glorious future. A friend of mine, a shoe-maker, decided to come and I thought I would come too. I have an elder brother who will inherit the Perth business. Altogether there were eight of us on *HMS Hermia*. All different trades. If I may say so, sir, you could do with a fine, new pair of boots. His name is MacGillivray, just around the corner, do say I recommended him. I'm hoping he will choose to stay here whatever happens. I think we shall have to find a local partner to add..." he pauses as if seeking the exact phrase, "verisimilitude. I think that's it!" His mouth twists, "most of the others have already gone back."

"I will, and thank you. Tell me, is your name really Golden Treasure?"

"Strictly it is Alan Treasure but my father, as he aged in Perth, was nick-named 'Silver' Treasure so - more in keeping with my own situation, I have adopted the name Golden. Now sir, how will you pay?"

He leaves the shop and goes to find Mr.MacGillivray's premises. Two carpenters are producing the front of a fairly large new shop. There is a central door with display windows either side already showing a number of different styles and colours. The labels are in both Spanish and English. *Home visits always a pleasure,* runs the sign. Glancing up at what the men are working on he notices the title of *Zapotero* after the name MacGillivray. Eager to show off his limited Spanish, he knows there should be two 'A's in the word. He rests a hand on the man's ladder and calls up. "Pardon me, but would you be Mr.MacGillivray?"

The man instantly stops working and nips down the ladder.

"Aye sir, MacGillivray the Boot! And, if I may say, sir, I can see immediately what it is you require!"

"I believe you are showing an error in your heading there. I have it on the best authority that a shoe is *Un Zapato,* it follows that a shoemaker is *Un Zapatero.* Not the way you have it written."

"Losh, I thankee, I must be checking that. Are ye sure?"

They sit inside and discuss Lauchlin's situation before moving to styles of shoe. Several are brought forward. Lauchlin has spent so many months clumping around in heavy army boots, that he finds even a substantial pair of city boots too light and failing to give him the degree of protection to which he is used. But the leather quality is fine.

"The leathers here are superb but they are not as skilled in the tanning and finishing. Losh, if I could get my cousin Fergal out here..." He pauses stroking the boot admiringly. The colour – a deep, chestnut – wins Lauchlin over. He decides to delay their collection until he has his new suit. The same Regimental authorization should cover the cost of the boots.

MacGillivray looks down at the signed document promising to pay the bearer *on demand* the sum of five guineas. He will share the authorization with his friend Golden Treasure. But MacGillivray is concerned at the political outlook. "D'ye think we're safe here, sir? I had a wee boy shouting at me yesterday afternoon. His mother shook him up but I didn'a think there was much affection in the look she gave me."

Thinking back to the time when they had been trying to bring the wagon and mules through the city, Lauchlin remains optimistic. "Well, some of them see us as invaders. When they realize that we are merely freeing them from Spanish oppression, I feel sure they will be grateful."

"But can ye be sure that we will let them have their independence? I hear rumours that encourage me to thoughts of a new British empire."

"It is a beautiful country, MacGillivray, and full of potential for someone like yourself, but too big and too far for Britain to control."

MacGillivray looks doubtful and rubs his chin. "Well we did hold on to the North-Americas, didn't we. And d'ye think the army's just going to leave us here?"

Recognizing an honest touch of insecure homesickness, Lauchlin tries to reassure him. "There'll always be some of the army here. And I think you'll be one of the leaders to benefit from your early presence. In time there will be thousands!" He pauses at the door thinking of Treasure's remark, "you might find it an advantage to join with a local *Zapateria,* MacGillivray y Santos or something!"

Thinking little more about the problem, he leaves the shop to seek out the returning boat.

For a number of reasons, he is kept on board the *Monarch* for several more days. He is looking forward to wearing the suit but apprehensive about the brown boots. On Sunday morning when he is wondering if the two tradesmen will be at their places of business, he is shocked to hear musket-fire from the town. Simultaneously the *Bosun's* Whistle summons the crew aloft to make sail. He sees John Dirleton on the Quarter Deck and manages to ask him what was happening. He summons him up the steps. Lauchlin sees his face is pale. "General Whitelocke seems to have abandoned the Northern side of the river and his troops are coming across to Buenos Aires.

"But what's the shooting all about, is he suddenly intent on making a full conquest?"

"Hard to say. We aren't familiar with his orders. I shouldn't think there'll be a lot of trouble, but you never know!"

His first reaction is pleasure at the thought that the country will become part of the Empire after all and that they will remain to police it. But from what Dirleton tells him, he learns that the Spanish army has been augmenting and training the Colonists' Militia. "So you see, we aren't able to tell what the new General's orders are. Stay or leave? You try and forecast the future!"

As the ship begins almost to drift into mid-channel, the shooting dies down to sporadic musketry in the distance. Lauchlin thinks of the British traders and, particularly, of his new clothes.

"Can we just get a boat ashore to rescue the traders?" He asks Dirleton.

"Good old Mackinnon," he chuckles, "what are you up to? Is there a wee lassie there? Always thinking of others. You should go far." He asks the lieutenant on watch, who turns away from him, busy with his duties. Dirleton leans across. "Not a good time, Mackinnon, maybe try again when we've learned a bit more about the situation."

As the day wears on they hear no more shooting. The church bells toll as normal on a Sunday and the sun sets in a warm, pleasant haze as if reminding all that spring is just over the horizon.

The ship has anchored again, further out but closer to the port offices. He counts fourteen other British ships but knows there must be many others in the area. But the ship is not the clean, bright efficient ship to which he had become accustomed. They have been anchored uselessly for too long.

Once again he seeks an answer to his question. The Watch has changed and the lieutenant on duty seems more approachable.

"We're sending a boat ashore at about eight bells to see if there's any more orders or despatches from the General. You can go with it but Heaven help you if you miss its return!"

He turns to John Dirleton. "Do you think the shops will still be open?"

"What's the matter with ye, d'you want to buy a souvenir of your visit? If it's the Brits I imagine they sleep with their wares so they'll be there until we have to drag all their goods back on board." He turns away then mutters over his shoulder: "If it should come to that."

Half an hour later he sees the boat's crew preparing to launch. He hurries over to the Petty Officer and explains he would like to go ashore with them. He merely receives a shrug in reply.

The boat is rowed over to a small pier adjacent to the Port Office but there is no longer a British Pennant announcing its presence. A local official sits outside enjoying the warmth of the sun. Lauchlin has further to walk round to Treasure's tailoring shop. The Petty Officer is off-hand but says they will probably be thirty minutes, but one of the others calls out: "Oh yes, and the rest!" He finds the shop and knocks heavily on the outer door. 'Golden' Treasure appears after a minute or two.

"Oh my goodness, thank Heavens it's you! There was shooting earlier today, did you hear it? I started packing up all my stock – then I thought a bit more and decided not to!" He waves Lauchlin in and scurries about opening boxes. "A fine suit I've made of it…where is it now? Finest Scotch wool…A little wider at the foot so that it hangs really well. I want to see that the jacket hangs properly in front even without buttons. Ah yes, here it is! Oh please, do try it on here… I prefer to see my sewing on the model, if you know what I mean."

Conscious of the boat's time-table and of his wish to visit MacGillivray as well, Lauchlin advises that he needs to carry it with him but 'Golden's' face drops with such obvious disappointment that he changes his mind. He throws off his old boots and removes the dirty and worn uniform. His shirt is not the cleanest it has ever been but he hurries to step into the trousers. "A new pair of suspenders I think, these are shrivelled like a piece of fried bacon!" He slides away and starts to rummage through his boxes again. "I'm sorry, I knew where everything was until that horrible shooting this morning. Ah yes, here we are…" he returns with a fine pair of elasticated suspenders and fusses around fixing the ends to the buttons. He murmurs to himself as he makes minor adjustments. "Need your boots on, young sir. Have to make a proper fit now…"

As soon as he is able Lauchlin slides into the jacket. It feels fine but Mr.Treasure has to check everything minutely. He takes a piece of fine chalk and starts to draw on Lauchlin's shoulder line.

"Yes, I think the young gentleman has broadened since we last saw him. Not a problem, we can let that out…"

"No, no! I must be away. The boat will leave without me and I want to fetch my new boots from Mr.MacGillivray!"

"Ah well, that will be perfect. Leave this with me. Ten minutes and I'll have it perfect. Off you go to MacGilliuvray's. Did you tell him I had recommended him? Get your fine new boots and by the time you're back here this will be all ready for you!"

Feeling that he has little choice, Lauchlin gets back into his old clothes and hurries off towards the door. As he reaches it he sees a collection of dress swagger canes. One in particular with a silver top catches his fancy. He pulls it out and tests it for size. He returns with it to 'Golden' and asks him to add it to his suit. He knows he has spent nothing for weeks and is entitled to a little extravagance.

Back in the street he walks smartly towards the shoe shop. As he turns the corner someone seems to shout at him but he cannot see the source and hurries on. The shop is as he remembers it although the windows on either side of the main door are now bare. In response to his knocking, a somewhat flustered MacGillivray opens up.

"By Heaven! What is this commotion all aboot? I wondered what it was a-banging on my door. Ye'll be having a wee dram will ye no?" MacGillivray has clearly been calming himself to excess. But he recognizes his visitor. "Ye're very welcome, sir, ye've come for yer boots?"

"Aye, I have that!" in spite of his months of trying to lose his accent, Lauchlin suddenly finds that the urgency and the greeting make him revert to his old form of speech. He hastens to correct himself. "I am in urgent need of my new boots and I would thank you for all possible speed in order that I am able to return to 'Golden' Treasure for my new suit!"

"And a very fine pair they are indeed, sir. If you will but be seated there, I shall proceed to fetch them at once." There is a half-filled glass on a table near the door. "Now, another tumbler I'm thinking…" he searches around in a disorganized manner.

Lauchlin sits to remove his worn and stained service boots. Filthy cotton stockings expose a toe but that is something that cannot be helped. MacGillivray has different ideas. Returning with the boots he shakes his head with disapproval.

"Och, dearie me, it's a nice new pair of stockings ye'll be wanting, am I not right?" He turns away pursing his lips then goes into the adjacent room. Lauchlin is relieved that thoughts of another glass have now left him. He is away for no more than three or four minutes but Lauchlin is getting frantic. When he returns he has a selection of cotton stockings hanging over one arm. "I have a fine choice, sir. Now what was the colour of your new garments?"

"It is a darkish grey, I believe it is called 'clerical' grey. So I suppose a grey pair would be best."

"Ah I see you have excellent taste, sir, but if I might just demonstrate… the grey into this chestnut boot…perhaps a sample in the deepest purple… oh beautiful…perhaps a ruby red?"

Lauchlin feels trapped. The boat will be going without him. Will he be able to find another, even if it is to the flagship? He buys three pairs of stockings and shows McGillivray the authority from the Commisariat. He studies it intently muttering to himself while taking careful note of the several numbers and signature.

"Losh – but where do I tak' this if the ships are all awa'?"

Expressing a confidence he does not entirely feel, Lauchlin replies "Oh there'll be Navy ships a'plenty here – mark my words!" In his turn, he signs MacGillivray's invoice book.

Carrying his parcel Lauchlin makes his escape and returns to the tailor. He calculates that some forty minutes must have elapsed since he went to the shoe shop.

'Golden' is seated cross-legged on the floor using a low table to hold his work. He springs up as Lauchlin enters.

"There we are, young sir. All is ready and a fine sight you'll make! Are those the new boots? Very nice. Some new stockings, perhaps would not go amiss…oh." His face falls slightly.

Once more Lauchlin changes his clothes. Throwing caution to the winds he decides on a new shirt as well. The feeling as the silk slides over his shoulders smoothes away his worries about his profligacy and even about the boat's departure. After signing all the papers again, he collects his cane. Mr.Treasure packs up all his old clothes and, with a parcel under his arm, the dandified Lauchlin proceeds to parade his way towards the Port Office.

He steps out at a good pace. The new boots seem to speed him along. *Lightness of foot* he smiles to himself. A hundred yards ahead he sees the Port Office and, to his huge relief, the boat is still there. As he gets nearer he notes how the crew are already in their places and about to cast off. He quickens his pace and hails the Petty Officer.

"Sorry I have delayed you – as you may see, matters to attend to!"

Amid some admiring cat-calls from the rest of the crew, the Petty Officer holds up his hand to say: "We must get back at once, orders from the flagship, back before sundown – they've started some kind of evening curfew!"

With his new cane under an arm and protecting his precious clothes, Lauchlin climbs in, thankful to have made it in time. As he gives the signal to start rowing, the Officer says casually: "You didn't meet up with Sergeant Matthews then?"

"Frank Matthews? No, why do you ask?"

By this time they are five yards from the pier. The Petty Officer stops the rowing. "He came from the *Monarch.* Looking for you. Bit desperate I thought. Told him we didn't know where you were going..."

"But do you mean he's still ashore, looking for me?"

"I assume so, didn't see him again. There was a bit of shooting as you will have heard."

Lauchlin is thrown into confusion. Suddenly he knows he cannot go back aboard without knowing what has happened to Frank. "I'm sorry, please, put me back on the pier – I must go and look for him!" After some moments of doubt they turn the boat around and he leaps ashore again. They throw his parcel to him. With his thoughts in a turmoil, he calls out "will you tell the Officer of the Watch that I am still ashore. I'll try and find Frank Matthews and we'll sleep with MacGillivray the Boot! Perhaps they can send another boat in the morning." He turns away. The sun is setting. He feels completely alone. With his eyes searching all around him he steps back towards the town centre.

The street is strangely deserted. Perhaps Frank has gone to MacGillivray's. He makes his way in that direction.It is turning into a fine twilight evening, what his mother would call the gloaming. His new boots fit so well that he imagines himself a kind of Mercury with wings at his ankles. He holds his parcel under one arm and uses the cane in an exaggerated fashion, stylishly swinging down the empty street in a manner he once saw in an illustration. The thought is cut off as he hears a voice shouting:

"Che, Veni a ver un pedito aqui!" The Spanish is too fast for him to

understand what is a cheerful summons to come and see this little fart below!

"Eh Tonto! Que haces ahi?"

He looks up to see two men laughing down at him. They are on the roof of the building about ten feet above him. He ignores the call which he had not understood and turns the corner. One of the men descends by outside steps and challenges him again. He sees a brass plate on the door he has just passed. It is some kind of Spanish or Provincial Bureau. The man starts being aggressive. He clearly wants Lauchlin to join him and his friends on the roof.

"Aqui hay toque de queda!" Que haces ahi?"

Trying to smile pleasantly, Lauchlin shows that he is in a hurry and begs to be excused. Then he hears musketry firing again in the distance. It is a shock. But the men's gestures are unmistakeable as is the shove he receives which forces him into the wall. Conscious of his new suit, Lauchlin is both annoyed and alarmed. The latter sentiment becomes the stronger when another man trips down the steps to join them. He is carrying a primed musket.

They interrogate him, demanding to know who he is and where he is going. To all of this he can only shake his head and smile. He thinks it better not to admit to being a British soldier. The sounds of firing are now even nearer. They grab hold of him and drag him up the steps. There are about ten men prone with muskets having an excellent field of fire even covering the roofs of adjacent buildings. He is still cautious about spoiling his new clothes and this increases their suspicions. They take his parcel and tear it open. Although soiled and stained, there is no mistaking the deep red of the uniform jacket. The boots add weight to his unmasking.

A new man who appears to be some kind of leader now appears. "You…Ingles *soldado*…no?...*Si*!"

He can only hang his head and admit the fact.

"Why you…*vestido*….like this? You an *espia* ….you come watch we do. You to be *fusilado!* Here we have…curfew – yes!"

There is a small door in the corner giving access to an internal staircase descending to the offices. They thrust him into a small room and he hears the lock turn. He has lost his precious cane. They chatter excitedly to each other as they go back to the roof. Lauchlin feels around him. It is very dark. He appears to be in a large cupboard. He holds his arms out feeling his way around. He finds one wall covered in shelving holding heavy books or ledgers. His feet stumble into a chair in a corner. It has a rush seat. He sits and finds it exceptionally low and clearly designed for use while consulting documents on lower shelves. He remembers Treasure sitting cross-legged on the floor. *Where the hell is Frank Matthews and why was he looking for him?*

It is absolutely dark with no sign of light even under the door. He stands and takes off his new jacket hoping to avoid creases or dust but, after feeling his way around the walls again and finding no hanging place, decides to wear it. He sits in the low chair again trying to think things through. It is unlikely that he will be posted as having deserted. The boat's crew will report that he remained to find "a comrade". What will they decide then? What is the shooting all about? The darkness is beginning to press in on him. He remembers his first few nights in the rear sail locker on *HMS Scottish Flame.* But there they could always open the door. He stands again and tests the lock without success. *If only there was more light…* Raising his hands he finds the ceiling. It is about seven feet above him. He seems to be immediately below the roof, tiled with flat paving and the rope-soled feet make little sound. The tiles are placed directly over timber trusses. If he had a heavy tool of some sort he might be able to break through. *They would hear, of course. Do they ever go off duty? It must be getting dark in the street now. Perhaps eight o'clock. Where the hell is Frank Matthews?...*

He hears musketry again. The men above him are now firing. The reports are loud. *What can they be shooting at?* It can only be British or Spanish troops, presumably the former. What was the latest news on the flagship before he left? General Whitelocke was besieging Montevideo before coming to take control of the city. He sits in the chair again. *Things seem to be quieter now.* The door key rattles and light from a couple of lamps pours in, temporarily blinding him.

A youthful voice that reminds him of someone speaks in Spanish which he does not understand. Then it breaks into English and he recognizes the speaker.

"In the morning we takes you up on the roof…you wear again the red uniform over these fancy clothes – we shoot you. It will be announced as execution for spying!"

His eyes adjusting, Lauchlin recognizes the speaker as Juan Manual Rosas. He forces himself to smile and speaks to him in English, "Ah Juan Manuel, what a pleasure to see you – *un placer!*"

He receives little more than a snarl in return. "Iss no a pleasure for me – nor you. You be shot as spy in morning, with your friend."

The last three words make no impact at first. Shot, as a spy! He remembers James Urquhart's remark when they first met. Surely this was just to frighten him.

In the morning they take him out of the cupboard and down to one of the offices below. He is given a gourd of *mate* with some sugar and a dry bread roll. He is very hungry. There is no sign of Juan Manual. He is questioned by the man on the roof who talked to him last night. He tries to explain that his uniform was so dirty and torn that he had gone for new clothes. The man, whose name appears to be Pedro, merely sneers. "You to be trialed wiz your friend, then fusilado!"

"What do you mean – my friend?"

"The one we catched first – he is uniforme – he already fusilado. Maybe he die quick!"

"Where is he? What is his name?"

"I know nada. You wait here!"

That last instruction is shouted as more heavy musketry breaks out. Pedro hurries upstairs. Another man locks the office door. There are windows set very high in one wall and chairs for him to sit at a table. The sounds of firing are all around. He takes a chair to stand on while he tries to see out of the windows but they are too high. To his horror he hears the loud detonations of a howitzer. It sounds as though it is being aimed personally at him. He thinks of squatting under the table but dismisses that as cowardly. There is the unmistakable sound of musket balls hitting the walls outside. The frightening situation continues. Suddenly he becomes conscious of a skidding sound increasing in volume as it approaches. It seems to be frozen in time although it can only have lasted for a fraction of a second. It ends in a huge explosion on the roof above him. Changes in air pressure make his ears hurt. He can hear nothing and the room is filled with smoke. He watches, almost like a disinterested witness, as the ceiling collapses slowly towards him. Senseless for a moment, his recovery is impeded by difficulty in breathing through the choking dust. Lying semi-conscious his mind drifts to scraping his arm on the side of the ship where it was subsequently hit by a musket ball. He feels no pain, indeed he feels entirely relaxed. He is in a long corridor with light ahead. Stupidly he thinks about his new clothes and brings up an arm to pat off the dust. It is the same arm now bleeding through the sleeve. It is hard to see the cause but he knows he has been cut in several places by flying glass broken by the Howitzer shell which must have killed everyone else in the building. He rests there almost comfortable as his mind wanders. There is more musketry but it seems to be withdrawing. Gradually the firing dies down. He thinks he hears faint cheering but has no way of knowing its source.

He struggles, trying to stand. Pieces of shelving are lying across him and using his left arm hurts so that he thinks there must still be glass in there. He manages to kneel and tries to open the door but it is firmly stuck. He remembers that it opens towards him. The shouting he had heard before comes nearer. It sounds like a cheering mob. Sections of it appear to stop and try to enter his building. There are blows on wood as if by an axe. Then voices converse quite close to him. They have used the outside steps to gain the roof and that appears to have been demolished together with the floor above him where he was locked in the cupboard. Pieces of tile come raining down on him in a shower of dust. He calls out.

"Help!" But it comes out as a croak. He tries to call in Spanish but the language has momentarily gone. He hears more talking as they pick over the ruin. At length he sees daylight and several men passing heavier items of stone and timber between them. He tries to hail them again and they shout out between themselves and to someone in the street.

It seems that the corridor outside his door has been destroyed. A face appears in a small gap near the wall. It rattles off questions in Spanish. He finds he is unable to reply.

The face studies him for some moments then makes vigourous movements towards the table that still stands in spite of the explosion having moved it some six inches.

"Ande alla! – Bajo de la mesa" – it is clearly telling him to get under it. Using the knuckles of his right hand like a gorilla he carefully picks his way and squats under the heavy timber top. They proceed with a will to remove

large sections of the roof and ceiling. At length they lower a ladder through a hole and one of them climbs down. With a sinking heart Lauchlin sees he is wearing the uniform of a Spanish officer. He speaks to him gently in words which Lauchlin cannot understand although the sentiment comes across. "We'll soon have you out of there – don't worry."

"I was shopping – went to buy a new suit!" But he realizes he is making no sense. The shock has robbed him of his senses. They cannot understand him but they carefully help him climb the ladder to the roof. It is badly damaged and there is a lot of blood but the defenders' bodies have been removed. They help him down the steps to the street and offer him a stretcher. Silently he tries to show he can walk, but the effort makes him giddy and he virtually falls down as directed. Four men carry him away and gradually he realizes that they do not know who or what he is.

They carry him for some hundred and fifty metres, laying him down in the central square in front of the old fort. Many injured lie here. As his head clears, Lauchlin realizes that they consider him a gallant *guerrillero* who has been shocked into losing the power of speech. He also becomes aware that there has been a tremendous battle but he cannot guess at the outcome. First aiders are moving from body to body. Most are lying on the ground, he is in a minority having a stretcher. The most urgent are being taken to a make-shift hospital. As the medical orderlies reach him, Lauchlin rolls off the stretcher to release it for a more serious case. As he does so he sees that he has been lying in pools of blood. The men shake their heads in sympathy and lay a clean sheet on the ground for him. One squats down and starts to remove his jacket. He stops as he sees the glint of glass pieces penetrating the fabric. The other orderly opens his case and takes out a large pair of scissors. Lauchlin tries to withdraw but they hold him down as they gradually cut all his new clothes off – including the silk shirt. With tweezers and even bare hands they start pulling out the shards still sticking out of his body. They take great pains to examine him all over and wipe the myriads of shallow cuts with a disinfectant which burns and stings. They stand again and prepare to move on to the next patient.

"You've been very fortunate. Just lie there and let the air at the scabs. We'll bring you a blanket in a while but for now let the air do its work."

He understands not a word but makes gestures of gratitude while they leave him on the sheet, stripped to the waist.

He sleeps a little wondering how he will escape from this situation. He wakes to the sounds of loud cat-calling and booing.. He sits up to note a small crowd showing its disfavour as a troop of British soldiers is paraded and marched without its weapons under a white flag. He finds difficulty in understanding that they have surrendered. His weakness continues and he lies back and sleeps once more. Four hours later they walk him, dressed only in a blanket, to a large tent where interviews with those less seriously hurt are establishing the nature of the local victory and the extent of the losses.

Lauchlin sits on the small chair before the two men taking the record. *"Su nombre, por favour!"* They ask his name. He rolls his eyes at them showing he is still in shock. They shake their heads in sympathy and call for a nurse to escort him and find him some clothes.

He is given a pair of pyjama-type trousers which tie at the waist, a coarse cotton shirt and a pair of rope-soled slip-ons. He is fed a rich *Puchero* stew with fresh bread and led to a neighbouring house which has agreed to take him in for the night. The middle-aged housewife who welcomes him shows him to a pleasant bedroom and points out the washing and privy arrangements. With grateful nods, Lauchlin chooses to fall into the bed and sleep.

He sleeps until nine the next morning. When he puts in an appearance she serve him a welcome breakfast of bread rolls, honey and the gourd of *mate* to drink. Lauchlin is feeling much relaxed and invigorated by the food. He is planning to absent himself by going for a walk and simply not returning. He will make his way to the port and try to obtain a means of getting aboard one of the ships that will surely still be there.

His plans are interrupted by a knocking on the outer door. After some polite murmurings with the caller the door to the *sala* opens and he sees two men. With a shock he recognizes one of them. It is Don Ortiz Leon de Rosas, his host at the dinner so long ago and the father of Juan Manual Rosas.

As soon as Rosas sees him he is forced to lean on a chair before pulling it round and seating himself. He and Puerridon, his companion this morning, have chosen to make routine calls on those citizens recorded as wounded and whose details were collected the day before. As senior members of the Town Council they are trying to check the situation as well as securing some general support.

"You…?" He gasps. Lauchlin's plans collapse. He feels like a beggar at the door asking for water and being caught in the front room holding a pearl necklace. "I am sorry, Don Leon, I was planning to visit the Provincial Offices this morning."

"Ha! You was zere yesterday. *Quizas* you are the *demonio responsabil* for zaire *destruccion!"*

Their discussion takes a meaningful time and the lady of the house hurries to offer them coffee which is declined with an oath which leaves her feeling offended. Puerridon is someone who had been better disposed towards the British through his dealings with Beresford but one who is now angered by the actions of what is assumed to be a detachment of General Whitelocke's army across the river. They talk together at a speed that Lauchlin is unable to follow. At the end Don Leon stands and speaks to the woman. Then he turns to Lauchlin and does his best to explain that he will now be taken to prison, the *carcel,* where he will be held until he is brought before a public inquiry.

Lauchlin tries to ask what has happened to the British army but Rosas merely shakes his head and makes a flicking action with his hands. "Some have come – *prisonieros* now. – finished – destroyed – *muchos muertos!"*

Left alone, Lauchlin is shocked as much by the news as by the woman's attitude to him. Where she had been considerate and motherly she is now angry and bitter. He is led into a bare room and locked in. It is little more than an empty pantry. There is no light and nowhere to sit. He can only lean against a wall and contemplate his fate. "A public inquiry" Don Leon had said; what did that mean? A trial? On what charge? Spying?

He wonders how the British could have been defeated. The ships must still be there. It had not sounded like a major assault. Perhaps it was merely a small detachment. This General Whitelocke must still be planning his battle.

But what can have happened to Frank Matthews? Did he get back to the ship? This sets him to thinking about 'Golden' Treasure and McGillivray. Did they make it? And what about their wares, or are they still planning to stay?

These thoughts and others like them keep him occupied for some two hours before he is collected by a small group of militiamen. One takes a delight in punching him whenever he can. The others are less direct but somehow their icy formality is more frightening. They walk him some two miles to the port area. The largest of his cuts have been re-opening and he feels the slight trickles of blood from several sources. His feet are sore in the rope-soled slippers.

They reach the river frontage and Lauchlin is astonished to see only one of the ships still present. It has sails set and is moving slowly to pass before him from left to right. Faintly on the breeze he can just hear a lone piper playing a sad lament. Although not accustomed to the sound it immediately makes him think of his family; his grandfather, lying in his bed constantly talking of the 'skirl' of the pipes. Strangely it brings tears to his eyes. For the first time in his life he understands the full meaning of a "Lament". He has never felt so lonely and so fearful of the future.

Chapter 23

They bring him to a brick-built outbuilding virtually on the river's edge. The plastered wall has been painted yellow but is dirty and pock-marked where musket balls have chipped it. On the landward side it has a window some twelve inches square with an iron bar bisecting it diagonally. The whole structure is about eight metres by five with an entrance alley leading down before a left turn to a wooden door facing the river. It is twisted with years of exposure to the sun and rain. A sliding panel opens an examination hole at head height, but Lauchlin is intrigued to note a hinged opening in its base. He is pushed into the cell, the door is dragged shut before being locked by an iron key hanging outside on a nail.

Lauchlin is no stranger to unpleasant smells but here he is physically affected by the odour of rotting damp, human waste and putrefaction. He rushes back to the door and vomits. His expulsions trickle down the inside of the door where they gather around the curious gap in its bottom and slowly pass through to the stony beach.

Bricks on the floor outline three bed areas each with a wooden block for a pillow. Two of these are occupied by what he assumes are mounds of old clothes. The floor is slippery with seaweed and wet slime flowing towards the flap under the door which permits ingress by the river at high tide.

One of the mounds of old clothes makes a slight move and croaks for water: *"Agua....agua."*

With the foul smell and taste still in his mouth, Lauchlin repeats the request calling out through the unglazed window but hears only a coarse laugh and a reply which he only half understands about the tide. Other than the bed shapes on the floor, the room is completely bare. He has no clothes and the simple apparel he was given by the medical orderlies will not be enough to keep him warm at night. He squats on one of the remaining bed shapes and leans against the wall. After a while, his knees demand relaxation. The space beneath him where he is presumably expected to lie is wet and cold.

Suddenly one of the two shapes lets out a piercing scream. It sits up and shouts at the top of its voice in Spanish. It continues like a soul in torment, then switches to barking like a dog. From the other mound a voice calls out in unmistakeable North-American: "For Heaven's Sake stop yer noise or I'll belt ya!"

"Frank? Is that you? Look at me. Can it be…? Am I glad to hear that voice!"

It is indeed Frank Matthews, taken two days ago by the colonists as he searched for Lauchlin. He sits up on hearing his name called. His face is dirty and his uniform damp, torn and mud-smeared but it is certainly Frank. One hand is roughly bandaged.

"Man oh man, Frank! I never thought to find you in a place like this! Where have you been?"

Frank climbs heavily to his feet and the two friends embrace. They exchange stories. Frank tells how he wanted to warn Lauchlin about the curfew when he was suddenly shot by what must have been a British musket. "It made a hole right through my hand – the pain was sharp but I was stunned. They found me before I was fully conscious and threw me into this stinking hell. It's awful, Lochy and this poor soul is well gone". He tells of watching through the window as a detachment of the army was marched under a white flag to board a ship and of how they are now "nearly all gone". Lauchlin corrects him as he tells of the last ship's departure.

"They brought me this screaming banshee to keep me company yesterday. He's mad as a village idiot. Serves us right to see the other side – he has a small bayonet wound in his thigh. He's tall and I call him 'Longshanks', and I caint understand a word he says but I kinda stroke him when he barks!"

Lauchlin sees that Frank is, himself, traumatized by his experiences and embraces him again. They both turn to look at the wild man as he starts to scream again. The voice is piercing and Lauchlin has to cover his ears. But Matthews bends over him and gently tucks his scraps of bedding round him. "Now Longshanks, I've told ya, I've got a headache with yer catterwailing. Go to sleep - there's an officer present!"

'Longshanks' settles down to sleep again as the two continue talking. "There'll be nothing to eat until tonight and then it'll only be raw vegetables!"

Lauchlin silently blesses the full meal he had last night and the hot *mate* this morning, even though so much of it is still drying inside the door with the rest washed away by the river.

"It'll be a cold night for ya, Lochy, dressed like that. I caint offer help as this is all I've got. The river only surges in when the wind really blows at high tide. But ye'll find we need it since it's the only damn cleaning agent we've got! Yon Longshanks is not the cleanest in the calaboose. Also, it's the only way to quench yer thirst though it's a mite salty and what it does to our insides is anyone's guess!"

After a while Lauchlin sees that Frank needs to rest some more and lets him sleep. He feels thirsty and the water lapping in under the door looks clean. With his hand he laps some up like an animal. It is fresh and cold but there is the faintest taste of salt which he hopes may help to keep it pure. He looks out of the window. The grey clouds chase each other across the sky. There is little human activity to see. Eventually he gathers his clothing around him and lies on the cold stone surface. He feels the wetness penetrate almost immediately. He wraps his hands around his arms and wishes he could have hung on to the thin blanket he had first been given to replace his clothes. Somehow he contrives to get through the afternoon. As the sun begins to set he hears the guards returning. Frank calls out to him:

"It's nothing to get excited about but it's better than starving!"

'Longshanks' hears them too and starts barking again. The guards enter with a wooden crate of carrots, onions and spinach which they simply lay on the floor. They laugh at the barking and one of them pokes him with a wooden truncheon. Lauchlin is furious and complains using all his recollected phrases. But they merely giggle some more and leave the cell, locking the outer door as they go.

The vegetables have not been peeled and are barely washed. Frank takes a carrot and bites into it. "Ye'll find the small ones are the softest and sweetest. This monkey always takes the biggest!"

The food requires a lot of chewing and for over three hours they take their pick. Once the light has gone they can only feel their way. The diet has the expected effect on their digestive systems. Longshanks is the first to relieve himself and Lauchlin is glad that the darkness permits an element of privacy. Eventually they settle again and blessed sleep helps overcome the endless terror of the night.

At ten the following morning, Doña Agustina de Rosas decides on a small *paseo* in her modest open carriage. She has been shocked at all the shooting and reports of an army preparing to fall on them from Montevideo. As her husband is seeking re-election on the Regional Council she feels it would be appropriate and helpful to his cause if the family were seen to be acting normally and offering sympathy and assistance to those of their fellow citizens who have been hardest hit. She decides to take her daughter, Alicia, with her and they sit facing one another in the small carriage. They take boxes of grapes from the estate to distribute. Leaving one of the larger First Aid posts near the Centre, they happen to pass a small group of armed militia taking three prisoners to the newly set up Law Office and Court. It is in the same building adopted for the Regional Council to replace that demolished by a British shell. It is of special interest to them since hopefully it will be Don Leon's new chambers. Alicia is filled with sympathy for the three prisoners now walking towards them and comments on them to her mother. They are dirty, thinly clad and have their hands bound. The tall one in particular catches Doña Agustina's attention and their eyes momentarily meet. As they come level, he jumps towards her. Putting his left foot on the carriage step he is able to lean over the door and bury his head in her lap. He screams and sobs before starting to bark like a mad dog. Alicia takes one of the wooden grape boxes and tries hitting him. His guards are taken by surprise. They cannot fire because of the proximity of the ladies. Fortunately one of the other prisoners, in spite of his bound wrists, is able to grasp his friend by his waist band and pull him back to the ground. The horse rears up in fear and swings round to fall over in the road. The resulting chaos is frightening; the animal is down, its eyes rolling and, still in its traces, is trying to regain its feet. The coachman has fallen to the ground, his smart hat has flown away and he has cuts on his head. Both of the ladies have been around animals all their lives. In spite of her shock, Doña Agustina alights from her seat and goes to help the driver. As he staggers to his feet saying he is quite unhurt, Alicia starts speaking calmly to the horse while releasing it from the mass of reins and harness. The barking prisoner has been dragged away by the other prisoners and is now sitting, crying, with his back against the wall while they tell him to behave. As the coachman takes over the release of the horse, Doña Agustina turns to thank the guards and, particularly, the other two prisoners. One of them is faintly familiar but he is so dirty and dishevelled that she soon dismisses the thought. Not however Alicia. She recognizes Lauchlin immediately. She has often thought about him. She had recovered the brass button he left with her from the floor where it had been thrown and studied it. The horse, *Romano*, is soon standing again and shivering with shock. She goes to add her comforting tones while stealing another glance in Lauchlin 's direction. The guards recover their prisoners and one kicks at 'Longshanks' leg. It is the one injured by the bayonet thrust and he collapses dragging the others with him. The kicking is redoubled and all three soon move away.

They arrive at the Court House. It is an old building that escaped serious damage and is being converted to its principal role as Council Chamber, offices and law court. They are pushed downstairs to a cellar-like room where they are to be guarded until sent for.

Frank looks down at Longshanks: "You're goin' to get us all in trouble, Longy, if ye don't stop yer carrying-on!" Dragging all their hands up he pats him on the head adding, "good boy there!" The single guard looks at them all with complete incomprehension. They sit themselves on the floor, it might be a long wait.

Lauchlin's thin clothing remains quite wet. He is cold, smelly and shivering. He thinks back longingly to being clean and wearing his silk shirt and new suit. His grand new boots will be lying in the dust of the demolished building. He wonders what happened to his smart walking cane.

They can hear people assembling upstairs and he prepares to stand and deliver the short speech in Spanish which he has planned. But there is no descent to fetch them. Merely a droning sound, as of bees, of jurymen and officials being sworn in. They sit there for another hour before being summoned. They are pushed up narrow stairs through a solid door into a small room which has been converted into a court with lines of benches seating spectators. One of the heaviest is bolted to the floor at the back with a chain before it. They are herded into it. Longshanks sits between them and grips the chain with a determined look. Frank cautions him to keep quiet.

There are signs of a Spanish crest having been chipped off the wall. Now three judges or magistrates sit at a desk in the front. All are unknown to the prisoners although, in fact, Ernesto Puerridon is the central one and therefore probably the most influential.

A man of about fifty stands to address the court. It is all incomprehensible to at least two of the prisoners. He speaks at high speed for some seven minutes after which Puerridon asks the prisoners if they have anything to say. He repeats the question in his attempt to speak English, at which the original speaker protests but is waved down.

Lauchlin stands: "I thank you sir. Two of us are British soldiers captured in battle and we would like to be repatriated. The third of our number is one of your own militia who has suffered from the same fighting and should be placed in a hospital!"

There is heated discussion in Spanish. Puerridon looks at Lauchlin,

"Eef you fighting in battle – where your uniform?"

"I was wounded, sir, and it was removed in the hospital."

The original advocate or prosecutor had seemingly been asking for the death penalty on the grounds that they are spies and he describes again the many dead citizens and damage to the city. There is an angry buzz of agreement among the public, and those who have come seeking revenge are muttering among themselves. The door at the back is opened and a note is passed up to Puerridon. He is irritated and puts on his small wire-framed glasses to read it. He looks up and makes something of a performance in removing the spectacles while he shows the note to his colleagues. He announces that there has been a development in the case and the three judges will retire to deliberate. In the meantime, the prisoners will be returned to the *carcel* under guard where they will be kept until a final decision is reached.

Unexpectedly, Longshanks leaps to his feet, defeating Frank's attempt to keep him down. He tries to spread his arms and shouts out his grateful thanks to everyone here present and especially to God...

"Gracias a todos; Gracias al Gran Dios!"

It is so obviously local Spanish that many of the small crowd now believe that he should be nursed back to health not put in prison. However, the judges have spoken and the three are soon escorted back to their dank dungeon.

Lauchlin calculates that there are about four hours to get through before their sunset 'supper'. They all discuss the happenings of the morning. Frank tries questioning Longshanks about what was said but they remain doubtful over the result.

Some two hours later they hear arguing outside the door. One voice that they recognize as belonging to a guard is trying to refuse the pleas of another visitor whose voice is unknown. The guard soon gives in and they hear him grumbling as he unlocks the door. Their visitor is Ticho, the Rosas' garden slave. He has brought a barrow piled with plates and a tureen of warm soup. The guard assists in carrying it in but he helps himself to tasty morsels of sliced cold meat while doing so.

Lauchlin spreads his arms wide and grasps Ticho's hands: *"Ticho, muchas Gracias!"* He continues expressing his thanks in English while telling Frank about him. Whilst shocked at his unexpected reception, Ticho makes it clear that the food is the gift from Doña Agustina. He bows repeatedly to Lauchlin with expressions of goodwill as he helps to serve the food including crisp, freshly baked bread.

Dinner that night for the Rosas family is a small affair for the four of them and Father Ignacio. There is discussion about how soon things can get back to "normal" after the dislocation caused by the fighting. The priest hopes that the schools will open again within the week. Several teachers have been away with the militia so that a re-distribution of the teaching staff may be necessary. Don Leon looks down at his plate as he reminds them that there may yet be more fighting if the British are successful in Montevideo.

A little nervously, Doña Agustina recounts the tale of being attacked in the street by the wild-eyed prisoner. Her husband is outraged. How is this the first he has heard of it? The fact that he was up-country all day visiting outlying *estancias* and *chacras* is an explanation but he remains unhappy. Alicia, ever the apple of his eye, is more courageous and gives him fuller details and confesses that she sent Ticho to the prison with some small helpings of food in her mother's name. This adds to his feelings of outrage and he demands to know who the prisoners were.

Gently his wife tells him about the tall one who was clearly a lunatic and affected by the fighting. "He buried his face in my lap and sobbed, calling me his *mama!*"

Juan Manuel, their son, is the fourth member of the family there. He looks across at Father Ignacio and says with a grimace, "From what I heard, people were admiring mother because she was more concerned about poor *Romano* who had taken them all round the town and was then lying in the road!"

His mother smiles at him for introducing a calming note. "Actually it was Alicia who got *Romano* on his feet again. But he is all right, just grazed a knee. They made a big fuss of him in the stables when we got him home."

"But who were these prisoners?" Don Leon demands, "They could have killed you! I must speak to Don Rafael in the morning, these people need more careful guarding!"

Alicia speaks very quietly. "The one who pulled the mad one off us was the Englishman who came to dinner with us in Ibicoy."

There is a stunned silence across the whole table. It is broken by Don Leon. He is completely astounded. "We must be rid of these outlaws and thieves. I believe Puerridon was hearing cases today – I shall speak with him in the morning. This is disgraceful!"

The priest looks around at all of them. "I remember that Englishman, he preferred to be called a Scotch man, he was a good man. Now we hear he saved Doña Agustina. We must thank God for sending him to us."

Don Leon looks down again. He mutters quietly, "I don't know, we'll see. Now, let's talk no more about it!"

Don Leon rides into town the next morning determined to ascertain the facts. He will see Puerridon privately, ensuring that these three villains are properly dealt with. Father Ignacio, who has learned to read Don Leon like a book, asks to go with him.

Puerridon is glad to see him. This is a tricky matter and Don Leon is closely involved since it was his family that was attacked. Also, he is the most senior of the Town Councillors and his opinion is important.

They sit over a glass of wine. Don Ignacio the priest sits with them. They discuss Don Leon's visits yesterday. The farms all seem to have been undamaged and their business can continue as before. Shops in the city are a different matter. Apart from the buildings, much of their stock has been damaged. A lot of it is insured in Madrid but the Insurers always take a long time to settle claims.

They come to the question of the three prisoners. "As you know, Don Leon, I had a good relationship with that General Beresford. I believed his assurances that they were here merely to secure our independence from Spain. I think he was honest with me. He told me that they had certain short-term objectives and would be away. The British are fighting the French and at present… Spain is under French control. He told me the soldiers were needed to free Spain and then finish with Bonaparte. I think his superior, Admiral Popham, was less honourable and I wrote to London about him." He takes another swallow of his wine. "They won't have received my despatch yet. As for that General Whitelocke, we know little but he is attacking Montevideo with determination!..."

"Yes Ernesto," Don Leon agrees, "enough said. Now, these prisoners…"

"Well, to tell the truth we were fairly well agreed to hang the two Englishmen and let that mad one go back to his home if we can find it… but then that letter from your family came in…"

"Letter from my family? What are you talking about? I knew nothing about the matter until last night." The priest pulls at his arm gently and murmurs some quiet words.

"Oh yes, that is so… I saw him when he was put in the safe house with Doña Anna he wasn't in uniform and had an injured arm…and bleeding scars all over his body…mmm…poor man, he is very young…"

"What was he doing in the Regional Offices when he was blown up?"

"No way of telling. All the men who were there were killed. He was locked in our old stock-room. Perhaps a prisoner."

Puerridon shows him the letter sent in to the court-room.

"This has Alicia all over it!" Don Leon smiles fondly. "She is her mother's daughter!"

Puerridon strokes his chin deep in thought. "You realize the chances are the British will come again – this new General Whitelocke is not going to be satisfied with Montevideo."

"Mmm…Then we'll have to beat them off all over again!"

The priest plays with his sleeve, getting his robes to sit neatly. "I always say you can't have too many friends, Don Leon, a couple of their members looking outwards from our side might be useful."

"Oh you were always an old softie! Keep them in eggs and steak I s'pose!"

"I only say that they might be useful - especially if we treat them kindly!"

They discuss the matter some more and reach a conclusion.

Chapter 24

Back in their cell, Longshanks starts to behave worse than ever. In between sobbing and crying for his mother, he screams and barks constantly. For the first time they are virtually sleepless and Lauchlin feels his tolerance being stretched to breaking point. There is no repetition of the food sent in by Doña Agustina and the stone hard vegetables take time to consume and digest with the resulting diarrhoea making it difficult to maintain any sense of dignity.

The following morning they hear the tread of the guard stepping down the alley outside the door. When it is opened he sees he is accompanied by two men whose rope-soled shoes make no sound. They are dressed in white and one of them carries a canvas contraption with long straps. It is soon clear that they have come for Lonshanks whose real name is Robertito. He screams with fear and hangs on to Frank for protection, but they are big men and accustomed to resistance. It was obvious that there could be only one outcome and, as gently as possible, he is forced into the strait-jacket and the straps tightened behind. Frank is affected by this treatment. For the several days when they were together, he began to care for the deranged young man, treating him almost like a puppy even to the extent that he required house-training.

He pats him on the head and embraces him saying "you be a good boy, now, Longshanks and don't let us hear any more of your nonsense."

As they remove him and lock the door again, Lauchlin can see that his friend is upset.

"He'll be all right, Frank, those men are clearly from some kind of hospital."

"Yeah, but I'm stuck with thinking that it may have been one of my own attacks that turned him into what he has become."

"Oh come now, that's a bit of a long shot!"

"Maybe, Lochy but if not him – someone else. I think back to a number of men I've hit or shot… I fear they may have been permanently damaged if not actually killed!"

"I suppose that's war, Frank. We do what we're told or we get punished ourselves."

Frank sits down on the wet slab only recently vacated and pats it, feeling the slight residual warmth and shakes his head. "I don't reckon I can ever do it again, Lochy. That poor guy has left his mark on me."

Lauchlin remains silent. He has some similar feelings himself: *'you do things to your fellow man at a distance but you have to be trained to do it face to face'.*

Later that day they receive another selection of dry vegetables. As the sun sets, around eight o'clock, they compose themselves for sleep. Lauchlin is now kept largely awake by his own sneezing. The damp cold and lack of clothing and proper food have left him debilitated so that he sleeps badly. He tosses and turns for most of the night hugging his arms around himself trying to get warm. The grey dawn arrives slowly and he cannot control his shaking. Neither of them sees any point in getting out of the sleeping troughs.

Later that morning they hear the guard again. He is more expansive and waves an arm around while addressing them unintelligibly. He gestures them to follow him up the short alley. At the top they see the small carriage of the Rosas family. The coachman is not wearing his smart hat and is not particularly friendly. He remains on his high box seat and watches their approach with a barely suppressed sneer.

As they ascend the step to the carriage he sees the state of their clothing and climbs down shouting. He fusses about in the box at the back until he finds a horse blanket that is relatively clean. Muttering to himself about the state people let themselves get into, he spreads the blanket over one of the seats and indicates that they should sit together.

The two are mystified. They recognize the carriage from the excitement of the day of their trial and guess the Rosas family are involved but cannot imagine how.

For Don Leon the problem discussed with Puerridon about the prisoners' disposal was slowly encroaching on the difficulties of his family business. For many months, years even, he had discussed with his son, Juan Manuel, how this could be developed. They had even gone so far as to use a Spanish contact in Madrid to report on the possibilities of an export market. Don Leon was mainly interested in leather and hoped that the hides they produced could be improved to the standards of Cordoba. But Juan Manuel had become obsessed with international food markets. He had studied the situation in Europe and was convinced that the war would leave huge areas starving. *Hides, yes, he told his father, but Meat is the thing!*

They spent many evenings after their dinner analysing the future of the business. What were their principal aims and current barriers if, as they believed, the Spanish war was ending. Often the discussions involved his mother and even the priest but Doña Agustina complained if such conversations threatened the meal. Even Alicia, his daughter, was not shut out of the debates. Don Leon was frequently impressed by the depth of her understanding.

"This old Vice-royalty of the River Plate must soon make its mind up about where to go next!" Juan Manuel was vociferous in his ideas about how future affairs should be handled. Primarily he believed real growth could only come from foreign markets. Their hopes of exporting livestock or carcases or even meat products, were made more difficult by the absence of a European agent and the disappointment at the results obtained by their Spanish agent.

But Juan Manuel pointed out what was supposed to be their considered opinion: that the principal limiting factor at present was that the expansion of their grazing territories was being hindered by the resistance of certain indigenous peoples who acted as though the lands were their own, particularly a tribe led by an unpleasant man known as 'El Chichon'.

"You know our own gauchos will not face up to them, either from fear or because they have relatives among them."

The father nods in agreement. "But even if we could raise enough local support to wipe them out, we would be unpopular with city indian lovers who talk of the romance of these filthy natives!" Thoughtfully he repeats his son's maxim. "The war between the French and other European nations cannot continue for ever. There will be enormous opportunities. We had hoped for a peaceful resolution of our fight here with the British but that has been impeded by stupidity – I make no judgments as to which side made the biggest errors!" He draws heavily on his after dinner cigar and looks Juan Manuel full in the face.

"I am over sixty now. Sometimes I wonder if I shall be able to make Father Ignacio's 'three-score years and ten' but, either way, Juan Manuel, the business will soon be yours – you must think about which way to go. It seems to me we have here two soldiers who could sort out 'El Chichon' and his friends - do our work for us and take the blame if the God-bothering Bible punchers complain. Then, when they go home again, back to Europe, we send them loaded with goodwill and samples of our meats."

Juan Manuel remains deep in thought. He had never realized his father could think on such long-term bases.

The small carriage drawn by Romano at last arrives at the Ibicoy estate. The only brief has been a despatch to Francisco the foreman which Tomasin the carriage driver has brought with him.

Francisco cannot be found and is assumed to be out in the fields. Tomasin is anxious to get back to the city. After a long debate with himself, he hands the despatch to Lauchlin telling him it is for Francisco. With a curt clicking of his tongue he leaves them where they are. They make their way to the barn where they spent the night when the detachment passed through so long ago. They push the big door open.

"Not a lotta change here, Lochy!"

Lauchlin is puzzling over why they have been brought here. Their duty is to return to their own country and continue the fight against Napoleon. They have spent this time in prison with the result that all the Naval ships have gone. But their duty remains - somehow to return home. It is further from the city port where they might hope to find a trading privateer in which they could either buy a passage or work their way to Europe. The first need is to obtain some clothes, especially for himself. He knows he is filthy and they still feel damp.

His thoughts are interrupted by an exclamation from his companion who has been poking about in a corner.

"Damn me, Lochy, look what I've found!" He holds up a single white stocking now very dirty. "That scrubber Ickerson said he'd lost one when we paraded. I threatened him with a charge but didn't in the end." He looks pensive. "I wonder where they are now. Did they get away on the ships or are they still around."

"Oh I imagine they were all included in the repatriation agreement. You might have seen them under the white flag!" But Lauchlin is not as confident as he sounds and worries about the fate of their old comrades. They settle themselves on a bale and wait.

Eventually faint whinnying presages the sound of horses' hooves. They leave the barn and see Francisco and two other gauchos down at the fenced-off corral. They lead in what must be a newly caught feral horse. It is struggling with rope lassoes twice around its neck. It continues trying to rear up in spite of the two hanging on. Francisco talks gently to it trying to get it to take something from his hand. Lauchlin and Frank lean on the fence watching every move. Francisco is astonished to see them and gives a wave but cannot leave the new pony.

Gradually the young animal becomes tired and stops fighting. But his eyes are wild and still flash with hate and anger. During a peaceful interlude, one of the gauchos, who appears to be called Jorge, takes the three other horses back to the stables. Francisco continues to follow the colt round the corral holding out his hand. But each time he gets within a metre of the animal it draws on reserves of strength and rears up threatening to crush him with its front hooves. The duel continues for nearly an hour before he can get his hand near its nose. Its eyes are still rolling but a frothy tongue emerges and quickly snatches the tasty sugar with which he has been tempting it. After another half-hour, during which his calming tones continue, he is able to rub its face and get the animal used to his smell. He removes both of the lassoes and makes a big show of throwing them on the ground and stamping on them. As time passes with him talking to it and letting it lick his fingers, he slowly passes his hand down its mane and strokes its back. Jorge has returned with a sheepskin mat and enters the corral slowly. He hands the soft rug to Francisco who gradually gets the horse to accept it on its back. Lauchlin is fascinated to watch the procedure and it is a further hour before it accepts a saddle and permits Francisco to mount up. Once again the horse bucks and rears in protest but Francisco stays on and gradually, without the use of any whip or chastisement, the animal calms down and he rides it round to the stable with everyone following.

"Sombrero", Francisco calls out in Spanish. "We shall call him Sombrero because he came to us on a day with very little sun!" They all

nod in agreement as Jorge rubs the animal down with a dry cloth. They lock him in with the other horses, providing him with water, a bag of hay, carrots and calming companionship.

With a final display of affection, Francisco tells it "later in the field with fresh grass you can make more friends!" Then he takes the letter Lauchlin offers him and reads it through carefully. "You know, what here?" He demands pointing at the despatch.

"No – we were brought here by Tomasin." He thinks better of telling him where they have spent the previous three days.

"Hmm…it say you to work here. First to become *limpios* – how you say clean? Then some proper clotheses! Then to learn riding of horse – you know eh?"

He leads the way back to the barn and tells them to clean themselves up while he fetches appropriate clothes. Although still feeling weak from lack of food, they both decide to wash themselves off in the river. Lauchlin's 'pyjama' bottoms virtually disappear as the water takes away the mud. Back in the barn they dry themselves with handfuls of hay. Francisco returns with bundles of loose trousers, rough shirts and footware. He offers them a selection of rope-soled slip-ons. Then he throws each of them a bundle of mixed working apparel.

"Here *Calzones!* You place inside trouser – like zis!"

They are crude cotton underbreeches but so untailored as to make them virtual wrap-arounds.

"Now the *Bombachas* like every gaucho!"

They are the loose 'plus-fours' which they had observed on almost every workman.

"Now we go horsing, eh?"

Lauchlin smiles and indicates that they are only novices. Jorge and Chapa have been hanging on every word; they chuckle at the suggestion of novices learning to ride. Chapa is a young lad, perhaps fifteen but his face is burnt a dark brown under the coarse felt hat tied around his neck. Jorge is older and probably number two to Francisco. His eyes are small brown buttons hidden deep in his face. He has a moustache and what appears to be three days' growth of beard but Lauchlin will learn that it is always the same, never more nor less. All three, as the two British will learn, are kindly and gentle with the animals in their care.

"You sleep there -!" He points at the barn, "stored grass nearly gone – is good eh?"

They both agree that it is quite satisfactory.

"Now we go choose horses. One likes you. You not *cruel* "He pronounces it in the Spanish way, is good eh?"

The five proceed to the stables again. There is a lot of drumming of hooves as the animals become agitated and turn around to see what is happening. The new arrival is not yet fully settled in his stall. Francisco takes a handful of sugar from his pocket and leans confidentially towards him, whispering endearments: "Eh 'Sombrero', You like the fresh air eh. Soon, maybe tomorrow."

He looks the horses over then confers with Jorge. After a while they all nod their heads and call out two horses – *'Durazno'* and *'Lechuga'*.

Francisco leads the way while the other two bring up the selected rides. 'Durazno', named after her peach colour is a fairly large mare of apparent gentle disposition. Francisco tells them she is over eight years old and has had a filly which works well on another site. For Frank they are proposing 'Lechuga' a very pale tan colour.

Francisco gives the two novice riders a handful of sugar and gestures to them to make friends. Lauchlin tries imitating what he saw Francisco doing earlier but 'Durazno' keeps drawing back. Francisco roars with laughter and slaps her back then, without any sugar, is nuzzling up to her face telling her to be polite to the Englishman. Chapa now brings up two saddles and sheepskin rugs. All have seen better days. Without any difficulty or objection he puts sheepskin and saddle on each horse and, with reins and bridle, completes their 'dressing'. Lauchlin tries to recall what he was taught by Sergeant Robinson at Cork, such a long time ago. He approaches 'Lechuga' but is instantly called back by Francisco.

"No No! Durazno for you – Lechuga his, and don't creep up behind her – she kick you.." He hands the reins to Lauchlin and commands: "You go – up now!"

He puts his left foot in the stirrup and gives a mighty heave to get his right leg across but his time in the prison hut has taken its toll. He fails to clear Durazno's rear giving her a light kick on her behind. She lunges forward and he releases the reins and is left dangling with one foot in the stirrup. A nasty incident is prevented by Chapa leaping forward to hold the horse while Francisco helps Lauchlin out of his predicament.

"You no muscles eh? Must get over – is good eh?"

He forms his hands together and hoists Lauchlin into the saddle placing his feet in the stirrups. "Please now, you walk a little!" The stirrups are slightly too high and he feels unbalanced and insecure. But the mare is gentle and recognizes a novice permitting him to walk her up and down in the damp yard. It is not an enjoyable experiemce; he feels dangerously high off the ground and the saddle is hard forcing his thighs apart. Nevertheless he continues with the exercise while they introduce 'Lechuga' to her new rider. Slightly irritatingly, Frank looks more settled and soon both horses are walking side by side.

Frank leans over to him causing Lauchlin to veer away nervously. "What say we ride off over the hill and back to the city!" He laughs, enjoying the idea. Lauchlin realizes that his companion is already a passable rider. Through clenched teeth he asks him where he learned to ride. "Hey, on the farm we had three horses and I was learned the hard way! This is a fine filly. I think she and I're going to be great friends!"

Chapa looks up at him. "You think you good rider, eh?"

He calls out another brown filly. It is skittish and he shouts at it causing the animal to rear up with the white of its eyes flashing. Chapa slaps its bare rump and as the animal bolts away he grasps its mane and leaps upon its back. After a run of some twenty metres he leaps off running alongside before launching himself on to its back again. He laughs with delight as he comes back to them.

"There – that good horse riding! You do soon!"

After an hour Lauchlin is so saddle-sore that he is certain he will not be able to walk. There is a call from Chapa. He uses the one word and points over his shoulder to a small field behind the main house:

"Asado!"

Francisco comes and shows them where to put the horses into one of the main fields where about a dozen others are grazing. Those animals immediately adopt an investigative attitude guarding their leadership against the new arrivals. The saddles, bridles and sheepskins are put into a barn and they are shown where their equipment should go. There is a clear seniority in the position on the wooden bar and strong ownership about each saddle. Most of the gauchos decorate their equipment with silver bands which they regularly check. Lauchlin subsequently learns that most of these are gained and lost gambling with dice and cards.

Francisco has evidently decided to give an 'asado' in their honour. They learn that unlike milk producing farms, here they are as interested in male calves as females. All are sterilized with the rare exception of those with particularly fine ancestry which, on Don Leon's authority alone, are kept for breeding. Each animal is branded on the left ear with an "R" inside a rose.

The scent of grilling meat is carried on the breeze over the fields and buildings. Half of a calf with its head still in place and four hooves poking through the ironwork, has been spread in an upright position over an iron griddle with white-hot embers of wood beneath. It almost seems to stare right at him and Lauchlin is affected with pity for the dead animal but knows he must conceal this strange 'European' trait. There are only seven of the field workers to feed, in addition to two of the female house-maids or slaves. With the two '*ingleses*' the total numbers just eleven. A big loaf of bread made from strong flour is the sole accompaniment to the meat. Using their own knives, each one is to cut off the joints that specially appeal. Francisco, as the senior person, goes first and cuts out the tongue then he hands each of his two guests a new knife in a coarse leather scabbard which he indicates they should always have on their person; it must be kept clean and, perhaps above all, sharp. As the men proceed to carve pieces off the joint, the 'guests' wait politely for the serving maids to precede them but this causes confusion and Francisco yells at them to stop wasting time.

As they find a corner to sit in, the distant sound of cantering hoof-beats permeates the gathering. It is a rhythm they will come to know well. The horsemen of the plains seem able to canter their steeds all day at a rate which although below the gallop is faster than a trot. Francisco looks up.

"Ah! It is Jacinto. Good, he was due back today. Make room for him he has been away three days!"

Lauchlin watches as the new arrival cares for his animal before carrying the saddle into the barn. When he comes closer, Lauchlin sees an arrogant, unfriendly face under the hard leather hat secured around his throat. He nods to the company before turning an aggressive gaze towards the two newcomers. He wears boots with a pronounced heel and he has a scar running down one cheek suggesting the near loss of an ear.

Francisclo rises to embrace him. There is a definite respect in his manner, before he explains to the soldiers, "Jacinto is a true gaucho. He cares for Don Leon's beasts in areas far from here. He spends much of his life alone." With an index finger pulling below an eye, he adds knowingly: "he keeps an eye on the Indians."

He murmurs brief details about the two strangers. Lauchlin is aware of a searching examination before the man takes an enormous slice of rib cage and fillet before squatting down comfortably by himself.

Lauchlin surreptitiously feels again the saddle sores caused by a short morning's work and wonders how this man can do it all and every day. His own gaucho trousers are very thin and the "underpinnings" will almost certainly be stained from the riding.

Francisco points at a stack of tin plates and gestures that they are for 'ze juices!' and laughs. Lauchlin recognizes Juancito who had ridden with the troop when they first received their recall from General Beresford. He waves at him but Lauchlin suspects he is more interested in one of the house maids who is giggling over something he has said. He wonders about their ranking and whether they are "slaves".

There is a carboy of red wine covered in wickerwork. Some of the diners have a metal cup, others merely hoist the container to their lips. Lauchlin starts by cutting off a section of the rib and is soon delighted with the tender, succulent meat. With Frank he returns and removes a larger section. As he goes back he notices a tin salt dispenser. The flavours are the best he has ever eaten, the result of his hunger and the fresh air. The wine is light and although slightly coarse lubricates the meal. The others watch them, clearly delighted with their appreciation.

After the meal, gourds of *mate* are passed around. A kettle of boiling water tops up the contents as the libation goes down, sucked through a shared silver straw *bombilla,* it is freely used by everyone. Frank looks over at Lauchlin. "My my, that's a meal like I hardly remember! Cain't be doin' much this afternoon!"

The workers collect their own cups and plates and start returning to their duties. The pit is still smoking and, leaning back, Lauchlin notices for the first time three large dogs closely watching their activities. Francisco smiles: "They will not attack you – they want the meat. We 'ave short *siesta* now - they will fight and burn their noses!"

Forty minutes later, Lauchlin and Frank pay for their hefty appetites by some harsh digestive problems, the inevitable consequences after days of near starvation. They return to the barn in some discomfort to sleep. Lauchlin is woken later to find Francisco standing over them. He has the letter in his hands.

"You know to shoot, yes?"

"Er yes, we know the best way to fire a broadside of muskets…"

"No no!" He is interrupted. Francisco sits down on a bale. He seems strangely troubled. "You know Kentucky rifle?"

Frank leans forward. "I have used one. Very accurate but a bit complicated to clean and oil and needs special ball, or bullets as they're called."

"Si si!...Hmm…." He looks pensive. "This letter say you learn to ride horse. Also, you go Father Ignacio and speak the *Castellano.* Two weeks – is right? You learn ride, you learn Spanish. Then Don Leon and Juan Manuel say what to do!"

He stands, looking down on them. Then he nods and walks out of the barn. Frank rises and stretches.

"Well, I guess we've been told what's what. The ridin' don't bother me but speakin' Spanish...I picked up a bit in Florida but it ain't somethin' that's goin' to further my career – no siree!"

Lauchlin massages his rear and thighs, then rubs his stomach to ease the aching. "Where do we meet up with Father Ignacio? He's a decent fellow and I suppose we'll have to go along with it but I'm a wee bit fearful of the riding…"

"Little and often." Frank prepares to walk out. "I'm for the privy again after which we'd better have another go with the hosses!"

"Oh hell." Lauchlin curses as another spasm hits him. "I fear you're right but why did he ask about our experience with rifles?"

They walk out of the barn together. "Yes, I don't like the sound of that too much. A rifle's a deadly weapon. You fire one bullet and it never misses, but sometimes they take an age to load. It'll never replace our lads in a line of muskets firing together and demolishing everything in front of 'em!"

"Mm. I wonder where our lads are now…I'd like to think we might have a chance some time of checking that they did get away."

They go to fetch their bridles and saddles and go on to the field where *Durazno* and *Lechuga*, their mounts of the morning, are grazing with other horses. It is a big field with wire fencing and a wooden gate.

"This wire is interesting…" Frank muses as he feels it. They rest the heavy saddles on the gate while they think what to do. Chapa comes out of a workshop to join them. In Spanish he explains that he is supposed to stay with them. After a couple of clarification questions they understand.

Lauchlin points at his saddle then out at *Durazno* who has given no welcoming sign or trotted over to see him. He thinks *Lechuga*, Frank's horse, is staring in their direction with twitching ears.

"You call her, and whistle!" Chapa continues. He puts two fingers in his mouth and gives a shrill call. One of the other horses shows an immediate reaction and starts to move towards the gate.

"*Llame, llame!"* You call. Chapa laughs. Lauchlin tries to whistle but has only a limited success. Frank is better at it but Chapa has already opened the gate and strides towards the animals. They close the gate behind them and follow.

Chapa gets a hold on *Lechuga* and they manage to put his saddle on but every move Lauchlin makes towards *Durazno* is countered by her gently side-stepping away. At length, by constant replenishing of his sugary hand, he gets the mare to come to him and makes a great fuss of her but he notes that she continues to pay more attention to Frank. Once saddled Lauchlin is helped up and they spend the next two hours walking gently down the river path they had all marched along so bravely.

At five the next morning Father Ignacio is pounding on the door. Frank feels his way through the dark barn and opens it to the still star-lit dawn.

"Sleepy-heads!" He c huckles, "It is time for your Spanish lessons. We shall have two hours before I leave for school."

They stumble into their clothes and cross to the main house. It is a cold, crisp morning and they are to study with the priest in front of the kitchen fire before the first meal, following which Father Ignacio will ride North to the school he has set up near the Indian village. He tells them of Don Leon's instructions contained in the despatch to Francisco. When they have attained the necessary riding skills – two weeks' maximum – they are to join him for intensive extra lessons at the school. One month later they must be fully capable of undertaking conversations in Spanish and their proper employment will come into effect.

Lauchlin looks at him. "What does proper employment mean?"

The priest's face falls. He looks down and pauses. "I do not know but Don Leon has certain ambitions… No doubt it will all become clear in God's good time!" He Crosses himself as he leads the way.

It is not an inviting prospect and both of them are apprehensive about the situation. But they see no alternative. It seems that the pleasant country life that Lauchlin had pictured is not to be.

The learning programme is strictly followed. It is clear that Don Leon's word is law and everyone seems aware of their time-table. Lauchlin finds the riding difficult. He cannot fault *Durazno* – she is well-behaved and loyal. But he has developed bruises on top of skin lesions and muscular strains from his ankles to the back of his neck. He has fallen off on every kind of surface and the fact that *Durazno* invariably stops for him hardly helps.

Conversely, it is the academic study of the new language which causes Frank the greater difficulty. He and *Lechuga* make a fine couple and he shows off his skills by jumping gates and riding off at speed. But in spite of his knowledge of some Spanish phrases from his days fighting them in Florida, he soon falls behind Lauchlin's ability to converse in the language.

At the end of two weeks Lauchlin finds himself more comfortable. He can now manage a canter of twelve miles, if not with ease, at least he can stay on, and his abilities in spoken Spanish have advanced very considerably as a result of the total immersion.

It is that distance of twelve miles they have to ride every morning now accompanying the priest to his school. It is a single building constructed of bricks made by baking a mixture of mud and straw, with a crude window on each side, an entrance at the end shows a number of roughly made wooden benches. It is roofed with rushes which, to judge from the sounds they emit, contain several families of cicadas, lizards and birds. The building was erected on Don Leon's instructions in an attempt to disarm the tribe of *Coacha* Indians that impeded the expansion of his estates. The Indian village is about three miles away from the school and stands on the banks of a tributary of the major river Lauchlin and his men had previously explored. He feels some guilt that he had known nothing of its existence when he was supposed to be surveying the area. Privately he wonders why it did not feature on the maps Don Leon had given him.

Now with Frank he is seated on a bench at the back staring at a collection of indigenous people being addressed on basic Christian principles in a language that is some eighty per cent Spanish and twenty per cent Guarani. By the end of the first day he is wondering what purpose he is serving in this knowledge of scraps of native *patois*. The "class" is composed of a dozen men and boys all of whom totally ignore their attempts at friendly introduction. They are dressed in a variety of what seem to be cast-off gaucho attire with rope-soled canvas shoes in place of the 'regulation' leather boots. On their heads they wear rough cotton caps beneath which greasy, dirty hair hangs in a cascade.

Although the composition of the "classes" varies slightly from day to day, by the end of the second week, Lauchlin has perceived that their leader is a man perhaps in his mid-thirties. He speaks good Spanish and is presumably there to absorb the teachings of Christ. But his face carries none of the compassion such learning should imprint. He sits on a bench at the front and glowers at Father Ignacio throughout his sermons. Lauchlin mentions this apparent contradiction to the priest.

"Yes, that is *Chino,* he is *El Chichon's* brother. It is very important for me to get my message across to him." He clicks with his tongue as he digs his sandalled feet into the horse's side. "El Chichon" is the leader in the village. What he says, goes!"

"Why do they come to the classes? Is there an inducement?"

"They have some nervousness about Don Leon's plans for the area. I think they want to show they are reasonable." After a short pause he adds, "also, they receive baskets of bread and clothes. These are useful".

"I have been trying to make friendly overtures to Chino but he seems determined to maintain a barrier between us."

The priest says nothing more on the subject but he looks troubled as he canters back with them.

At the end of their month's "education" at the school, they return one evening to find the family wagons being unpacked. Francisco tells them that they have all returned from the city. Alicia has brought a friend,

Encarnacion, with her. "She is of good family and perhaps they are hoping for her to make a match with Juan Manuel. He has not returned with them as he has joined the army."

"The army? Which army?"

"Well, the British are still at Montevideo and Spanish are trying to regain control of the Region but we, the *Platinos,* are developing our strengths in secret." He snatches at a fly in his ear. "As a fine horseman, Juan Manuel is, of course, in the *Caballeria.* I imagine he will soon be in command!" Francisco wanders away leaving Lauchlin to wonder if the outburst of humour did not conceal some irritation with his youthful master.

They are not invited to dine with the family but take their meal as usual in the kitchen with Francisco and the senior household staff. Through a half-glassed door he sees Ticho and other outside staff – or slaves – eating together. It troubles him although they seem to receive the same food.

At this time of year most people seem to retire to sleep soon after dinner. Gradually Lauchlin and Frank have fallen in with this habit; they rise early and sessions at the school have prevented the after-lunch siestas. Francisco enjoys a small cheroot after his evening meal and they have begun sitting with him for some thirty minutes. This evening he has a message from Don Leon: They are all to join him in a briefing in his library. They wait while Francisco collects certain weapons from the small armoury.

The *Caudillo* is smoking his customary post-prandial cigar sitting in a high-backed armchair with a tray of coffee on a side table. It is the first time Lauchlin has seen the room. It is lined with leather-bound, gold-toothed books on fine wooden shelves. He does not rise to greet them but points to a set of chairs against the wall and offers them a cup of coffee. Francisco has brought a long soft leather case which Lauchlin guesses contains a musket. Don Leon leans down and shows them a heavy pistol.

"Have you ever seen one of these?" Lauchlin and Frank both reply in the affirmative. He remembers General Beresford praising its automatic action when in Dover Harbour. Frank examines it carefully when it is handed to him. After checking that it is not loaded, he points it away and pulls the trigger. It makes a satisfactory sound as of smooth machinery.

Don Leon hands him a small cotton sheet to wipe his hands. It has been packed away heavily covered in oil.

"Francisco, your rifle please!" Lauchlin realizes the Foreman is trembling with nerves and wonders if he is always like this in his master's presence or is it the rifle.

Francisco undoes the straps on the leather case and takes out what Lauchlin assumes is the so-called 'Kentucky' weapon that Frank had said would never replace the musket. Don Leon continues:

"If you hold this up and look through the barrel you will see the rings that cause the bullet to 'rifle' or to spin as it leaves the barrel. Being fast, it is far less affected by the wind. It can be loaded with up to five bullets at a time. It is 'sighted' by putting these elements in line when pointed at the target. You make an allowance for the distance." He nods as he handles the weapon. "It is a deadly machine and very accurate. I have seen an *Hornero* brought down at fifty metres!" Lauchlin wonders why one should want to bring down a small bird with no culinary value but shows he is impressed.

"I have bought five of these from the North Americans. They are expensive and you must ensure that they do not fall into the wrong hands!"

"Wrong hands? Don Leon, whose hands would they be?"

Frank is always a mite direct for Lauchlin's taste but the Caudillo just smiles,

"Well, the British for a start!"

He tells Francisco to fetch him some maps off a nearby table. He looks through them and, after making some space, spreads out the local area and points to the river and Ibicoy.

-"This is where we are sitting. Right?" He places it on the floor and finds another map of the Northern area that abutts it.

"This is all my land, registered in Buenos Aires with the Spanish and the Regional Authority. You see just here the occasional location of the Indian village - I say occasional deliberately. They move around. They are not constructive; they move their animals on to good land until it is exhausted then they move again. They leave the country totally destroyed and ridden with disease. They grow almost nothing but they attack my animals. They eat them – of course they are better! They deny it but they use the skins to make their crude adobe houses and we have seen our brands. Francisco will tell you about their *Pozo negros* – the holes they dig for their waste. They are disgusting people and have no right to be on my lands!"

He pauses to re-light his cigar and puffs away at it. He is becoming agitated. "I built that school for them and have tried to encourage them to become Christians and to settle on their own land properly…but it is a hopeless task. Their leader is one Chichon. I have tried to make him friendly – even given him gifts, but to no avail. He just consults *Sietemesina La Vieja,* you remember her, Lauchlin, our local witch! She tells him it is right so he thinks they can continue to wander at will over my property spreading their filth and disease everywhere!"

Lauchlin stirs his coffee as he thinks the matter over. "And our task, Don Leon?"

"You can shoot, I know. I will give each of you one of these fine Kentuckies. I want you to move those Indians off my lands. They can be just as happy if they are re-located two hundred kilometres to the north. Jacinto has told me there is plenty of land available there."

Frank leans forward. "But are those lands quite free, Don Leon? If they are registered in someone else's name, there could be trouble."

Lauchlin becomes more conscious of Francisco's nervousness. He is clearly trembling and his coffee cup rattles as he tries to drink. It would be useful to know why. Is he a Coacha himself? "Can we take any of your men to help us, Don Leon?"

The cigar takes longer to light this time. At length he looks down at the maps.

"I have some forty gauchos in my employ. They are all trained horse soldiers. But they have wives and children. In total I feed about one hundred and ten of them." After a pause he looks directly at them: "TThey are all Coachas!"

He takes a quick glance at Francisco. "All except one, anyway. They are frightened of *El Chicho*n and *Sietemesinas La Vieja* who speaks against an attack. Do you think they would fight against their own tribe?"

"Can we offer them any extra inducements? Regular food perhaps if they moved on."

"And how should this 'regular food' be provided if they are two hundred kilometres away?" Lauchlin recognizes the beginnings of contempt in Don Leon's face as he responds to Frank's question.

"Some money perhaps, or a stock of animals? Or clothes?"

The Caudillo's face darkens and he shakes his head.

"You don't seem to realize. These are not normal people. They have little concept of personal ownership. They are thieves. They simply help themselves to whatever they want."

Lauchlin takes the bull by the horns. "But can just two of us handle a whole tribe?"

"You must make an early impression! You have weapons and firepower that they have never even seen. You must make it clear that they either leave my properties for ever or they will die. You sir!" And his eyes fix firmly on Lauchlin. "You are an officer and you will know how to handle inferior people like these!"

"What weapons do they have?"

"Oh spears and home-made bows and arrows – knives of course. Are you becoming afraid? I thought if I had you trained to ride properly and to speak Spanish, I would be employing two professional soldiers who would be able to clear this evil off my property! Am I wrong? Is it quite beyond the abilities of the British? These are not Christian people – they have no souls!"

Frank looks up at him: "We're not just professional killers, sir!"

He does not hide his anger and rises making sweeping movements with his hands. The interview is at an end.

Lauchlin and Frank spend the next day making plans and, particularly, learning how to load and fire the Kentucky rifles.

Chapter 25

They leave the following morning. They carry blankets and cooking utensils, a small sack of flour, some smoked bacon, sausage and the two Kentucky rifles in holsters together with ammunition amounting to two boxes each of twenty rounds. Frank also takes a musket, powder and shot, trusting in old, established methods. They will live largely off the land – hares or birds. Each carries his knife in a scabbard and about forty metres of rope coiled at the front of the saddle but neither has much faith in his skill with the lasso.

It is a bright morning with the first faint promise of Spring. Big splashes of blue in the sky are reflected in the river which assumes a friendlier hue. The horses seem to be pleased to be on an outing. They take the track along the river's edge that they now know so well. The animals assume they are going to the school as usual. Lauchlin hears a whoop calling out to them. Over on their left he sees the two girls, Alicia and Encarnacion, out for a pre-breakfast canter. He has a moment's regret that they are not going in the same direction. He and Frank trot onwards and discuss their plans.

"We'll leave the guns in the holsters and try to talk with this *El Chichon*."

Frank sniffs dismissively. "I don't get the impression that he's much of a talker – certainly if he's anything like his brother! If these lands really do belong to Rosas why can't he get the army or whatever law enforcing agent there is?"

"I imagine that is exactly what he thinks he is doing - Us! We're to enforce the law. But we'll start with being nice and polite."

From the school there is a clear path away from the river leading to the village. Suddenly a figure walks out in front of them waving her arms and calling out:

"Peligro! Peligro! No pasen a la muerte! (Danger! Danger! Do not proceed towards Death!)

Lauchlin realizes this must be the old witch, *Sietemesinas,* that Don Leon had warned them about. Frank tries to ignore her and ride past but she fixes her gaze on his horse which stops dead, nearly toppling him: *"Lechuga! No pases aqui!"* They cannot get their animals to progress and are forced to dismount.

Lauchlin challenges her for stopping two riders going about their lawful business. Her face is so lined he finds himself remembering Don Leon's comments that she was elderly when he was a boy. She scuttles to the side making gestures that they must follow. The horses stand as if frozen and the men clamber through a thicket of fresh-smelling flowers to a small hut which is where she evidently lives. Lauchlin is impressed with its cleanliness. The floor is lined with a rug of plain design but with strange stick-like symbols on its perimeter. She squats down very easily as if she were twenty years old, inviting them to join her.

"You – much danger!" She looks directly into Lauchlin's face. He sees eyes of wisdom yet tinged with sadness. Her Spanish is not perfect – she has an accent that is impossible to place. "You going but will cause much death and injury – even to you! Better you go back!" With those words she hoists herself into a standing position without any use of her hands. "Go now – you leave!"

Lauchlin feels shocked and has a moment's breathlessness. They find their horses are now quite calm and relaxed, cropping the grass as if on home ground. Lauchlin looks at Frank. "What do you make of that?"

"Well, you were the one she warned!" Frank gives a little grin as if dismissing the whole event. "I don't fancy going back to Don Leon and telling him we've changed our minds."

It has put Lauchlin into a rather pensive mood but he merely gives a quiet nod and they mount up again to continue their journey.

As they ride into the encampment they are immediately conscious of the enmity in every gaze. About forty or fifty box-like structures built up by leather hides enclosing adobe blocks are erected in a roughly circular pattern.

Frank shakes his head and murmurs, "If they only had a few trees they could live in proper tepees like real injuns!"

The river has meandered in this direction and formed a gently flowing pool with a net laid right across, although at first sight they cannot see if it contains fish. Some women dressed in coloured cottons are washing clothes below the fishing net and a number of small children are running around or sitting by the water completely naked. In the distance they see men around a crude corral dressed like the ubiquitous gaucho, training a pony. Nearer the homes are four unattended smoking fires.

In his best Spanish Lauchlin addresses one of the older women. "Good day, Señoras. Is it possible to speak to Don Chichon?"

There is no reply but one of the younger women rises and runs towards the men. The visitors remain in the saddle. The washing has stopped and they remain the focus of about seventeen pairs of eyes. The silence is only broken by *Durazno* pawing the ground like a child digging up a small pebble. Eventually three of the men walk towards them. Lauchlin dismounts. "Good day, Señores, we are hoping to talk with your leader, Don Chichon."

A man of about forty looks at him. "Who are you?"

"My name is Lauchlin." He chooses to stress the last syllable, hoping to make it sound more in keeping with local usage. "We have come from Don Leon Ortiz de Rosas." As he speaks the name there is an immediate murmur. The man who had spoken simply raises his hand.

"Not possible. Chichon very busy."

Retaining his polite stance, Lauchlin nods before asking "When is he likely to be less busy?"

"Chichon always busy!" All the men laugh and turn to walk away in a dismissive and insulting manner. The women merely continue to stare totally immobile. Lauchlin feels helpless. How can he negotiate with these people if they refuse even to talk?

With a huge heave he manages to get back into the saddle. "C'mon," he says to Frank. They urge the animals to follow the men, walking behind until they are very close to them. Durazno is sniffing at the back of a man's head. He cannot resist turning to see what is happening. "You show us Chichon please. Today we are polite and gentle!"

This time there is some talk among them. This is something they had not prepared for. Chichon will not be pleased.

The silence continues. Durazno plays her part. She lunges forward and licks the spokesman's ear as if he had wiped it with a sweetness. He jumps away in surprise and the three start hurrying again towards the group who have been watching while pretending to be concentrating on the pony.

Some forty metres away, in the direction of the big river, there is a kind of chicken run, fenced in by dried hides. Lauchlin can tell how they move it every few days allowing the birds a fresh range. The old run can be seen alongside, it is scratched and dusty. It is an apt simile for what Don Leon had said of their whole encampment.

One man now comes towards them. He is tall and looks muscular under the thin cotton shirt. His face is oval with a prominent forehead under black hair pulled back into a single tail. He has a long straggly moustache under a beak of a nose. He is frowning, clearly displeased and in no way intimidated.

"What you want?"

Lauchlin dismounts again, wondering if he will be able to regain his seat without assistance. "Are you Don Chichon?"

"I Chichon. We have no *titulos* here. Who you?"

"I am Lauchlin. We are sent here by Don Leon de Rosas. Where can we talk privately?"

"No privately here. All same man!"

"And woman – and children – all same?"

But the slight criticism hits no target. The Indian merely twitches an eyebrow and looks coldly back at them.

"Don Leon says this is his land. He needs it for his cattle."

This time there is a perceptible sneer on Chichon's face. "This Coacha land since sun appear in sky. We many land. Sometimes we here sometimes we move to land of brown river, sometime to Grey Rock. We many land – many year!"

"But this land is registered with the Regional Council as belonging to Don Leon. You must move away!"

Chichon turns to the men at his side. Speaking Guarani which Lauchlin only partially understands, he laughs as he explains: "Little man in city have paper with names so this no longer Coacha lands!" The other men join him in laughing.

Lauchlin hangs on to Durazno's reins and leans towards the Chief, saying softly: "the law is on Don Leon's side." He suggestively strokes the rifle's leather saddle-bag while fixing his eyes firmly on the Indian. "If there is a war you will be out-numbered!" Turning away in a relaxed way, he adds, "suppose he gives you a nice present – cattle perhaps, or clothes – or even money!"

Chichon's face is a mask. "He give us school when he first come. We leaving that soon – but we not be going far!" He turns away signifying that the interview is over. Lauchlin is reminded of Don Leon.

He tries once more. "Chichon, you have many women and children here. You have a responsibility for them. If you do not move north as Don Leon instructs, men will come with guns. Many hurt!"

"And this your Jesus? Your Doctor Ignacio he teach us all men same and loved by Lord Jesus." He is not always easy to understand but Lauchlin gathers the sense as he continues: "We liken man seen by good Samarian – if we need help doctor say good Lord Jesus come rescue us!" He laughs coarsely then shakes his head and spits before turning away. The men join him in giving all their attention to the horse.

Frank, who has been sitting silent in the saddle quietly leans down and pulls out the Kentucky from its holster. He loads it and aims quickly at one of the hens scratching in the grass where it can just be seen through a gap in the hide screen. There is an explosion as he pulls the trigger and the hen is carried some five metres by the blast where it flaps around in its death throes.

Chichon looks at Frank with utter disdain. "Is useful. Maybe we go get some."

Lauchlin tells him "they are not easy to obtain – or use! We need to see you making moves to leave. We shall be back!"

This time Chichon really shows that the meeting is over by walking off and entering one of the squat mud huts.

Lauchlin feels deflated. Chichon has shown his complete contempt for them and their talk of land registration. With as much dignity as possible, he puts his left foot in the stirrup and manages to heave himself up. As he says to Frank later, he could swear Durazno leant over to help him. They ride back the way they came.

Lauchlin still hopes that in time Chichon will come to a different conclusion. In order to keep an eye on the encampment, they decide to settle themselves within two or three miles. There is a slight incline giving them a view of the village. They hobble the horses with ends of rope; there is grass and water in abundance. They make themselves a late lunch by frying some of the hunks of bacon and then settle down for a restful day or two keeping a watch to see if Chichon makes a move.

Thin clouds turn to a light drizzle and their failure to pack capes minimizes their idyll. There is no shelter but the horses look quite content.

Chapter 26

Two days later Alicia and her guest take their ponies out for their customary early morning canter. Encarnacion Ezcurra is a city girl but her wealthy father with roots in Spain has always ensured that his daughter is familiar with horses and knows how to ride. The two had met at their small private school in Buenos Aires and Alicia's father, Don Leon, is always quick to identify suitable marriage partners for his family. 'Money should marry money' is one of his favourite sayings.

Francisco supervises Juancito in bringing out the two horses and fitting them up with saddles and bridles. They hold them in the yard while waiting for the young ladies to emerge. It is a glorious morning after rather a damp and cold night. The animals sniff the air and are eager to be on their way. But Encarnacion is not to be hurried. Barely seventeen she is quite aware of the need for a young lady to be immaculately turned out in every respect. Whilst both girls are competent riders with conventional stirrups, Encarnacion, ever mindful of her appearance, prefers to be seen riding side-saddle and Alicia follows suit. At last they appear. Encarnacion wears a black, full-length billowing silk skirt that totally obscures her fashionably tiny feet in their elegant, highly polished boots. Over it she has chosen a black velvet jacket and white blouse with a frilled front. On her head she sports a black formal straw *sombrero* and a veil held in place by a small but exquisite diamond and gold brooch pinned to her jacket. Black kid gloves complete her perfection.

Alicia is not to be out-done and wears a similar outfit in dark green. She cannot be bothered with a veil and wears a simple headscarf. The men cup their hands and hoist the ladies into position. For appearance they each sport a small stock whip. With superbly straight backs they click their tongues and the horses leave the cobbled yard and make their way down towards the river path. Alicia has chosen this route as she secretly hopes Lauchlin may be camped somewhere along the eight or so miles they plan to canter through. She has a romantic vision of having the men serve them with coffee.

There is no sign of the two British soldiers so they turn left up the hilly drove track leading away from the river, planning to ride back along the soft grassy field at the top where the horses can be safely urged into a gallop. They reach this spot with the horses breathing heavily from the climb. They hear a soft whoop behind them. Encarnacion turns her head to see five mounted gauchos urging their ponies towards them.

"Whatever do they think they're doing, Alicia. Cannot they see we are here?"

As their faces become clearer, Alicia quickly realizes they are Coacha and not from their own *estancia*. She is not especially alarmed.

"Oh these people are around the area quite often – take no notice."

Although she knows her father hates them and wants them moved away, Alicia has been familiar with them for much of her life. She knows how the younger males like to show off so the two girls urge their mounts to the side so that the Indians can overtake without coming too close. Alicia thinks they always smell strongly with a unique odour difficult to describe.

Instead of riding past, Chichon who is leading them, makes a noise deep in his throat and the others reach out and grasp the girls' bridles before turning and pulling the horses behind them, back down towards the river. Alicia gives a shout – she is not frightened but shocked and angered.

Encarnacion, however, feels seriously threatened and cries out: "Whatever do these filthy savages think they are doing? Go away!" She uses her small whip to try and shake off the hands holding her bridle. She shouts at them to let go but sitting side-saddle has to hold on to her own pommel to avoid being thrown off. Alicia carefully feels for the decorated gaucho knife in its smart scabbard fixed to her belt. She always considers it an essential part of her '*Countryman's*' attire.

Riding as swiftly as they can, the Indians drag them to the village. As they enter they ignore the women permanently washing clothes in the lake below the fish-net, exactly as before. In the centre of the encampment Chichon dismounts and watches as the captive girls are dragged off their saddles and frog-marched into his hut. Alicia secretly draws her knife and stabs one of the men's hands. He draws away in shock but the others grasp her and seize the weapon. They have their wrists bound behind them. One of the Indians is so fascinated by the folds of clothing around Encarnacion's ankles that he begins to bind them while forcing her clothing up towards her knees but Chichon stops him with a curt order before leading the men out.

Alicia remains lying on her left side conscious of a hard belt buckle digging into her side. She now curses the vanity that made her choose to wear it. The scabbard without the knife has slipped down with the belt and is now hidden in her skirt somewhere under her thigh. She has difficulty in sitting up, her hands are tied so firmly that she can only use her shoulder as a pivot to twist round to see her friend. It is fairly dark inside the hut; she can just see that Encarnacion has her eyes tightly shut her mouth a thin line of pain. Alicia asks if she is hurt. Through a grimaced mouth she replies in a whisper Alicia can barely hear:

"I am contaminated! Those filthy natives have touched me, tied my hands, felt my clothes. My father's nobility and ancient lineage are insulted – he may be forced to reject me!" Her voice rises, "I smell of them now – it is in my hair, my skin, my clothes! Oh what is to become of me?"

Three miles away, Lauchlin and Frank feel guilty and angry in equal measure as they load the Kentucky's and mount up. Lauchlin had been walking back towards the small hill commanding a reasonable view over the village. He had hoped to see them folding their blankets and hides before making moves in line with Don Leon's commands. He had seen Chichon ride out with four companions and his initial feeling was one of satisfaction, in the hope that this was the vanguard of a general exodus. To keep them in view he had moved round and down the hill.

When he sees them turn back in a southerly direction he assumes they are merely a hunting party. This is irritating. He will have to return to the village and confront them more forcibly. Frank has gone forward to observe the other side. He retraces his steps thinking about the best way to handle this disobedient chief. Lauchlin had been considering waving to the two young girls as they left the river and moved up the track towards their homeward gallop, but they were too far away. Suddenly he sees the Indians again, riding hard behind the girls. With horror he hears their shouts and his first reaction is to run to Durazno and head them off before they reach the village. But there is no time. Frank quickly returns to join him and they shout suggestions to each other as they saddle the horses.

They have no way of knowing what Chichon plans to do. Is it a considered plan or just a spot decision that only occurred to him when he saw them? Lauchlin feels that the first thing is to let the whole of the small tribe know what the outcome of such an outrage will be, that the action has been witnessed and that they will all be held responsible for whatever happens.

Frank counters the argument, "Chichon may consider them simply a couple of gaucho women and relatively unimportant. He may not know who they are. If he begins to think they're important to us, won't that strengthen his hand and encourage him to stay?" They discuss the several elements as they hurry towards the village.

Once again they are ignored by the women near the entrance bent over their washing. Approaching the centre Chichon steps out in front of them with his arms folded across his chest in a halting and commanding way.

"Ah Chichon, you are still here. Why are you not making moves to leave as the owner of the land has instructed?"

"Chichon not move. This our land! We stay here. We have two captives. You cannot send soldiers now maybe hurt women prisoners."

Lauchlin bursts out: "Women prisoners! Pah! Servants -What is that to us? Great Chief like Chichon will know that noble Spanish families like Don Leon Ortiz de Rosas take small account of females! Now, if you had captured Juan Manuel – his eldest son – that would be something else. But young girl servants – pah!"

Chichon looks doubtful. Frank's horse starts to wander about as if seeking a blade or two of grass to nibble. He seems to be trying to get it to behave. Chichon watches then looks up belligerently, "These pretty women. Make good playthings for my young men!" He starts to walk away then turns back: "They not dressed like servants – yes…nice shapes under clothes…my men like…perhaps me too!"

"Then they would be of even less value or interest to Don Leon. No Chichon, you must leave here, Don Leon has decided. You go or you all die."

The shaft goes home. Lauchlin can see the troubled look. Chichon walks away, then suddenly swings back again. "You want to hear squealing and crying from captive women? You wait there - I start asado – maybe we cook them first!"

They turn their horses away immediately. "That is a matter of utter indifference to us Chichon. We shall have to go and tell Don Leon that you are refusing to move and have stolen two of his women. He will come soon with many soldiers. Great chiefs do not hide behind women!"

They ride back past the featureless washerwomen and children. They regain the main river path and continue until they are out of sight.

Frank shakes his head. "I don't know. If we had more men with us we could mount an immediate attack. You saw the way those injuns acted – the ladies may get raped!"

Lauchlin is making up his mind. "We've got to rescue them at once anyway! Chichon will think we're on our way back to Ibicoy to report. He'll think he's got at least five or six hours, probably more if an army has to be put together…I just wish it was dark…"

Frank looks at him. "You know you have begun to look much like any other gaucho… Perhaps I'm the same…"

"Mmm…I wonder… you think… If we slim down to just shirt and baggy trews and perhaps make a few rips and tears…muddy our faces… get in by the other side…what's it like, you've been there."

"There's a slight slope up from the stream, little bit of cover from rushes. I'm pretty sure they're in the big brick-shaped squat just off the centre. It's bigger than the others – has a small window in the side - perhaps it's Chichon's. I let *Lechuga* wander towards it and I think I caught a whiff of perfume – nothing like the stink those filthy injuns give off!"

They determine a plan of attack. They must ride out of sight well above the village until they can approach it from the northern end. The horses must be kept out of sight yet near enough for a rapid escape. They will try to approach the huts without being noticed and get the girls out, perhaps the window can be used. Then back to the horses…easy? If only it were dark. How long before the girls' delayed return is noticed and a search initiated?

The first part is straightforward. When above and hidden from view they alter their appearance. They jettison all the food and utensils from the horses keeping only the coils of rope and the two Kentucky rifles which they load with the maximum of five bullets each and hide the remaining rounds in their pockets.

They hobble the horses as before, concealing them in a small rocky ravine where the stream descends sharply from the village before making another gentle pool on its way to the big river.

Although their appearance has been altered, they must not be seen. A simple incline accompanies the stream as it reaches back to the gentle slope of plain where the adobe huts are sited. The slight fall of shallow water makes a constant gurgling sound over the stones that fails to drown the ever-present bird song.

As he reaches the top, Lauchlin finds a total lack of cover. Although there is a cold wind, the sun is shining clearly and would glint brightly on a rifle or knife blade which could expose their presence.

Frank remains hidden in the grass at the bottom of the slope. He keeps both rifles by his side. Lauchlin goes forward trying to imitate the movements of a local. His right hand hides the knife which has been regularly honed and is now razor-sharp. For a few moments he has some difficulty in registering his position. There is a hut close to him and he moves carefully around it. Other than the stream there is little sound. He holds his head close to the hut but hears nothing and the entrance flap is tied shut. He moves forward between two more squats before he can see the back of Chichon's larger hut. Facing him there is the flapping gap of a window.

The hut has thick wooden stakes. He wonders for a moment where they had come from in this almost tree-less plain. There is a hole in the roof presumably to let smoke out and some ropes hang down to carry hides which are tightly attached. But those at the base are hard and dry; his knife makes little impression.

He hears soft murmuring from within. He tries to use the window but although flapping in the breeze it is tied shut with thick hides that are much heavier than he had expected. To reach the entrance he must expose himself to everyone in the centre of the village but there is no alternative.

Casually he slides round from the rear and enters the hut. He hears a shout in the distance. As his eyes adjust from the light outside, he makes out the figures of the two girls lying on their sides. Alicia is facing him. At first he is merely a figure against the light but as he moves into the hut her eyes open in amazement. He signs to her to keep silent. She swivels round to show him the bindings on her wrists, they are red and raw where she has been trying to loosen them. The bindings are thick hide and at an angle that prevents the knife from cutting away from her hands. He cannot risk cutting her. Running feet are approaching. He ducks down behind Alicia's voluminous skirt. There is a blanket almost under her. By forcing himself behind her and half hidden by the blanket he ducks down.

"You cheap women stay here eh!" It is a voice he does not recognize. He can just see the silhouette against the light in the entrance. The figure moves towards Encarnacion. "You cheap woman eh, I feel you all over when Chichon have sleep!" He squats down and makes small moaning sounds as if he had already started. Encarnacion shrieks in horror.

"Urgh! Go away! Stop!" She screams more loudly and uses her feet to try and kick him. Suddenly Chichon comes in. He is angry and shouts at the man in their own language. They leave the hut with Chichon still roaring his disapproval.

Lauchlin remains half under the blanket as he tries to turn Alicia over to find a better place for his knife to cut the wrist bindings. In doing so he braces his left arm to give him better leverage. She turns easily her slight figure yielding to his pressure. She gives a small grunt of disapproval and he realizes with horror that his hand had been pressing hard on her upper thigh. He moves it away as if scalded but he has her wrists now and can slice through the leather ties. With her hands free she turns to him and, in English, whispers in his ear. "Oh zank you!" He is left with a delicate scent that, for a moment, overpowers the rotten smell in the hut.

Silently he rolls towards Encarnacion. Her eyes have stayed tightly shut so that she is unaware of the rescue attempt. As soon as he tries to turn her on her front to reach the bindings, she starts howling. "No, no! Don't touch me – filthy animals!"

Alicia does her best to silence her but the screaming continues and she keeps refusing to allow him to reach her hands. In exasperation he puts down the knife and grasps her shoulders with both hands forcing her to turn over burying her mouth in the folds of her skirt and the filthy floor blanket. The screaming continues, although now muted and she manages a good kick in his groin. Alicia helps hold her down but for a full minute he cannot find the knife. At last, with relief he sees it and is able to saw through the dried hide. An Indian walking within ten paces of the entrance calls out at them to keep quiet.

Alicia helps her friend to stand up. Lauchlin whispers what they must do. Sadly, escape via the window at the back is impossible. Fortunately their clothes are dark. He puts his knife away before taking a quick look outside. He pushes them through the door before taking one of their hands and pulling them as fast as he can towards Frank's hiding place. He hears a roar from behind but they reach the top of the incline safely. They make the girls descend to the horses. He tells Alicia to unhobble them and to mount up. In line with their plan, Frank will take the lighter girl, Alicia, in front of him on *Lechuga*. They take the loaded rifles and lie hidden some ten metres apart. He hears the girls arguing below and knows that the hysterical Encarnacion wishes to ride off, abandoning their rescuers, but Alicia will have none of it.

There is whooping from the first of the Indians. Chichon appears riding a pony bareback. Frank fires first and the horse goes down. Hopefully it will have trapped its rider but they have no opportunity to check. A small hail of arrows comes down near them but they are not aimed as every head that shows itself is shot at and the Indians are quick to draw back. Lauchlin knows their ammunition is nearly exhausted and signs to Frank that they should leave. Both the girls are in the saddles, their skirts pulled up to allow their legs to grip. With the rifles in their right hands the men mount up. Lauchlin somehow scrabbles up behind Alicia and holds her as they all kick the animals into movement.

Lauchlin is on *Durazno* frantically feeling for the stirrups. Alicia shouts at him to hang on to her while she controls the animal. Her years of riding now show their value. Simultaneously kicking his sides and shouting in *Durazno's* ear she demonstrates her mastery. The horse's response is immediate and they are soon in a gallop while Lauchlin desperately hangs on. Her hat has gone and her hair is flying back into his face. He has difficulty in staying in the saddle but her body is so settled and firm that he holds on to her feeling her warmth.

Frank is behind on *Lechuga f*everishly gripping the reins while clutching Encarnacion to his chest. She is still in a confused state but she sits lightly and he kicks his horse to follow *Durazno.*

Without further delay they are soon on the South side of the village approach where it nears the river path. But they are now under a more organized attack with several of the Indians on ponies. They are bound to overtake. It is a matter of a moment for the horses to be pulled up, for Lauchlin to take Frank's rifle and tell them to go on to the estancia and organize a rescue. Alicia is tempted to argue but Frank slaps *Durazno's* side and they move quickly on.

Lauchlin flings himself to the ground as he sees five Indians galloping towards him. He takes up a position where the river reeds conceal him although they offer little protection. He loads both rifles – ten bullets with three left in one pocket. He must conserve these but he has to hold the Indians back until Frank can reach the estancia. An arrow sings past his head. He is surprised at its speed – they are clearly lethal. He aims carefully at the leading horseman and is relieved to see him drop. One of the horses has halted allowing its rider to use the height to obtain a better view. He has an arrow fixed in the bow and releases it at the same moment as Lauchlin fires. The man is blown backwards out of sight but his arrow hisses into Lauchlin's left thigh, piercing the fleshier part roughly half-way between his knee and groin. The pain is intense, the head almost through but he must keep firing. The action seems to cease for some moments. He slides backwards into the water, shifting his situation by three or four metres. The water is cold and gives him some relief. He grits his teeth knowing he must not give in. The water is nearly chest high to him and he takes the last of the bullets out of his right hand pocket leaving both rifles trembling on the top of the reeds. He has five rounds in one rifle and three in the other. In the moment of silence he suddenly thinks of the old witch, *Sietemesinas* and herwarning to him.

Suddenly, in a concerted attack six Indians rise up together, shooting their arrows into his old position. He empties one rifle and thinks three were hit. It causes the action to cease again momentarily. Then another Indian stands about to launch a spear. Lauchlin turns to fire; it twists his wound and the pain causes him to miss. He gives a curse and repeats the action for the man to disappear. Lauchlin now has just two rounds left in the chamber. The pain in his thigh is becoming overpowering. He lets the empty rifle sink in the water.

There is movement on the other side of the path. The Indians must have managed to creep around him and now have a commanding position.

'Well, so be it' he thinks. Should he use one of the bullets on himself? There is a shout and the movement becomes a rider waving. He is about to aim when he sees it is Jacinto, the man who scouts the far corners of Don Leon's lands, spending days on his own.

Jacinto stands in the stirrups, fully exposed, and bellows at the Indians with real anger. In his hands he holds three long spears. He gives a roar of challenge and hate as he launches his horse in the Indians' direction. He stands in the stirrups to throw a spear. Lauchlin cannot see it land but there is a cry of agony as Jacinto disappears in the direction of the village.

While feeling in the water for the lost rifle, Lauchlin pulls himself towards the path. By luck his hand falls on it and he uses it to help support him. He wishes he could break the arrow but knows he cannot do it alone.

Jacinto returns shouting at him to climb out. The Indians have fled – for the moment at least – their realization that other parties are joining in has sapped their confidence.

Lauchlin staggers on his right leg. He is cold, wet and suffering from reaction. Jacinto sees the blood pouring out of his trousers to drip on the ground. Dismounting he takes hold of Lauchlin's arm and supports it across his shoulder to help him towards the horse. But there is no way that this will succeed. Ignoring the patient's protests he takes his knife and in one move cuts his trousers from waist to foot. He clicks his tongue, looking about him for a large stone, before forcing Lauchlin to sit while he places the stone under the arrow. With his knife in his teeth he grasps Lauchlin's thigh and holds it down firmly. Then, without a moment's delay he chops his knife down hard on the feathered end of the arrow. It falls away but the pain and shock make Lauchlin pass out. Jacinto takes an end of rope and binds a tourniquet to stop the bleeding then takes off his own shirt and wraps it around the wound. He avoids the area of the arrowhead which he can clearly see almost through the leg. He whistles for his horse, *Esquinal.* It quickly responds, its ears still twitching at the shooting and the excitement. Jacinto's plan is to hoist himself into the saddle and hold Lauchlin before him but the lifeless body proves an insurmountable weight. The horse sheers away from the scent of blood. There is no alternative but to ease him on to the animal's back while he runs alongside with one hand holding the reins and the other propping up Lauchlin's almost senseless body.

Frank had made good time and the party reached Ibicoy within four hours. Francisco is appalled at the news and within twenty minutes an army of ten gauchos is galloping back along the river path. They are lightly armed with just their knives and a couple of axes but are fully prepared to take on the whole village. They soon meet up with Jacinto so that caring for the still barely conscious Lauchlin becomes the prime concern.

With Encarnacion occupying the best room, Alicia insists on the next-best guest-room for Lauchlin. Large pincers have reduced the feathered end to the skin but removing the buried head will call for serious surgery. Arrangements have already been put in hand for Doctor Fuselio, their usual Practitioner, to come out from Buenos Aires in the morning to ensure the best possible treatment for Encarnacion. With the advancing hour there is small prospect of him coming to Ibicoy this evening but a message is sent advising him of the needs of a new patient and urging him to make all possible speed in the morning.

There is little sleep in the house that night. Alicia is beside herself with worry for the man who saved her life. All the ladies, from Doña Valenciana through Doña Agustina to the elderly cook, have recipes which will help mitigate the pain and prevent infection. Semi-stupefied, Lauchlin politely swallows the various potions but they have little effect. Jacinto's shirt has been removed and the rough rope tourniquet replaced by boiled vegetable cord which is carefully replaced every ten minutes or so when the blood gushes out once again. Because of the personal position of the wound, Alicia is banned from attending such treatments but she insists on sitting with him through the night. Most of the nursing is done by Francisco whose rough, scarred hands have been scrubbed sore.

The following morning both Don Leon and his son come to Ibicoy. Tomasin the coachman has brought the father together with two doctors but Juan Manuel has taken a short leave from the army and arrives separately. The doctors go into an immediate huddle over the patient after which they withdraw to discuss the matter with Don Leon in his study.

"This is a serious operation, Don Leon; happily the arrow missed the femoral artery but it is awkwardly positioned behind the bone." He draws a small sketch, "it is lying like this and will virtually require simultaneous surgery at the front and the rear." He looks into Don Leon's eyes: "To be frank, it would be easier for everyone to simply remove the whole leg at the hip." Don Leon's face is horrified.

Doctor Fuselio pauses again, getting his thoughts in order. "Few patients can survive the shock. It is also..." he gives a small deprecatory cough, "very expensive and we understand that he is not a member of the family..."

Don Leon looks up angrily. "Do not talk to me about cost! This man carried out a supreme service to me and I must have the best possible care for him!" The doctors bow their understanding.

Doctor Arriego is the more experienced surgeon and now takes over. "He is a young man and presumably in good health. We will find the best room for the surgery and do the work tomorrow morning." He turns to his colleague: "I must send for my instruments and I think it best if we have Julio bring them. We will probably be in need of his strength."

Two hours later they return to Don Leon and outline their plan. They have found a substantial work table in the kitchen area: a marble slab on plain legs which are fixed firmly to the ground. They will require the whole area to be covered with clean sheets and wish to have the room emptied for their use. Julio, Dr. Arriego's assistant, will lie the patient down on the slab and tie him firmly with lengths of rope which they would like to be washed and boiled overnight. "We shall require twice this length as we shall have to turn the patient over on to his front when we need to make the rear incisions."

Don Leon shakes his head over the list. "It will be a terrible experience for him. How can we reduce the pain?"

"Well, the traditional way is to make him so drunk that he knows little about what is happening. Perhaps that can be arranged. I have heard of the use of chemicals and gases to make the patient unconscious, but..." he chuckles mirthlessly, "the reports I get tell only of the patient dying so I think we'll just have to proceed the conventional way and hope for the best. A Tetanus infection is the principal danger!"

Lauchlin finds that sitting up in the bed keeping the leg immobile and clear of any weight is not too painful. He gets accustomed to the strange effects of the tourniquet although its release every ten or fifteen minutes is agony. As the day wears on, it gets colder and he needs the comfort of a light blanket but they keep bringing him glasses of various cordials and the slight light headedness is welcome. He is conscious of Alicia's presence and, although they speak mostly in Spanish, he giggles at some of her English. When she bends over him with a glass to his lips she is careful to avoid choking him. Even in his dazed condition he is aware of the perfume of her hair. Once, on a rare occasion when they are alone, she shows him a small brooch on a chain around her neck; he recognizes the button he presented at their first meeting.

Lauchlin is wandering about in a blinding storm of pain. He is back on *Scottish Flame* but fallen overboard and the waves continually knock him in various directions. He cannot breathe. He knows he is drowning as he chokes to death and hears voices calling to him. He wakes lying on his front with his face buried in a towel soaked in vomit. An agonizing pain runs from his left shoulder to his foot. Someone wipes his face and a heavy, gorilla of a man turns him round on his back. A glass is offered to his lips; he drinks and throws up. He lives in excruciating pain. He passes out again and tries to fight the fearful beast with its jaws clamped around his thigh.

It is two days before he recovers proper consciousness. They try to feed him with a meaty soup but he prefers the cognac which helps to dull the pain. Alicia talks to him in English. He can only groan in reply. A day later he realizes she is crying as she holds his hand; it jerks him back to a kind of civilized behaviour. On the following morning he is aware that the surgeon is back and everyone in the room is beaming.

Doctor Arriego is sniffing a bandage he has just removed. "Yes, I think it's a great success. The stitches I put in have held well. Of course, he will always have a scar there…I remember a bull-fighter I did once… very similar. Yes, I think I can report to Doctor Fuselio that things have gone well!"

Chapter 27

After three weeks Lauchlin is able to get out of bed on his own. The relief goes some way to compensate for the discomfort of his wound. The embarrassment of intimate attention from male members of staff had slowly become acceptable, especially when the ever-solicitous Francisco hands over those elements to Ticho the garden slave who is now devoted to him. Frank regularly comes in just before the dinner hour but he is clearly being kept busy and invariably brings the conversation round to how much he wishes to return to the army. North America now seems less alien land to him. Alicia comes every day but always now accompanied by her mother and the visits are stilted. Not having shaved for well over a month, he has grown a fine, almost blonde beard. When her mother leaves the room for a moment, Alicia lightly strokes him under the chin and whispers – "I've often wondered what it would be like to kiss a man with a beard." He is about to reply when her mother returns. Several times he asks after Father Ignacio but the answers seem evasive.

He is forced to stay in his room although gradually he becomes adept at putting weight on the leg and, with the help of crutches or sticks, begins to get around. On the fiftieth day following the operation he is able to join the family at dinner. He finds that Frank is still confined to the barn and to taking his meals with the senior staff. He asks to speak with Don Leon in his study when he thanks him sincerely for the medical attention given him but informs him that he would now prefer to join Frank in the barn. They had arrived together and he hopes they can leave together.

Don Leon seems to wince at this last statement, and counters "Why are you so determined to leave? You have the possibility of a good career here." He appears to be busy with some papers on his desk but then looks up. "You must know that I am deeply grateful to you for saving my only daughter..." he coughs, clearly embarrassed, "there is nothing that the family will not do for you...!"

"But my home – my family, are in Scotland! They will be wondering what has happened to me."

Don Leon nods, but almost dismissively as he mutters "they can always come out here and visit." He stands to collect two books off a shelf. "These are two of my account books. I seem to remember you saying that you understood accounting." The book falls open at the current page and he leafs back some way. "Juan Manuel always does the figures. He started when he was nine years old, see, here are his first entries!" The father is proud. Lauchlin leans on the table to look. There are some ink blots but the figures are clear and another hand has ticked various figures in pencil. Don Leon continues,

"Father Ignacio used to do the auditing – see, there in pencil!"

"Where is Father Ignacio? I haven't seen him since my injury!"

"Ah...yes...now do you think you could do these figures for me? It would be a real help."

Lauchlin studies the books more closely. "It has been a long time, Don Leon but, yes, I think so...You have one hundred *centavos* to the gold Real. We have a system of two hundred and fifty-two pennies to the Guinea."

"Ha! That seems a curious method – you will find our system easier, I think."

"It should be, Don Leon, perhaps Father Ignacio could look over my first efforts."

Don Leon just mumbles at this, then continues. "The account books are all here in my study. Please look them over and let me know your thoughts about auditing them. After that I will arrange for all Debtor and Credit Bills to be passed to you."

In fact Lauchlin is pleased to have a worthwhile task to do while unable to ride. He takes all the accounts to a separate table and soon finds their several patterns. They are very like the books he kept for the Master Tailor, Francis Reardon, in Edinburgh so long ago. He wonders how he is. A nice man who had been forced to sell his business.

His decision to sleep in the barn with Frank is not propitious. It soon becomes obvious that one of the house servants has been partnering him. Also, the opportunities to wash are not as good and he is aware of the need to keep his wound dressings clean. He allows himself to be coaxed back into the main house.

After three months he is generally recognized as the Accountant. Juan Manuel flits in and out. The army is taking up much of his time but Lauchlin learns he is continuing to experiment with methods of preserving beef. He is now keen on finding ways of packing food for the army. Francisco proudly announces that he is perfecting a kind of shredded and salted beef they are calling *Tasajo*****.

Lauchlin perseveres with exercises and, after some days, is assisted into the saddle; support is provided by a sheepskin and the left stirrup is raised although he remains nervous about putting weight on it. But it is the gentle forays with Frank that lead to his learning of all that has been happening.

"Juan Manuel is with his Spanish cavalry regiment, I haven't seen him for months although they tell me he's around. They still talk of attacking the British but, as you know, my Spanish ain't as good as yours and I can't figure out where we're supposed to come from although I did hear we've been stuck in Montevideo for ages!"

As day follows day his riding becomes more adventurous. When out along the river path he mutters "we must be getting near the village – are things better there now or have they moved away?"

Frank nearly chokes. "Of course – that's another thing…!" Frank tells him how Juan Manuel and a group of gauchos from the *Arraña* tribe had gone up to the school. "The place had been trashed and set on fire and in the corner they found poor old Father Ignacio. They must have set about the place shortly after our little adventure. I guess he tried to stop them… anyway…" he pauses as Lauchlin interrupts.

"My God Frank, that's awful! Alicia and the family must have been terribly shocked. I wonder why they never told me…"

"Didn't want to upset you, I guess. But…err that's not all… The very next day all the men went up there…axes, knives even a couple of Kentucky rifles…"

"What happened?" Lauchlin is shocked.

"I never heard the full details but I can just imagine…they wiped out the whole tribe and burned all their huts – stole their horses but let the

---

**** Tasajo: A kind of jerked beef that became very popular.

chickens go. Seemingly Chichon was laid up, probably because we shot him, but anyway, they killed them all – women and children – the lot!"

There is silence for a while. Frank mumbles, "not Christians, you see…"

After a while he continues. "Shouldn't have taken the women… punishment, or revenge – whatever – was inevitable.Those *Arraña* fighters, you know, once they've been wound up…they don't come down again in a hurry. I think even Don Leon was a bit shocked!" He smiles ruefully, "He gave an Asado for them when they got back. I was advised not to get involved but they went on drinking and dancing all night!"

"And Alicia, how did she take it?"

"Well, to be honest I only saw her in the distance. You remember the fair Encarnacion?"

"Oh yes, what about her?"

"Well, she recovered and Alicia went home with her in the carriage. We all had to swear that the nearest any of Chichon's tribe got to her was to touch the merest fold of her dress. Don Leon agreed and, as she hadn't really been hurt at all, reckoned her worth as the daughter of a *Grande* was still as great as ever. I think Juan Manuel is still sniffing around! A bit different, I think, if she had been raped. Anyhow, Don Leon now has the clear mandate to occupy the northern lands he has always craved and some of the animals are already there." He grunts sarcastically, "maybe a few hens too!"

There is a sharp difference in the way Lauchlin is being treated. Where before he was an employee brought in to carry out a particular task, and a rather low-grade undertaking at that, he is now recognized as the girls' saviour, wounded on their behalf. As the accountant he is now almost an associate in the family business.

Frank's sleeping accommodation is moved into the house merely to satisfy Lauchlin, who needs to be in his old quarters, but Frank continues to eat with Francisco whilst Lauchlin enjoys the family dinners and the prospect of chatting in English with Alicia. But these opportunities are rare as the rest of the family cannot understand and it is clearly the height of bad manners to pursue such delights in front of them. In any event, most of the discussion is about their return to the city and they press him to accompany them.

Suddenly their departure is delayed by "a few days". Don Leon keeps the family at Ibicoy. Juan Manuel has already gone back to his unit. Don Leon is evasive about the reason. His explanation is that he wishes to manage the movement of animals himself, to the lands around the old Indian village. He invites Lauchlin to join him and explains how the soil there will be very different to that in other parts of the estancia. It has not been a good Summer and now that the March winds and Autumn rains have come, it will be necessary to keep checking the stock there for diet deficiencies as well as diseases they may pick up from infections left by the Indians' animals or, indeed, by the people themselves. But Lauchlin feels that there is something else.

The delay in moving back to Buenos Aires continues. Lauchlin makes plans to draw the accounts off every month instead of annually. He enjoys the precision of figures and it does not take up much of his time. He finds a book in the study that he reads principally to improve his Spanish. It introduces him to the symptoms and causes of disease in cattle. He finds the illustrations helpful and gets drawn into the veterinary side, increasingly going out with Francisco and becoming involved in animal husbandry. The cattle are generally in a healthy condition but occasional accidents and odd outbreaks of illness possibly caused by mineral deficiency have to be treated promptly to avoid any spread. Lauchlin often finds himself marvelling at the gauchos' skills.

Alicia continues with her morning ride, invariably using a conventional saddle with stirrups. She has decided that none of the female house staff ride well enough to accompany her. The young groom, Juancito, acts as a chaperone as she occasionally arranges "accidental" meetings with Lauchlin. Their relationship advances and Juancito knows better than to hang around too visibly when the pair dismount to examine a view or to discuss some serious matter. But sometimes he is questioned by the senior house staff who may have to answer matters posed by Alicia's mother.

In truth, Alicia's curiosity about him and enjoyment of his company started even before her rescue from Chichon. But the nursing process had accelerated that closeness. Bringing him a drink one day she had playfully kissed his bearded cheek. It seemed natural and was as light as a butterfly's breath but he had immediately looked in her eyes.

"That will help the healing a lot. I feel a surge of magic. I think you should do that more often." What starts for him as innocent banter with a girl who is little more than a child, changes as he comes to appreciate that her age of nearly eighteen is at least as mature as his own if not more. They keep their relationship secret from all but Alicia's strict upbringing soon warns her that they are playing with fire. But she enjoys the experience and her outdoor life has made her a healthy, even passionate young woman.

Her reputation is intact largely because they are so rarely alone. The thrill of his touch when helping her to dismount and the gentle breath of her kiss on his cheek is as far as they are able to go. But Lauchlin knows that his constant longing for her company is indicative of a passion that is far away from any giggling or fondling that he has ever enjoyed with the opposite sex. They cannot totally hide the signs and it is clear that her mother, Doña Agustina, would like her daughter to go and stay with friends and away from Lauchlin, but Don Leon forbids any talk of her going to the city.

A dramatic change occurs within twenty-four hours. Don Leon joins him in the study; the *Patron,* as Lauchlin is learning to call him, is anxious and hurried in his speech.

"Ah, err…Lauchlin, I have serious news from the city. We must go together at once!"

In response to his enquiry Don Leon confirms that Frank must come with them but the family will be staying at Ibicoy.

"I am summoned to a meeting of the Council. It involves the British and you and Señor Franco may be needed as interpreters. Also, he may be able to rejoin his army and, who knows, even return to his home!"

Lauchlin's heart leaps at the news. He assumes General Beresford and the other British prisoners are to be released. The prospect of seeing his mother and family again fills him with delight. For a moment he wonders why it is only Frank whom the *Patron* describes as possibly able to rejoin "his" army but soon dismisses the thought.

He is told that Alicia is out on her morning ride. Don Leon is adamant that they must leave at once. Lauchlin's mind starts turning somersaults. How can he leave without saying goodbye? Would they pass her on their way towards the city? He knows that is unlikely. In any event, they cannot have a final meeting in front of other people!

Nevertheless, escorted by four of the more belligerent gauchos, Don Leon rides his huge black stallion to lead them out within the hour. Frank is eager to leave but neither he nor Lauchlin knows anything about the major historical events that have led to this summons.

Chapter 28

At a Cabinet meeting in February, 1807, the members receive a confidential despatch from Lord Cornwallis, the First Minister's special envoy to Europe. He has spent months endeavouring to negotiate an alliance with the Kingdom of Spain, or at least a truce. His latest despatch states in unequivocal terms that the First Consul, as Napoleon is now calling himself, is laying plans for the removal of the king of Spain, replacing him with his own brother, Joseph. The whole peninsula of France, Spain and Portugal is to be conjoined. In the longer term the common language of French will ensure their eternal fraternity.

After some furious debate, there is recognition that the war with Spain is entering a deeper phase. In some ways it could be counted upon as a new ally; but the truth is that it remains Britain's foe. Instructions are finally issued for army detachments temporarily held in several stations to go forward immediately to the Spanish Vice-royalty of the River Plate in accordance with their original orders. The Cabinet is uncertain as to the whereabouts of Brigadier Auchmuty, who was held at the Cape Verde Islands with his two thousand fusiliers, carabiniers and cavalry. He is now ordered to proceed at once in line with Sir David Baird's original despatches. Colonel Robert Craufurd is promoted Brigadier and sent out from England immediately with a force of some five thousand men together with cavalry and heavy guns.

Auchmuty finally arrives in the River Plate with men that have spent months aboard the heavy transports awaiting these orders. Living on naval rations and lacking proper exercise their condition is best described as "indifferent". That of the horses is even worse since landing them for exercise has been almost impossible. But it is their morale that causes their commander the greatest concern. Even the officers under him have voiced their displeasure at the vacillations of the Government.

As a first stage Auchmuty moves his force to the port of Colonia, remaining on the North side of the river, but well to the West of Montevideo. It has been held by British Infantry ever since Beresford's capture of Buenos Aires nearly a year earlier. The new arrivals are exercised heavily to restore their fighting skills. Auchmuty has been informed that further forces are on their way to the River Plate and he knows that a new Commander-in-Chief has been appointed. He decides to mount an early attack on the fortifications of Montevideo thus securing the whole Northern bank of the river.

But Montevideo is more difficult to overcome than expected. Captain Santiago de Liniers, although French by birth, is capitalizing on the general recognition of his assumption of Commander-in-Chief of the whole Vice-royalty. With the departure of the Spanish Viceroy, government over the area has been in the hands of the self-appointed Council. Now, with new prospects of war, the people demand a more experienced commander. Since Beresford's surrender he has been collecting every available member of the Spanish army, together with colonial *Patricios* as they are beginning to be known, and trained them in musketry and field-craft. Most of the Spanish are elderly, clerks and custom men, and not trained fighting troops, but he has been building a sense of pride and laying in stocks of ammunition and powder, training them, above all, in the ability to shoot down from flat roofs upon soldiers in streets below. There is advice on how to throw hot fats and cooking oils down on troops in the streets.

The fort at Montevideo was originally built centuries before to watch over the entrance to the river. It is surrounded on three sides by water and guns of heavy calibre are in position to mount a strong defence.

In the first wave of the attack, Auchmuty's *Forlorn Hope,* an initial, specially trained detachment, is beaten back with heavy losses from carronades of grape-shot. The defensive guns are brought to bear on the ships which are prevented from firing back by the sand bars and are forced to withdraw. The British attack is a failure and they abandon their position to consolidate at Colonia and to replenish their supplies.

The siege of Montevideo continues through a hot Summer into the Autumn and the British troops are relatively comfortable in their defence of Colonia and the continuing, relatively half-hearted offensive they maintain at Montevideo.

Finally, early in June, just before the middle of the Southern Winter, the new Commander-in-Chief arrives in the Plate with a brigade of fresh troops. The new arrivals are largely untrained fusiliers but they do include some forty cavalry. Major General Whitelocke has spent the last two years as Inspector General of the Army. This has exposed him to several theatres of the war against Bonaparte although without any personal responsibility for operations. Some front-line officers believe that he has a higher opinion of his abilities than his experience strictly merits.

Around the middle of July, the Winter rains set in with a vengeance born of a long dry spell. The siege of Montevideo has inevitably caused considerable hardship to the townsfolk. Eventually a form of surrender is agreed and the new Commander-in-Chief is able to send despatches to London reporting his success. He now concentrate on his principal objective.

After listening to the reports of the several scouting and Intelligence-gathering parties that have been active over recent months, he decides on an early attack to secure the more important city of Buenos Aires. In line with his somewhat academic background, the most detailed plans are made and orders issued with line by line details. He decides that the troops will disembark at the small coastal town of Ensenada. This is further from the city than Point Quilmes which was used by General Beresford and it may be that he chooses to avoid Quilmes for that very reason. In his despatches he explains that this point of landing will be less observed by the Spanish. It will, however, involve the Infantry and Artillery in marching a considerable distance, through largely unknown territory, before engaging the enemy. He informs his officers that he does not anticipate any great resistance.

"The Spanish are beaten and the locals will recognize us as liberators!"

Each Brigade will follow in line; the vanguard under his second-in-command, Brigadier General Gower, will be responsible for capturing and holding the several bridges that have been identified and mapped.

The forces at Whitelocke's disposal are considerable, as is the strength of senior officer capability, since it contains four Brigadier-Generals, some of whom have spent months in the area. Brigadier Craufurd is in charge of the Light Brigade of whom much is expected in the street fighting that may follow the previous practice.

Every man is issued with rations for three days by which time the operation will have been completed.

A Major in the 48th Brigade – Lord Muskerrow – who was not part of the Staff planning process, but who has been active in the onslaught ever since General Beresford's original invasion, declares boldly: "No-one but a madman would land at Ensenada in Winter!" This opinion comes to the ears of the C-in-C who immediately decides that Major the Lord Muskerrow will remain with his Companies at Montevideo and have no part in the successes that are bound to follow.

The plans envisage a landing before the middle of August but fog settles in the area and landing the men from ships' boats is impossible. The fog remains for a further three days resulting in many of the men consuming their rations.

The delay enables Liniers, the Spanish Commander who has now adopted the rank of army general, to assess the changes in the British attack. By a quirk of fate, as a young officer, Liniers had been Port Captain at Ensenada and he is familiar with the country around. He moves the bulk of his fighting men from Montevideo to Buenos Aires. He uses light-weight sailing and rowed craft manned by fishermen that can circumvent the mud flats and they pass the British ships undetected in the fog. Then he mobilizes his defences at Buenos Aires so that the citizenry are prepared to receive their "new visitors".

As the gloomy Winter fogs lighten, day by day, ships' boats begin ferrying the troops ashore. The rains come again and the sandbars in the river cause navigational difficulties. The first men ashore are soaked from the waist down. The landing area has been narrowed by the torrential rains which have widened small streams and troops must vacate the small beach quickly so that those behind have the necessary space. Wet and cold they commence a hard climb away from the river. The ground is heavy and the several narrow tracks become more difficult when traversed by hundreds of pairs of boots. At one stage the hill levels out to a swamp of waist-deep water under gorse-like bushes. Brigadier Gower's men are forced to push themselves some seven miles before finding easier progress. But the slow disembarkation continues behind them. During a rest break, the Vanguard is attacked by a small force of cavalry and a protective line of Infantry dug in with three guns protecting the first major bridge. A short, sharp volley secures some British casualties but they charge with the bayonet; the Spanish retreat and the guns are captured - as is the bridge - still intact.

Following this initial success, Brigadier Gower decides to bivouac on the Northern side of the River *Chuelo.* He is informed that the city is only three miles or so ahead and it is considered advisable to wait for further troops to come up. The rain continues torrential and many of the men are now without rations.

The disembarked army is spread out, more or less in single file, over a distance of ten miles. General Whitelocke remains on board his Command ship in order to be central to the operation. All hope of a secret landing has been lost and many of the men are seriously exhausted, being unused to heavy marching after their weeks on board the transports. Following a wet night the troops are roused early, without breakfast, and ordered to continue the march.

As his men are now so close to the target and, being aware of their poor condition, Brigadier Gower orders that all of their kit is to be abandoned under guard, excepting only their weapons and ammunition. Without heavy packs and 'bum-bags' they should find it easier to cover the ground. After securing the next bridge over the smaller river *Melonia,* the vanguard is rested to enable the next Brigade under Brigadier General Auchmuty to come up with them.

The city occupies a position roughly on the South-western bank of the River Plate and the army is approaching it from the South. In accordance with their orders, both of the first Brigades move around to the Northern side of the city with Auchmuty covering the extreme North and ordered to capture the *Plaza de Toros* which, being built on a slight hill, will give him an overall view of the city. Planners envisage this as an initial headquarters. The other two Brigades are under orders to clear the streets on the Southern side. Their objective will be the old *Cabildo* Fort in the *Plaza Mayor* familiar to General Beresford as his headquarters. When that has been secured they will be within half a mile of the river frontage and be able to communicate with the ships which can then move up river to join them.

Auchmuty's Brigade is the first to come under a heavy and sustained fire from the flat roofs of the buildings. They break in to any house that they think has a dominant position. These tend to be the larger properties so that as they break down a door they are met by a hail of fire from an open patio, sometimes with an overseeing balcony. This causes many casualties. With the bayonet they fight their way to the roof hoping to secure a commanding position from which to clear other roof-tops. But progress is necessarily slow and losses mount on both sides.

The Brigades engaged in clearing the South side of the city have an even harder time. The *Patricios* fight tooth and nail to protect their homes. Overall it is a brutal engagement and the fusiliers who reach the Plaza in front of the old fort are subjected to particularly heavy fire from cannon on the roof bombarding them with grape-shot.

At mid-day General Liniers sends an emissary under a white flag to the senior officer he can observe from his headquarters in the fort. This demands surrender. It happens to be Brigadier Craufurd who rejects the offer immediately. He is uncertain about the progress of the other brigades and his men are breaking down the doors of many houses in their approach to the square so that he hopes to have a dominant position shortly. Some of the residences even overlook the roof of the fort and British marksmen are soon trying to deal with identified targets although they themselves remain under a heavy fire.

Meanwhile, Auchmuty's Brigade has captured the Bull-ring which increasingly serves as a reception point for the wounded. Its thick walls offer a degree of protection of which the troops quickly take advantage.

Shortly after his lunch, General Whitelocke comes ashore with his senior staff. Even their horses make heavy work of the journey but they meet up with Brigadier Gower as night begins to fall.

Whilst acknowledging the difficulties encountered, Gower's opinion remains optimistic. He fears the losses have been heavy but they still have a substantial force and are almost in control of the city. However, during their evening meal in a tent looking over the river, Whitelocke receives a letter from General Liniers. This informs him that he has captured General Crauford with over one thousand of his men. He offers that if Whitelocke surrenders and takes his forces away, Liniers will restore all the prisoners captured, including those held since General Beresford's original landing.

The letter adds that in view of the many colonist *Patricios* killed, wounded and whose homes have been destroyed, should General

Whitelocke reject his offer, the matter will be handed over to the Provincial Council and he could not be held responsible for the result.

After consulting his senior colleagues, including an exchange of despatches with Brigadier Auchmuty in the *Plaza de Toros,* Whitelocke sends General Gower to reject the demand outright but to counter with a request for a twenty-four hour truce to enable the wounded to be collected and treated. This is agreed.

As the casualties are brought in, it becomes clear that the losses have been greater than calculated. Including those captured by the Spanish, the total lost numbers over three thousand men. Nevertheless, Gower maintains that they still have over six thousand troops of all ranks and have captured over thirty guns. Also, as he thumps the table, they have themselves captured over a thousand prisoners and, what is more, they are now virtually in possession.

Auchmuty points out that even with the capture of the city they are not in possession of the whole province; to complete the operation they would need at the very least a further five thousand experienced troops, plus cavalry and artillery to maintain the country thereafter. This would require more resources than the Government would be willing to grant.

Whitelocke asks for the truce to be extended by a further three days. This is agreed on condition that no moves are made to improve their military situation.

Chapter 29

As Don Leon and his team ride in to the first of the city's streets, the scenes that meet their eyes make the gauchos angry. They start by being silent, as if overcome with horror, but this soon turns to voluble exchanges and Lauchlin recognizes that he and Frank are part of the target.

Don Leon curtly tells them to keep quiet but he shakes his head as ruined properties become commonplace. There are occasional troupes of British soldiers mainly standing at street corners as if supervising the cleaning up of the city. The wounded have been taken away but there is still ample evidence that this was a battlefield. Although they are without weapons, their muskets are stacked within easy reach.

The party is stopped by a Spanish guard in his green uniform. Don Leon briefly explains their mission and he directs them to the Plaza Mayor and the Cabildo fort. They appear to be late for a meeting that has already begun. Don Leon directs his gauchos to take all the horses to their city mansion – Lauchlin hears that they have followed the French habit of styling their home *Hotel Rosas.* He suggests that Frank should make his way to the army headquarters but is particularly anxious that he should dine with him tonight in order that their farewells can be properly fulfilled. He asks Lauchlin to stay with him.

"Without Father Ignacio we shall be very short of interpreters. I can only ask that you act as fairly as possible and tell me what is said!"

There are armed British and Spanish soldiers guarding the main doors. Two sergeants, one from each army, check Don Leon's documents, especially the letter he received in summons this morning. They look hard at Lauchlin but permit him to enter.

It is a large room and the light through the windows does not enable Lauchlin to make out much detail. As his eyes adjust he sees that six tables have been drawn up, three on each side facing each other with another two at one end, placed at right angles. Someone, whom Lauchlin subsequently learns is Martin Pueyrredon, stands and gestures for Don Leon to take a seat next to him about a third of the way along one side. Facing him, in the centre, is a figure in the full-dress uniform of a British general. He has four other senior officers at his side; other chairs at the back are presumably occupied by clerks, interpreters and advisers. Lauchlin takes a chair behind Don Leon and listens as Pueyrredon tells him about the proceedings thus far.

"We haven't advanced much. Mostly arguing about the seating arrangements. You know that is Liniers at the end. He has decided to chair the meeting and he has a clerk with him trying to record all that is said. I think you know Don Bernardo de Amuñecar at his side – is he any good?. The English general seems to be a sort of schoolmaster, wanting everything set out on easels at the side. That is stupid, we wouldn't be able to see anything at this distance..." He breaks off as Liniers stands and appears to continue.

"When the English General Beresford surrendered to me I made him certain promises that he would be able to take his soldiers back with him. Unfortunately, as Don Martin de Pueyrredon..." he turns towards the man in question, "will recall, the Council would not agree. As the military commander I gave my word and it was odious that the Council chose to imprison him with his senior officers!"

A man at the end of the table stands and furiously interrupts. "You had no right to offer those butchers such generous terms. After all the damage they did they deserved to be executed!" He gives a rude snigger before adding, "of course you, as a Frenchman, would know nothing of such things!"

"Please, Don Fernando, my job here today is hard enough without resorting to insults!"

General Whitelocke rises to his feet. Putting up a hand in interruption he speaks impatiently. "My gallant and esteemed colleague, General Beresford, granted the citizens of this Province many benefits and improvements which they did not have under the Spanish!" After a short pause for translation, he continues, "I mean, of course, freedom of religion, the abolition of slavery, free trade throughout the world – not confined to Spain or her master Napoleon!"

There is a buzz of anger and opposition as he enumerates benefits that actually upset the lives of many of those present. Their long-standing contracts with Spanish houses had been abruptly terminated and finding new customers to replace them could take years.

Lauchlin is looking hard at the man seated with Liniers. In the uniform of a Spanish officer, there is something about him that strikes a chord. Then he hears the name – Don Bernardo – of course! He had been a guest at Ibicoy when it was hinted that he might be a suitable husband for Alicia. Lauchlin now studies him closely. Physically he compares reasonably well with other Spaniards, somewhat short but muscular and, in a way, delicate in his movements as if such tasks as handling reports and summaries were normally carried out by subordinates. Would Alicia marry him after Lauchlin's departure? Backwards and forwards his mind ranges.This is no suitable husband for her. He has to pull himself together.

The English general is speaking again and Lauchlin translates as fast as he can for Don Leon and his friend. The British claim that they only came to fight their principal enemy – Bonaparte – who was in regular receipt of precious metals from the mines at Potosi. The British aim had been to achieve independence for the Viceroyalty and, apart from an increase in general trade, had no pecuniary interest in the campaign.

A man seated three places up from Don Leon now stands waving a paper. He is addressed as Don Martin de Alzaga and Lauchlin gathers that he had been a sort of Mayor. He protests that what has just been said is lies. When the British had first arrived, the Viceroy had fled to Cordoba taking all the city's treasure. The British had sent a fast column of cavalry after him and captured everything. But did they return it to the city? They did not! It was all sent to London as spoils of war!

The charges and counter-charges continue. Increasingly, Lauchlin gains the impression that Liniers is determined to allow the British to leave. He wants them gone and power restored to the old regime. Others demand compensation for the destruction of the city and for the loss of its treasure. They decide on a pause in the proceedings to see if any new proposals develop. It is nearly lunch time.

Don Leon suggests he should approach the English General and arrange for Frank's and his own reinstatement "If...." And he looks hard at him with his penetrating blue eyes, "you are really set on leaving us!"

As Lauchlin moves down the room behind the British group a hand slaps him hard on the shoulder: "My hat – if it isn't the theatrical Pierrot Mackinnon! What role are you made up for today?"

Major James Urquhart has found him again. He holds him by the upper arms. "My, it is good to see you! We thought you were dead – instead I see you've gone native!"

They sit together in a corner and bring each other up to date. It was natural for Urquhart, a Spanish speaker, to be part of General Whitelocke's team. "It's not looking too good for us, is it Lauchy. How do you view things from the other side, so to speak?"

"Well, thank you for that! But listening here I recognize that both sides need a benefit. Independence from Spain is good but that's not totally in the British gift, is it? This would be a terrific gain if they became part of the King's Empire!" An idea begins to form in Lauchlin's head.. "If some good British tradesmen decided to stay here and help create the new state, it might be possible to steer it in our direction. This is an agrarian country - and big!" He adds unnecessarily, "they need scientists, accountants I s'pose...woollen mills...meat processors – perhaps salt and ice producers – everything really – coach makers", he adds thinking of the Rosas carriages built in Spain.

"My hat! That's a good notion. I must put it to the General. Come and meet him!"

General Whitelocke is seated with two other officers. A bottle of brandy is half empty and the glasses in front of them testify as to where it has gone. Urquhart breaks in to introduce him. "Lieutenant Lauchlin Mackinnon, General, been deeply immersed in the local life here for a year. Has some thoughts!"

"Bugger me – I've never seen a British lieutenant dressed like that. Shouldn't you have washed and changed before coming to see me? 'Deeply immersed' you say – is that another way of saying 'deserted in the field'?" Someone sniggers.

Urquhart does his best to explain the situation and introduces Lauchlin's ideas about suitably qualified British being encouraged to bring industrial developments to this largely agricultural economy. Perhaps a regiment to defend them at first and train their army. One of the officers laughs. Urquhart ignores him.

"Perhaps specialists could be sent out here, General, each one with say, twenty pounds…" As he sees Whitelocke's face creasing up before him, he reduces the sum to "ten guineas each – provided by the Government, free passage…"

"Oh shit – now we're turning into a politician are we." He joins in the mocking laughter. "Didn't someone say that a company of bloody highlanders had decided to remain – up North somewhere. He turns his back very deliberately, "sod off until you can come up with a helpful suggestion!"

Urquhart's face darkens. He pulls Lauchlin away. "Come on, we'll get little sense here." He fumes silently before exploding: "What a dreadful man! Is this what our country is coming to? You'd do better to stay here!"

As they walk towards the exit, they have to pass Don Leon, sitting with Pueyrredon and two others whom Lauchlin does not know. As he passes, Don Leon stretches out a hand. "We don't think there is going to be any progress today, Lauchlin. Let me introduce you." He explains the presence of the young man and Lauchlin introduces them to Major Urquhart who is in uniform.

In good Spanish Urquhart passes on Lauchlin's proposals. They look pensive. "We would need good fighting men to protect us – for a year at least!"

Don Leon nods appreciatively. "It's a thought. We'll put it to the Council this afternoon. It must be down to us – not Liniers! Go with Franco and make your arrangements, have some *ensalada* and a glass. Then make your way to Hotel Rosas, I'm told it is still in good order. I would like to see you and Señor Franco for dinner there." He tells him how to find the house, "Look out for the *Plaza de España* in front!"

Urquhart tells him that none of the 71st Regiment will still be around. He promises to make some enquiries and will be able to advise Lauchlin at tomorrow's meeting. Urquhart thinks it inadvisable to parade in public dressed as he is. They part.

Chapter 30

At Ibicoy, Alicia returns from her morning ride and is disappointed to find that Lauchlin's mount, *Durazno,* is not in its usual paddock nor anywhere in the stables. She notes the absence of her father's black stallion but that is not unusual. Going into the house she learns that the men have all rushed off to the city which is under a renewed British attack. It is rumoured that the two *ingleses* will leave.

Her imagination begins turning cartwheels. She had never really expected Lauchlin to make his home at Ibicoy but had thought she could enjoy his company for some months more before he left – and she could always hope. But surely he would not leave without saying goodbye.

Her mother and grandmother keep themselves much to themselves. Her grandmother, Doña Valenciana, is occupied with a large tapestry of Christ at Emmaus which she had promised Father Ignacio would be completed before her death. Now it is an icon dedicated to his memory. Her mother sits in her sitting-room endlessly writing letters.

Alicia feels banks of misery building up like rain-clouds on the hills. Some weeks earlier she had been stupid enough to raise the subject of marriage with her parents. Her mother had thundered in disapproval.

"In your veins runs the blood of kings and queens of Spain! Do you really think it appropriate for 'Doña Alicia' as you will be, to be married to a common foreigner!"

"But with God's help he could be a great man like my father."

"But he has not the Rosas name! Can you not understand? If Juan Manuel marries Encarnacion, as we are beginning to hope, it will continue a great lineage. Would they then want him as a brother?"

Her father had interposed gently: "Do you think you are in love with this...Englishman?"

She had felt her face colouring. "I do not know, father, but I like him very much – anyway, he is a Scotchman, not an Englishman."

"Love – Ha…that has nothing to do with marriage. Your father and I will find some suitable husband for you. Until then you must be careful to protect your reputation. Now, do not speak to us again of this foolish notion."

Her father had been somewhat subdued in the exchange but she knew better than to raise the matter again. Nevertheless, the thoughts had grown in her mind. Now, finding him gone she feels a desperate loneliness and a physical emptiness such as she has never experienced before. Without waiting to change her clothes she rushes off to find Tomasin.

* * *

After leaving Urquhart, Lauchlin makes his way to the Rosas' house on foot. He has much to think about. He feels somewhat low. This General Whitelocke is a different sort of man to General Beresford. What kind of a reception is he going to receive in the army? He knows he has matured greatly through his experiences. He longs to see his mother and the family again but travelling around the world with the regiment no longer appeals. He needs work that stretches him. He feels a depression pressing in on him and tries to shake it off.

He finds the park easily and stands facing the Rosas mansion. Don Leon had explained that the land belonged to him but was now gifted to the city.

"For many years Spain was under the control of *Los Moros.* Although not Godly they left much in my country that is noteworthy. One is the traditional *Allahrago,* part of the cultural legacy of *El Andaluz,* an open space in the city for people to rest and refresh themselves. That is now a permanent feature in front of my property. There should be water – one day I'll produce a spring. It will be my gift to God." He had smiled almost shame-facedly.

In spite of his low mood, Lauchlin has to agree that the open space brings air into the city. It sets the house off nicely and, who knows, may have saved it from ruin during the attack. He stares about him, one of Don Leon's dreams… his gift to God. The grass is unkempt and littered presumably the result of the battle. An elderly couple are sitting on the grass, quietly sobbing in each others' arms. Then, with horror, he sees signs of blood lying across a path. It still looks wet. What was the invasion about? How creditable has this mission been?

He moves away to leave the two in privacy and studies the house.It is an impressive site. There are entry and exit gates for a carriage and the drive continues under an arch to stables at the back. Dressed the way he is he avoids the main door and walks round to the kitchen area to bang on the glass.

His arrival is not welcomed by the maid who opens it. She is very black and dressed in white. The chain around her neck identifies her as a house slave. She is busy with preparations for Don Leon's return. It reminds him of Ticho who had nursed him kindly at Ibicoy. He wonders about their dreams. Was she born here or brought from Africa? Or merely purchased, like a horse.

She eyes his clothes up and down, preparing to shut him out. By good fortune he sees Tomasin, the carriage driver, sipping a *mate* at a table. He jumps up and verifies him. Lauchlin has no changes of clothes but assumes that they will be provided before dinner. He will have to freshen up too but cannot bring himself to care very much.

He is shown to a room on the first floor, overlooking the park. It is finer than his room at Ibicoy being larger with an armchair and small table by the bed. A shaving stand holds a washing bowl surmounted by a mirror and there is a razor folded with soap and flannel. He examines his face wondering why that stupid General had accused him of being unwashed. Certainly the face staring back is brown and the hair badly needs his mother's knife. He decides it is a sad face and tries to improve it by smiling. He looks at his teeth then shakes his head in the realization that it is all a stupid act. What is he to do?

He will stay here one night. For dinner and the required valedictory meeting with Don Leon. Assuming that he will not be required in the morning, he and Frank can simply make their way to the British offices and hand themlselves in – come what may. Urquhart can testify that they did everything they could to return by General Beresford's deadline. Then he had gone ashore to look for Frank who was there himself looking for him. What a mess! He stands looking out of the window. He knows that his thoughts keep steering him towards Alicia. Strictly to himself he has begun to think about marriage and of life at her side. But the Rosas family is powerful and Juan Manuel is as enthusiastic and ambitious as his father. They may not allow him, let alone welcome him, into their circle. Yet, somehow, he feels that Don Leon and the older family members have warmed to him; he is uncertain about Juan Manuel. But he has been away with his regiment for a long time.

He wonders what the time is; it must be about four. If he decides to stay, it will be years before he can see his family again. That is disloyal. Should he remain in the army? *The English army!* as Grandfather had put it. Is he still alive? Yes, it will be good to see them again – surely he will find a promising career with all his experience. His heart sinks again. How can he leave without saying goodbye to Alicia? He thinks of her being married to Don Bernardo. He is tortured by his imagination. The truth forces itself to the surface. He does not want to leave and she is the principal reason; the only reason? What about the work? That would be better as well but the prime reason – the full, factual, unequivocal reason - is Alicia.

There is a breath of air through the room and a click from the door behind him. He turns quickly and cannot prevent a gasp of near pain. She is walking across the room towards him – she stands by the bed facing him, taking off her small gloves which she throws on a chair.

"How could I let you go without saying goodbye?" She is in his arms; she clutches him tightly. Her hair is dishevelled. She is wearing her long, riding habit over a white blouse.... a little silver necklace seems to highlight the small brooch made from the button he gave her at their first meeting.

He kisses her gently on the forehead. It is level with his mouth. He lowers it to her eyes, they seem to be wet with tears. She whispers in his ear, the scent of her excites him.

"We must be silent, only Tomasin knows I am here!"

"But how did you get here – where have you been?"

"I came in the carriage with Tomasin. Juancito is coming with *Paloma...* I had to see you – you're not upset with me are you?"

He takes her in his arms and holds her firmly. His lips gently caress her ear as he murmurs, "your father would kill me if he knew!" His left hand strokes the back of her neck while his right fondles her back gently, pulling her towards him.

"No he won't! I've thought about it. When it's done he'll have to accept it and we'll be married!" Her arms curl around his neck and she pulls his face down to hers. She kisses him on the mouth. It is the first time. He holds her with both arms and pulls her firmly towards him as her excitement rises.

He feels unable to control himself. He undoes the small buttons on her shirt and lets his hand explore. She has on some kind of thin bodice and he tries to raise it to feel her bareness. She gives a gasp and pulls him towards the bed. She kicks off the boots. Her split skirt is held up by a leather belt. He cannot loosen it with one hand; she helps him and his hand gently enters. He can smell her passion and his pulse is throbbing. He kneels on the floor and whispers "When what is done?"

"Oh", she moans softly. "When my reputation is done with…after tonight…we'll tell them…oh…don't stop!"

With a sudden realization his mind turns to Encarnacion and the attack by Chichon. He imagines the faces of the two ladies, of her father, of Juan Manuel, he even remembers Father Ignacio. He takes his hand away. How can he do that to the girl he loves? How can he repay the kindness he has found in the family in this manner?

"No!" He is almost sobbing. He takes hold of her again and sits her up. "I cannot do this. I will win you with your family's approval! You will see. This is not the right way!"

She sobs quietly. "Oh Lauchlin…" she still stresses the last syllable, "do you think so little of me then?"

"No, no! I love you Alicia but we should not start in this way. It will break your family's heart and in the end it will not be the best way for us. Yes, I want you here and now but I want to marry you and I know this is not the right way." He kisses her again but gently. He feels her tears.

She sits up on her own but makes no move to adjust her dress. He can see her trembling and feels heartbroken himself. He kneels in front of her again.

"You will see. This is not the way for our future happiness." He takes one of her hands and kisses each finger. "You must dress now and go to your room. Maybe we can ride together in the morning."

He helps her to dress and put on her boots. As she stands again he pulls her towards him and kisses her with growing passion. She responds, holding him tightly while pressing herself against him. Then, desperately she pushes him away. "No, you're right! We mustn't start all this again – I must return to my own room!"

The floor creaks as he takes a hand and opens his door. He watches as she makes her way down the corridor.

He sits and tries to think. The incident goes round and round in his mind. He is tortured by his desires and by a desperate ache in his lower stomach.

Alicia sobs to herself. She feels dirty and cheapened. What had she done? Would he now be so contemptuous of her that he would not want to see her again?

Chapter 31

Don Leon is surprised to be told that Alicia had ridden up to town and angry at her having only taken Tomasin as the driver and escort.

"These are dangerous days. You must promise me that you will never do such a thing again!" He arranges for someone to ride back at once to reassure the two ladies about Alicia's safety. But he is not totally satisfied and keeps eyeing his daughter through the meal, noting her high colour. What is going on? He will have to talk to her later.

After the meal the three men discuss the events of the day. Frank explains that he feels he must make his way back to North America.

"There is the scent of independence all over this continent, Don Leon. I must return and make my peace. Who knows? Land will be cheap and one day I'll have my own farm and practise those things I've learned here."

"And you, Lauchlin? Will you want to be seeing your family again?"

"Oh yes" he mumbles, slightly taken off guard. Don Leon's eyes stay on him. Those steady blue eyes that Lauchlin has grown to know so well.

Frank discusses his departure. Not surprisingly Don Leon nods as though he has been expecting something of the sort.

"I am not surprised, Señor Franco, your country calls you away in a manner that I do not see in Lauchlin. I think sailings up the coast to the North will be frequent." He glances out of the window. "Not true, perhaps, of Europe…the war and so on." He turns back to Frank. "You must go when you wish and it will be with my thanks. There is one matter that I would very much like to discuss." He proceeds to spell out the worth of Frank's work in the past ten or eleven months. "I have calculated it in local currency that may not be suitable for you. I have arranged with our agent here that this sum be converted into gold for you. Who knows – it may help buy a farm for you!"

Frank is deeply grateful and tries to express his thanks but Don Leon waves them aside. "You may feel that there will be an opportunity for some of Juan Manuel's processed meats and herbs to be sold in your country; although most of your work has been with Francisco, caring for the animals, you are familiar with his developments. The salt content has been carefully calculated and they sell quite well in Spain and Portugal, still largely with the army but the name is spreading. Do you believe they could be acceptable on the dinner tables of North America?" He coughs and smiles, seemingly slightly embarrassed as he adds, "perhaps you could carry a chest of these as samples in your baggage…if they sell well… perhaps you could become our agent." He gets more excited as he adds, "remember, that as the seasons in your country are upside down to ours, some of our pickled products, in time, perhaps olives, perhaps peppers and choclos, could be included." He turns to the window as the breeze causes a twig to rub against the glass. "Ideally, we should have a canning factory but that will take time."

Frank nods slowly, anxious to agree, "My part of Georgia is still a poor country, Don Leon and it will need time to recover…"

Don Leon interrupts him. "Many parts of Spain are also poor, and remember, up in the mountains it is cold. But the *Fiambres* and *chorizos* are much demanded as well as many of the smoked meats. They are an economical and nourishing meal!"

Lauchlin thinks Frank is preparing to argue and thinks about how to save the situation but Frank cuts across him. "I find your suggestions most interesting, Don Leon, and much in line with my own recent thoughts!" He pauses to look out of the window, "You will understand that it will take me some time to get established again."

Lauchlin's jaw falls; this is the first he has heard of Frank having thoughts about importing such products into North America. As he considers the question he begins to see the logic in it. But Frank could, of course, learn to make the products himself. Would that be dishonest?

After an early breakfast, Lauchlin has a hurried whispered conversation with a shame-faced Alicia agreeing that they had said their farewells last night. Escorted by the four gauchos who came up with Don Leon yesterday she rides home to Ibicoy.

During the long ride she keeps herself to herself. From what was said at dinner it is clear he intends returning to his family. She has cheapened herself and is no longer fit for society. She had offered herself to him and he had rejected her. She feels at turns angry at him, then at herself and sorrowful. She feels in need of a bath. On reaching home she goes straight to her room and firmly shuts the door.

Lauchlin accompanies Don Leon to the meeting. The British are now offering commercial aid if the *Patricios* reject the Spanish and French. They offer defensive and training aid to the amount of two regiments of fusiliers, about one thousand men, under a Colonel as Army Commander-in-Chief. In return they demand right of passage for their ships carrying away all their men, equipment and heavy guns. Montevideo is to be retained as a British possession. Those men and guns captured from the Colonists will be released.

With the exception of the retention of Montevideo, these are largely the terms agreed. At first Liniers as a General in the Spanish army is viewed as the hero of the hour. As weeks pass he is accused of being French and of having sold out the Colonists without any compensation.

But that is for the future. The Council offers General Whitelocke and four of his senior officers, lunch in the *Cabild*o while the documents are drawn up. As a mere Major, Urquhart is required to utilize his language skills in vetting and composing the wording of the Agreement. Lauchlin is able to have ten minutes alone with him during a short intermission.

"Whitelocke is no gentleman, Lauchlin, and I fear these terms will be repudiated by our Government once they get the troops home. He has no authority to say he'll post a couple of regiments here to help them defend themselves. Above all, to give up Montevideo is a cruel blow to the men who died for it!"

"Didn't you say some of General Beresford's Highlanders had opted to stay here rather than return to Scotland?"

Urquhart snorts. "That's old hat! I hardly think that'll count. Who knows where their loyalties lie now. They were not exactly lovers of England, were they. Anyhow, I don't know how many were involved and their kit will probably be useless! But, more to the point, what about you?"

"Frank Matthews now wants to return to North America. You will frecall he was one of the Loyal Americans but now feels that his home is there."

"I remember him well – a good man. That's understandable but the army will do nothing to aid his passage home. He'll have to make his own way. Could even walk I s'pose…There's a few have done that." He rubs his chin. "A pity, there were some really good men there." He swings round. "I'll have to go back in there soon. I've made some enquiries about the 71st Regiment. Most are out in Portugal with Beresford," with a twinkle in his eye, he adds, "he specially asked for them!" He looks hard at Lauchlin. "How about yourself? You're the mystery man it seems to me. The army will welcome you back – you might make Captain! The regiments are enlarging with the war in Europe and there will be vacancies - But you'll have to be quick!"

"Oh I'll be going back, of course. This place is all dreams!" They part again and Lauchlin makes his way back to the *Hotel Rosas.*

Next morning he accompanies Frank to the Port area. The only shipping is the British warships and there is no news regarding the arrival of neutral shipping although the Port Captain says they will return very quickly once the current emergency is over. After leaving details of Frank's requirements with him, they decide to return to Ibicoy. Lauchlin must collect his property and he wishes to say proper farewells to everyone there.

They ride back on *Durazno* and *Lechuga.* They have become attached to the two animals and Lauchlin pretends to himself that the affection is returned.

When they arrive they are welcomed as heroes. The four gauchos who escorted Alicia home yesterday had told everyone that they were making plans to return to Europe. Francisco proposes an asado for the following evening so that everyone can attend.

The exception is Alicia. Lauchlin is saddened to hear that shortly after her return she had packed up some changes of clothing and departed to stay at a neighbouring estancia some forty-five miles away.

Although Don Leon is still in the city, Doña Agustina allows the employees to proceed with the asado. The gauchos present gifts in appreciation for Frank's work over the year. Whilst there seem to be no gifts for Lauchlin, he is too troubled by Alicia's absence to notice.

A conversation between Jacinto and one of the house staff mentions a visit the young servant had made to *Sietemesinas La Vieja.* Such visits were generally frowned on but all loved to hear her tales of forecast. The old witch had evidently been at her fanciful best and made mention of the young soldier from afar who would marry the beautiful princess in the tower. The story makes the rounds but never reaches Lauchlin.

He is touched by their apparent affection but collects up his kit in a dispirited mood. Frank's gifts are impressive. Pride of place goes to a pair of soft leather boots, made to measure against his favourite work-boots by a house-worker.

Francisco presents him with a fine steel knife in a leather holster. He says in terrible English: "This cut you very real gaucho!"

Frank whispers to Lauchlin that what he would really have liked is one of the treasured Kentucky rifles but has to be satisfied with the new knife. To much humour, Francisco continues to struggle speaking English as he quotes Don Leon: "He say in your country they like many pistol shootings and sometime Indians!"

Three days later Frank receives a message from the Port Captain that a Spanish coaster is calling to unload coffee, cotton and other cargoes from the North. It will be returning, perhaps as far as Panama. He is not yet aware if it will be loading cargo so if Frank is interested he should make his way to the port within thirty-six hours.

Lauchlin has spent hours tormented by his doubts and self-recriminations. At one stage he tells himself that his duty lies in returning to the regiment and, hopefully, of seeing his family prior to being sent on to Portugal to join General Beresford. But, he argues, is his worth in that great enterprise comparable with his value in this country where he knows his work is valued and useful. He tries to keep thoughts of Alicia away from this equation. But they keep intervening. When he is honest with himself he acknowledges that she is the principal reason. Sometimes he casts a dice, promising that if the value is greater than three he will stay. But when it shows him ones and twos he rejects the system.

On the following morning he packs up all his property and accompanies Frank to the city. It is a fine, clear morning as they set off in Tomasin's wagon on the fifty or so miles. Don Leon's case of samples has been added to their personal luggage so that the wagon is a heavy load for the two small ponies. Frank is quiet as he surveys a countryside he has come to appreciate.

"Am I doing the right thing, Lochy? Those people really seemed to like us."

"I'm sure that's right, Frank," Lauchlin is ill at ease. He is not pleased to have this question posed at him yet again. What is he going to do? "We have to remember they're not our people and we'll always be foreigners to them. Also, when they see the condition of the city they'll question how we could do such things and why we came in the first place."

Frank is quiet for some moments. Lauchlin stares at the river reeds outside Las Conchas. Is this the last time he'll see them? Why did Alicia disappear like that? He tells himself that in time he will forget about her.

The wagon takes them straight to the Port where the luggage is unloaded and left in an outside office. The Spanish ship is called *La Santa Catalina* and the smell of coffee pervades the area. The Port Captain tells them that the ship left Funchal in Madeira in April and delivered grapes, wine and fruit to the Cape Verde Islands where it loaded salt. It then sailed to Merida in Mexico for rice, spices, fruit and cocoa which it carried to ports down the East Coast before loading coffee. He continues, "Captain Dorrego is a very skilled Master and, after leaving the last of his coffee here, now plans to load sacks of grain and perhaps some wool for a northern port, probably Venezuela."

They go on board to discuss terms with the captain. They find a short, bright-eyed man in a dirty cap with a small 'goatee' beard. He agrees to carry Frank and shows him his cabin which is vastly superior to what he had been expecting. His price for taking him as far as Venezuela would be thirty Reales and conveying him further North would require another evaluation. Walking on the main deck consists of treading in spilt coffee beans. Dorrego is irritated.

"In the same way as every hour in port costs me money, so does broken casks or bales. Some shore workers will break open a bale just so that they can steal some of the contents!"

Back in the Port office, Frank is handed a note that has been sent down from Don Leon. It invites them both to dinner. He hopes Juan Manuel will join them for a last meal.

A last meal - Lauchlin looks at Frank. There is a realization that he is losing his only friend. There are still three British warships collecting wounded men. Lauchlin watches as several stretchers at a time are laid on floating pontoons, towed out to the ships and taken on board with minimum disturbance. But, even at this distance, Lauchlin can hear screams of agony. He wonders which ship will carry him home. A heavy transport loaded with dead and dying does not appeal. But Alicia has shown by her absence that he means little to her.

They walk back to the house each lost in his own thoughts. After the long ride in the wagon they feel tired and the prospect of a good meal is inviting. As they walk up the short drive Frank shakes his head slowly. "I didn't think I'd be back in this city again as soon as this!"

"Ah well, it's not for much longer and you'll be back in Georgia."

"Not sure what's waiting for me there!"

"You can always come back, you know. I shall miss you like hell." Lauchlin speaks without thinking.

"Sure thing, but of course you'll always have Alicia to comfort you!"

Lauchlin is quiet. *Alicia to comfort you* …if only.

The ground floor reception rooms comprise a *salon* with a number of elegant paintings of Rosas antecedents. French windows look out on a terrace which commands the garden. The dining-room contains a large table capable of seating thirty diners. Don Leon's study adjoins his office where during the day two clerks record the progress of the business. The accounts which Lauchlin has been keeping so assiduously thinking he was making a real contribution are merely a part of what goes on here. Not such a major contribution after all. It adds to his depression. He has no-one to talk with about his plans or intentions. A voice seems to whisper: *Best to go back to the Regiment.*

A notable addition to the building is a water closet providing a bucket of water with which to flush the waste out to the bottom of the garden where a large septic system processes animal, garden, human and kitchen waste. The kitchens and staff quarters are downstairs and partly dug into the foundations of the house. When the family wishes to eat and talk confidentially, food from the kitchen to the dining-room is by a manually controlled hoist.

Juan Manuel joins them for a light dinner. He is still in the army but is casually dressed to let them feel at ease. On his father's instructions he has brought a quantity of gold pieces in payment to Frank. They comprise a variety of currencies. Some are Reales minted in Callao; there are some golden Napoleon pieces from Paris and even some from the kingdom of Portugal. It is a generous settlement and Frank is fulsome in his thanks.

Juan Manuel waves the matter away as if it is of little consequence. He is pleasant to them both but now concentrates his attention on Lauchlin.

"I need good management I can trust! This country is to be totally re-organized and I must be free to play my part. Spain is now under British control and will have to give up its interests here. The Vice-royalty of the River Plate will be ended. We shall be independent!" He looks down at some notes he has prepared. Clearly it is his father he wishes to impress more than his British guests.

"But where will the seat of government lie? This is an enormous country to be ruled as one central entity!" Lauchlin is impressed with the thought that has gone into these statements. He wonders to himself *'just how do you set about governing a huge territory?*

"To begin with, Buenos Aires will rule a state – such as is happening in North America, or a province. It will be as big as many European countries! After that – we shall expand the government piece-meal!"

It is a subject about which he is passionate. Lauchlin can understand his ambitions with regard to the farming and even regarding the processing of the beef but politics is another thing entirely and the discussion continues after dinner, even when they retire to the terrace with imported French cognac and Cuban cigars.

The next morning Juan Manuel returns to his cavalry regiment. As they wait for his horse to be brought round, he embraces them both and urges Lauchlin to immerse himself in the management process at Ibicoy. "My father is now elderly and needs looking after. As I indicated last evening, I must be free to help build this nation!" He would have said more but his stallion is brought round and he easily slips an immaculately polished boot into the left stirrup and mounts into the saddle. With a friendly wave he clatters out through an arch.

Lauchlin smiles ironically. "Who would have thought that was the same man who tried to frighten us off his father's lands fifteen months ago."

Frank nods thoughtfully. "Yup, He clearly thinks the world of you. Let us see what transpires."

After collecting the last of his luggage, Frank is ready to leave. Lauchlin walks him down to the ship. Frank shows him his cabin. "My home for – who knows how long!" There is a ninety minute delay as the tide rises to its highest point. The Captain eventually shouts that Lauchlin should leave the ship. The two old friends embrace and, with a heavy heart, Lauchlin stands on shore as the *Santa Catalina* raises its anchor and hoists its old, stained sails to catch the land breeze. A watery sun breaks out below the clouds making Frank's last view of him a shimmering silhouette as the captain calls for the hoisting of more sail.

Saddened and dispirited Lauchlin watches as the ship is slowly swallowed by the horizon. He turns away from the river to make his lonely way back to the Hotel Rosas.

As he walks up the hill, shielding his eyes against the setting sun, he sees a figure in a familiar riding habit pushing her hair away from her face as she waves and calls to him.

About the Author

Roderick Bethune has dual British and Argentine nationality and is particularly proud of his Scottish descent. After education in both countries, he served as a Pilot Officer in the Royal Air Force before joining the Argentine army as a private soldier. Subsequently, he crossed the ocean as a Merchant Seaman. He spent many years in commerce and industry, becoming a senior executive in one of the world's largest paper and packaging groups.

Printed in the United States
by Baker & Taylor Publisher Services